HERO IN THE SHADOWS

Also by David Gemmell

The Drenai books
Legend
The King Beyond the Gate
Waylander
Quest for Lost Heroes
Waylander II: In the Realm of the Wolf
The First Chronicles of Druss the Legend
The Legend of Deathwalker
Winter Warriors

The Jon Shannow books
Wolf in Shadow
The Last Guardian
Bloodstone

The Stones of Power books
Ghost King
Last Sword of Power
Lion of Macedon
Dark Prince

The Hawk Queen books
Ironhand's Daughter
The Hawk Eternal

The Rigante books
Sword in the Storm
Midnight Falcon

Individual titles
Knights of Dark Renown
Drenai Tales
Morning Star
Dark Moon
Echoes of the Great Song

DAVID A. GEMMELL

HERO IN
THE SHADOWS

BANTAM PRESS

LONDON · NEW YORK · TORONTO · SYDNEY · AUCKLAND

TRANSWORLD PUBLISHERS
61–63 Uxbridge Road, London W5 5SA
a division of The Random House Group Ltd

RANDOM HOUSE AUSTRALIA (PTY) LTD
20 Alfred Street, Milsons Point, Sydney,
New South Wales 2061, Australia

RANDOM HOUSE NEW ZEALAND
18 Poland Road, Glenfield, Auckland, New Zealand

RANDOM HOUSE SOUTH AFRICA (PTY) LTD
Endulini, 5a Jubilee Road, Parktown 2193, South Africa

Published 2000 by Bantam Press
a division of Transworld Publishers

A catalogue record for this book is available
from the British Library
ISBNs 0593 044355 (cased)
0593 044533 (tpb)

Typeset by Hewer Text Ltd, Edinburgh
Printed in Great Britain by
Clays Ltd, St Ives plc

1 3 5 7 9 10 8 6 4 2

Hero in the Shadows is dedicated with much love to Broo Doherty, with thanks for the years of support, encouragement and flawless good humour. Be happy, Broo!

ACKNOWLEDGEMENTS

MY THANKS TO MY TEST READERS, JAN Dunlop, Tony Evans, Alan Fisher, Stella Graham, and Steve Hutt, whose observations and advice were invaluable, and to my editors, Ursula Mackenzie, Liza Reeves and Steve Saffel. I am also more than grateful to Tim Walker, and the crew at Active Computers, Bexhill, who stepped in when my computer turned rogue and died during the final run up to deadline. Their swift assistance – and the loan of a new computer – ensured that Waylander's latest adventure made it to the publishers on time.

Special thanks to Dale Rippke and to Eric Harris, who have made planning the next Drenai novel an even greater pleasure.

PROLOGUE

MERCENARY CAPTAIN CAMRAN OSIR REINED IN HIS MOUNT AT THE crest of the hill and swung in the saddle to stare back down the forest trail. The twelve men under his command rode from the trees in single file, and paused while he scanned the horizon. Removing his iron helm, Camran ran his fingers through his long blond hair, enjoying, momentarily, the warm breeze evaporating the sweat on his scalp. He glanced at the captive girl on the horse beside him. Her hands were tied, her dark eyes defiant. He smiled at her, and saw her blanch. She knew he was going to kill her, and that her passing would be painful. He felt the warmth of blood pulsing in his loins. Then the feeling passed. His blue eyes narrowed as he gazed over the valley, seeking sign of pursuit.

Satisfied that no one was following, Camran tried to relax. He was still angry, of course, but calmed himself with the thought that his riders were ill-educated brutes, with little understanding of civilized behaviour.

The raid had gone well. There were only five men in the little farming settlement, and these had been killed quickly, with no wounds or losses among his own men. Some of the women and children had managed to escape into the woods, but three young women had been taken. Enough, at least, to satisfy the carnal urges of his riders. Camran himself had captured the fourth, the dark-haired girl on the sway-backed horse beside him. She had tried to run, but he had ridden her down, leaping from his horse and bearing her to the ground. She had fought silently, without panic, but one blow to the chin had rendered her unconscious, and he had thrown

1

her over his saddle. There was blood now upon her pale cheek, and a purple bruise was showing on the side of her neck. Her faded yellow dress was torn at the shoulder and had flapped down, almost exposing her breast. Camran jerked his thoughts from her soft skin, turning his mind to more urgent concerns.

Yes, the raid had gone well. Until that idiot Polian had incited the others to set fire to the old farmhouse. Wanton destruction of property was anathema to a man of breeding like Camran. It was criminally wasteful. Peasants could always be replaced, but good buildings should be treated with respect. And the farmhouse was a good building, soundly constructed by a man who cared about quality work. Camran had been furious – not only with them, but with himself. For instead of merely killing the captured women he had allowed his needs to override his common sense. He had taken his time, enjoying the screams of the first, luxuriating in the desperate pleading of the second, and the subsequent cries of agony of the third. With each of them dead he had turned his attentions to the dark-haired girl. She had not pleaded, or made a sound after returning to consciousness to find her hands and ankles bound. She was to be the richest harvest; her cries, when they came, would be the purest and sweetest.

The smoke had billowed over him just as he was unwrapping his ivory-handled skinning knives. Swinging round, he saw the fires. Leaving the bound girl where she lay, he ran back to the scene. Polian was grinning as Camran came alongside him. He was still grinning as he died, Camran's dagger plunging between his ribs, skewering his heart.

This sudden act of savagery cowed the men. 'Did I not tell you?' he thundered. 'Never property! Not unless directly ordered. Now, gather supplies and let's be gone.'

Camran had returned to the young woman. He thought of killing her, but there would be no pleasure in it now, no slow, pounding joy as he watched the light of life fade from her eyes. Gazing down at the six small skinning knives in their silk-lined canvas pouch, he felt the dead weight of disappointment dragging at him. Carefully he rolled the pouch, tying it with black ribbon. Then he hauled the girl to her feet, cut the ropes around her ankles and lifted her to the dead Polian's mount. Still she said nothing.

As Camran rode away he gazed back at the burning building, and

2

a deep sense of shame touched him. The farmhouse had not been built speedily, but with great patience, the timbers lovingly fashioned, the joints fitting to perfection. Even the window-frames had been carved and embellished. Destroying such a place was an act of sacrilege. His father would have been ashamed of him.

Camran's sergeant, the hulking Okrian, rode alongside him. 'Wasn't in time to stop them, sir,' he said.

Camran saw the fear in the man's eyes. 'It is what happens when one is forced to deal with scum,' said Camran. 'Let's hope there are better men available when we reach Qumtar. We'll earn little commission from Panagyn with only eleven men.'

'We'll get more, sir. Qumtar is crawling with fighters seeking employment with one or other of the Houses.'

'*Crawling* is probably an apt description. Not like the old days, is it?'

'Nothing ever is,' said Okrian, and the two men rode in silence, each lost in thoughts of the past. Camran remembered the invasion of Drenai lands eighteen years earlier, when he had been a junior officer in the army of Vagria, serving under Kaem. It had been, Kaem had promised, the dawn of a new empire. And, for a time, it was true. They crushed all armies sent against them, forcing the greatest of the Drenai generals, Egel, into the vastness of Skultik Forest, and besieging the last fortress, Dros Purdol. But that had been the high point of the campaign. Under the command of the giant Karnak, Purdol had held, and Egel had broken from Skultik, descending upon the Vagrian army like a storm. Kaem himself had been slain by the assassin Waylander, and within two years Drenai forces had invaded Vagria. And it had not ended there. Arrest warrants were issued against many of the best Vagrian officers, charging them with crimes against the populace. It was laughable. What crime was there in killing your enemies, whether they be soldiers or farmers? But many officers were taken and hanged.

Camran had escaped north into the lands of the Gothir, but even here agents of the Drenai continued to hunt him. So he had drifted east, across the sea into Ventria and beyond, serving in numerous armies and mercenary bands.

At thirty-seven he was now in charge of recruitment for House Bakard, one of the four ruling Houses of Kydor. There was no outright war for them to fight. Not yet. But each of the Houses was gathering soldiers, and there were many skirmishes in the wild lands.

3

News from home rarely reached Kydor, but Camran had been delighted to hear of the death of Karnak some years previously. Assassinated as he led a parade. Wonderful! Killed, apparently, by a woman wielding the bow of the legendary Waylander.*

Jerking his mind once more to the present, Camran gazed back at his recruits. They were still frightened now, and anxious to please, hoping that when they made camp Camran would let them have the girl. He would soon dash those hopes. His plan was to use her, skin her, and leave the men to bury the body. He glanced once more at her, and smiled. She looked at him coolly and said nothing.

Just before dusk Camran swung from the trail and selected a campsite. As the men unsaddled their mounts he took the girl deeper into the forest. She made no resistance as he pushed her to the ground, and she did not cry out as he took her. As he was reaching his climax he opened his eyes and found her staring at his face, expressionless. This not only removed any pleasure from the rape; it also ruined his erection. Anger roared through him. Drawing his knife, he laid the edge on her throat.

'The Grey Man will kill you,' she said, slowly, no trace of fear in her voice. The words carried certainty and he paused.

'The Grey Man? Some demon of the night, perhaps? A protector of peasants?'

'He is coming,' she said.

He felt the prickle of fear on the nape hairs of his neck. 'I suppose he is a giant, or some such?'

She did not reply. A movement came from the bushes to his left. Camran surged to his feet, heart pounding. But it was Okrian.

'The men were wondering if you'd finished with her,' said the sergeant, his small eyes focusing on the peasant girl.

'No, I have not,' said Camran. 'Maybe tomorrow.'

The sergeant shrugged and walked back to the campfire. 'One more day of life,' Camran told the girl. 'Are you going to thank me?'

'I am going to watch you die,' she said.

Camran smiled, then punched her in the face, hurling her back to the ground. 'Stupid peasant,' he said.

But her words kept coming back to him, and the following morning's ride found him constantly scanning the back trail. His

* From *Waylander II: In the Realm of the Wolf* (1993)

4

neck was beginning to ache. Camran was about to heel his horse forward when he took one last look back. For a heartbeat only, he saw a shadow moving into the trees some half a mile down the trail. He blinked. Was it a horseman, or merely a wandering deer? He could not be sure. Camran swore softly, then summoned two of his riders. 'Go back down the trail. There may be a man following. If there is, kill him.'

The men swung their mounts and rode away. Camran glanced at the girl. She was smiling.

'What's happening, sir?' asked Okrian, nudging his horse alongside Camran's mount.

'Thought I saw a rider. Let's move on.'

They rode through the afternoon, stopping for an hour to walk the horses, then made camp in a sheltered hollow, close to a stream. There was no sign of the two men Camran had sent out. He summoned Okrian to him. The big mercenary eased himself down alongside his captain and Camran told him about the girl's warning. 'Grey Man?' he said. 'Never heard of him. But, then, I don't know this area of Kydor well. If he is following, the boys will get him. Tough lads.'

'Then where are they?'

'Probably dawdling somewhere. Or, if they caught him, they're probably having a little fun with him. Perrin is said to be somewhat of an artist when it comes to the Blood Eagle. The men say he can open a man's ribs, pin the guts back with twigs, and still leave the poor bastard alive for hours. Now, what about the girl, sir? The men could use a little diversion.'

'Aye, take her,' said Camran.

Okrian hauled her up by her hair and dragged her back to the campfire. A cheer went up from the nine men gathered there. Okrian hurled her towards them. The first man rose and grabbed her as she half fell. 'Let's see a little flesh,' he shouted, tearing at her dress.

Suddenly the girl spun on her heel, slamming her elbow into the man's face, crushing his nose. Blood spurted over his moustache and beard and he staggered back. The sergeant came up behind the girl, curling his arms around her and dragging her back into a tight embrace. Her head snapped back into his face, striking him on the cheekbone. He grabbed her hair and savagely twisted her head. The first man drew a dagger and advanced towards her. 'You puking bitch,' he snarled, 'I'm going to cut you bad. Not enough so we can't enjoy you, you little whore. But enough to make you scream like a gutted pig.'

The girl, unable to move, stared with undisguised malevolence at the knifeman. She did not beg or cry out.

Suddenly there was a crunching thud. The knifeman stopped, his expression bemused. Slowly he reached up with his left hand. As he did so he fell to his knees. His questing finger touched the black-feathered bolt jutting from the base of his skull. He tried to speak, but no words flowed. Then he pitched to his face.

For a few heartbeats no one moved. The sergeant hurled the girl to the ground, and drew his sword. Another man, closer to the trees, grunted in shock and pain as a bolt speared his chest. He fell back, tried to rise, then gave out a gurgling scream as he died.

Camran, sword in hand, ran back to the fire, then charged into the undergrowth, his men fanning out around him.

All was silent, and there was no sign of an enemy.

'Make for open ground!' shouted Camran. The men ran back to their horses, saddling them swiftly. Camran grabbed the girl, forcing her to mount, then clambered up behind her and rode from the hollow.

Clouds drifted across the moon as the men raced through the forest. In the darkness they were forced to slow their flight. Camran saw a break in the trees, and angled his mount towards it, emerging on to a hillside. Okrian came close behind. As the other men broke through Camran counted them. Including himself and his sergeant, eight men were now clear of the trees. Flicking his gaze around the milling group he counted again. The killer had taken another victim during the flight.

Okrian removed his black leather helm and rubbed his hand across his balding pate. 'Shem's balls,' he said. 'We've lost five men and we've seen no one!'

Camran glanced around. They were in a circle of clear ground, but to progress in any direction they would have to re-enter the forest.

'We'll wait for the dawn,' said Camran, dismounting. Dragging the girl from the saddle, he swung her round. 'Who is this Grey Man?' he asked. She did not reply and he slapped her hard. 'Talk to me, you bitch,' he hissed, 'or I'll cut open your belly and strangle you with your entrails!'

'He owns all the valley,' she said. 'My brother, and the other men you killed, farmed for him.'

'Describe him.'

'He is tall. His hair is long, mostly grey.'

'An old man?'

'He does not move like an old man,' she said. 'But, yes, he is old.'

'And how did you know he would be coming?'

'Last year five men attacked a settlement north of the valley. They killed a man and his wife. The Grey Man followed them. When he returned he sent out a wagon and the bodies were brought back and displayed in the market square. Outlaws do not trouble us now. Only foreigners such as yourself would bring evil to the Grey Man's land.'

'Does he have a name?' asked Camran.

'He is the Grey Man,' she said. 'That is all I know.'

Camran moved away from her, and stared back at the shadow-haunted trees. Okrian joined him. 'He can't be everywhere at once,' whispered Okrian. 'Much will depend on which way we choose to travel. We were heading east, so perhaps we should change our plans.'

The mercenary captain drew a map from the pocket of his saddlebag and opened it out on the ground. They had been heading towards the eastern border and Qumtar, but now all Camran wished to see was an end to the tree-line. On open ground the assassin could not overcome eight armed men. He studied the map in the moonlight. 'The nearest edge of the forest is to the north-east,' he said. 'Around two miles away. Once it is light we'll make for it.' Okrian nodded, but did not reply.

'What are you thinking?'

The sergeant took a deep breath, then rubbed his hand across his face. 'I was remembering the attack. Two crossbow bolts, one close upon the other. No time to reload. So, either there's two men or it must be a double-winged weapon.'

'If there'd been two men we'd have seen some sign as we rushed the undergrowth,' said Camran. 'They couldn't both have avoided us.'

'Exactly. So it is one man, who uses a double crossbow. One man – one skilled assassin who, having already killed the first two we sent, can then take out three tough men without being seen.'

'I take it there is a point to this?' muttered Camran.

'There was a man, years ago, who used such a weapon. Some say he was killed. Others claim he left the lands of the Drenai and bought himself a palace in Gothir territory. But perhaps he came instead to Kydor.'

Camran laughed. 'You think we are being hunted by Waylander the Slayer?'

'I hope not.'

'Gods, man, we're two thousand miles from Gothir. No, this is just another hunter using a similar weapon. Whoever he is, we're ready for him now,' said Camran. 'Put two men on watch and tell the rest to get some sleep.'

Camran moved to the girl, retied her hands and feet, then settled down on the ground. He had served in six campaigns and knew how important it was to rest whenever possible. Sleep did not come instantly. Instead he lay in the darkness thinking about what Okrian had said.

Waylander. Even the name made him shiver. A legend back in the days of his youth, Waylander the Slayer was said to be a demon in human form. Nothing could stop him; not walls or armed guards, not spells. It was said that the terrifying priests of the Dark Brotherhood had hunted him. All had died. Were-beasts, created by a Nadir shaman, were sent after him. Even these he had slain.

Camran shivered. Get a grip on yourself, he thought. Back then Waylander was said to be a man in his late thirties. If he was following them now he would have to be a man close to sixty, and an old man could not kill and move as this one did.

No, he decided, it could not be Waylander. With that thought he slept.

He awoke suddenly and sat up. A shadow moved across him. Hurling himself to his right he ducked and scrabbled for his sword. Something struck him on the brow and he pitched back. Okrian shouted a battle cry and sprinted forward. Camran surged to his feet, sword in hand. Clouds covered the moon once more, but not before Camran saw a shadowy figure merge into the darkness of the trees.

'Who was on watch?' shouted Camran. 'By the gods I'll cut his bastard eyes out!'

'No point in that,' said Okrian, pointing to a sprawled figure. Blood was pooling around the man. His throat had been slashed open. Another dead man was hunched by a boulder. 'You've been wounded,' he said. Blood was dripping from a shallow cut in Camran's brow.

8

'I ducked at the right moment,' said the captain, 'otherwise his blade would have opened my throat.' He glanced at the sky. 'Another hour and it will be light.' Pulling a handkerchief from his pocket he held it to the bleeding wound on his brow.

'I think I cut him,' said Okrian. 'But he moved fast.'

Camran continued to dab at his wound, but the blood was flowing freely. 'You'll have to stitch it,' he told Okrian.

'Yes, sir.' The hulking sergeant moved to his horse, removing a medicine pouch from his saddlebag. Camran sat very still as Okrian went to work. He glanced at the four other surviving conscripts, sensing their fear. Even as the sun rose there was no lessening of tension. For now they had to ride back into the forest.

The sky was clear and bright as Camran stepped into the saddle, the hostage girl seated before him. He swung to his men. 'If he attacks in daylight we'll kill him,' he said. 'If not we'll be clear of the trees soon. He'll stop following us then. He'll not tackle six armed men on open ground.'

His words did not convince them. But, then, they didn't convince him either. They moved slowly towards the trees, found the trail, then picked up the pace, Camran in the lead, Okrian just behind him. They rode for half an hour. Okrian glanced back to see two riderless horses. He shouted an alarm. Panic touched them all then and they began to ride faster, lashing their horses.

Camran emerged from the trees and hauled on the reins. He was sweating now, and could feel his heart beating wildly. Okrian and the other two surviving men drew their swords.

A rider on a dark horse moved slowly from the trees, his long black cloak drawn closely around him. The four warriors sat very still as he approached. Camran blinked back sweat. The man's face was strong, and somehow ageless. He could have been anywhere from his thirties to his fifties. His grey hair, lightly streaked with black, was shoulder-length, held back from his face by a black silk band tied about his brow. He was expressionless, but his dark eyes focused on Camran.

He rode to within ten feet of them, then drew back on the reins, waiting.

Camran felt the sting of salt sweat upon his cut brow. His lips were dry and he licked them. One grey-haired man against four warriors. The man could not survive. Why, then, the terrible fear causing Camran's belly to cramp?

9

In that moment the girl threw herself from the saddle. Camran tried to grab her, missed and swung back to face the rider. In that briefest of moments the rider's cloak flickered. His arm came up. Two crossbow bolts slammed into the riders on either side of Okrian. The first pitched from the saddle, the second slumped forward, sliding over his horse's neck. Okrian heeled his mount forward and charged at the rider. Camran followed, his sabre extended. The man's left hand flashed forward. A shining streak of silver light sped through the air, punching through Okrian's left eye-socket and into his brain. His body tipped back, his blade flying from his hand. Camran's sabre lanced out towards the assassin, but the man swayed in the saddle, the blade missing him by mere inches. Camran swung his mount.

Something struck him in the throat. Suddenly he couldn't breathe. Dropping his sword, his hand came up. Grabbing the hilt of the throwing knife, he dragged it clear of his flesh. Blood bubbled over his tunic. His horse reared, dumping him on the grass. As he lay there, choking on his own blood, a face appeared above his own.

It was the girl.

'I told you,' she said.

The dying man watched in horror as her bound hands lifted the blood-drenched throwing knife, raising it above his face. 'This is for the women,' she said.

And the blade swept down.

CHAPTER ONE

WAYLANDER SWAYED IN THE SADDLE, THE WEIGHT OF WEARINESS
and pain bearing down on him, washing away the anger. Blood from
the gash in his left shoulder had flowed over his chest and stomach,
but this had halted now. The wound in his side, however, was still
bleeding. He felt light-headed, and gripped the saddle pommel,
taking slow, deep breaths.

The village girl was kneeling by the dead raider. He heard her say
something, then watched as she took up his throwing knife in her
bound hands and rammed it into the man's face over and over again.
Waylander looked away, his vision blurring.

Fifteen years ago he would have hunted down these men and
emerged without a scratch. Now his wounds throbbed and, with the
fury gone, he felt empty, devoid of emotion. With great care he
dismounted. His legs almost gave way, but he kept hold of the
pommel and sagged against the steeldust gelding. Anger at his
weakness flared, giving him a little strength. Reaching into his
saddlebag he pulled out a small pouch of blue linen and moved
to a nearby boulder. His fingers were trembling as he opened it. He
sat quietly for a few heartbeats, breathing deeply, then unfastened his
black cloak, letting it drop back to drape over the boulder. The girl
came alongside him. Blood had splashed to her face, and into her
long, dark hair. Waylander drew his hunting knife and cut the ropes
binding her wrists. The skin beneath was raw and bleeding.

Twice he tried to sheath his blade, but his vision was misting, and
he placed the knife on the boulder beside him. The girl peered at his
torn leather tunic shirt, and the bloodstains upon it. 'You are hurt,'
she said. Waylander nodded. Unbuckling his belt, he reached up with

11

his right hand and tried to pull his shirt over his head. But there was no strength left. Swiftly she stepped in, lifting the garment clear. There were two wounds, a shallow cut from the top of his left shoulder and down past the collarbone, and a deeper puncture wound that had entered just above his left hip and exited at the back. Both holes were plugged with tree moss, but blood was still oozing. Waylander reached for the crescent needle embedded in the blue linen pouch. As his fingers touched it darkness swept over him.

When first he opened his eyes he wondered why the needle was shining so brightly, and why it was floating before his eyes. Then he realized he was staring at the crescent moon in a clear night sky. His cloak had been laid over him, and beneath his head was a pillow fashioned from a folded blanket. A fire was burning close by, and he could smell the savoury scent of woodsmoke. As he tried to move, pain erupted in his shoulder, stitches stretching against tortured flesh. He sagged back.

The girl moved alongside him, stroking his hair from his sweat-drenched brow.

Waylander closed his eyes and slept again, floating in a sea of dreams. A giant creature with the face of a wolf bore down upon him. He shot two crossbow bolts into its mouth. A second came at him. With no weapons to hand, he leapt at the beast, his hands grasping for its throat. It shifted and changed, becoming a slender woman whose neck snapped as his hands gripped hard. He cried out in agony, then looked around. The first dead beast had also changed. It had become a small boy, lying dead in a meadow of spring flowers. Waylander looked at his hands. They were covered in blood, which flowed up over his arms, covering his chest and neck, streaming over his face and into his mouth, choking him. He spat it out, struggling for breath, and staggered to a nearby stream, hurling himself into it, trying to wash the blood from his face and body.

A man was sitting on the bank. 'Help me!' called Waylander.

'I cannot,' said the man. He stood and turned away, and Waylander saw two crossbow bolts jutting from his back.

The terrible dreams continued, dreams of blood and death.

When he awoke it was still dark, but he felt stronger. Moving with care to protect the stitches, he rolled to his right and pushed himself to a sitting position. The second wound above his hip flared with pain and he grunted.

'Are you feeling better?' the girl asked him.

'A little. Thank you for helping me.'

She laughed.

'What is so amusing?' he asked.

'You rode after thirteen men and suffered these wounds to come to my rescue. And you thank *me*? You are a strange man, Lord. Are you hungry?' He realized that he was. In fact, he was ravenous. She took a stick and rolled three large clay balls from the fire. Cracking open the first with a sharp blow she knelt down and examined the contents. Looking up at him, she smiled.

It was a pretty smile, he thought. 'What do you have there?' he asked.

'Pigeons. I killed them yesterday. They are a little too fresh, but there was no other food. My uncle taught me how to cook them in clay, but I have not tried it in years.'

'Yesterday? How long have I been sleeping?'

'On and off for three days.'

Satisfied that the first pigeon was cooked, she cracked open the other two balls. The smell of roasted meat filled the air. Waylander felt almost sick with hunger. They waited impatiently until the meat had cooled, then devoured the birds. The flavour was strong, the texture not unlike aged beef.

'Who is Tanya?' she asked.

He looked at her, and his eyes were cold. 'How do you know that name?'

'You cried out in your sleep.'

He did not answer at first, and she did not press him. Instead she built up the fire and sat quietly, a blanket around her shoulders. 'She was my first wife,' he said at last. 'She died. Her grave is a long way from here.'

'Did you love her greatly?'

'Aye. Greatly. You are very curious.'

'How else does one find out what one wishes to know?'

'I cannot argue with that.' She was about to speak, but he raised his hand. 'And let that be an end to questions on this matter,' he said.

'As you will, Lord.'

'I am not a lord. I am a landowner.'

'Are you very old? Your hair is grey, and there are lines on your face. But you move like a young man.'

'What is your name?' he asked her.

13

'Keeva Taliana.'

'Yes, I am old, Keeva Taliana. Older than sin.'

'Then how is it that you could kill all those men? They were young and strong and fierce as devils.'

Suddenly he felt weary again. She was instantly full of concern. 'You must drink lots of water,' she said. 'My uncle told me that. Loss of blood, lots of water.'

'A wise man, your uncle. Did he also teach you to use your elbow as a weapon?'

'Yes. He taught me many things. None of which was terribly useful when the raiders came.'

Fetching a canteen from a saddle on the ground close by, she held it out to him. Waylander took it from her and drank deeply. 'Do not be so sure,' he said. 'You are alive. The others are not. You stayed cool and you used your mind.'

'I was lucky,' she said, a note of anger in her voice.

'Yes, you were. But you planted the seed of fear in the leader. For that he kept you alive.'

'I don't understand.'

'You told him the Grey Man was coming.'

'You were there?'

'I was there when he told his sergeant what you had said. I was about to slay them both when the sergeant grabbed you by the hair and dragged you back to the fire. That caught me out of position. Had you not crushed that man's nose I would not have had time to come to your aid. So, yes, you were lucky. But you made the best use of that luck.'

'I did not see you or hear you,' she said.

'Neither did they.' Then he lay back and slept again.

When he awoke she was snuggled down alongside him, sleeping peacefully. It was pleasant to be this close to another human being, and he realized he had been alone too long. Easing himself away from her, he rose to his feet and pulled on his boots. As he did so, a group of crows detached themselves from the bodies of the dead and rose into the air, cawing raucously. The sound woke Keeva. She sat up, smiled at him, then moved away behind the boulders. Waylander saddled two of the horses she had tethered, the effort causing his wounds to throb.

He was still angry about the first wound to his shoulder. He should have guessed the leader would send out a rearguard. They almost

14

had him. The first had been crouched on a tree branch above the trail, the second hiding in the bushes. Only the scraping of the first man's boot upon the bark above had alerted him. Bringing up his crossbow he had sent a bolt into the man as he leapt. It had entered at the belly, slicing up through the heart. He had fallen almost on top of Waylander, his sword slashing across his shoulder. Luckily the man was dead as the blow struck, and there was no real force in it. The second man had lunged from the bushes, a single-bladed axe in his hand. The steeldust gelding had reared, forcing the attacker back. In that moment Waylander sent the second bolt through the man's forehead. You are getting old and slow, he chided himself. Two clumsy assassins and they almost had you.

It had probably been this anger that had led him to attack their camp – a need to prove to himself that he could still move as he once had. Waylander sighed. He had been lucky to escape with his life. Even so, one of the men had managed to slam a blade into his hip. An inch or so higher and he would have been disembowelled, a few inches lower and the blade would have sliced the femoral artery, killing him for sure.

Keeva returned, smiling and waving as she came. He felt a touch of guilt. He had not known, at first, that the raiders had a captive. He had hunted them purely because they raided his lands. Her rescue, though it gave him great pleasure, was merely a fluke, a fortunate happenstance.

Keeva rolled the blankets and tied them to the back of her saddle. Then she brought him his cloak and weapons. 'Do you have a name, Lord?' she asked. 'Apart from the Grey Man.'

'I am not a lord,' he said again, ignoring her question.

'Yes, Grey Man,' she said, with an impudent smile. 'I will remember that.'

How resilient the young are, he thought. Keeva had witnessed death and destruction, had been raped and abused, and was now miles from home in the company of a stranger. Yet she could still smile. Then he looked into her dark eyes, and saw beneath the smile the traces of sorrow and fear. She was making a great effort to appear carefree, to charm him. And why not? he thought. She is a peasant girl with no rights, save those her master allows her. And these were few. If Waylander were to rape and kill her, there would be no inquest and few questions asked. In essence he owned her as if she were a slave. Why would she not seek to please him?

15

'You are safe with me,' he said.

'I know that, Lord. You are a good man.'

'No, I am not. But you can trust my words. No further harm will come to you, and I will see you safely home.'

'I do trust your words, Grey Man,' she replied. 'My uncle said that words were just noises in the air. Trust deeds, he told me, not words. I will not be a burden to you. I will help with your wounds as we travel.'

'You are not a burden, Keeva,' he said softly, then heeled his horse forward. She rode alongside him.

'I told them you were coming. I told them you would kill them. But I didn't really believe it. I just wanted them to know fear as I knew fear. Then you came. And they were terrified. It was wonderful.'

They rode for several hours, heading south and west, until they came to an old stone road leading to a secluded fishing settlement on the banks of a wide, flowing river. There were some forty houses, many of them stone-built. The people here looked prosperous, thought Keeva. Even the children playing close by boasted tunics without patches or any sign of wear, and all wore shoes. The Grey Man was recognized instantly and a crowd gathered. The village headman, a small, portly man with thinning blond hair, pushed his way through them. 'Welcome, sir,' he said, with a deep bow. Keeva could see fear in the man's eyes, and felt the nervous tension emanating from the small crowd. The Grey Man dismounted.

'Jonan, isn't it?'

'Yes, sir. Jonan,' answered the little headman, bowing once more.

'Well, be at ease, Jonan, I am merely passing through. I need some food for the rest of the journey, and my companion needs a change of clothing and a warm cloak.'

'It will be done instantly, sir. You are most welcome to wait in my home, where my wife will prepare some refreshment. Let me show you the way.' The little man bowed once more and turned towards the crowd. He gestured once at them, and they all bowed. Keeva climbed down from the tall horse and followed the two men. The Grey Man did not show any evidence of his wounds, save that there was still dried blood on his ripped tunic.

Jonan's house was of sand-fired brick, the frontage decorated with blackened timbers, the roof covered by red terracotta tiles. Jonan led them into a long living room. At the northern end was a large fireplace, also built with brick, and before it were set several deep

16

leather chairs and a low table. The floor was of polished timber, adorned with attractive rugs, beautifully crafted from Chiatze silk. The Grey Man eased himself into a chair, resting his head against the high back-rest. A young blonde woman entered. She smiled nervously at Keeva and curtsied to the Grey Man. 'We have ale, sir,' she said, 'or wine. Whatever pleases you.'

'Just some water, thank you,' he replied.

'We have apple juice, if that would be preferable?'

He nodded. 'That would be very fine.'

The headman shifted from foot to foot. 'May I sit, sir?' he asked.

'It is your house, Jonan. Of course you may sit.'

'Thank you.' He sank into the chair opposite. Keeva, unnoticed, sat down cross-legged upon a rug. 'It is a great pleasure and an honour to see you, sir,' continued Jonan. 'Had we known you were coming we could have prepared a feast in your honour.'

The woman returned, bringing a goblet of apple juice for the Grey Man and a tankard of ale for Jonan. As she backed away she glanced down at Keeva and silently gestured for her to follow. Keeva rose from the floor and walked from the room, through the hall beyond and into a long kitchen. The woman of the house was flustered, but she offered Keeva a seat at a pine table and filled a clay cup with juice. Keeva drank it.

'We did not know he was coming,' said the woman nervously, sitting down opposite Keeva. She ran her fingers through her long, blond hair, pushing it back from her eyes, and tying it at the nape of her neck.

'It is not an inspection,' said Keeva softly.

'No? You are sure?'

'I am sure. Some raiders attacked my village. He hunted them down and killed them.'

'Yes, he is a terrible killer,' said the woman, her hands trembling. 'Has he harmed you?'

Keeva shook her head. 'He rescued me from them. He is taking me home.'

'I thought my heart would stop beating when he rode in.'

'He owns this village too?' asked Keeva.

'He owns all the lands of the Crescent. Bought them six years ago from Lord Aric, though he has been here only once in that time. We send him his taxes. In full,' she added quickly. Keeva did not respond to this. Surely no community paying full taxes could afford so many fine clothes, furniture and Chiatze rugs. Nor would they be so

17

nervous concerning inspections. But, then, withholding taxes was, in her limited experience, a way of life among farmers and fishermen. Her brother had always managed to squirrel away one sack of grain in twenty to sell at market in order to supply small luxuries to his family, like new shoes, or a better-made bed for himself and his wife.

'My name is Conae,' said the woman, relaxing a little.

'Keeva.'

'Did the raiders kill many in your village?'

'Five men and three women.'

'So many? How awful.'

'They came in at dusk. Some of the women managed to run, taking the children with them. The men tried to fight. It was over very quickly.' Keeva shuddered at the memory.

'Was your husband among them?'

'I am not married. I was living in Carlis with my uncle, and when he died last year I went to work for my brother. He was killed. So was his wife. And they burned down our house.'

'You poor girl,' said Conae.

'I am alive,' said Keeva.

'Were you close to your brother?'

'He was a hard man and he treated me like a slave. His wife was little better.'

'You could stay here,' said Conae. 'There are more young men than young girls and a pretty creature like you could find a good husband.'

'I am not looking for a husband,' said Keeva. 'Not yet,' she added, seeing the concern on Conae's face. They sat in uncomfortable silence for a little while, then Conae smiled awkwardly and rose. 'I'll fetch you some clothes,' she said. 'For your journey.'

As Conae left the room Keeva leant back in the chair. She was tired now, and very hungry. Am I evil not to mourn Grava's death? she wondered, picturing his broad face, and his small, cold eyes. He was a brute and you hated him, she told herself. It would be hypocrisy to pretend grief. Pushing herself to her feet, she moved across the kitchen, cutting herself a slab of bread and pouring another cup of apple juice. In the silence she could hear the conversation from the living room. Chewing the bread, she moved closer to the wall. There was a closed wooden hatch, crafted so that food could be passed from the kitchen. Putting her eye to the crack, she saw the Grey Man rise from his chair. Jonan stood also.

18

'There are bodies in the woods to the north-east,' said the Grey Man. 'Send out some men to bury them, and gather whatever weapons and coin they were carrying. These you can keep. You will also find horses. These will be brought to me at my house.'

'Yes, sir.'

'One other thing, Jonan. Your profits from smuggling are nothing to do with me. Taxes on goods shipped in from Chiatze lands are subject to the Duke's laws not mine. You should bear in mind, however, that punishment for smugglers is severe indeed. I am reliably informed that the Duke's inspectors will be sent out in the next month.'

'You are mistaken, sir. We don't . . .' His words tailed away as he met the Grey Man's gaze.

'If the inspectors find you guilty you will all be hanged. Then who will bring in the fish and pay me my taxes? Are you all blind here? You are a fishing settlement and yet your children wear clothes of the best wool, your women boast brooches of silver, and your own house has three rugs that would cost a year's profit from a good fishing vessel. If there are any old clothes left in this village I suggest you find them. And when the inspectors arrive make sure they are worn.'

'It will be as you say, sir,' said Jonan miserably.

Keeva pulled away from the hatch as Conae returned with a dress of blue wool, a pair of high-laced ankle-length shoes, and a brown woollen cloak lined with rabbit fur. Keeva put them on. The dress was a little loose, the shoes a perfect fit.

Jonan called out for the women and they both returned to the living room. The Grey Man was on his feet. Reaching into a pouch by his side, he gave Jonan several small silver coin, in payment for the clothes.

'That is not necessary, sir,' said Jonan.

Ignoring him, the Grey Man turned to Conae. 'Thank you for your hospitality, lady.'

Conae curtsied.

The horses were outside, the saddlebags bulging with food for the journey. The Grey Man helped Keeva to mount, then stepped into the saddle.

Without a word of farewell he rode from the settlement, Keeva following.

CHAPTER TWO

THEY RODE IN SILENCE FOR A LITTLE WHILE AND KEEVA SAW THAT
the Grey Man's face was stern. She guessed he was angry. Even so, she
noted that he studied the lands as he rode, always alert and watchful.
Clouds obscured the sun and a little light rain began to fall. Keeva
lifted her hood into place and drew her new fur-lined cloak about her.

The rain passed swiftly, sunlight spearing through a break in the
clouds. The Grey Man angled his horse up a shallow slope and
paused at the top. Keeva drew alongside. 'How are your wounds?'
she asked him.

'Almost healed,' he said.

'In such a short time? I don't think so.'

He shrugged and, satisfied the way was clear of danger, heeled the
steeldust forward.

Throughout the long afternoon they rode steadily, once more
entering the forest. An hour before dusk the Grey Man found a
campsite beside a stream and set a fire. 'Are you angry with the
villagers for cheating you?' asked Keeva, as the flames licked at the
dry wood.

'No. I am angry at their stupidity.' He looked at her. 'You were
listening?'

She nodded. The Grey Man's face softened. 'You are a canny girl,
Keeva. You remind me of my daughter.'

'Does she live with you?'

'No, she lives far away in another land. I have not seen her in
several years. She is married now to an old friend of mine. They had
two sons, last I heard.'

'You have grandsons.'

'In a manner of speaking. She is my adopted daughter.'

'Do you have children of your own?'

He fell silent for a moment, and in the firelight she saw a look of deep sadness touch him. 'I had children, but they . . . died,' he said. 'Let us see what food Jonan's wife prepared for us.' Rising smoothly he moved to the saddlebags, returning with a hunk of ham and some freshly baked bread. They ate in silence. Keeva gathered more dry wood and fed the fire. The clouds had returned, but the night was not cold.

The Grey Man removed his shirt. 'Time to draw these stitches,' he said.

'The wounds cannot have healed,' she told him sternly. 'The stitches should remain for at least ten days. My uncle . . .'

'. . . was a very wise man,' said the Grey Man. 'But see for yourself.'

Keeva moved closer to him and examined the wounds. He was right. The skin had healed, and already scar tissue had formed. Taking his hunting knife, she carefully cut through the twine, pulling each stitch clear. 'I have never heard of anyone healing this fast,' she said, as he pulled on his shirt. 'Do you know magic?'

'No. But once I was healed by a monster. It changed me.'

'A monster?'

He grinned at her. 'Aye, a monster. Seven feet tall, with a single eye in the centre of his forehead – an eye that had two pupils.'

'You are making fun of me,' she chided him.

The Grey Man shook his head. 'No, I am not. His name was Kai. He was a freak of nature – a man beast. I was dying and he laid his hands upon me and all my wounds closed, healed in a heartbeat. Ever since then I have known no sickness, no winter chills, no fevers, no boils. I think even time has slowed for me, for by now I should be spending my days sitting in a comfortable chair with a blanket around my knees. He was a fine man, Kai.'

'What happened to him?'

He shrugged. 'I don't know. Perhaps he is happy somewhere, perhaps he is dead.'

'You have lived an interesting life,' she said.

'How old are you?' he asked her.

'Seventeen.'

21

'Kidnapped by raiders, and taken away into the forest. There are some in years to come who will hear of this tale and say, "You have lived an interesting life." What will you say to them?'

Keeva smiled. 'I shall agree – and they will envy me.'

He laughed then, the sound full of good-humour. 'I like you, Keeva,' he said. Then, he added wood to the fire, stretched out and covered himself with a blanket.

'I like you too, Grey Man,' she said.

He did not answer, and she saw that he was already asleep.

She looked at his face in the firelight. It was strong – the face of a fighter – and yet she could detect no cruelty there.

Keeva slept, and woke with the dawn. The Grey Man was already up. He was sitting by the stream and splashing water to his face. Then, using his hunting knife, he shaved away the black and silver stubble from his chin and cheeks. 'Did you sleep well?' he asked, as he returned to the fire.

'Yes,' she told him. 'No dreams. It was wonderful.' He looked so much younger without the stubble, a man perhaps in his late thirties. She wondered momentarily how old he was. Forty-five? Fifty-five? Surely not older.

'We should be at your settlement by noon,' he said.

Keeva shivered, remembering the murdered women. 'There is nothing there for me. I was staying with my brother and his wife. They are both dead, the farmhouse burned.'

'What will you do?'

'Go back to Carlis and seek work.'

'Are you trained in some craft or skill?'

'No, but I can learn.'

'I can offer you employment at my home,' he said.

'I will not be your mistress, Grey Man,' she told him.

He smiled broadly. 'Have I *asked* you to be my mistress?'

'No, but why else are you offering to take me to your palace?'

'Do you think so little of yourself?' he countered. 'You are intelligent and brave. I also think you are trustworthy and would be loyal. I have one hundred and thirty servants at my home, administering often to more than fifty guests. You would clean rooms, prepare beds for those guests, and help in the kitchens. For this I will pay you two silvers a month. You will have your own room and one day a week free of all duties. Think on it.'

22

'I accept,' she said.

'Then let it be so.'

'Why do you have so many guests?'

'My home – my palace, as you call it – houses several libraries, an infirmary and a museum. Scholars come from all over Kydor to study there. There is also a separate centre in the South Tower for students and physicians to analyse medicinal herbs and their uses, and three further halls have been set aside for the treatment of the sick.'

Keeva remained silent for a while, then she looked into his eyes. 'I am sorry,' she said.

'Why would you apologize? You are an attractive young woman, and I can understand why you would fear unwelcome advances. You do not know me. Why should I be trusted?'

'I trust you,' she told him. 'Can I ask you a question?'

'Of course.'

'If you have a palace why are your clothes so old, and why do you ride out alone to protect your lands? Think of all you could lose.'

'Lose?' he asked.

'All your wealth.'

'Wealth is a small thing, Keeva, tiny like a grain of sand. It seems large only to those who do not possess it. You talk of *my* palace. It is not mine. I built it, I live within it. Yet one day I will die and the palace will have another owner. Then he will die. And so it goes on. A man *owns* nothing but his life. He holds items briefly in his hand. If they are made of metal or stone they will surely outlive him and be owned by someone else for a short time. If they are cloth he will – with luck – outlive them. Look around you, at the trees and the hills. According to Kydor law, they are mine. You think the trees care that they are mine? Or the hills? The same hills that were bathed in sunlight when my earliest ancestor walked the earth. The same hills that will still be covered in grass when the last man turns to dust.'

'I see that,' said Keeva, 'but with all your wealth you can have everything you want for the rest of your life. Every pleasure, every joy is available to you.'

'There is not enough gold in all the world to supply what I want,' he said.

'And what is that?'

'A clean conscience,' he said. 'Now, do you wish to return to the settlement to see your brother buried?'

23

The conversation was obviously over. Keeva shook her head. 'No. I don't want to go there.'

'Then we will push on. We should reach my home by dark.'

Cresting a hill, they began the slow descent on to a wide plain. As far as the eye could see there were ruins everywhere. Keeva drew rein and stared out over the plain. In some places there were merely a few white stones, in others the shapes of buildings could still be seen. Towards the west, against a granite cliff-face there were the remains of two high towers, which had crumbled at the base and crashed to the ground like felled trees.

'What was this place?' she asked.

The Grey Man gazed over the ruins. 'An ancient city called Kuan-Hador. No one knows who built it, or why it fell. Its history is lost in the mists of time.' He looked at her and smiled. 'I expect the people here once believed they owned the hills and the trees,' he said.

They rode down on to the plain. Some way to the west Keeva saw a mist rolling between the jagged ruins. 'Speaking of mists,' she said, pointing it out to her companion. Waylander halted his horse and glanced to the west. Keeva rode alongside. 'Why are you loading your crossbow?' she asked him, as his hands slid two bolts into the grooves in the small black weapon.

'Habit,' he said, but his expression was stern, his dark eyes wary. Angling his horse towards the south-east, away from the mist, he rode away.

Keeva followed him and swung in the saddle to stare back at the ruins. 'How strange,' she said. 'The mist is gone.'

He, too, glanced back, then unloaded his weapon, slipping the bolts back into the quiver at his belt. He saw her looking at him.

'I do not like this place,' she said. 'It feels . . . dangerous,' she concluded lamely.

'You have good instincts,' he told her.

Matze Chai parted the painted silk curtains of his palanquin and gazed with undisguised malevolence at the mountains. Sunlight was filtering through the clouds and shining brightly upon the snow-capped peaks. The elderly man sighed and pulled shut the curtains. As he did so his dark, almond-shaped eyes focused on the back of his slender hand, seeing again the brown liver spots of age staining the dry skin.

The Chiatze merchant reached for a small, ornate wooden box and removed a tub of sweet-smelling lotion, which he applied carefully to his hands, before leaning back against his cushions and closing his eyes.

Matze Chai did not hate mountains. Hatred would mean giving in to passion, and passion, in Matze's view, indicated an uncivilized mind. He loathed what the mountains represented, what the Philosopher termed the Mirrors of Mortality. The peaks were eternal, never changing, and when a man gazed upon them his own ephemeral nature was exposed to the light; the frailty of his flesh apparent. And frail it was, he thought, regarding his coming seventieth birthday with a mixture of disquiet and apprehension.

He leant forward and slid back a panel in the wall, revealing a rectangular mirror. Matze Chai gazed upon his reflection. The thinning hair, drawn tightly across his skull and braided at the nape of his neck, was as black as in his youth. But a tiny line of silver at the hairline meant that he would need to have the dye reapplied soon. His slender face showed few lines, but his neck was sagging, and even the high collar of his scarlet and gold robes could no longer disguise it.

The palanquin lurched to the right, as one of the eight bearers, weary after six hours of labour, slipped on a loose stone. Matze Chai reached up and rang the small golden bell bolted to the embossed panel by the window. The palanquin stopped smoothly and was lowered to the ground.

The door was opened by his *Rajnee*, Kysumu. The small warrior extended his hand. Matze Chai took it and stepped through the doorway, his long robes of heavily embroidered yellow silk trailing to the rocky path. He glanced back. The six soldiers of his guard sat their mounts silently. Beyond them the second team of bearers climbed down from the first of the three wagons. Dressed in livery of red and black, the eight men marched forward to replace the tired first team, who trudged silently back to the wagon.

Another liveried servant ran forward, bearing a silver goblet. He bowed before Matze Chai and offered him the watered wine. The merchant took the goblet, sipping the contents. 'How much longer?' he asked the man.

'Captain Liu says we will camp at the foot of the mountains, sir. The scout has found a suitable site. He says it is an hour from here.'

25

Matze Chai drank a little more, then returned the goblet, still half full, to the servant. Climbing back into the palanquin he settled himself down on his cushions. 'Join me, Kysumu,' he said.

The warrior nodded, pulled his sword and scabbard from the sash of his long grey robes, and climbed inside, seating himself opposite the merchant. The eight bearers took hold of the cushioned poles, raising them to waist height. At a whispered command from the lead bearer they then hefted the poles to their shoulders. Inside the palanquin Matze Chai gave a satisfied sigh. He had trained the two teams well, paying attention to every detail. Travel by palanquin was usually not dissimilar to sailing a small boat on choppy water. The cabin lurched from side to side and within minutes those with delicate constitutions would begin to feel queasy. Not so for those who travelled with Matze Chai. His teams were made up of eight men of equal height, trained for hours every day back in Namib. They were well paid, well fed, powerful young labourers; men of little imagination but great strength.

Matze Chai leant back in his cushions, transferring his gaze to the slim, dark-haired young man seated opposite him. Kysumu sat silently, his three-foot-long curved sword on his lap, his coal-black slanted eyes returning Matze Chai's gaze. The merchant had grown to like the little swordsman, for he spoke rarely and radiated calm. There was never a hint of tension about him.

'How is it you are not wealthy?' Matze Chai asked him.

'Define wealth,' answered Kysumu, his long face, as ever, expressionless.

'The ability to purchase whatever one desires, whenever one desires it.'

'Then I am wealthy. All I desire is a little food and water each day. These I can pay for.'

Matze Chai smiled. 'Then let me rephrase the question: how is it that your renowned skills have not supplied you with plentiful amounts of gold and coin?'

'Gold does not interest me.'

Matze Chai already knew this. It explained why Kysumu was the most highly prized *Rajnee* in all the lands of the Chiatze. All men knew that the swordsman could not be bought, and thus would never betray the nobleman who hired him. Yet it was baffling, for among the Chiatze nobility loyalty always came at a price, and it was

26

perfectly acceptable for warriors and bodyguards like Kysumu to change allegiance when better offers were made. Intrigue and treachery were endemic to the Chiatze way of life – indeed, among politicians of all races. Which made it even more curious that Kysumu was revered among the treacherous nobility for his honesty. They did not laugh behind his back, or mock his 'stupidity'. Even though it highlighted, in glorious colour, their own lack of morals. What a strange race we are, thought Matze Chai.

Kysumu had closed his eyes and was breathing deeply. Matze Chai looked at him closely. No more than five and a half feet tall, slightly round-shouldered, the man looked more like a scholar or a priest. His long face and slightly downturned mouth gave him a look of melancholy. It was an ordinary face, not handsome, not ugly. The only distinctive feature was a small purple birthmark on his left eyebrow. Kysumu's eyes opened and he yawned.

'Have you ever visited the lands of Kydor?' asked the merchant.

'No.'

'They are an uncivilized people, and their language is hard on both the ear and the mind. It is guttural and coarse. Not musical in any way. Do you speak any foreign tongues?'

'A few,' said Kysumu.

'The people here are offshoots from two empires, the Drenai and the Angostin. Both languages have the same base.' Matze Chai was just beginning to outline the history of the land, when the palanquin came to a sudden stop. Kysumu opened the panelled door and leapt lightly to the ground. Matze Chai rang the small bell and the palanquin was lowered to the rocks. Not smoothly, which irritated him. He climbed out to berate the bearers, then saw the group of armed men barring the way. He scanned them. There were eleven warriors, all armed with swords and clubs, though two carried longbows.

Matze Chai flicked a glance back to his six guards, who had all edged their horses forward. They were looking nervous, and this added to Matze's irritation. They were supposed to be fighters. They were *paid* to be fighters.

Lifting his yellow robes to keep the dust from the hem, Matze Chai moved towards the armed men. 'Good day to you,' he said. 'Why have you stopped my palanquin?'

A bearded man stepped forward. He was tall and broad-shouldered, a longsword in his hand, two long, curved knives sheathed in his thick belt. 'This is a toll road, Slant-eye. No one passes here without payment.'

'And what is the payment?' asked Matze Chai.

'For a rich foreigner like you? Twenty in gold.' Movement came from left and right as a dozen more men emerged from behind rocks and boulders.

'The toll seems excessive,' said Matze Chai. He turned to Kysumu and spoke in Chiatze. 'What do you think?' he asked. 'They are robbers and they outnumber us.'

'Do you wish to pay them?'

'Do you believe they will merely take twenty in gold?'

'No. Once we accede to their demands they will demand more.'

'Then I do not wish to pay them.'

'Return to your palanquin,' said Kysumu softly, 'and I will clear the path.'

Matze Chai returned his gaze to the bearded leader. 'I suggest,' he said, 'that you step aside. This man is Kysumu, the most feared *Rajnee* among the Chiatze. And you are, at this moment, only heartbeats from death.'

The tall leader laughed. 'He may be all you say, Slant-eye, but to me he's just another vomit-coloured dwarf ripe for the taking.'

'I fear you are making a mistake,' said Matze Chai, 'but, then, all actions have consequences and a man must have the courage to face them.' He gave an abrupt bow, which in Chiatze would have been insulting, and turned away, walking slowly back to his palanquin. He glanced back, and saw Kysumu walk forward to stand before the leader. Two robbers advanced from the group to stand alongside the bearded man. For a moment only Matze Chai doubted the wisdom of this course of action. Kysumu seemed suddenly tiny and innocuous against the brute power of the round-eye robber and his men.

The leader's sword came up. Kysumu's blade flashed into the air.

Moments later, with four men dead, the rest of the robbers scattering and running away into the rocks, Kysumu wiped clean his sword and returned to the palanquin. He was not out of breath, neither was his face flushed. He looked, as always, serene and at peace. Matze Chai's heart was beating wildly, but he fought to keep his face expressionless. Kysumu had moved with almost inhuman speed, cutting, slashing, spinning like a dancer into the midst of the

28

robbers. At the same moment his six guards had charged their horses into the second group, and they, too, had run for cover. All in all, a most satisfactory outcome, and one that justified the expense of hiring guards.

'Do you believe they will come back?' asked Matze Chai.

'Perhaps,' said Kysumu, with a shrug. Then he stood quietly waiting for orders. Matze Chai summoned a servant and asked Kysumu if he wished to partake of some watered wine. The swordsman refused. Matze Chai accepted a goblet, intending to take a sip. Instead he half drained it.

'You did well, *Rajnee*,' he said.

'We should be moving from here,' replied Kysumu.

'Indeed so.'

The cabin of the palanquin felt like a sanctuary as Matze Chai settled himself down on his cushions. Lightly striking the bell to signal the bearers to move on, he closed his eyes. He felt safe, secure, and almost immortal. Opening his eyes, he glanced out through the window and saw the setting sun blaze its dying light over the mountain peaks. Reaching up, he drew the curtains closed, his good-humour evaporating.

They made camp an hour later, and Matze Chai sat in his palanquin while his servants unloaded his night-time furniture from the wagons, assembling his gold-lacquered bed, and spreading upon it his satin sheets and thick goose-down quilt. After this they raised the poles and frame of his blue and gold silk tent, spreading out the black canvas sheet upon the ground, then unrolling his favourite silk rug to cover it. Lastly his two favourite chairs, both inlaid with gold and deeply cushioned with padded velvet, were placed in the tent entrance. When finally Matze Chai climbed from the palanquin the camp was almost prepared. His sixteen bearers were sitting together round two campfires set in a jumble of boulders, two of the six guards had taken up sentry positions to patrol the perimeter, and his cook was busy preparing a light supper of spiced rice and dried fish.

Matze Chai moved across the campground to his tent and sank gratefully into his chair. He was tired of living like a frontier nomad, at the mercy of the elements, and longed for the journey to be over. Six weeks of this harsh existence had drained his energy.

Kysumu was sitting cross-legged upon the ground close by, a section of parchment, pinned to a board of cork, resting on his knees.

29

Using a shaped piece of charcoal Kysumu was sketching a tree. Matze Chai watched the little swordsman. Every evening he would fetch his leather folder from the supply wagon, take a fresh section of parchment, and sketch for an hour. Usually trees or plants, Matze Chai had noted.

Matze Chai had many such drawings in his own home, by some of the greatest Chiatze masters. Kysumu was talented, but by no means exceptional. His compositions lacked, in Matze Chai's opinion, the harmony of emptiness. Kysumu's work had too much passion. Art should be serene, devoid of human emotion. Stark and simple, it should encourage meditation. Even so, Matze Chai decided, he should – at journey's end – offer to purchase one of the sketches. It would be impolite not to do so.

A servant brought him a cup of scented tisane and, with the temperature dropping, laid a fur-lined robe around Matze Chai's thin shoulders. Then two of the bearers, using forked wooden poles, carried an iron brazier, glowing with coals, into Matze Chai's tent, setting it down on a pewter base plate, to prevent cinders singeing the expensive rugs.

The incident with the robbers had proved spiritually uplifting. As the mountains spoke silently of the fleeting nature of man, the sudden peril had brought to the fore just how much Matze Chai enjoyed life. It made him aware of the sweetness of the air he breathed, and of the feel of silk upon his skin. Even the tisane he now sipped was almost unbearably fine upon the tongue.

Despite the discomforts of travel Matze Chai was forced to admit that he now felt better than he had in years. Wrapping himself in the fur-lined cloak he settled back and found himself thinking of Waylander. It had been six years since last they met, back in Namib. At that time, Matze Chai had recently returned from Drenan, where he had, upon Waylander's instruction, purchased a skull from the Great Library. Waylander had then sold his home and journeyed north and east, seeking a new land and a new life.

Such a restless soul, thought Matze Chai. But, then, Waylander was a man on a mission that could never be completed, a quest born in despair and longing. At first Matze Chai had believed Waylander to be seeking redemption for past sins. This was only partly true. No, what the Grey Man sought was an impossibility.

An owl hooted close by, breaking Matze Chai's concentration.

Kysumu finished his sketch, and replaced it in the leather folder. Matze Chai beckoned him to sit in the second chair. 'It occurs to me,' he said, 'that had the remaining robbers not panicked and run you would have been overwhelmed.'

'Indeed,' said Kysumu.

'Or, if my guards had not attacked the second group at just that instant, they could have run at the palanquin and killed me.'

'They could have,' agreed the swordsman.

'But you did not think it likely?'

'I did not think of it at all,' said Kysumu.

Matze Chai suppressed a smile, but allowed the feeling of warm satisfaction to flow through him. Kysumu was a delight. The ideal companion. He did not gush or chatter, or ask endless questions. He was, in truth, harmony itself. They sat thus for a little while. Then food was brought and they ate quietly.

At the conclusion of the meal Matze Chai rose from his chair. 'I shall sleep now,' he said. Kysumu rose, pushed his sword and scabbard into the sash around his robes, and strolled from the camp.

The captain of Matze Chai's guards, a young man named Liu, approached his master and bowed deeply. 'Might I enquire, Lord, where the *Rajnee* is going?'

'I would imagine he is seeking out the robbers, in the event that they might be following,' Matze Chai told him.

'Should some of the men not go with him, Lord?'

'I do not believe he has need of them.'

'Yes, Lord,' said Liu, bowing and backing away.

'You did well today, Liu,' said Matze Chai. 'I shall mention it to your father upon our return.'

'Thank you, Lord.'

'You were frightened, though, were you not, before the fighting began?'

'Yes, Lord. Did it show?'

'I am afraid that it did. Try to exhibit a little more control of your expressions should any similar incidents occur.'

The Grey Man's palace had initially both surprised and disappointed Keeva. Darkness had fallen as they arrived. They had ridden slowly up a dirt road through thick woods, emerging on to open ground and an area of well-trimmed lawn, bisected by a wide stone avenue.

31

There were no fountains or statues. Two spear-wielding guards were patrolling the front of a long, flat, single-storey building around two hundred feet long. There were few windows to be seen, and even these were dark. The only light Keeva could see came from four large brass lanterns hanging in the wide, marble-pillared entrance. It looks like a mausoleum, thought Keeva, as the Grey Man rode his horse forward.

The black doors opened and two young men ran out to meet them. Both wore grey livery. Weary now, Keeva dismounted. The servants led the horses away, and the Grey Man beckoned her to follow him inside. An elderly man was waiting for them, a tall, stooping figure, white-haired and long-faced. He, too, was wearing grey, an ankle-length tunic of fine wool. At the shoulder the image of a tree had been beautifully embroidered in black satin. He bowed to the Grey Man. 'You look tired, sir,' he said, his voice deep and low. 'I shall have a hot bath prepared.'

'Thank you, Omri. This young woman will be joining the staff. Have a room prepared for her.'

'Of course, sir.'

Without a word of farewell the Grey Man strode away across the marble-tiled hallway. He had said little since they had moved away from the ruins, and Keeva wondered if she had said, or done, something to annoy him. She felt confused and uncertain, and gazed around at the velvet hangings, the ornate rugs and the walls adorned by fine paintings.

'Follow me, girl,' said Omri.

'I have a name,' she said, an edge of irritation in her voice.

Omri paused, then turned slowly.

She expected an angry response, but he merely smiled. 'My apologies, young woman. Of course you have. So let us not keep it a secret. Pray share it with me.'

'I am Keeva.'

'Well, that was easily settled, Keeva. *Now* will you follow me?'

'Yes.'

'Good.' He moved across the hall, and turned right into a broad corridor, which led to a wide staircase that descended into shadow. Keeva paused at the top. She had no wish at all to spend the night in this ugly, flat dwelling. But to go underground? What kind of man would spend his wealth building a home burrowed under the earth? she wondered.

The servant Omri was a little ahead of her now and Keeva moved swiftly down the carpeted stairs. The whole building seemed dark and dingy, occasional lanterns casting sinister shadows to the walls. Within minutes Keeva felt hopelessly lost within a gloomy labyrinth. 'How can you live here?' she asked Omri, her voice echoing in the bleak corridor. 'It is an awful place.'

He laughed with genuine amusement. It was a good sound and she found herself warming to the man. 'It is surprising what one can become used to,' he told her. They passed several doors before Omri took a lantern from the wall and halted before a narrow doorway. Lifting the latch he stepped inside. Keeva followed him. Omri moved to the centre of the small room, took a candle from an oval table-top, and held the wick to the lantern flame. Once it was lit he replaced it in a bronze holder shaped like an open flower. Keeva looked around. There was a bed against the wall, a simple piece, unadorned and crafted from pine. Beside it was a small cabinet, upon which was placed another candle in a bronze holder. Heavy curtains covered the far wall. 'Get a little rest,' Omri told her. 'I will send someone to you tomorrow morning early to explain your duties.'

'What is it that you do here?' she asked him, her words tumbling out in her anxiety not to be left alone.

'I am Omri, the steward. Are you all right? You seem to be trembling.'

With a great effort Keeva smiled. 'I am well. Truly.'

Omri paused and ran his thin hands through his thinning grey hair. 'I know that he fought and killed the men who attacked your settlement, and that you were captured by them, and treated . . . badly. But this is a good house, Keeva. You are safe here.'

'How could you know all that happened?' she asked.

'One of our guests is a Chiatze priestess. She can see over great distances.'

'She practises magic?'

'I do not know if it is magic. There are no spells cast. She merely closes her eyes. But it is, I must admit, beyond my understanding. Now, get some rest.'

Keeva heard his footsteps echoing along the corridor. Safe she might be, but she was determined to stay in this awful place not one heartbeat longer than necessary. Never before had Keeva been afraid of the dark, but here, in this underground palace, she found herself

33

staring at the little candle, pitifully grateful for its flickering light.

Weary from the long ride, she removed the cloak, dangling it over the back of a chair, then slipped out of her dress. The bed was comfortable, the mattress firm, the blankets clean, the pillow soft and yielding. Keeva closed her eyes and slipped into a dream-filled sleep. She saw again the Grey Man ride from the forest to confront the raiders, but this time when he came to rescue her his face was bleached of all colour. He took her by the arm and led her to a wide hole in the ground, dragging her in. She screamed – and woke, heart pounding. The candle had guttered and gone out, leaving the room in total darkness. Keeva rolled from the bed and scrabbled for the door latch, dragging it open. In the corridor a distant lantern was still burning. Taking the second candle from the bedside cabinet she ran to the lantern and lit the wick from its flame. Then she returned to her room, and sat quietly, berating herself for her fear.

'In life,' her uncle had told her, 'there are two kinds of people: those who run from their fears, and those who overcome them. Fear is like a coward. If you back away it becomes a fearsome bully who will beat you into the ground. Face him and he shrinks to a tiny noisy insect.'

Steeling herself, she blew out the candle and, lying down, pulled the blankets back into place. I will not give in to night terrors, she told herself. I will not panic, Uncle.

This time she slept more peacefully, and when she awoke there was the faintest of lights within the room. Sitting up, she saw that the light emanated from a crack in the heavy curtains of the far wall. Rising from the bed, Keeva crossed the room and drew back the curtains. Sunlight flooded in – and she found herself staring out across the brilliantly blue Bay of Carlis, the morning sun glittering on the waves. Tiny fishing-boats dotted the water, their white sails gleaming in the light. Above them gulls swooped and dived. Astonished now, Keeva opened the wooden-framed glass doors and stepped out on to a curved balcony. All around her, on different levels, were similar balconies, most larger, some smaller, but all looked out over the beauty of the bay.

She was not underground at all. The Grey Man's white marble palace had been built on the side of a sloping cliff, and she had entered at the top, unable to see its true magnificence.

Keeva glanced down. Below the balcony she saw terraced gardens and walkways and steps angling down towards the distant beach, where a wooden ramp extended into the sea. A dozen sailing-boats were moored there, sails furled. Returning her gaze to the palace itself, she saw that two towers had been erected to the north and south, huge structures, each with its own terraces.

Everywhere gardeners were already at work among the scores of flower-beds, some clearing away dead plants, others sweeping leaves from the paths and gathering them into sacks slung over their shoulders. Still more were planting fresh border flowers or dead-heading the many rosebushes.

Keeva was so entranced by the beauty of the scene that she failed to hear the gentle tapping at her door, or the creaking of the latch as it opened.

'I think perhaps you should come inside and dress yourself,' said a voice. Keeva whirled and saw a young woman with braided blond hair. She was carrying a neat pile of folded clothes. The woman grinned at her. 'The priests might catch sight of you, and what would happen to their vows then?'

'Priests?' asked Keeva, stepping inside and accepting the clothes from the woman.

'Chiatze foreigners. They are studying the ancient books that the Gentleman keeps in the library of the North Tower.'

Keeva took a white cotton blouse from the pile, shook it out, then slipped it over her head. The material was very soft – like a summer breeze upon the skin. She shivered with pleasure, then stepped into the long grey skirt. It had a belt of silvered leather, and a bright silver buckle. 'These are mine?' she asked.

'Yes.'

'They are wonderful.' Keeva reached up and touched the em-broidered tree on the right shoulder of her blouse. 'What does this represent?' she asked.

'It is the Gentleman's mark.'

'The Grey Man?'

'In public we call him the Gentleman, since he is not a lord and far too powerful to be merely a landowner or a merchant. Omri says you came in with him last night. Did you bed him?'

Keeva was shocked. 'No, I did not. And you are very rude to ask such a question.'

The blonde woman laughed. 'Life is very different here, Keeva. We

35

speak freely and think freely – except in front of the Gentleman's guests. He is a very unusual man. None of us is beaten, and he does not use the young women as his personal slaves.'

'Then perhaps I shall like it here,' said Keeva. 'What is your name?'

'I am Norda, and you will be working with my team in the North Tower. Are you hungry?'

'Yes.'

'Then let us get some breakfast. You have a great deal to learn today. The palace is like a rabbit warren and most of the new servants get lost.'

Some minutes later, after what was for Keeva a bewildering journey through endless corridors and several sets of stairs, the two women emerged on to a wide, paved terrace. A long breakfast table was covered with a score of deep dishes containing cooked meats, vegetables, smoked fish, cheeses and fruits. Fresh-baked bread had been set at one end, and flagons of water and fruit juices at the other. Keeva followed Norda's lead and took a plate, heaping it with bread, a slab of butter and some smoked fish. Then they walked to a table by the terrace wall and sat down to eat.

'Why did you ask if I'd slept with the Grey Man?'

'The Gentleman!' corrected Norda.

'Yes, the Gentleman.'

'There is great harmony here between the servant girls. The Gentleman does not play favourites – and neither does Omri. Had the Gentleman bedded you it would have caused discord. Many of the young women would like to . . . enchant him.'

'He is a strikingly attractive man – but he is very old,' said Keeva.

Norda laughed again. 'Age has little to do with it,' she said. 'He is handsome, strong – and immensely rich. The woman who captures his heart would never want for anything, even if she had ten lives to live.'

'From what you say it is surprising he has taken no wife,' observed Keeva.

'Oh, he has taken many.' Norda leaned in close, dropping her voice. 'Gold wives.'

'He *pays* for his pleasures?' asked Keeva, astonished.

'Always. Isn't that weird? Most of the girls here would rush to his rooms at the merest gesture from him. Yet he sends his carriage to bring whores from the town. Oh, fancily dressed and bedecked with jewels, but whores nonetheless. For the last year his favourite has been Lalitia – a red-headed strumpet from the capital.' Norda's face reddened, and Keeva saw her pale blue eyes grow cold.

'You obviously don't like her.'

'Nobody *likes* Lalitia. She rides around in a gilded carriage, with liveried servants whom she treats abominably. In her house she has been known to thrash the maids when the mood takes her. She is a vile creature.'

'What does he see in her?' asked Keeva.

Norda laughed aloud. 'Oh, you'll recognize it when you lay eyes on her. Loathe her as I do, even I have to admit she is astonishingly beautiful.'

'I would have thought him a better judge of people,' offered Keeva.

'You don't know much about men, do you?' said Norda, with a quick smile. 'When Lalitia passes by you can hear the sounds of jaws striking the ground. Strong men, bright men, scholarly men, even priestly men all fall under the spell of her beauty. They see what they want to see. Women, on the other hand, see her for what she is – a whore. And not as young as she pretends. I'd say she was closer to forty than the twenty-five she claims.'

Other servants had begun to arrive, gathering their food and finding places to sit and eat. A young man in a grey mailshirt approached them. Removing his helm he smiled at Norda. 'Good morning,' he said. 'Will you introduce me to the newcomer?'

Norda smiled. 'Keeva, this is Emrin, the guard sergeant. He thinks he's more handsome than he is and will do everything in his power to lure you to his bed. It is, sadly, his nature. Do not judge him too harshly.'

Keeva glanced up at the man. He had a round, good-looking face and blue eyes. His hair was light blond, short and tightly curled. Emrin extended his hand and Keeva shook it. 'Do not believe everything Norda says about me,' he told her. 'I am really a gentle soul, seeking the perfect partner for my heart.'

'Surely you found him the first time you looked in a mirror,' said Keeva, with a sweet smile.

'Sadly that is true,' said Emrin, with disarming honesty. Taking her hand he kissed it, then turned his attention to Norda. 'Be sure to tell your new friend what a great lover I am,' he said.

'I will,' said Norda. She glanced at Keeva. 'The best ten heartbeats I've ever experienced.' Both women laughed.

'I think I should leave,' Emrin said, 'while I have a modicum of dignity left.'

'Too late,' said Keeva. The man grinned and moved away.

'Neatly done,' said Norda. 'He will pursue you with even greater vigour.'

'Not something I desire,' Keeva told her.

'Oh, don't rule him out,' said Norda. 'As he says, he really is quite good in bed. Not the best I have known, but more than adequate.'

Keeva burst into laughter, and Norda joined in.

'So who was the best?'

She knew it was the wrong question as soon as she spoke: the good-humour faded from Norda's face. 'I am sorry,' said Keeva, swiftly.

'Don't be,' Norda told her, laying her hand over Keeva's. 'Now we'd better finish breakfast for there is much to do. There are several more guests due to arrive today, and one of them is a Chiatze. Believe me, there is no race so fussy.'

CHAPTER THREE

USING LONG, LAZY STROKES WAYLANDER SWAM THROUGH THE cold water. He could feel the warmth of the sun on the skin of his back, and he dived deep, through shoals of silver-backed fish, which scattered before him. Rolling and twisting, he felt a surge of joy. Here there was silence and – almost – contentment. Relaxing, he let his body float upward towards the sun. Breaking clear of the surface, he drew in a deep breath, tossed back his head to clear the hair from his eyes and trod water while he gazed around the bay.

At the harbour opposite a dozen ships were unloading their cargoes, while anchored further out on the bay were twenty more, waiting for the signal to dock. Twenty-eight of the ships flew under the flag of the Tree. His ships.

It seemed incredible to Waylander that a man, like himself, without a great understanding of the subtleties of commerce should have become so ridiculously wealthy. No matter how much he spent now – or, indeed, gave away – more gold flowed in. Matze Chai, and other merchants, had invested Waylander's money well. But even his own ventures had paid handsomely. It is all a grand nonsense, he thought, as he floated in the water. He had lost track of the number of ships he now owned. Somewhere above three hundred. Then there were the mines – emerald, diamond, ruby, gold and silver – scattered from the hinterlands of Ventria to the eastern Vagrian mountains.

He swung in the water and gazed up at the white marble palace. He had commissioned it six years ago following an idle conversation with a young architect who had talked passionately about the overwhelming and delightful problems of construction, and of his

39

dream to create a marvel. 'Why should we always seek out flat ground?' asked the young man. 'Where is the wonder in that? Great buildings should make an observer gasp.'

Three years in construction, the White Palace was indeed a wonder, though the young architect had not lived to see it finished. A nobleman from House Kilraith, he had been stabbed to death one night by assassins from a rival House. Such was life among the nobles of Kydor.

Waylander swam for the beach and emerged on to the white sand. His steward Omri left his seat beneath the olive tree and walked out to meet him, a long linen towel folded over his arm. 'Was the swim beneficial, sir?' he asked, extending the towel and draping it over Waylander's shoulders.

'It was refreshing,' said Waylander. 'And now I am ready for the pressing matters of the day.'

'The Lady requests an audience with you, sir,' said Omri, 'when you have the time.'

Waylander looked at the older man closely. 'Is something bothering you, Omri?'

'Were you aware she is a mystic?'

'No, but it is not surprising. I have known many priests with Talent.'

'I find it unsettling,' admitted Omri. 'I rather feel she can read my thoughts.'

'Are your thoughts so terrible?' asked Waylander, with a smile.

'Occasionally, sir,' admitted Omri, straight-faced. 'But that is not the point. They are *my* thoughts.'

'Indeed so. What else requires my attention?'

'We have received a message from Lord Aric saying he will visit in ten days on his way to the Winter Palace.'

'He needs more money,' said Waylander.

'I fear so, sir.'

Dry now, Waylander moved into the shade of the olive tree and pulled on a black silk shirt and a pair of soft leather leggings. Tugging on his boots, he sat back and gazed once more over the bay. 'Did the Lady say why she wished to see me?'

'No, sir. But she did tell me of your fight with the raiders.'

Waylander caught the note of criticism in the old man's voice. 'It is too fine a day to be chided, Omri,' he said.

'You take great risks, sir. Largely unnecessary risks. We have thirty guards here, and a dozen tough foresters. They could have been sent after the robbers.'

'Very true. But I was close by.'

'And you were bored,' said the old man. 'You always ride off into the wilderness when you are bored. I have come to the conclusion that you do not enjoy being rich. It is, I must say, hard to understand.'

'It is a terrible thing, boredom,' said Waylander. 'It has come to me over the years that wealth and tedium are great bedfellows. When one is rich there is nothing to strive for. Every pleasure I desire is available to me.'

'Obviously not every one, sir, otherwise you would not be bored.'

Waylander laughed. 'That is true. Now, enough of this soul-searching, my friend. What other news is there?'

'Two retainers from House Bakard were murdered in Carlis two days ago, supposedly by men hired by House Kilraith. There is great tension in the town. The merchant Vanis has requested an increase to his loan. He claims to have lost two ships in a storm and is unable to meet his debt payments. Also . . .' Omri pulled a slip of parchment from the pocket of his grey robe and perused it '. . . the surgeon Mendyr Syn has asked if you would be prepared to hire three extra students, at a cost of six silvers a month, to assist him. There are now no spare beds in the infirmary and Mendyr has been working for fifteen hours a day trying to aid the sick.' Omri folded the parchment, returning it to his pocket. 'Oh, yes, and . . . er . . . Lady Lalitia has invited you to attend a celebration of her birthday in three days.'

Waylander sat in the shade, staring out at the fishermen casting their nets in the bay. 'Call in the loan on Vanis,' he said. 'This is the third time in a year he has furnished an excuse for non-payment. His debts have not prevented him buying three racing stallions and extending his eastern estate. Increase the funds to Mendyr Syn and tell him he should have requested help much earlier. And send a message to Lady Lalitia that I will be delighted to attend her celebration. Purchase a diamond pendant from Calicar and have it delivered to her on the day.'

'Yes, sir. Might I point out two things? Point one: Vanis has many friends in House Kilraith. Foreclosing his debt will bankrupt him and be seen as a slight upon the House.'

41

'If he has that many friends,' said Waylander, 'let them pay his debts. Now, what was the second point?'

'If memory serves me correctly is this not the third birthday that Lady Lalitia has had in the past fifteen months?'

Waylander laughed. 'Yes, it is. Make it a *small* diamond pendant.'

'Yes, sir. By the way, the young woman you brought in has been put to work with Norda's team. Do you wish for any special treatment towards her?'

'Give her a little leeway for she has suffered much. She is a strong girl, but even so she has witnessed the murder of her family, been treated cruelly and threatened with death. It would be remarkable were she to suffer no after-effects. Watch her closely and give her a little support. If she does not prove to be a good worker, dismiss her.'

'Very well, sir. And what message shall I send the Chiatze Lady?'

'No message, Omri. I will go and see her presently.'

'Yes, sir. Would it be considered a discourtesy to ask her how long she and her retainers plan to stay?'

'I am more interested to know why they came here – and how,' said Waylander.

'*How*, sir?'

'A priestess in robes of embroidered silk, with three retainers, appears at our gates. Where was the carriage? Where were the horses? From where did they come? They did not stay in Carlis.'

'Obviously they walked from elsewhere,' said Omri.

'And yet attracted little dust to their clothing, and showed no sign of weariness.'

Omri made the Sign of the Protective Horn. 'Regardless of the discourtesy, sir, I would gratefully appreciate knowledge of their departure date.'

'I do not believe there is any need to fear them, Omri. I sense no evil in her.'

'That is good to hear, sir. But some of us have little choice concerning what we fear. I have always been a frightened man. I don't know why.'

Waylander laid his hand on the old man's shoulder. 'You are a gentle soul and a good man,' he said. 'You care about people and their happiness. That is rare.'

Omri looked embarrassed. 'I would have liked to have been more

'. . . manly, shall we say? I was a terrible disappointment to my father.'

'Most of us are,' said Waylander. 'Had my father seen what I have done with my life he would have burned with shame. But that is neither here nor there. We live in the *now*, Omri. And *now* you are a steward, valued and respected – even loved by those who serve under you. It should be enough.'

'Perhaps,' said Omri, 'but then you are loved and respected by those who serve you. Is it enough for you?'

Waylander gave a rueful smile, but did not reply. Moving away, he climbed the terrace steps towards the North Tower.

Minutes later he reached the top of the circular stair to the largest of the library rooms. It had originally been designed as a large state room, but as his collection of ancient scrolls and books grew, so too did the need for added space. There were now five smaller libraries within the palace, as well as the huge museum in the South Tower. Pushing open the door, he stepped inside and bowed to the slender woman sitting at the long, oval table, scrolls spread out around her. He found himself marvelling once more at her beauty, the pale gold of her flawless skin, and her finely boned Chiatze features. Even the shaven head only emphasized her exquisite good looks. She seemed almost too frail to bear the weight of the heavy robes of red and gold silk adorning her body.

'What are you studying, Lady?' he asked.

She looked up. Her slanted eyes were not the deep chestnut of the Chiatze, but tawny gold, flecked with blue. They were disconcerting eyes that seemed to stare deep into the recesses of his soul. 'I have been reading this,' she said, her gloved hand lightly touching an ancient scroll of dry and faded parchment. 'It is, I am told, a fifth-generation copy of the sayings of a writer named Missael. He was one of the most extraordinary men of the New Order, following the destruction of the Elder Races. Some believe his verses contain prophecies for the future.' She smiled. 'But, then, words are so imprecise. Some of these verses could mean anything.'

'Then why do you study them?'

'Why does one study at all?' she countered. 'For greater knowledge, and with it greater understanding. Missael tells how the old

43

world was destroyed by lust, greed, fear and hatred. Did mankind learn from the destruction?'

'Mankind does not have a single set of eyes,' said Waylander. 'A million eyes see too much and absorb too little.'

'Ah, you are a philosopher.'

'A poor one at best.'

'From your words you believe mankind cannot change for the better, evolve and develop into a finer species?'

'Individuals can evolve and change, Lady. This I have seen. But gather together any large group and within a few heartbeats you can have a howling mob, intent on murder and destruction. No, I do not believe mankind will ever change.'

'That may be true,' she agreed, 'but it leaves the taste of defeat and despair. I cannot countenance such a philosophy. Please sit.'

Drawing up a chair, he reversed it and sat opposite her. 'Your rescue of the girl, Keeva, does you credit,' she said, her voice low, almost musical.

'I did not at first know they had taken a hostage,' he admitted.

'Even so. She now has a life – and a destiny – that would otherwise have been robbed from her. Who knows what she may achieve, Waylander?'

'Not a name I use now,' he told her. 'And not one by which I am known by any in Kydor.'

'No one shall hear it from me,' she told him. 'So, tell me, why did you ride after the bandits?'

'They attacked my lands and my people. What other reason did I need?'

'Perhaps you needed to prove to yourself that you are still the man you were. Perhaps, beneath the hard, worldly exterior, you felt for the pain and the loss of the villagers, and were determined that those evil men would never again cause such distress. Or perhaps you were thinking of your first wife, Tanya, and how you were not present when the raiders came to kill her and murder your children.'

His voice hardened. 'You asked to see me, Lady. Your messenger said it was a matter of some importance.'

She sighed, then looked once more into his eyes. When she spoke her voice was softer, the tone regretful. 'It distresses me to have caused you pain, Grey Man. Forgive me.'

'Let us understand one another,' he said coldly. 'I try to hold my

44

pain in a private place. Not entirely successfully. You opened a window to it. I would consider it a courtesy if you did not open it again.'

'You have my word upon it.' She sat silently for a moment, her golden eyes holding to his gaze. 'It is sometimes difficult for me, Grey Man. You see, nothing is hidden from me. When I meet someone for the first time I see all. Their lives, their memories, their angers and pains are all laid bare to me. I try to close myself to myriad images and emotions, but that is painful and exhausting. So, in the main, I absorb them. It is why I avoid crowds, for it is like being trapped under an avalanche of roaring emotion. So let me say again that I am sorry to have offended you. You have been most kind to me and my followers.'

Waylander spread his hands. 'It is forgotten,' he said.

'That is most generous of you.'

'And the matter you wished to speak of?'

She averted her eyes. 'This is not easy for me,' she said, 'for I need to ask your forgiveness a second time.'

'I have already said—'

'No, not for my earlier words. In coming here I may have placed you in some . . . danger. My followers and I are being hunted. It is possible – though I hope unlikely – that we will be found. I felt obliged to inform you of this, and to offer, with genuine intent, to leave immediately, should you desire it.'

'You have broken some Chiatze law?' he asked.

'No, we are not law-breakers. We are seekers of knowledge.'

'Then who hunts you, and why?'

Now her eyes met his. 'Bear with me, Grey Man, while I explain why I cannot yet tell you. As I have already shown, your thoughts and memories are known to me. They blaze from you like the rays of the sun, and like those rays they radiate out over the land. All human thoughts do this. The world is awash with them. Far beyond this palace there are minds attuned to such thoughts, seeking out a resonance that will lead them to me. If I told you the names of those hunting me they would form part of your thinking. And merely by thinking them you might alert those who seek to kill me.'

Waylander smiled. 'Since I do not understand the ways of magickers let us move on,' he said. 'Why did you come here?'

'Partly because you are here,' she said simply, then fell silent.

'And the other part?'

'That is even more complicated.'

Waylander laughed. 'More complicated than magical enemies who can read thoughts over great distances? It is a bright morning, with a fresh breeze and a blue sky. I am fresh from a cooling swim. My mind is clear. Speak on, Lady.'

'This is not the only world, Grey Man.'

'I know. There are many lands.'

'That is not what I meant. We dwell at this time in Kydor. But there are other Kydors, an infinite number of them. Just as there are an infinite number of Drenai worlds. Many have identical histories, many are different. In some the assassin Waylander killed the Drenai king and the land was overrun by Vagrian forces. In others he killed the king and the Drenai won. In some he did not kill the king and there was no war. You follow?'

Waylander's good humour seeped away. 'I murdered the king. For money. It was unforgivable. But it happened. I cannot change it. No one can change it.'

'It happened *here*,' she said softly. 'But there are other worlds. An infinite number. Somewhere, at this moment, in the vastness of space there is another woman, sitting with a tall man. The scene is exactly as this one, save perhaps that the woman is wearing a blue robe and not one of gold. The man may be bearded, or dressed differently. But she is still me, and he is still you. And the land they dwell in is called Kydor.'

Waylander took a deep breath. 'He is not me. I am me.'

'I am sure *he* is saying exactly that.'

'And he is right,' said Waylander. 'He might also be about to ask the point of this conversation. What does it matter if there are two Waylanders, or two hundred, if they never meet or interact?'

'A good question. I have seen some of these worlds. In all of them, no matter what the outcome, the man known as Waylander has a part to play.'

'Not in this world, Lady. Not any longer.'

'We shall see. Do you wish us to go?'

'I will think on it,' he told her, rising from his chair.

'That is kind of you. One other small matter . . .'

'Yes?'

'You did not ask Keeva how she killed the pigeons she cooked for you.'

46

'No, I did not.' He gave a wry smile. 'I had other matters on my mind.'

'Of course. She used your crossbow. She missed with the first bolt, but then killed all three – the last as it took flight.'

'Impressive,' he said.

'I thought that it would interest you.'

He paused in the doorway. 'In all your studies have you come across anything about the ruins to the west?'

'Why do you ask?'

'I was there yesterday. I . . . did not like the feel of the place. And yet I have passed through it many times. Something today was different.'

'You felt in danger?'

He smiled. 'I felt fear, and yet all I saw was a mist.'

'I know that the ruins are five thousand years old,' she said. 'Perhaps you sensed the spirit of someone long dead. But if I find anything of interest I will call upon you, Grey Man,' she told him.

'It is probably nothing. But it was too warm for a mist, and it seemed to be flowing against the breeze. Had the girl not been with me I would have investigated the phenomenon. I do not like mysteries.'

Then he turned and was gone.

As the Grey Man left the library a small door opened and a slender, round-shouldered man stepped into the presence of the priestess. Like her he was shaven-headed, and wearing an ankle-length robe. It was of white wool, with matching gloves and boots of thin, pale grey leather. His tawny eyes cast a nervous glance towards the outer door. 'I do not like him,' he said. 'He is a savage just like them.'

'No, Prial,' she said. 'There are similarities, but he does not have their cruelty.'

'He is a killer.'

'Yes, he is a killer,' she agreed. 'And he knew you were beyond the door.'

'How could that be? I scarcely even allowed myself to breathe.'

'He knew. He has an unconscious talent for these matters. It is, I think, why he has survived so long.'

'And yet he did not know one of the raiders was hiding in a tree above him?'

The priestess smiled. 'No, he did not. But he had strung his crossbow minutes before, and was holding it ready when the man leapt. As I said, it is an unconscious talent.'

'I thought for a moment you were going to tell him,' said Prial.

She shook her head. 'I am hoping still that I do not have to. Perhaps they will not find us before we have completed our mission.'

'You believe that?'

'I *want* to believe it.'

'As do I, Ustarte. But time is short, and we still have not found the way. I have scanned over two hundred tomes. Menias and Corvidal have at least equalled me in this, and there are still more than a thousand to study. Has it occurred to you that these people have long forgotten the truth of Kuan-Hador?'

'They cannot entirely have forgotten,' said Ustarte. 'Even the name of the land remains similar. We have come across references to demons and monsters, and heroes who fought them. Fragments, mostly, but somewhere there will be a clue.'

'How soon will the gateway begin to open?' he asked her.

'Within days rather than weeks. But the creatures of the mist are already here. The Grey Man sensed their evil.'

'And now the deaths will begin,' said Prial sadly.

'Yes, they will,' she admitted. 'And we must continue our search with hope in our hearts.'

'I am fast losing hope, Ustarte. How many worlds must we see fall before we admit we are too weak to save them?'

The priestess sighed and rose from her chair, the heavy silk gown rustling as she moved. 'This one world *did* defeat them three thousand years ago. They drove them back through the gateways. Despite the power of their sorcery, and the allies they brought with them, they were beaten back. Even the *Kriaz-nor* could not save them.'

Prial did not look her in the eyes. 'Five years we have been searching and have found nothing. Now we have – perhaps – a few days. Then they will send an *Ipsissimus* and he will sense our presence.'

'He is already here,' she said softly.

Prial shivered. 'You have seen him?'

'There is a cloak-spell around him. I cannot see him, but I can sense his power. He is close.'

'Then we must flee while we have the opportunity.'

48

'He does not yet know we are here, Prial. There is some power left in me. I also know how to cloak our presence.'

He stepped forward, taking her gloved hand in his and raising it to his lips. 'I know that, Ustarte. But you cannot stand against an *Ipsissimus*. If he has not found us it is because he is not yet looking for us. When he does he will kill us.' Prial began to tremble, and she felt his gloved fingers close tightly about her hand.

She watched him closely, and saw him take a deep, shuddering breath. 'I am calm,' he told her. 'Truly I am.' Then he pulled away from her, embarrassed by his show of weakness. 'These clothes chafe me,' he complained. Opening his robe he pushed it back from his shoulders. Ustarte moved behind him, scratching her fingers through the thick grey fur of his back and shoulders.

His tawny eyes closed, and he grunted with pleasure, his terror subsiding.

But it would return, she knew.

Keeva was tense and more than a little angry as she reached the unusual buildings set aside for the Grey Man. Despite Norda's directions, she had lost herself twice in the maze of corridors and stairs, and had emerged on a lower level, only to see that the building she sought was one storey above and to the right. Climbing a set of stone steps, which cut through a rockery, she finally arrived at the entrance. She stood for a moment, surprised by what she saw. The Grey Man's dwelling place was set back into the cliff, the stone facing roughly fashioned and blending with the natural rock around it. This made it virtually invisible from the bay side of the palace. It looked stark and unprepossessing – not the home of a rich man at all.

Her disquiet grew. Keeva had told the Grey Man she would not be his mistress, but now, within a day, he had summoned her to his rooms. Keeva's anger subsided, and she felt a sudden sadness. For a little while today she had allowed herself to believe she might be happy here. She liked Norda, and the other girls of the team had been friendly. They all spoke highly of old Omri, and the atmosphere among them had been full of good humour. Ah, well, she thought, best get it over. Stepping forward she tapped on the door.

The Grey Man opened it. He was dressed in the same manner as when first she had seen him, dark leggings over riding boots, and a shirt of thin, supple leather. He wore no rings, or chains of gold, and his clothes boasted no brooches and no embroidery. He beckoned her inside. 'Come through,' he said, swinging away from her and strolling into the main living area. It was a rectangular room with only two hide-covered chairs and an old rug. There were no shelves or cabinets, and the fireplace was bare of ornament. A pile of logs was set beside it and a blackened iron poker. The Grey Man wandered through the room and out through a door at the rear. Keeva followed him, expecting to see a bedroom. Her anger began to rise once more.

She crossed the doorway and paused, surprised. It was no bedroom. The thirty-foot wall on the left was panelled with pine, and upon it hung many weapons: longbows, crossbows, Chiatze war darts, swords, knives of all descriptions, some small, others long and double-edged. The right-hand wall was set with six lanterns, their light casting flickering shadows over an array of wooden frames and curious apparatus. Targets had been placed around the room, some round, others crafted from straw, string and old clothing into the forms of men.

The Grey Man moved to a bench table from which he took his crossbow. Loading it with two bolts, he carried it back to Keeva. Then he pointed at the round target some twenty feet away. 'Direct two bolts into the centre,' he told her.

Keeva's arm came up, her hand settling into the worn pistol grip, her fingers on the two bronze triggers. As she had learnt when shooting at the pigeons, the weapon was front heavy, and as the triggers were depressed it tipped slightly downward. Adjusting for this, she loosed both bolts. They flew across the room, slamming into the small red centre of the target. The Grey Man said nothing. Relieving her of the weapon, he moved to the target, retrieving the bolts. Returning the crossbow to the bench he took up two throwing blades. They were diamond-shaped and around four inches in length. There were no hilts, but grooves had been cut into the metal for greater grip.

'Handle this with care,' he said, passing her a blade. 'It is very sharp.' She took it gingerly. It was heavier than it appeared. 'It is not just about direction and speed,' he told her, 'but about spin. The blade must reach its target point first.' He pointed to a nearby straw man. 'Hit that.'

'Where?'

'In the throat.'

Her hand came up, the arm snapping forward. The blade struck the throat area hilt first then bounced away. 'I see what you mean,' she said. 'Can I have the second?' He passed it to her. This time the blade sliced home through the straw man's chin. 'Damn!' she swore.

'Not bad,' he said. 'You have a good eye and excellent co-ordination. That is rare.'

'In a woman, you mean?'

'In anyone.' Moving to the straw target he extracted the blade, picked up the second from the floor and returned to her side. 'Turn your back to the target,' he said. Keeva did so. The Grey Man handed her a blade. 'At my command spin and throw – aiming for the chest.'

He stepped back from her. 'Now,' he said softly. Keeva whirled, the blade slashing through the air to cannon from the target's shoulder and strike the far wall. Sparks flashed briefly from the stone.

'Again,' he said, offering her the second blade. This time it thumped home – once more in the shoulder, but closer to the chest.

'Why are we doing this?' she asked.

'Because we can,' he answered, with a smile. 'You are very talented. With a little work you could be exceptional.'

'If I wanted to spend my life throwing knives,' she observed.

'You told me you had no craft, but were willing to learn. Skilled marksmen can earn a good living at market fairs and celebration days. Not one man in a hundred could have brought down three pigeons in four shots with an unfamiliar weapon. Not one in a thousand could have achieved it without some rudimentary training. In short, like me, you are a freak of nature. Mind and body in harmony. The gauging of distance, the balancing of weight, the power of the throw – all these require precise judgement. For some it takes a lifetime to acquire. For others it can be learnt in a matter of moments.'

'But I missed the chest. Twice.'

'Try again,' he said, gathering up the fallen blade.

She spun – and sent it hurtling into the target.

'Straight through the heart,' he said. 'Trust me. With training you can be among the best.'

'I do not know that I want to be skilled with weapons,' she told him. 'I loathe men of war, their posturing, their arrogance and their endless cruelties.'

Removing the knives from the target the Grey Man took them to the bench and began to clean them with a soft cloth. Placing them in sheaths of black leather he turned again to Keeva. 'I was once a farmer. I lived with a woman I adored. We had three children, a boy of seven and two babes. One day, when I was out hunting, a group of men came to my farm. Nineteen men. Mercenaries seeking employment between wars.' He fell silent for a moment. 'I rarely speak of this, Keeva, but today it is strong in my mind.' He took a deep breath. 'The men tied my Tanya to a bed then – after a little time – killed her. They also killed my children. Then they left.

'When I rode out that morning I recall the sound of laughter in the air. My wife and my son were playing a chasing game in the meadow, my babes were asleep in their cots. When I returned all was silence, and there was blood upon the walls. So I, too, loathe the men of war and their cruelty.'

His face was terribly calm, and there was no sign of the emotional struggle Keeva guessed was raging below the surface. 'And that is when you became a hunter of men,' she said.

The Grey Man ignored the question. 'My point is that there will always be vile men, just as there will always be men of kindness and compassion. It should have no bearing on whether you choose to develop your talents. This world is a troubled, savage place. It would, however, be even more ghastly if only evil men took the time to master weapons.'

'Was your wife skilled with weapons?' she asked.

'No. And before you ask, it would have made no difference had she been the finest archer in the land. Nineteen killers would have overpowered her and the result would have been the same.'

'Did you go after them, Grey Man?' she asked softly.

'Yes. It took many years, and in that time some of them committed other foul deeds. Others married, settled down and raised families of their own. But I found them all. Every one.'

It was suddenly quiet in the room, the air heavy. Keeva watched the Grey Man. His gaze seemed far away, and upon his face was a look of infinite sadness. In that moment she understood this grim and gloomy dwelling place, set alongside the gleaming white marble of his palace. The Grey Man had no home, for the home of his heart had been destroyed a long time ago. She glanced around at the targets of straw and the array of weapons upon the walls. When she looked back she met his gaze. 'I do not wish to learn this craft,' she said. 'I am sorry if that disappoints you.'

52

'People long ago ceased to disappoint me, Keeva Taliana,' he told her, with a rueful smile. 'But let me ask you this: how did you feel when you killed the raider captain?'

'I do not want to talk about it.'

'I understand.'

'Do you? You have been a killer so long I wonder if you do.' She reddened as she realized what she had said. 'I'm sorry if that sounds disrespectful, Grey Man. I do not mean it to be. You saved my life and I will be for ever in your debt. But what I mean is that I do not want to experience again the feelings I had when I killed Camran. What I did was needless. He was dying anyway. All I did was to inflict a little more agony. If I had the time again I would merely have walked away from him. What hurts and angers me is that, in those few heartbeats, I allowed myself to be dragged down in the filth of his evil. I became him. You understand?'

He smiled sadly. 'I understood *that* long before you were born, Keeva, and I respect what you say. Now you had better return to your duties.'

Yu Yu Liang was not a happy man. A little distance away the arguments were still raging among the dozen survivors and Yu Yu struggled to hear what they were saying. His understanding of the round-eye tongue was merely fair, and he found that many of the words and phrases sailed by him before his ears could catch them and his mind translate them. He was concentrating hard, for he knew it was only a matter of time before someone pointed an accusing finger at him.

Sitting on the rock, his stolen sword in his lap, the former ditch-digger did his best to look silently ferocious – like the warrior he pretended to be. Yu Yu had only been with the group for three days. In that time he had heard many fine promises from the now dead leader, Rukar, about life on the road, and the riches to be made from passing merchants. Instead Rukar had been cut down by the *Rajnee* and Yu Yu had moved faster than ever in his twenty-three years to escape the swinging swords of the charging horsemen.

Truth to tell, he felt a little stab of pride that it had been a Chiatze who had cowed them – a true *Rajnee*. Not a fraud with a stolen blade. Yu Yu shivered. Six years of training before a *Rajnee* could own a blood-tempered blade, and a further five years of philosophical study before he was allowed to fight. But only the very, very best were allowed to wear the grey robes and black sash sported by the man who killed Rukar. As soon as Yu Yu had seen him he had carefully eased himself to the back of the second group and was primed to flee the moment the horsemen charged.

The reality was that Rukar had been a dead man from the moment the *Rajnee* approached him.

'One little swordsman,' someone said, 'and you all run like frightened rabbits.' Yu Yu understood the word *rabbits* and guessed the moment of truth was approaching.

'I didn't notice you standing up to him,' another man pointed out.

'I was caught up in the rush,' the first responded. 'It was like being in a stampede. If I hadn't run I'd have been crushed to death.'

'I thought we had our own Chiatze *Rajnee*,' put in a third voice. 'Where in Shem's balls was *he* when we needed him?'

Here it comes, thought Yu Yu Liang miserably. He turned his bearded face towards the twelve men in the group and glowered. 'Well, he ran past me like his arse was on fire,' someone observed. A ripple of laughter sounded.

Yu Yu rose slowly to his feet, his double-handed sword glinting as he swept it left and right in what he hoped might look a menacing fashion. Plunging the blade into the ground dramatically, he drew himself up to his full height. 'Any man think me afraid?' he asked, lowering his voice. 'Do you?' he thundered, leaping forward and stabbing his finger at the nearest, who, surprised by the suddenness of the move, fell backwards. 'Or you?' No one spoke. Yu Yu breathed an inner sigh of relief. 'I am Yu Yu Liang!' he shouted. 'Feared from Blood River to shores of Jian Seas. I kill you all!' he bellowed.

In that instant he saw their faces change, from surprise to stark horror. It was very satisfying. Suddenly one of them scrambled to his feet and ran towards the south. Immediately the others followed, leaving behind their meagre possessions. Yu Yu laughed and threw his hands in the air. 'Rabbits!' he shouted after them. He expected the men to retreat a little distance, but they carried on running. Surely I cannot have been that terrifying, he thought. Must have been the firelight glinting on the muscles of my arms and shoulders, he reasoned, looking down and clenching his fists. Ten years of ditch-digging had honed his upper body beautifully. This warrior life is really not so hard, thought Yu Yu. Bluff and bravado could achieve wonders.

Even so, their reaction was unusual, to say the least. He squinted into the distance, looking for signs of their return. 'I am Yu Yu Liang,' he shouted again, keeping his voice gruff. Then he laughed, and swung back to where he had left his sword.

Standing quietly in the firelight was the little grey-garbed swordsman.

Yu Yu's heart skipped a beat. He leapt backwards, his heel landing in the fire. He swore and jumped forward, then scrabbled for the sword, yanking it from the ground and waving it furiously back and forth, while at the same time shouting a battle cry. It would have been more impressive, he realized, had it not burst forth in a shrill falsetto.

The *Rajnee* stood very still, watching him. He had not drawn his sword. Yu Yu, still holding his sword aloft, glared at him. 'I am Yu Yu Liang . . .' he began, this time in Chiatze.

'Yes, I heard,' said the swordsman. 'Are you left handed?'

'Left-handed?' echoed Yu Yu, bemused. 'No, I am not left-handed.'

'Then you are holding the sword incorrectly,' observed the *Rajnee*. Moving past Yu Yu he glanced towards the south.

'Are you going to fight me?' Yu Yu asked him.

'Do you wish me to?'

'Isn't that why you came here?'

'No. I came to see if the robbers were planning another attack. Obviously they are not. Where did you find the sword?'

'It has been in my family for generations,' said Yu Yu.

'May I see it?'

Yu Yu was about to hand it to the man. Then he jumped back again, slashing it through the empty air. 'You seek to trick me?' he shouted. 'Very clever!'

The *Rajnee* shook his head. 'I am not trying to trick you,' he said quietly. 'Farewell.'

As he turned away Yu Yu called out after him. 'Wait!' The *Rajnee* halted and glanced back. 'I found it after a battle,' Yu Yu said. 'So I took it. The owner didn't care. Most of his head was missing.'

'You are a long way from home, Yu Yu Liang. Is it your ambition to be a robber?'

'No! I want to be a hero. A great fighter. I want to strut through the market towns and hear people say, "There he is. That's—"'

'Yes, yes,' said the *Rajnee*, 'Yu Yu Liang. Well, all journeys begin with a single step, and at least you have mastered the strutting. Now I suggest you follow me.' With that he walked away.

Yu Yu sheathed his sword, and looped the baldric over his shoulder. Then, grabbing the carrysack containing his meagre possessions, he ran to catch up with the departing *Rajnee*.

The man said nothing at first, as Yu Yu marched along beside him, but after walking for almost an hour the *Rajnee* paused. 'Beyond those trees is the camp of my master, the merchant Matze Chai.' Yu Yu nodded sagely and waited. 'Should anyone recognize you what will you tell them?'

Yu Yu thought about this for a moment. 'That I am your pupil, and you are teaching me to be a great hero.'

'Are you an imbecile?'

'No, I am a ditch-digger.'

The *Rajnee* turned towards him and sighed. 'Why did you come to this land?' he asked.

Yu Yu shrugged. 'I don't really know. I was heading west when I found the sword, then I decided to swing north-east.'

Yu Yu felt uncomfortable under the man's dark gaze and the silence grew. 'Well,' he said, at last, 'what are you thinking?'

'We will talk in the morning,' said Kysumu. 'There is much to consider.'

'Then I am your pupil?'

'You are *not* my pupil,' said Kysumu. 'If you are recognized you will tell the truth. You will say you are not a robber and that you were merely travelling with them.'

'Why was I travelling with them?'

'What?'

'If they ask.'

The *Rajnee* took a deep breath. 'Just tell them about your desire to strut.' Then he strode away towards the campfires.

CHAPTER FOUR

THE FIRST OF THE OUTLAWS DRIFTED BACK TO THE FADING campfire, moving in warily, terrified that the grey-robed *Rajnee* would be hiding somewhere close by, ready to leap out and rip their lives from them with his wickedly curved sword. They had seen Rukar's body opened from shoulder to belly, his entrails spilling out, and had no wish to share his grisly fate.

Satisfied that the swordsman had gone, one of the men gathered up some dead wood, throwing it on to the fire. Flames licked out, the light spreading.

'What happened to Yu Yu?' said another man, searching the ground for signs of a struggle.

'He must have run,' said another. 'There's no blood.'

Within an hour nine men had gathered around the fire. Three were still hiding out on the plain. It was growing colder, and a fine mist had begun to seep across the land, swirling like pale smoke.

'Where did you hide, Kym?' someone asked.

'There are some ruined walls. I lay down behind one.'

'Me too,' said another. 'Must have been a big settlement here once.'

'It was a city,' said Kym, a small man with sandy hair and buck teeth. 'I remember my grandfather used to tell stories about it, great stories. Monsters and demons. Wonderful stuff. Me and my brother used to lie in bed and listen to them. We'd be terrified.' The man laughed. 'Then we wouldn't be able to sleep and our mother would start shouting at Grandfather for scaring us. Then the following night we'd beg him to tell us more.'

'So what was this place then?' asked Bragi, a stoop-shouldered figure with thinning black hair.

57

'It was called Guanador, I think,' said Kym. 'Grandfather said there was a great war and the entire city was destroyed.'

'Where did the monsters come in?' put in another man.

Kym shrugged. 'There were magickers, and they had great black hounds with teeth of sharpened iron. Then there were the man-bears, eight feet tall with talons like sabres.'

'How come they got beat, then?' asked Bragi.

'I don't know,' said Kym. 'It's only a story.'

'I hate stories like that,' said Bragi. 'Don't make any sense. Who beat 'em, anyway?'

'I don't know! Wish I'd never mentioned it.'

The mist thickened and edged into the camp. 'Man, it's cold,' said Bragi, taking up a blanket and wrapping it around his shoulders.

'You're always complaining about something,' said a powerfully built man with a shaven head and a forked beard.

'A pox on you, Canja,' snapped Bragi.

'He's right, though,' said someone else. 'It is damned cold. It's this mist. Feels like ice.' Rising from the ground, the men sought out more wood, building up the fire. Then they sat, wrapped in their blankets.

'It's worse than winter,' said Kym.

Moments later the cold was forgotten as a terrible scream echoed in the night. Kym swore and drew his sword. Canja leapt to his feet, dagger in hand, and peered out past the fire. The mist was so thick that he could see no more than a few feet.

'I bet it's that *Rajnee*,' he said. 'He's out there.'

Canja moved a little way into the mist. Kym was watching him.

A curious noise began. The men looked at one another, then clambered to their feet.

'What the Hell is that?' whispered one. It sounded like scratching on the rocky ground just beyond the line of their sight.

The mist was even thicker now, flowing across the fire, causing it to hiss and splutter. Then came a sickening sound, followed by a grunt. Kym swung round to see Canja tottering back towards the fire. Blood was gouting from a huge hole in his chest. His mouth was open, but no sound came forth. Then something white closed around the dying man's head, wrenching it from his body. Bragi spun on his heel and ran several steps in the opposite direction. A huge white form loomed from the mist, and a taloned arm swept down. Bragi's face disappeared in a crimson spray. Talons ripped into his belly, hurling him high into the air.

Kym screamed, and backed away to the fire, dragging out a blazing brand, which he waved around in front of him. 'Get away!' he shouted. 'Get away!'

Something cold curled around his ankle. He glanced down to see a white serpent slithering over his boot. He leapt back – straight into the fire. Flames licked around his leggings. The pain was terrible, but even through it he could see huge white forms approaching the blaze on every side.

Dropping the brand, Kym drew his dagger and turned the point towards his throat. Closing his eyes he rammed it into his jugular.

Something struck him in the back, and he fell from the fire. Gurgling on his life blood he felt sharp teeth rip into his side.

And the mist closed over him.

Kysumu was sitting on the ground, cross-legged, his back against the tree. He was not asleep but in a meditation trance, which served to revitalize his tired muscles. It took many minutes to establish the trance, for the snoring of Yu Yu Liang beside him was a constant irritant, rather like the buzzing of an insect around one's face on a summer's day.

Many years of training served Kysumu well, for he calmly put aside all thoughts of Yu Yu and honed his concentration. Once established he released it in a blaze of emptiness, holding only to the image of a blue flower, bright and ethereal against a backdrop of endless black space, unlit by stars. Slowly – so slowly – he began mentally to recite the Mantra of the *Rajnee*. Thirteen words, set in a child's rhyme.

> *Ocean and star,*
> *Each am I*
> *Broken my wings*
> *And yet I fly.*

With each repeated verse Kysumu grew calmer, his mind expanding, feeling the blood flowing through his veins, the tension easing from his body. One hour of this every day and Kysumu had little need of sleep.

Yet tonight something was disturbing his trance. It was not the sleeping Yu Yu, or even the growing cold. Kysumu was hardened to extremes of cold or heat. He struggled to hold the trance, but it receded from him. He became aware of the scabbarded sword in his lap. It seemed to be vibrating gently under his fingers.

Kysumu's dark eyes flicked open. He glanced about the camp. The night had turned very cold and a mist was seeping through the trees. One of the horses whinnied in fear. Kysumu took a deep breath, then glanced down at his sword. The oval bronze fistguard was glowing. The *Rajnee* placed his slender hand over the leather-wrapped hilt and drew the sword from its black-lacquered scabbard. The blade was shining with a bright blue light so powerful that it hurt the eyes to gaze upon it. Rising to his feet the swordsman saw that Yu Yu Liang's stolen sword was also shining.

Suddenly a sentry screamed. Kysumu threw aside his scabbard and ran across the camp, cutting round the back of the supply wagon. No one was there. But the mist was rising now and Kysumu heard a crunching noise from within it. Dropping into a crouch, he examined the ground. Something wet touched his fingers. By the brilliant light of the sword he saw that it was blood.

'Awake!' he shouted. 'Awake!'

Something moved beyond the mist. Kysumu had the merest glimpse of a colossal white figure. Then it disappeared. The mist rolled over his legs. Icy cold touched his skin. Instinctively Kysumu leapt back. His sword slashed down. As it touched the mist, blue lightning rippled through the air, crackling and hissing. A deep, angry growl sounded from close by. Kysumu jumped forward, plunging his sword into the mist. Once more blue lightning sparked, and thunder boomed over the camp.

Another guard yelled from somewhere to the left. Kysumu glanced back to see Yu Yu Liang hacking and slashing at the mist, lightning blazing from his sword. The guard was on the ground, close to the edge of the trees. Something white was wrapped around his foot, dragging him from the camp. Kysumu sprinted across the clearing. The guard was screaming at the top of his voice. As Kysumu reached him he saw what appeared to be the tail of a great white worm looped around the man's ankle. He hacked at it, cutting deeply into the albino flesh. Yu Yu Liang appeared alongside him. With a high-pitched cry he slammed his blade into the worm. It released the guard, who scrabbled back to the relative safety of the camp. The worm slid back into the mist.

Yu Yu bellowed a battle cry and gave chase. Kysumu's left hand snaked out, grabbing the collar of Yu Yu's wolfskin jerkin, yanking him back. Yu Yu's legs shot into the air and he landed heavily.

'Stay with me,' said Kysumu calmly.

'You could have just asked me!' grumbled Yu Yu, rubbing furiously at his bruised backside.

Kysumu backed away to the centre of the camp. The guards and bearers had all gathered here, and were gazing fearfully at the mist, and listening in silent horror to the strange sounds, clicking and tapping just out of vision.

The mist swirled up. Kysumu cut his sword into it. Blue lightning flashed once more, and weird howls of pain could be heard from within the fog.

Yu Yu appeared alongside him. 'What is this?' asked Yu Yu, swinging his sword.

Kysumu ignored him. Two of the horses screamed and went down. 'Stay here! Keep the mist back,' said Kysumu, turning and running across the clearing. The mist parted before him. Something moved to his left. Kysumu dived to his right, rolling and coming to his feet in one smooth motion. A long taloned arm slashed down towards his face. Kysumu swayed back, and sent the glittering sword straight through the limb. There was a howl of agony, and – for a heartbeat only – Kysumu saw a ghastly face, with huge protruding red eyes and wickedly curved fangs. Then it was gone, back into the mist.

The sky began to lighten, the mist flowing back towards the trees.

Within moments the sun shone above the mountains, and the clearing was calm. Two of the horses were dead, their bellies ripped open. Of the missing sentry there was no sign.

As sunlight bathed the scene Kysumu's sword ceased to shine, fading back to silver steel.

On the ground at his feet the taloned arm continued to writhe. Then, as sunlight touched it, the skin blistered and turned black, peeling away from grey bone. Smoke rose from it, the stench filling the air.

Kysumu walked back across the clearing. Yu Yu Liang joined him.

'Whatever they were,' said Yu Yu happily, 'they were no match for two *Rajnee*.'

Matze Chai opened the flap of his tent and stepped out into the open. 'What is the meaning of this noise?' he asked.

'We were attacked,' said Kysumu quietly. 'One man is dead and we lost two horses.'

'Attacked? The robbers came back?'

'No, not robbers,' Kysumu told him. 'I think we should move from here. And swiftly.'

'As you wish, *Rajnee*.' Matze Chai leaned forward and peered at Yu Yu Liang. 'And who is this – this person?'

'I am Yu Yu Liang. And I helped fight the demons.' Yu Yu raised his sword and puffed out his chest. 'When the demons came we leapt and cut—' he began excitedly.

'Stop!' said Matze Chai, raising a slender hand. Yu Yu fell silent. 'Stand still and say nothing.' Matze Chai turned his attention to Kysumu. 'You and I will continue this conversation in my palanquin once we are on our way.' Casting a malevolent glance at Yu Yu the merchant disappeared back inside his tent. Kysumu walked away.

Yu Yu ran after him. 'I didn't know these swords could shine like that.'

'Neither did I.'

'Oh. I thought you could explain it to me. We make a good team, though, hey?'

Kysumu wondered briefly if he had committed some great sin in a former life, and Yu Yu was a punishment for it. He glanced up into the taller man's bearded face, then walked away without a word.

'Good team,' he heard Yu Yu say.

Walking back across the camp Kysumu could find no trace of the severed arm, but on the edge of the woods he found many tracks of three-toed taloned feet. Liu, the young captain of the guard, approached him. The man's eyes were frightened and he cast nervous glances into the woods. 'I heard your pupil say they were demons.'

'He is not my pupil.'

'Ah, forgive me, sir. But you think they were demons?'

'I have never before seen a demon,' said Kysumu softly. 'But we can discuss it once we are on the road and away from these woods.'

'Yes, sir. Whatever they were it was fortunate that your – your friend was on hand to aid us with his shining sword.'

'He is not my friend,' said Kysumu. 'But, yes, it was fortunate.'

Matze Chai sat in his palanquin, the silk curtains drawn shut. 'You think they were demons?' he asked the little swordsman.

'I can think of no alternative. I cut the limb from one and it burned in the sunlight as if in a furnace.'

'I have not heard of demons in this part of the world but, then, my knowledge of Kydor is limited. My client said nothing of them when he invited me here.' Matze Chai fell silent. He had once used a sorcerer to summon a demon and kill a business rival. The rival had been found the following morning with his heart torn out. Matze Chai had never really known whether the supernatural was genuinely involved, or whether the sorcerer had merely hired a killer. The sorcerer himself had been impaled two years later, following an attempted coup against the Gothir emperor. It was said that a horned demon had appeared within the palace and killed several guards. Could it be, he wondered, that one of Matze's many enemies had hired a magicker to send the creatures in the mist to kill him? He dismissed the thought almost immediately. The murdered sentry had been at the far end of the camp, furthest from his tent, as had the butchered horses. Surely a spell aimed at Matze Chai himself would have focused upon the tent where he lay? A random incident, then, but a disquieting one. 'Liu tells me that your sword shone like the brightest moonlight. I have not heard of this before. Are the swords of the *Rajnee* magical?'

'I had not thought them to be,' said Kysumu.

'Can you think of an explanation?'

'The rituals of the *Rajnee* are ancient. Each sword is blessed with one hundred and forty-four incantations. The iron ore is blessed before smelting, the steel is blessed, the armourer-priest tempers it with his own blood after three days of fasting and prayer. Finally it is laid upon the temple altar at Ri-ashon, and all the monks join together in that most holy of places to give the sword its name and its final blessing. The swords of the *Rajnee* are unique. No one knows the origins of many of the incantations, and some are spoken in a language no longer understood, even by the priests who utter them.'

Matze Chai sat silently as Kysumu spoke. It was the longest speech he had heard from the normally laconic swordsman. 'I am not an expert in military matters,' said Matze Chai, 'but it seems to me that the swords of the *Rajnee* must have been created originally for a purpose other than merely battling enemy swordsmen. Why else would they display such mystical properties when demons are close?'

'I agree,' said Kysumu. 'It is a matter I must ponder upon.'

'While you do so, might you explain the appearance of the loud oaf in the foul-smelling wolfskin?' asked Matze Chai.

'He is a ditch-digger,' answered the *Rajnee*, his face expressionless.

'We were aided by a ditch-digger?'

Kysumu nodded. 'With a stolen *Rajnee* sword.'

Matze Chai looked into the swordsman's face. 'How was it that you happened upon him?'

'He was one of the robbers who attacked us. I went to their camp. The rest ran away, but he stood his ground.'

'Why was it that you did not slay him?'

'Because of the sword.'

'You feared it?' asked Matze Chai, his surprise making him momentarily forget his manners.

Kysumu seemed untroubled by the remark. 'No, I did not fear it. When a *Rajnee* dies his sword dies with him. It shivers and cracks, the blade shattering. The sword is linked to the soul of the bearer, and travels with him to the world beyond.'

'Then perhaps he stole it from a living *Rajnee* who still hunts for it.'

'No. Yu Yu did not lie when he said he took it from the body of a dead *Rajnee*. I would have known. I believe the sword chose him. It also led him to this land and, ultimately, to our campsite.'

'You believe the swords are sentient?'

'I cannot explain it to you, Matze Chai. I underwent five years of intensive study before I began to grasp the concept. So let me say this, by way of explanation. You have wondered since we met why I accepted this assignment. You came to me because you were told I was the best. But you did not expect me to agree to journey from the lands of the Chiatze. Not so?'

'Indeed,' agreed Matze Chai.

'I had many requests to consider. As I was taught, I went to the holy place and sat, with my sword in my lap, to meditate, to request the guidance of the Great One. And then, when my mind was purged of all selfish desire, I considered the many offers. When I came to yours I felt the sword grow warm in my hands. I knew then that I had to journey to Kydor.'

'Does the sword then yearn for peril?' asked Matze Chai.

'Perhaps. But I believe it merely shows the *Rajnee* a path towards the will of the Great One.'

'And these paths inevitably carry you towards evil?'

'Yes,' said Kysumu.

'Hardly a comforting thought,' said Matze Chai, deciding he had

64

no wish to elicit further explanation. He disliked excitement, and this journey had already contained too many incidents. Now, it seemed, the mere presence of Kysumu guaranteed further adventure.

Pushing thoughts of demons and swords from his mind he closed his eyes, picturing his garden and the scented, flowering trees. The image calmed him.

From outside the palanquin came a raucous noise. The ditch-digger was singing in a loud, horrible discordant voice. Matze Chai's eyes snapped open. The song was in a broad northern Chiatze dialect, and concerned the physical endowments and unnatural body hair of a young pleasure-woman. A small pain began behind Matze Chai's left eye.

Kysumu rang the bell and the palanquin came to a smooth halt. The *Rajnee* opened the door and leapt lightly to the ground. The singing stopped.

Matze Chai heard the loud oaf say, 'But the next verse is really funny.'

Lalitia was a woman not easily surprised. She had learnt all there was to know about men by the time she was fourteen, and her capacity for surprise had been exhausted long before that. Orphaned and living on the streets of the capital at the age of eight, she had learnt to steal, to beg, to run and to hide. Sleeping on the sand beneath the wharf timbers, she had sometimes huddled in the dark and watched the cut-throats drag victims to the water's edge before knifing them viciously and hurling the bodies into the surf. She had listened as the cheap tavern whores plied their trade, rutting with their customers in the moon shadows. On many occasions she was close by when the officers of the watch came round to collect their bribes from the tavern women, before taking it in turns to enjoy free sport with them.

The red-headed child learnt swiftly. By the age of twelve she was leading a gang of juvenile cutpurses, operating throughout the market squares, paying out a tenth of their earnings to the watch, ensuring they were never caught.

For two years Lalitia – Sly Red, as she was known then – hoarded her own takings, hiding the coin where no one would find it. She spent her spare time crouched in alleyways watching the rich enjoying their meals in the finer taverns, noting the way the great ladies moved and spoke, the languid grace they displayed, the faint air of boredom they assumed when in the company of men. Their backs were always straight, their movements slow, smooth and assured. Their skin was creamy white, untanned – indeed, untouched – by the sun. In summer they wore wide-brimmed hats, with gossamer veils. Sly Red watched, absorbed their movements, carefully storing them in the vaults of memory.

At fourteen her luck had run out. While running from a merchant, whose money pouch strings she had neatly sliced, she slipped on a piece of rotten fruit and fell heavily to the cobbles. The merchant had held her until the watch soldiers arrived, and they had dragged her away.

'Can't help you this time, Red,' said one of them. 'You just robbed Vanis, and he's an important man.'

The magistrate had sentenced her to twelve years. She served three in a rat-infested dungeon before being summoned one day to the office of the gaol captain, a young officer named Aric. He was slim and cold-eyed, even handsome in a vaguely dissolute manner. 'I saw you walking by the far wall this morning,' he told the seventeen-year-old girl. 'You do not appear to be a peasant.'

Sly Red had been using her hour of daylight to practise the movements she had observed among the great ladies of the capital. She said nothing to the captain. 'Come closer, let me look at you,' he said. She stepped forward. He moved in – then recoiled. 'You have lice,' he said.

'Aye,' she said huskily, 'and fleas. I think the bath in my apartment is out of order. Perhaps you could assign a servant to repair it.'

He grinned at her. 'Of course, my lady. You should have brought it to my attention sooner.'

'I would have,' she said, adopting a languid pose, 'but there are so many calls upon my time.'

Aric summoned the guard and had her returned to her cell. An hour later two soldiers came to collect her. She was marched through the prison to a private wing, and brought to a bathroom. In it was a bronze hip tub, brimming with perfumed water. Two female prisoners were waiting beside it. The male guards ordered her to disrobe and she removed the filthy dress she wore and stepped into the tub. One of the women poured warm water over her greasy red hair, then massaged a sweet-smelling soap into it. The other woman began to scrub her skin. The feeling was exquisite and Sly Red closed her eyes. Tension seeped from her muscles.

When the bath was completed, her hair dried, combed and braided, she was dressed in a green gown of faded satin.

The larger of the two women leant in to her. 'Don't get too used to this, dearie,' she whispered. 'Not one of his girls lasts more than a week. He is easily bored.'

Sly Red lasted a year, and at eighteen was given a full pardon. Aric at first amused himself with her, then began teaching her the more esoteric secrets of noble behaviour. The pardon was hard-earned, for Aric's carnal desires were wide-ranging and sometimes painful. In return for the pardon Sly Red agreed to become a plaything for men Aric needed to impress, or rivals he desired to exploit, or enemies he was determined to destroy. In the years that followed Lalitia, as Sly Red became, found men only too eager to surrender their secrets. It seemed that arousal loosened tongues and brains in equal measure. Bright and brilliant men became like children, anxious to please. Secrets long hidden spilled out as they sought to impress her with their cleverness. Stupid men!

In his own way Aric had been good to her, allowing her to keep the gifts her lovers bestowed. Within a few years Lalitia was close to wealthy. Aric even gave his blessing when she married the old merchant Kendar. He died within a year. Lalitia was overjoyed. Now she could have the life she had always desired. Kendar's wealth should have been enough for two lifetimes. Except that Kendar's wealth had been bogus. He died massively in debt, and once more Lalitia found herself surviving on her wits and her physical charms.

Her second husband had the bad grace not to die, despite being over seventy when she married him. This had necessitated drastic action. The thought of poisoning him occurred to her, but she dismissed it. He was a pleasant enough man, even kind. Instead Lalitia fed him a diet spiced with powerfully aphrodisiac herbs, acquired at great cost. When he finally expired, the surgeon summoned to pronounce him dead could not fail to remark that he had never seen a happier corpse.

Lalitia was now truly rich.

And set about becoming poor with a speed that beggared belief. She began with a series of investments in merchant enterprises, all of which failed, then bought land, which she was convinced would multiply in value. It fell sharply. One day her dressmaker sent a message to say that no further clothes would be forthcoming unless all bills were paid. Lalitia was amazed to discover she had no funds to cover the debt.

She had contacted Aric, who once more made use of her services.

Now, at thirty-five, she had funds, a fine house in Carlis, and a lover so rich he could probably buy the whole of Kydor and not notice the difference.

Leaning back on the satin pillow she gazed at the tall, powerfully built man standing by the window. 'Did I thank you for the diamond pendant, Grey Man?' she asked.

'I believe that you did,' he told her. 'Quite eloquently. So, tell me, why do you not wish to attend my banquet?'

'I have not been feeling well these last few days. It would be better for me to rest, I think.'

'You seemed well a few moments ago,' he observed drily.

'That is because you are such an exquisite lover. Where did you learn such skills?'

He did not answer, but transferred his gaze back out of the window. Compliments slid from him like water from slate. 'Do you love me?' she asked him. 'Even a little?'

'I am fond of you,' he said.

'Then why do you never tell me anything about yourself? You have been coming to me for two years now and I don't even know your real name.'

He turned his dark gaze towards her. 'Nor I yours,' he said. 'It does not matter. I must be going.'

'Be careful,' she said suddenly, surprising herself.

He looked at her closely. 'Of what?'

She was flustered. 'There is some talk in the town . . . You have enemies,' she concluded lamely.

'Vanis the merchant? Yes, I know.'

'He could . . . hire men to kill you.'

'Indeed. Are you sure you will not attend my banquet?'

She nodded. As always he walked across the room without any farewells. The door closed behind him.

Stupid! Stupid! Stupid! she railed at herself. She had heard from Aric that Vanis was considering assassination. With his creditor dead Vanis would stave off bankruptcy. Aric had warned her to say nothing. 'It should be a surprising evening,' he had said, 'the rich peasant slaughtered in his own palace. Quite a memorable event, I would think.'

At first Lalitia had been annoyed, for now the gifts would cease, but she knew, after two years, there was no hope of the Grey Man proposing marriage. And she already knew he was seeing another courtesan in the south of the town. Soon he would stop coming to her. But, as the day wore on, she couldn't stop thinking about his demise.

Aric had always been good to her, but she knew that if she betrayed him he would have no hesitation in ordering her killed. And yet she had almost risked it. Almost told the Grey Man that the killers were waiting.

'I do not love him,' she said aloud. Lalitia had never loved anyone. Why then, she wondered, did she want to save him? Partly, she thought, it was that he never sought to possess her. He paid for his pleasure, was never cruel or dismissive, never judgemental or dominating. He did not seek to question her life, or offer her advice.

She rose from the bed and walked naked to the window where he had stood only moments before. She watched him ride the steeldust gelding through the open gates, and the heavy weight of sadness bore down on her.

Aric called him the rich peasant, but there was nothing of the peasant about the man. He radiated power and purpose. There was something elemental about him. Unyielding.

Lalitia smiled suddenly. 'I do not think they will kill you, Grey Man,' she whispered.

The words, and the accompanying lift to her spirits, astonished her.

Life, it seemed, still had the capacity to surprise.

Keeva had never attended a Noble Gathering, though as a child she had seen the elaborate carriages of the wealthy, and caught glimpses of the ladies in their silks and satins as they attended such events. Now she stood by the western wall of the Great Hall, a silver tray in her hands, bearing a selection of delicately crafted pastries, some filled with cheese, others with spiced meats. She was one of forty servants moving among the Grey Man's two hundred guests.

Never had Keeva seen so much satin, so many jewels: golden bangles encrusted with precious stones, ear-rings that sparkled in the light cast by a hundred lanterns, dresses or tunics embroidered with pearls and edged with silver, glittering tiaras, and even shoes decorated with rubies, emeralds and diamonds.

A young nobleman and his lady paused before her. The man was wearing a short cape edged with sable, over a red satin jacket embroidered with gold thread. He reached out and took a pastry. 'These are wonderful. You should try them, dearheart,' he said to the woman beside him.

'I'll try a taste of yours,' she said, her white satin gown rustling as she moved in closer to her lover. He grinned at her and placed a small portion of the pastry between his teeth. She laughed, leant in and took it from him with a kiss. Keeva stood very still, aware that she was invisible to them. It was a curious feeling. Not once did their eyes meet hers, and they moved away into the crowd without ever registering her presence. Other guests flowed by, some pausing to take a pastry, others merely moving towards the dance floor. Her tray empty, Keeva edged around the wall and down the short staircase to the long kitchens.

Norda was there, refilling goblets with fine wine. 'When does the Grey Man arrive?' asked Keeva.

'Later,' she said.

'But it is his Gathering.'

'He is here already,' said Norda. 'Have you not noticed a steady stream of people moving through to the Small Hall beyond?'

Keeva had, but had not thought about it. The young sergeant, Emrin, was stationed at the rear door and Keeva was determined not to be seen looking at him. She wished to give the man no reason to pursue his interest in her.

'Most of the nobles and merchants here this evening will be seeking some favour from the Gentleman,' said Norda, 'so, for the first three hours, he sits in the Walnut Room and receives them. Omri is with him, and he will be writing down their requests.'

'So many people wanting favours,' said Keeva. 'He must be very well loved.'

Norda's laughter pealed out. 'Idiot,' she said, as she took up her tray and moved back to the stairs.

Keeva was confused, and she glanced around and saw some of the other girls smiling. Embarrassed, though she did not know why, Keeva refilled her tray and returned to the Great Hall.

Twenty musicians were playing now, the music fast and lively, and dancers whirled on the polished floor. It was warm in the hall, but all the wide doors leading to the terrace were open, and a fresh sea breeze was filtering into the room.

For another hour the dancing continued, and the hall was filled with the sounds of music and laughter. Keeva's arms began to ache from holding the tray. Few people were now eating. Norda moved carefully around the edge of the hall. 'Time to exchange that tray for refreshments,' she said.

Keeva followed her downstairs. 'Why did you call me an idiot?' she asked, as the blonde woman began to fill crystal glasses with wine.

'He is not loved,' said Norda. 'He is hated by them all.'

'But why, if he grants them favours?'

'That is why. Do you know nothing about the nobility?'

'Obviously not.'

Norda paused in her work. 'He is a foreigner and immensely wealthy. They envy him, and envy always leads to hatred. It doesn't matter what he does, they will always hate him. Last year when there was a failure of the crops in the east the Gentleman sent two hundred tons of grain to be distributed among the starving. A fine deed, yes?'

'Of course.'

'Well, this fine deed prevented the cost of grain from soaring, and thus reduced the profits the nobles and merchants could have made. You think they would thank him for that?' Norda smiled. 'You'll learn, Keeva. Nobles are a different breed.' Her smile faded, and her eyes became cold and angry. 'I wouldn't piss on one if he was on fire.'

'I do not know any,' said Keeva.

'Best to keep it that way,' replied Norda, her voice softening. 'They bring nothing but grief to the likes of us. We'd better get back.'

Carrying a tray of drinks, Keeva returned to the Great Hall, and began moving through the throng. The musicians had ceased playing briefly, and were partaking of refreshments, and most of the nobles had gathered in small groups. They were chatting and laughing, and the mood was a happy one. There was still no sign of the Grey Man, though Keeva saw the one noble she did recognize: Lord Aric of House Kilraith. Resplendent in a grey and black striped tunic shirt of heavy silk, edged with silver braid, he was standing close to the terrace, talking to the young woman Keeva had earlier seen taking the pastry from the mouth of her companion. The two were laughing, and Keeva saw Aric whisper something in the woman's ear. He was a handsome man, slim and elegant, his features fine, though his nose a little long, thought Keeva. He looked younger than she remembered, his hair uniformly dark. Keeva seemed to recall that he had had grey in his hair when he had ridden through the settlement last year. And his face had seemed puffier. He has probably dyed the hair, she thought, and lost a little weight. It suited him.

Just behind them stood a black-bearded man, tall and broad-shouldered with deep-set eyes. He was wearing an ankle-length robe of deep blue velvet edged with silver thread. In his right hand was a long staff, topped with an ornate twist of silver. The man was standing quietly, holding the hand of a young, blond-haired boy around eight years of age. Keeva moved towards them. The tall bearded man stepped away from the shadows of the terrace doorway and Keeva felt his gaze upon her. It was a shock, for she had become used to being invisible to these people. His eyes were dark and large beneath hooded lids.

'Drink, sir?' she said.

The tall man nodded. His face was broad, made even wider by the heavy black beard. He released the boy's hand and took a crystal goblet filled with red wine. 'I much prefer it white,' he said, his voice low. He smiled at her and held up the goblet. Immediately colour began to drain from it, becoming first a bright scarlet, then a deep pink, until, at last, it looked as clear as water. Keeva blinked. The man chuckled, then sipped the changed wine. 'Excellent,' he said.

She glanced down at the silent boy. His bright blue eyes met hers and he gave a shy smile. 'Can I fetch something for your son?' she asked the bearded man.

He smiled and ruffled the boy's hair. 'He is my nephew and my page, not my son. And, yes, that would be most kind.'

'We have cordials made from apples, or pears or peaches,' she told the boy. 'Which would you prefer?'

The child glanced up into the face of the bearded man, who turned to Keeva. 'He is very shy, but I know that he likes pear juice. Let me relieve you of your tray while you fetch it.'

Instantly the tray floated up from Keeva's hands, hovering in the air, before lowering itself down to a small side-table. Keeva clapped her hands in delight, and the small boy smiled.

72

'Come now, my friend,' said the Lord Aric. 'You must save your entertainments for those who will most appreciate them.'

Keeva moved swiftly downstairs, filled a goblet with cooled pear juice and returned to the ballroom. The boy accepted the drink with a smile of thanks and sipped the contents.

Lord Aric took the bearded man by the arm and led him away towards the centre of the hall. A breath of breeze whispered through the terrace doorway. Keeva sighed with relief, for her clothes were sticking to her in the heat. Not only was it a warm summer night, but the lantern flames and the hundreds of bodies in the hall were producing almost intolerable warmth.

In the centre of the hall Lord Aric ordered two servants to pull a table across the floor. Then he sprang upon it and lifted his arms in the air. 'My friends,' he called out, 'by your leave, I have brought a little entertainment to amuse you. I ask you to offer your warmest greetings to Eldicar Manushan, recently arrived from our Angostin homeland.' With that he reached down, and the tall bearded man took his hand and climbed to the table. The nobles and their ladies politely applauded. Aric leapt down from the table and Eldicar Manushan gazed out over their faces. 'It is a trifle warm, dear people,' he told them. 'I can see that some of the ladies are feeling faint, and that their wrists will soon begin to burn from overuse of their fans. So let me begin with a small rearrangement of the weather.' Laying the long staff at his feet he clasped his hands together, raised them high, then opened his fingers and drew his arms apart. What appeared to Keeva to be a white mist floated from his palms, and rose into the air.

Eldicar made a circular motion with his hand, and the mist rolled itself into a ball and began to grow. With a gesture he made it float across the room to where a small group of noblewomen were fanning themselves. As it hovered above them their faces changed, and they squealed with delight. The ball split into two. One remained above the women, the other bobbed in the air, then floated to another group. Each time it stopped it split itself, though neither of the globes lost any size.

People underneath them began to applaud, while those they had not yet reached looked mystified. Keeva watched as one of the globes spun gently towards her. As it came close she felt suddenly cool, as if a breeze, filtered over snow, was blowing through the room. It was

73

both refreshing and exhilarating. Soon there were white globes all around the Great Hall, and the temperature had dropped dramatically.

All conversation ceased. Eldicar Manushan lowered his arms. 'Now,' he said, 'the entertainment can begin. But first, my friends, let me thank you for your welcome. It is extremely gratifying to see such grace, beauty and culture so far from home.' He bowed to them, and they applauded the compliment with great enthusiasm. 'Might I also thank Lord Aric for his courtesy and his generosity in inviting me to share his home during my stay in Kydor.' Again they applauded. 'And now,' he said, 'a little entertainment to amuse you. What you are about to see are images. They cannot touch you. They cannot see you. So please do not be alarmed. Especially when you notice there is a huge black bear among you!' He suddenly pointed to the western wall.

A massive form reared there, and a bloodcurdling roar sounded from it. Those closest to the ferocious animal screamed and backed away. In an instant the bear dropped to all fours and broke into a dozen pieces. Each of the pieces then bounded out on to the dance floor, and Keeva saw that they were all black rabbits. Laughter echoed around the hall – most loudly from those terrified only moments before. Eldicar Manushan clapped his hands, and the rabbits became blackbirds, which flew into the air and out through the terrace doorway.

A lion bounded in. People scattered, but without real fear now. Rising on its hind legs it pawed at the air, and growled menacingly. Then it padded around the room. A young woman reached out as it loped by, her hand sinking into the beast and passing through it. The lion turned towards her and reared up. She cried out – but the lion shattered, becoming a flock of golden doves, which circled the room.

The crowd cried out for more, but Eldicar Manushan merely bowed. 'I have promised Lord Aric to reserve my finest – shall we say? – tricks for the Duke's Feast at the Winter Palace in eight days. It was merely my duty tonight to whet your appetite. I thank you for your applause.' He bowed again, and this time the clapping was thunderous.

Climbing down from the table he retrieved his staff and walked back to where Keeva and the boy were standing. Taking another goblet he twirled it in his hands before sipping the wine. Then he glanced at Keeva. 'Did you enjoy the entertainment?' he asked her.

'I did, sir. I will be sorry to miss the Duke's Feast. What is your page's name?'

'His name is Beric. He is a good boy, and I thank you for your kindness to him.' Raising her hand to his lips he kissed it. At that moment there was a stir from the far side of the hall. Dressed in a black satin tunic shirt, dark leggings and boots, the Grey Man made his entrance. He was immediately seen by several women, who smiled and curtsied. He bowed, exchanged pleasantries and moved across the room.

Keeva watched him, and was struck by the easy, confident way in which he greeted his guests. He stood out from them by his lack of adornment. He wore no brooches or rings, and no gold or silver glistened from his tunic. Even so, he looked every inch the lord of the palace, she thought. Around him the other men seemed as flamboyant as peacocks.

Moving from group to group he made his way to the far end of the hall, where Keeva stood holding her tray. Lord Aric and his friend, Eldicar Manushan, stepped forward and greeted him.

'I am sorry to have missed your display,' the Grey Man told the magicker.

'I do apologize, sir,' he said, with a bow. 'It was remiss of me to begin while you were not present. However, you will see something far greater at the Duke's Feast.'

The music began again, and dancers took to the floor. Several of the guests approached the Grey Man. Keeva could no longer hear the conversation, but she watched his face as he listened to them. He was attentive, though his eyes had a faraway look, and it seemed to Keeva that he was not enjoying the festivities.

At that moment Keeva's attention was caught by a young noble edging closer to the Grey Man. He looked tense, and there was sweat upon his brow, despite the cool breeze still emanating from the white globes that hung above the revellers. Then Keeva saw a second man detach himself from a nearby group, and also move towards the Grey Man. Their movements seemed furtive and Keeva found her heart beating faster.

The Grey Man was talking to a young woman in a red gown as the first of the men came up behind him. Keeva saw something glitter in the man's hand. Before she could cry out a warning the Grey Man spun on his heel, his left arm blocking a knife thrust, his right hand, fingers extended, slamming into the assassin's throat. The man gagged and fell to his knees, the long-bladed knife clattering to the floor. The second man ran in, knife raised, but collided with the woman in the red dress, who was trying to back away from the scene. The assassin pushed her aside and she fell heavily. The music had stopped now, and all the dancers were standing staring at the knifeman. Keeva saw the guard, Emrin, run at the assassin, but the Grey Man waved him back. The assassin stood very still, knife extended towards his intended victim. 'Well,' said the Grey Man, 'are you intending to earn your pay?'

'I do this for the honour of House Kilraith!' shouted the young noble, charging forward.

The Grey Man sidestepped, slapped away the knife arm, and tripped the young man, who sprawled headlong to the stone floor. He hit hard, but rolled and came to his knees. The Grey Man moved in and kicked the knife from the assassin's hand. The young noble surged to his feet, and ran for the terrace. 'Let him go,' the Grey Man ordered Emrin and two other guards who had joined him.

Turning his attention to the first of the assassins, the Grey Man knelt by the still body. Keeva glanced down. The man's bladder had released its contents, which had stained the expensive grey leggings he wore. His eyes were open, staring sightlessly up at the ornate ceiling. The Grey Man rose and turned to Emrin. 'Remove the body,' he said. Then he strolled from the room.

'An unusual man,' said Eldicar Manushan.

Recovering from her shock, Keeva glanced down at little Beric, who was staring wide-eyed at the dead man.

'It is all right,' she said, kneeling and putting her arms around his slim shoulders. 'There is no danger.'

'Will he be all right?' asked Beric, his voice trembling. 'He is very still.'

'They will take care of him,' Keeva assured him. 'Perhaps you should leave.'

'I shall take him to his room,' said Eldicar. 'Once again my thanks to you.' Taking the boy by the hand the magicker walked across the hall and vanished into the crowd.

The musicians, not knowing what to do, started to play once more, but the music faded away when no one moved. Then the first of the nobles began to leave the area.

Within minutes the Great Hall was deserted and Keeva and the other servants cleared away goblets, tankards and dishes, before returning with mops, buckets and cleaning cloths. By the time they had finished there was no sign that hundreds of guests had danced and dined there.

In the kitchens, as they washed the dishes and cutlery, Keeva listened to the other girls talking about the failed assassination. She learnt that the two young men were nephews of the merchant Vanis, but no one had any idea why they should seek to kill the Gentleman. The girls talked about how lucky the Gentleman had been, and how fortunate that his blow had killed the first assassin.

As the dawn was breaking Keeva made her way to her room. She was tired, but her mind whirled with the events of the night, and she sat for a while upon her balcony, watching the sunlight gleaming like gold upon the waters of the bay.

How had he known he was in danger? she wondered. With the noise of the music there was no way he could have heard the man move up behind him. Yet his arm had been moving to block the blow even as he turned. His movements had been unhurried and smooth. Picturing the scene again, she shivered. There was no doubt in Keeva's mind that the death blow to the young man's throat had not been, as the other girls believed, a fortunate strike. It had been delivered coldly and with deadly intent, in a move that spoke of long practice.

What are you, Grey Man? she mused.

Waylander left the Great Hall and strode down the second-level corridor leading to the South Tower. As he turned the first corner he pushed aside a velvet hanging and pressed a stud on the panelled wall beyond. There was a faint creak as the panel opened. Stepping through he pulled it shut behind him and stood in the near-total darkness. Then, without hesitation, he began to descend the hidden steps. He was angry now, and made no attempt to stifle it. He knew both the young men who had attacked him, had spoken to them on several occasions while they had been in the company of their uncle, the merchant Vanis. They were not of great intelligence, nor were they stupid. To all intents and purposes they were merely pleasant young nobles who should have been considering a lifetime of possibilities.

Instead one was lying in a darkened room waiting for someone to

77

collect his body and place it in the cold ground to feed worms and maggots. And his shade would be wandering the Void, frightened and alone. The second was somewhere out in the night, contemplating his next move, and probably not realizing that he was facing death.

Waylander descended the steps, counting them as he went. One hundred and fourteen had been cut into the cliff, and as he reached the hundredth he saw the faintest gleam of moonlight dappling the lower wall.

He paused at the hedge that disguised the lower entrance, then edged his way around it and stepped across the rocks leading to the winding path. The sky was clear, the night warm. He glanced up at the windows and terrace of the Great Hall far above. There were still people there but they would be leaving soon.

As indeed would he.

Tomorrow he would see Matze Chai and reveal his plans. The Chiatze would be horrified, he knew. The thought lifted him briefly. Matze Chai was one of the few people Waylander both trusted and liked. The merchant had arrived just before the Gathering. Waylander had sent Omri to show Matze Chai the suite of rooms assigned to him, and to convey Waylander's apologies for not being present to greet him. Omri had returned looking flustered and annoyed.

'Were the rooms to his liking?' Waylander had asked.

'He indicated they would *suffice*,' answered Omri. 'He then had one of his servants move around the suite wearing a white glove, which he used to see if there was any dust upon the shelves.'

Waylander laughed aloud. 'That is Matze Chai,' he said.

'I did not find it amusing, sir. In fact, it was extremely annoying. Other servants stripped the satin sheets from the bed examining it for bugs, while still more appeared with cloths and began cleaning and perfuming the bedroom. All the while your friend sat upon the balcony, saying nothing to me, but relaying his instructions through the captain of his guard. You told me that Matze Chai speaks our language perfectly, and yet he did not say a word to me. Most discourteous. I wish you had been there, sir. Perhaps he would have acted in a more civilized manner.'

'You dislike him?' asked Waylander.

'I do, sir.'

'Trust me, Omri, once you get to know him you will *detest* him.'

'What is it, may I ask, that *you* like about him?'

'A question I ask myself constantly,' answered Waylander, with a smile.

'I do not doubt it, sir, but – if you don't mind me saying – that is no answer.'

'A full answer would only confuse you more, my friend. So let me say this. There is only one fact that I know for certain about Matze Chai. His name is not Matze Chai. He is an invention. My guess is that Matze was low born, and clawed his way up from the lowest levels of Chiatze society, reinventing himself at every stage.'

'You mean he is a fraud?'

'No, far from it. Matze is like a living work of art. He has transformed something he perceived as base into a flawless Chiatze noble. I doubt he even allows himself to remember his origins.'

Waylander walked on through the moonlight, angling towards his own quarters. He paused at the edge of the cliff and stared out at the dark sea. The moon was reflected there, broken and shimmering upon the gentle waves. He stood in silence as a sea breeze blew gently across his face, and wished that he had been as successful as Matze in reinventing himself.

He gazed at the two moons, the high perfect light in the sky, and the fragmented twin upon the waves. As he did so he recalled the words of the seer: 'When you close your eyes and think of your son, what do you see?'

'I look down upon his dead face. He is lying on the meadow and there are spring flowers around his head.'

'You will not know happiness until you look *up* into his face,' the old man had told him.

The words had been meaningless then, and were meaningless now. The boy was dead, murdered, and buried. Waylander would never be able to look up into his face. Unless the seer had been talking about picturing him in some spiritual paradise high above the stars. Waylander took a deep breath, then moved on along the cliff path.

Ahead were a series of terraces, covered by flowers and screened by scented bushes. Waylander slowed, then stopped. 'Come out, boy,' he said wearily.

The young blond noble rose from behind a bush. In his hand was a golden-hilted shortsword – a light ceremonial blade, worn at official functions. 'Did you learn nothing from your brother's death?' asked Waylander.

'You killed him?'

'Aye, I killed him,' said Waylander coldly. 'I crushed his throat and he choked to death on the floor. As he died he pissed himself. That is what happens. That is the reality. He is gone – and for what?'

'For honour,' said the young man. 'He died for the honour of the family.'

'Where are your wits?' snapped Waylander. 'I loaned your uncle money, and when he could not repay I loaned him more. I did this because he made me promises – promises he failed to keep. Whose is the dishonour? Now your brother is dead. And all so that fat Vanis can avoid financial ruin. A man of his stupidity faced ruin anyway.' Waylander stepped in close to the young man. 'I do not want to have to kill you, boy. The last time we met you talked of your engagement to a young woman you adored. You spoke of love and a small estate by the coast. Think on it. If you walk away now I will take this matter no further. If you do not you will certainly die, for I offer no second chances to my enemies.'

He looked into the young man's eyes, and saw the fear there, and also the pride. 'I do love Sanja,' said the noble. 'But the estate I spoke of belongs – belonged – to my uncle. Without it I have nothing to offer her.'

'Then I shall give it to you as a wedding gift,' said Waylander softly, knowing even as he spoke that it was to no avail.

Anger shone in the noble's eyes. 'I am of House Kilraith!' he snapped. 'I do not need your pity, peasant!' He leapt forward, the sword slashing through the air. Waylander moved in to meet him, throwing up his left arm to block the blow at the noble's wrist, and curling his right hand up and behind the sword arm, clamping to it and dragging it back. The noble screamed, the sword dropping from his fingers as his arm snapped. Waylander pushed him away and swept up the fallen blade. The young man fell heavily and rolled to his knees. As he started to rise he felt the cold iron point of the blade against his throat. 'Don't kill me,' he begged.

A great sadness descended on Waylander as he looked into the frightened blue eyes. He took a deep breath. 'Too late,' he said. The blade plunged home, slashing through the jugular. Blood gouted from the severed vein and the noble fell back, his legs kicking out.

Waylander let fall the sword and, turning his back, walked the last few steps to his quarters.

Another man was waiting there, sitting quietly, cross-legged upon the ground. He wore a pale grey, chequered robe, and a long Chiatze blade, scabbarded, was resting in his lap. He was a small man, round-shouldered, his face thin. He looked up as Waylander approached. 'You are a hard man,' he said.

'So they say,' replied Waylander coldly. 'What do you want?'

The Chiatze rose, pushing his scabbarded sword into the black sash at his waist. 'Matze Chai will be returning to his home soon. It is my desire to stay in Kydor. He said you might have need of a *Rajnee*. I see now that you do not.'

'Why do you wish to stay?' asked Waylander. 'Is there not employment enough within Chiatze lands?'

'There is a mystery I must solve,' the *Rajnee* told him.

Waylander shrugged. 'You are welcome here as long as you wish to stay,' he said. 'If you arrived with Matze Chai you will already have been given lodging. But I can offer no work for a swordsman.'

'That is most kind, Grey Man.' The *Rajnee* sighed. 'I must, however, inform you that I am carrying a . . . a burden.'

At that moment, from the path behind them, came a cry of shock and surprise. Waylander turned. A stocky, bearded Chiatze ran into view carrying a long, curved sword. He was wearing a roughly made garment fashioned from wolfskin. 'There's a body!' he said, his voice shrill. 'On the path. Had his throat cut!' He peered around at the surrounding vegetation. 'There are assassins,' he added. 'They could be anywhere. We should get inside. Call the guards!'

'This,' said the *Rajnee*, 'is Yu Yu Liang, the burden of which I spoke.'

'We fought demons together,' said Yu Yu.

Waylander glanced at the *Rajnee*. 'Demons?'

The man nodded. 'That is part of the mystery.'

'Come inside,' said Waylander, moving past the man and opening the door to his quarters.

Moments later they were seated by the fire, the room bathed in the glow of lanterns and firelight. Yu Yu Liang sat on a rug, while the other two men occupied the only chairs in the room. 'The man who owns palace should give you better rooms,' Yu Yu told Waylander. 'I walk through palace. Much silver and gold, and velvet and silk. Probably he is rich bastard, and mean with money?'

81

'This man *is* the owner of the palace,' said the *Rajnee* in Chiatze.

Yu Yu glanced around the bare walls and grinned. 'And I am the emperor of the world.'

'You mentioned demons,' said Waylander. Briefly, and with no hint of melodrama, the *Rajnee* told him of the attack, the coming of the mist, and the strange creatures who walked within its depths. Waylander listened intently.

'The arm! Tell him about the arm!' said Yu Yu.

'I cut a limb from one of the creatures. The skin was pale, white grey. When sunlight touched it the flesh began to burn. Within a few heartbeats it had vanished entirely.'

'I have not heard of any such creatures in Kydor,' Waylander told him, 'nor any attacks of the kind you describe. I do recall reading about swords of bright light. I cannot remember the tome, but it is in the North Library. I will search for it tomorrow.' He looked into the *Rajnee*'s dark eyes. 'What is your name, swordsman?'

'I am Kysumu.'

'I have heard of you. You are welcome in my home.'

Kysumu bowed, and said nothing.

'Recently I saw such a mist as you describe,' said Waylander. 'I sensed there was evil in it. We will discuss the mystery further when I have searched my library.'

Kysumu rose. Yu Yu scrambled to his feet beside him. He tugged at Kysumu's robe. 'What about assassins?' he asked.

'The dead man *was* the assassin,' said Kysumu.

'Oh.'

Kysumu sighed. He bowed again to Waylander. 'I will send your guards to fetch the body.'

Waylander nodded, then walked away from the two men, entering a lantern-lit room at the rear of the building.

CHAPTER FIVE

MATZE CHAI SLEPT WITHOUT DREAMS, AND AWOKE FEELING refreshed and invigorated. The suite of rooms assigned to him had been decorated with sublime taste, the colours of the walls delightfully matched in pastel shades of pale lime and pink. Works of art by the most famous and sought-after Chiatze artists adorned the walls, and the hand-painted silk curtains filtered the morning light, allowing Matze Chai to appreciate the beauty of the dawn without the harshness of the sun's glare upon his delicate eyes.

The furniture was exquisite, embellished with gold leaf, the bed wide and firm beneath a silken canopy. Even the pot beneath the bed, which Matze had used three times during the night, was embellished with gold. Such elegance almost made the trip worthwhile. Matze Chai rang the golden bell alongside his bed. The door opened and a servant stepped inside, a young man employed by Matze for the last two years. He couldn't remember his name.

The servant offered Matze Chai a goblet of cool water, but he waved it away. The young man left the room and returned with a ceramic bowl filled with warmed, scented water. Matze Chai sat up and the servant pulled back the covers. The old merchant relaxed as the boy helped him remove his night-shirt and hair-cap, allowing his mind to wander as the servant gently sponged and dried his skin. The boy then opened a pot of sweet-smelling cream.

'Not too much,' warned Matze Chai. The servant did not answer, for Matze Chai did not allow conversation so early in the day. Instead he lightly smoothed the cream into the dry skin of Matze Chai's shoulders and arms. After this he pulled loose the long ivory

83

pins in Matze Chai's hair, applied fresh oils, then skilfully combed and brushed the hair, drawing it back into a tight bun at the crown, before slipping the ivory locking pins into place.

A second servant entered, bearing a tray on which sat a small silver tisane pot and a ceramic cup. Setting the tray by the bedside, the second servant moved to a large wardrobe, taking from it a heavy gown of yellow silk, beautifully embroidered with gold and blue songbirds. Matze Chai stood and stretched out his arms. The servant expertly slipped the gown over them, moving to the rear to button the upper portion of the garment, before attaching the lower section to ivory hooks at Matze Chai's waist. Swinging the golden sash around his master's waist, the servant tied it, then stepped back with a bow.

'I shall take my tisane upon the balcony,' said Matze Chai. Instantly the first servant moved to the curtains, drawing them aside. The second gathered up a wide-brimmed hat of artfully fashioned straw.

Matze Chai stepped out on to the balcony and sat down on a curved wooden bench, leaning his back against a large, embroidered cushion. The air was fresh and Matze believed he could detect salt in it. The light, however, was bright and unpleasant, and he gestured to the man holding the hat. He ran forward and placed it on Matze's head, angling it so that his face was in partial shadow, before tying it under his chin.

The stone of the balcony was cold under the merchant's feet. Glancing down, he wiggled his toes. Brief moments later one of the men knelt down and placed fur-lined slippers upon his feet.

Matze Chai sipped his tisane and decided that all was well with the world on this fine day. Waving his hand, he dismissed the servants and sat quietly in the morning sunshine. The breeze was fresh and cool, the sky a clear, cloudless blue.

He heard movement behind him, and the merest touch of irritation disturbed his tranquillity. Liu, the young captain of his guard, moved into sight and bowed deeply. He said nothing, waiting for his master's permission to speak.

'Well?' asked Matze Chai.

'The master of the house requests an audience, Lord. His servant, Omri, suggests that he could attend you presently.'

Matze Chai leant back against his cushion. For all that he was a round-eyed *Gajin* Waylander's manners were perfect. 'Convey to the servant that I would be honoured to entertain my old friend,' he said.

Liu bowed again, but did not depart immediately. Irritation once more touched Matze Chai, but he did not show it. He looked quizzically at the young soldier.

'One more matter, Lord, that you should be made aware of. There was an attempt on your . . . old friend's life last night. At the ball. Two men with knives attacked him.'

Matze Chai gave the briefest of nods, then waved his hand to dismiss the soldier. Was there ever a time, he wondered, when someone was not attempting to kill Waylander? One would have thought they would have learnt by now. His cup was empty and he looked for a servant to refill it, then remembered he had dismissed them. And his golden bell was all the way across the room by the bedside. He sighed. Then, glancing round to see that he was not observed, filled the cup. Matze Chai smiled. To serve oneself was quite liberating. But not civilized, he chided himself. Even so his good mood was restored and he waited patiently for Waylander to arrive.

A different servant ushered him in, removed the pot of tisane and the empty cup, then departed without a word. Matze Chai rose from his chair and offered a deep bow to his client, who responded in similar fashion before seating himself.

'It is good to see you, my friend,' said Waylander. 'I understand your journey was not without excitement.'

'It was – regrettably – not as dull as one would have liked,' agreed Matze Chai.

Waylander laughed. 'You don't change, Matze Chai,' he said, 'and I cannot tell you what a delight that is.' The smile faded. 'I apologize for asking you to make this journey, but I needed to see you.'

'You are leaving Kydor,' said Matze Chai.

'I am indeed.'

'Where to now? Ventria?'

Waylander shook his head. 'Across the western ocean.'

'The ocean? But why? There is nothing there – save the end of the world. It is where the stars flow into the sea. There is no land, no civilization. And even if there is land it will be barren and empty. Your wealth would be meaningless there.'

'It is meaningless *here*, Matze Chai.'

The elderly merchant sighed. 'You have never been content to be rich, Dakeyras. This, in some strange way I have yet to fathom, is why you *are* rich. You care nothing for wealth. What is it, then, that you desire?'

'I wish I could answer that,' said Waylander. 'All I can say is that this life is not for me. I have no taste for it.'

'What is it that you wish me to do?'

'You already manage one sixth of all my ventures, and hold two fifths of my wealth. I shall give you letters to all merchants with whom I have business dealings. These will inform them that, from the time they receive my instructions, you will speak for me. I shall also tell them that if they do not hear from me within five years then all my ventures and capital become yours.'

Matze Chai was aghast at the thought. He struggled to come to terms with what Waylander offered. Already wealthy, Matze Chai would become instantly the richest man in all of Chiatze. What would there be left to strive for?

'I cannot accept this,' he said. 'You must reconsider.'

'You can always give it all away,' said Waylander. 'But whatever you choose I shall sail from this world and not return.'

'Are you truly so unhappy, my old friend?' asked Matze Chai.

'Will you do as I ask?'

Matze Chai sighed again, deeply. 'I will,' he said.

Waylander rose, then smiled. 'I will tell your servants to prepare your second pot of tisane,' he said. 'They really should have brought it by now.'

'I am served by cretins,' admitted Matze Chai, 'but, then, if I did not employ them their stupidity would see them starve in the streets.'

After Waylander had left Matze Chai sat lost in thought. He had long ago ceased to be surprised by his fondness for his *Gajin* client. When Waylander had first come to him, all those years ago, Matze Chai had been merely curious about the man. That curiosity led him to engage the old seer. Matze had sat upon the silken rug at the centre of the temple's inner sanctum and watched as the elderly priest cast the bones.

'Will this man be a danger to me?'

'Not if you do not betray him.'

'Is he evil?'

'All men carry evil within them, Matze Chai. The question is imprecise.'

'What, then, can you tell me of him?'

'He will never be content, for his deepest desire is unattainable. Yet he will become rich, and make you rich. Is that enough for you, merchant?'

'What is this unattainable desire?'

'Deep in his heart, far below the level of conscious thought, he is desperate to save his family from terror and death. This unconscious desire drives him on, forces him to seek out danger, to pit himself against the might of violent men.'

'Why is it unattainable?'

'His family are already dead, slain in a mindless orgy of lust and depravity.'

'Surely,' said Matze Chai, 'he knows they are dead.'

'Of course. As I said, it is an unconscious desire. A part of his soul has never accepted that he was too late to save them.'

'But he will make me rich?'

'Oh, yes, Matze Chai, he will make you richer than you could ever dream possible. Be sure, however, that you recognize the riches when you have them.'

'I am sure that I will.'

The stooping servant, Omri, was waiting in the corridor outside Matze Chai's apartments. As Waylander stepped out he bowed briefly. 'Lord Aric is waiting to see you, sir, along with the magicker, Eldicar Manushan,' he said. 'I have had refreshments served to them in the Oak Room.'

'I was expecting him,' said Waylander, his expression cold.

'I must say that he looks well. I believe he has dyed his hair.'

Together the two men walked back along the corridor, and up two sets of stairs. 'The bodies have been removed, sir. Emrin had them loaded on to a wagon and has driven it into Carlis. He will make a report to the watch officer, but I expect there will be an official inquiry. The incident, I should imagine, is the talk of Carlis. One of the young men was due to be wed next week. You even received an invitation to the ceremony.'

'I know. He and I spoke of it last night, but he was in no mood to listen.'

'A shocking incident,' said Omri. 'Why did they do it? What did they have to gain?'

'*They* had nothing to gain. They were sent by Vanis.'

'That is disgraceful,' said Omri. 'We must inform the watch officer. You should lay charges against him.'

'That will not be necessary,' said Waylander. 'I do not doubt that Lord Aric has a plan to resolve the situation.'

'Ah, I see. A plan that no doubt involves money.'

'No doubt.'

They moved on in silence, emerging into a wide, arched hallway on the upper floor.

As they reached the doors of carved oak Omri stepped back. 'I have to say, sir,' he said, in a low voice, 'that I am not comfortable in the presence of this magicker. There is something about the man that I find disturbing.'

'You are a good judge of character, Omri. I shall bear that in mind.'

Waylander pushed open the doors and entered the Oak Room.

The room, panelled with oak, had been designed in the shape of an octagon. Rare weapons from many nations hung on the walls, a battleaxe and several hunting bows from Vagria, spears and curved scimitars from Ventria. Angostin broadswords, daggers and shields vied with tulwars, lances, pikes and several embossed crossbows. Four armour trees had been placed around the room, boasting ornate helms, breastplates and shields. The furniture consisted of twelve deep chairs and three cushion-covered couches, set upon a scattering of Chiatze rugs of hand-dyed silk. The room was lit by sunlight streaming through the high-arched, east-facing windows.

Lord Aric was seated on a couch below the window, his booted feet resting on a low table. Opposite him was the magicker, Eldicar Manushan, his blond page standing beside him. Neither man rose as Waylander entered, but Aric waved his hand and gave a broad smile. 'Good morning, my friend,' he called. 'I am so glad you could find time to join us.'

'You are up early, Lord Aric,' said Waylander. 'I have always been led to believe it was considered uncivilized for a noble to rise before noon – unless a hunt was in the offing.'

'Indeed so,' agreed Aric, 'but, then, we have pressing matters to discuss.'

Waylander sat down and stretched out his legs. The door opened and Omri entered, bearing a tray on which was set a large silver pot of tisane and three cups. The men sat in silence as he filled the cups then departed. Waylander sipped the brew. It was camomile sweetened with mint and a little honey. He closed his eyes, enjoying the taste upon his tongue. Then he glanced at Aric. The slim noble was doing his best to appear at ease, but there was an underlying tension in him. Transferring his gaze to the black-bearded magicker, Waylander saw no sign of unease. Eldicar Manushan was drinking his tisane quietly, apparently lost in thought. Waylander caught the eye of the little blond boy, who smiled nervously.

The silence grew, and Waylander made no attempt to disturb it.

'Last night was most unfortunate,' said Aric at last. 'The two boys were well liked and neither of them had ever been in any kind of trouble.'

Waylander waited.

'Parellis – the blond boy – is . . . was a second cousin to the Duke. In fact, I understand that the Duke had agreed to stand alongside Parellis at his wedding. It is one of the reasons the Duke decided to bring the Winter Court to Carlis. You see the complications that are beginning to arise.'

'No,' said Waylander.

Aric seemed momentarily bewildered. Then he forced a smile. 'You have killed a relative of the ruler of Kydor.'

'I killed two assassins. Is this against the law in Carlis?'

'No, of course not, my friend. As to the first killing there were hundreds of witnesses. No problems there. But the second. . . . Well,' he said, spreading his hands, 'no one saw that. It is my understanding that there was only one weapon – a ceremonial sword belonging to Parellis. This would indicate you dispossessed him of that weapon and killed him with it. That being so, it could be argued that you killed an unarmed man, which, according to the law, is murder.'

'Well,' said Waylander easily, 'the inquiry will establish the facts then make a judgement. I will abide by that.'

'Would that it were so easy,' said Aric. 'The Duke is not a forgiving man. Had both boys been killed in the ballroom I think even he would have been forced to accept the outcome. But I fear that the relatives of Parellis will seek to have you arrested.'

Waylander gave a thin smile. 'Unless?'

'Ah, well, this is where I can help, my dear friend. As one of the leading nobles in House Kilraith, and the chief magistrate of Carlis, I can mediate between the factions. I would suggest some reparation to the bereaved family – merely as a gesture of regret over the incident. Say . . . twenty thousand gold crowns to the mother of the boys, and the cancelling of the debts owed by their uncle, the grieving Vanis. In this way the matter will be solved before the arrival of the Duke.'

89

'It touches me that you would go to such lengths on my behalf,' said Waylander. 'I am most grateful.'

'Oh, think nothing of it! It is what friends are for.'

'Indeed. Well, let us make it thirty thousand gold crowns for the mother. I understand she has two other younger sons and that the family is not as wealthy as once they were.'

'And Vanis?'

'By all means let the debt be cancelled,' said Waylander. 'It was a piffling sum.' He rose and gave a bow to Aric. 'And now, my friend, you must excuse me. Much as I enjoy your company I have other pressing matters of my own to attend.'

'Of course, of course,' said Aric, rising from his seat and offering his hand. Waylander shook it, nodded to the magicker, then left the room.

As the door closed Aric's smile vanished. 'Well, that was simply done,' he said coldly.

'You would have preferred it to be difficult?' asked Eldicar Manushan softly.

'I would have preferred to see him squirm a little. There is nothing quite so stomach-churning as a peasant with wealth. It offends me that I am forced to deal with him. In the old days he would have been dispossessed by his betters, his wealth used by those who understood the nature of power and its uses.'

'I can see how much it must grieve you,' said the magicker, 'to come to this man and beg for scraps from his table.'

All colour drained from Aric's thin face. 'How dare you?'

Eldicar laughed. 'Come, come, my friend, what else can it be called? Each year for the past five years this rich peasant has paid your gambling debts, the mortgage on your two estates, settled your tailor's accounts and enabled you to live in the style and manner of a noble. Did he do this of his own volition? Did he come running to your house and say, "My dear Aric, I have heard how fortune has fled you, so please allow me to pay all your debts?" No, he did not. You came to him.'

'I leased him land!' stormed Aric. 'It was a business arrangement.'

'Aye, business. And all the monies you have received since then? Including the five thousand crowns you requested last night?'

'This is intolerable! Beware, Eldicar, my patience is not limitless.'

'Neither is mine,' said Eldicar, his voice suddenly sibilant. 'Shall I ask for the return of the gift *I* gave you?'

90

Aric blinked. His mouth opened. He sat down heavily. 'Oh, come now, Eldicar, there is no need for us to argue. I intended no disrespect.'

The magicker leant forward. 'Then remember this, Aric. You are mine. Mine to use, mine to reward, and mine to dispose of if I see fit. Tell me that you understand this.'

'I do. I do understand. I am sorry.'

'That is good. Now, tell me what you observed during our meeting with the Grey Man.'

'Observed? What was there to observe? He came in, agreed to all my demands and left.'

'He did not just agree,' said Eldicar. 'He *raised* the sum.'

'I know that. The size of his fortune is a matter of legend. Money means little to him, obviously.'

'Do not underestimate this man,' said Eldicar.

'I do not understand that. I just plucked him like a chicken – and he offered no resistance.'

'The game is not over yet. You have just seen a man who can mask his anger brilliantly. His only slip was to show his contempt by raising the amount of the extortion. This Grey Man is formidable, and I am not yet ready to have him as an enemy. So when this game moves on you will take no action.'

'Moves on?'

Eldicar Manushan gave a small smile. 'Soon you will come to me with news and we will speak of it again.' Eldicar pushed himself to his feet. 'But for now I wish to explore this palace. I like it. It will suit me well.' Rising from his chair he reached out, took the hand of his page, and walked from the room.

There were those who believed fat Vanis the merchant was incapable of regret. Always jovial, he would talk often of the stupidity of those who insisted on reliving past mistakes; of worrying over them and examining them from every angle. 'You cannot change the past,' he would say. 'Learn from your mistakes and move on.'

And yet Vanis was forced to admit to himself a tiny feeling of regret – even sadness – at the death of his two stupid nephews. This was, of course, assuaged by the news from Aric that all debts had been cancelled and that an extra fortune in gold would soon be in the hands of his sister, Parla. The money would be passed immediately to

Vanis for investment, since Parla was even less intelligent than her departed children.

Thoughts of the gold, and what he would do with it, filled his mind, submerging the hint of sadness beneath a cascade of anticipated pleasures. Perhaps now he would be able to interest the courtesan Lalitia. For some reason she had rebuffed all his advances.

Vanis heaved his considerable bulk from the couch and wandered to the window, gazing down at the guards patrolling the walled perimeter of his house. Pushing open the window he stepped out on to the balcony. The stars were bright in a clear sky, and a three-quarter moon hung just above the tree tops. It was a fine night, warm yet not cloying. Two guard dogs loped across the paved entrance path, disappearing into the undergrowth. Ferocious creatures, they made him shiver, and he hoped all the downstairs doors were locked. He had no wish to find one of the beasts padding along his corridors during the night.

The iron gates to his home were chained shut and Vanis relaxed a little.

Despite his own philosophy he found himself thinking back over the mistakes of the past months. He had taken the Grey Man lightly, believing he would not dare to push the matter of the debts. After all, Vanis was highly connected within House Kilraith, and the Grey Man – being a foreigner – needed all the friends he could find in order to operate his business interests in Carlis. The miscalculation had proved costly. Vanis should have guessed that matters would not be so easily resolved when the debts had been lodged with the Merchants Guild, the promises of repayment written down and witnessed.

He moved back inside and poured himself a cup of Lentrian Fire, an amber spirit he had found to be more potent than the finest wines.

It was not his fault that the boys were dead. Had the Grey Man not threatened to ruin him none of this would have happened. *His* was the blame.

Vanis had another drink and walked across to the western window. From here he could see the distant palace of the Grey Man across the bay, shining white in the moonlight. Once more he moved out on to the balcony, checking on the guards. A blond crossbowman was sitting on the lower branches of an oak, his eyes trained on the garden wall. Below him two more guards were patrolling, and Vanis saw one of the black hunting dogs padding across the open ground. The merchant moved back inside and sank into a deep leather seat alongside the flask of Lentrian Fire.

Aric had laughed at Vanis's insistence on hiring bodyguards. 'He is a merchant like you, Vanis. You think he would risk himself by hiring killers to hunt you down? If any were captured – and named him – he would lose everything. We'd have his palace and whatever of his fortune rests hidden in the palace vaults. By Heaven, it is almost worth hoping that he *does* send assassins.'

'Easy for you to say, Aric. Did you hear about his hunting down of the raiders who attacked his lands? Thirty of them, it is said. And he killed them all.'

'Nonsense,' sneered Aric. 'There were around a dozen, and I don't doubt that the Grey Man had most of his guards with him. It is just a lie put about to enhance the Grey Man's reputation.'

'A lie, eh? I suppose it was a lie that he killed Jorna with a single blow to the neck and then slew Parellis with his own sword. As I understand it, he did not even break sweat.'

'Two stupid boys,' said Aric. 'Gods, man, I could have done the same. What possessed you to use such simpletons?'

'It was an error,' said Vanis. 'I thought they were planning to surprise him in the grounds of his palace. I did not expect them to make the attempt at a ball in front of a hundred witnesses!'

'Ah, well, it is over now,' said Aric smoothly. 'The Grey Man gave in without a struggle. Not even a raised word. Have you thought what you will do with Parla's fifteen thousand?'

'Thirty thousand,' corrected Vanis.

'Minus my commission, of course,' said Aric.

'There are those who might feel that your commission is a little excessive, my friend,' said Vanis, struggling to control his anger.

Aric laughed. 'There are also those who believe that, as chief magistrate of Carlis, I should be investigating what caused those two hitherto exemplary boys to commit such a deed. Are you one of those?'

'You have made your point,' muttered Vanis. 'Fifteen thousand it is.'

Even now, some hours later, the conversation left a bad taste in his mouth.

Vanis finished a third cup of Lentrian Fire, and heaved himself once more to his feet. Moving somewhat unsteadily across the room, he pulled open the door and staggered to his bedchamber. The satin sheets on his bed had been pulled back and Vanis peeled off his robe and slippers and sat down heavily, his head spinning. He fell back on to the pillow and yawned.

A shadowy figure moved to the bedside. 'Your nephews are waiting for you,' said a soft voice.

Three hours after dawn a servant brought a tray of fresh-baked bread and soft cheese to the bedroom of the merchant Vanis. There was no reply to his gentle tapping, and he knocked louder. Thinking his master in a deep sleep the servant returned to the kitchens. Half an hour later he tried again. The door was still locked, and no sound came from inside.

He reported this to the head manservant, who, with a duplicate key, opened the door.

The merchant Vanis was lying back on blood-drenched sheets, his throat cut, a small, curved knife held in his right hand.

Within the hour the chief magistrate, Lord Aric, was at the property, along with the dark-bearded Eldicar Manushan, two officers of the watch and a young surgeon. The magicker ordered the little page-boy, dressed now in a tunic of black velvet, to wait outside the door. 'Not a scene to be witnessed by a child,' Eldicar told him. The boy nodded and stood outside with his back to the wall.

'It seems fairly obvious,' said the surgeon, stepping back from the body. 'He cut his own throat and died within a few heartbeats. The knife, as you can see, is very sharp. There is only the one cut – a deep slash that opened the jugular.'

'Strange that he removed his robe first, don't you think?' offered Eldicar Manushan, pointing to the garment on the floor by the bed.

'Why strange?' asked Aric. 'He was getting into bed.'

'To die,' said the magicker. 'Not to sleep. This means he knew his body would be found. Let us face it, gentlemen, Vanis was not a handsome man. Bald, monstrously fat and ugly would be an accurate description. Yet he disrobes, sits down upon white satin sheets and ensures he will be found in the most disgusting of positions. One would have thought he would have left his clothes on. A second thought concerns the wound itself. Very messy and painful. It takes a man of great courage to open his throat. Just as effective would be to open the arteries at the wrist.'

'Yes, yes, yes,' said the surgeon. 'This is all very interesting. But what we have here is a man dead in a locked bedroom, the instrument of his demise in his hand. We will never know what was going on in his mind at the time of his death. I understand his beloved nephews were killed only days ago. His brain was obviously unhinged by grief.'

Eldicar Manushan laughed, the sound horribly contrasting to the bloody scene within the room. 'Unhinged? Indeed he must have been. For he was so frightened of the thought of being killed he surrounded his house with guards and dogs. Then, once he was safe, he cut his throat. I would agree that sounds unhinged.'

'You believe he was murdered, sir?' asked the young surgeon, icily.

The magicker walked to the window and gazed down at the grounds below the balcony. He swung back. 'If he was murdered, young man, then he would have to have been killed by a man who could move in utter silence through a screen of guards and vicious dogs, scale a wall, commit the deed and depart without being seen or scented.'

'Precisely,' said the surgeon, turning to Lord Aric. 'I shall send for the morgue wagon, my lord, and prepare a report.'

With that the young man bowed to Aric, nodded towards Eldicar Manushan, and left the room.

Aric looked at the grotesque bloated body upon the bed, then swung to the two officers of the watch. 'Go and question the servants and the guards. See if anyone heard or saw anything – no matter how inconsequential it may have seemed at the time.'

The men saluted and walked away. Eldicar Manushan moved from the window and pushed shut the bedroom door. 'Would you like to know what really happened?' he asked softly.

'He killed himself,' whispered Aric. 'No one could have got to him.'

'Let us ask him.'

Eldicar stepped to the bedside and laid his hand upon the dead merchant's brow. 'Hear me,' whispered the magicker. 'Return from the Void and flow once more into this ruined shell. Come back to the world of pain. Come back to the world of light.'

The bloated body spasmed, and a choking, gargling noise came from the throat. The body began to tremble violently. Eldicar thrust his fingers into the man's mouth and dragged out a rolled-up ball of parchment. Hissing breath blew from the dead man's lung, and the remnants of his blood bubbled from the wound in his throat.

'Speak, Vanis,' ordered Eldicar Manushan.

'Grey . . . Man . . .' croaked the corpse. The body sagged back, arms and legs twitching. Eldicar Manushan clapped his hands twice. 'Return to the pit,' he said coldly. All movement ceased.

The magicker glanced at the ashen face of Lord Aric, then lifted the wet ball of parchment he had pulled from the merchant's throat. He opened it and spread it on the bedside table.

'What is it?' whispered Aric, taking a scented handkerchief from his pocket and holding it to his nose.

'It appears to be the contract for the debt the Grey Man waived. It contains all the promises made by Vanis for repayment.' Eldicar laughed again. 'One might say that Vanis was forced to eat his words before his demise.'

'I shall have him arrested!'

'Do not be a fool. I told you the game was not yet over. What evidence will you offer against him? Will you say that the dead man spoke to you? I do not wish that to happen. Great events will soon be upon us, Aric. The dawn of a new age. This matter is closed. As the surgeon said, Vanis took his life in a moment of terrible grief.'

'How did the Grey Man do it? The guards, the dogs . . .'

'What do we know of him?'

'Very little. He came here some years ago from the south. He has business interests in all the great trading nations, Gothir, Chiatze, Drenan, Ventria. He owns a huge fleet of merchant vessels.'

'And no one knows where he comes from?'

'No – not for sure. Lalitia enjoys his favours, but when I spoke with her she said he never talks about his past. She believes he has been a soldier, though she does not know with which army, and he speaks with knowledge about all the countries with which he has dealings.'

'A wife, children?' asked Eldicar.

'No. Lalitia says he once spoke of a woman who died. But he has been bedding Lalitia for more than a year now, and still she has managed to elicit no useful information.'

'Then I fear it will remain a mystery,' said the magicker. 'For within a few days the Grey Man will be gone from this world – as indeed will many others.'

Just before dawn a blond-haired man wearing a red shirt, embroidered with the coiled snake emblem of Vanis the merchant, rowed a small boat to the edge of the beach below Waylander's palace. Stepping into the shallow water he dragged the boat free of the tide then walked up the steps and through the terraced gardens. As he approached the rooms of the Grey Man he pulled a black skull-cap from his head. The blond hair came away with it. Pushing open the door of his rooms Waylander returned the skull-cap to a hidden drawer at the rear of an old wooden cabinet, then stripped off his clothing. The red shirt he rolled into a ball and tossed into the fireplace, atop the dried logs. Taking a small tinder box from beside the hearth he struck flint and lit the fire.

Waylander's mood was dark and he felt the heaviness of guilt upon him, though he did not know why. Vanis deserved to die. He was a liar, a cheat and a would-be murderer who had caused the death of two innocent boys. In any civilized society he would have been placed on trial and executed, Waylander told himself.

So why the guilt? The question nagged at him.

Was it, perhaps, because the kill had been so easy? Moving through to the small kitchen, he poured himself some water and drank deeply. Yes, it had been easy. Always the miser, Vanis had hired cheap guards, getting one of his servants to conduct the negotiations. There was no guard commander, the men having been hired singly from the taverns and docks, and told to patrol the grounds. It was after dark when Waylander, dressed as a guard, had scaled the wall and made his way to the tall oak some twenty feet from the house. Once there he had sat quietly in plain sight, crossbow in hand, watching the wall. One by one the hired men moved below him, occasionally glancing up and waving. The dog handler had also been hired independently, but in order for his dogs not to savage the guards he had walked the beasts around the grounds, letting them pick up the scent of every man dressed in a red tunic shirt. Thus when the man was on his rounds Waylander climbed down, chatted to him and patted the dogs, who sniffed at his boots, then ignored him.

After that it had been simplicity itself, waiting in the tree until the depths of the night, then scaling the wall and hiding patiently behind the velvet curtains alongside the merchant's bed.

He had not made Vanis suffer. The kill had been swift – one fast sweep and he had sliced the knife through the merchant's jugular. There was no time for Vanis to make a sound and he fell back on the bed, his blood pumping to the satin sheets. As a last flourish

Waylander thrust the crumpled contract deep into the dead man's throat. Moving to the balcony he waited for the guards to pass, then climbed down to the gardens below.

Once over the wall he had strolled through the near-deserted streets of Carlis, climbed into the small boat he had left moored in the harbour, and rowed across the bay.

It was while in the boat that the guilt had come. He had not recognized the emotion at first, putting it down to the same malaise he had been suffering for months now; a dissatisfaction at his life of riches and plenty. But it was far more than that.

Yes, Vanis had deserved to die, but in killing him Waylander had returned, albeit briefly, to a way of life that had once filled him with contempt and shame: the dark days when he had been Waylander the Slayer, a killer for hire. He knew at that moment why the guilt was growing. The deed had reminded him of an innocent, unarmed man, whose murder by Waylander sparked a terrible war and the death of thousands.

There is no comparison, he tried to tell himself, between a Drenai king and a fat, murderous merchant.

Stepping naked into the dawn's golden light, Waylander made his way around the terrace to where a small waterfall was bubbling over the rocks. Wading into the shallow pool below it, he stood under the cascading water, half hoping that it would wash away the bitterness of his memories. No man could reshape the past, he knew. If it could be done he would ride back to the little farm and save Tanya and the children from the raiders. In his nightmares he still saw her tied to the bed, the gaping, bloody wound in her belly. In reality she had been dead when he found her, but in his dreams she was alive and crying for help. Her blood had flowed across the floor, up the walls and over the ceiling. Crimson drops fell like rain upon the room. 'Save me!' she would cry. And he would scrabble at the blood-drenched ropes, unable to untie the knots. Always he would wake trembling, his body bathed in sweat.

The waterfall flowed over him, cold and refreshing, washing the dried blood from his hands.

Leaving the water, he sat down on a white marble boulder, allowing the sun to dry him. A man could always make excuses for his actions, he thought, seeking some sense of self-worth for his stupidities or meanness of spirit. Ultimately, however, a man's actions were his own, and he would have to answer for them at the Court of the Soul.

What will you say? he wondered. What excuses will you offer?

It was true that had the raiders not killed his family Dakeyras would never have become Waylander. Had he not become Waylander he would not have taken the life of the last Drenai king. Perhaps then the terrible war with Vagria would never have happened. Hundreds of villages and towns would not have been burned, and scores of thousands would never have died.

Guilt merged with sorrow as he sat in the sunshine. It seemed incredible now to Waylander that he had once been a Drenai officer, in love with a gentle woman who wanted nothing more than to raise a family on a farm she could call her own. He could hardly even recall the thoughts and dreams of that young man. One fact was certain. The young Dakeyras would never have donned a disguise to butcher an unarmed man in his bed.

Waylander shivered at the thought.

He had, over the years, tried to change his life so many times. He had allowed himself to care for another woman, Danyal, and had helped her to raise the two orphan girls, Miriel and Krylla. After the Vagrian War he had built a cabin high in the mountains, and assumed the life of the peaceful Dakeyras, a family man. He had almost grown content. After Danyal died in a riding accident he had raised the girls alone. Krylla wed a young man and they moved away to a distant land to build a farm and start a family.

Then the killers had come into the mountains. Dakeyras had no idea why Karnak, the ruler of the Drenai, should send assassins after him. It made no sense. Until the day he discovered that Karnak's son had unwittingly caused the death of Krylla during a drunken chase. Terrified that this action would result in Waylander seeking revenge, Karnak took precipitate action. Assassins were despatched to kill him. They failed. They died. And the days of death and blood had returned.

Eventually Waylander moved to the distant Gothir city of Namib, where he tried to rebuild his life. Once more assassins came for him. He led them deep into the forests outside the city, killing three and capturing the fourth. Instead of executing the last man he made a deal with him. Karnak had offered a fortune in gold for the head of Waylander. Proof of the killing would come with the handing over of his famed double-winged crossbow. One of the dead assassins bore a passing resemblance to Waylander, so he cut the head from the corpse and placed it in a sack. Then he gave his crossbow to the survivor. 'With these you will become rich,' he said. 'Is our business concluded?'

'Aye, it is,' said the man, who returned to Drenan and pocketed his reward. The skull and crossbow had then been exhibited in the Marble Museum.

Once more Waylander had journeyed to far places, choosing the distant realm of Kydor and attempting to immerse himself in a life of riches and plenty.

Yet now he had become the assassin once more. Not through necessity but through false pride.

It was not a pleasant thought.

Perhaps, he thought, when the ship comes in ten days' time, and I journey across the ocean, I will find a life that does not involve violence and death. A world without people, a vast land of soaring mountains and trickling streams. I could be content there, he decided.

Deep inside he could almost hear the mocking laughter.

You will always be Waylander the Slayer. It is your nature.

Ustarte the Priestess stood by the window. Far below her she could see the Grey Man sitting beside the waterfall. Even from here she could feel his shame. She turned from the window. Her three shaven-headed acolytes waited silently at the table. Their thoughts were troubled, their emotions strong. Prial was the most fearful, for he was the most imaginative. He was remembering the cage and the whips of fire. His heart was beating wildly.

The powerful, brooding Menias also felt fear, but it was leavened by frustration and anger. He hated the Masters with all of his being, and dreamt of the day he could Change and tear into them, ripping the flesh from their bones. He had not wanted to escape through the gateway. He had urged them all to remain and fight on.

Corvidal was the calmest of the three, but then he was the most content. All he desired was to be in the company of Ustarte. The priestess felt his love, and though she could not return it in the way he desired she still found great joy in it, for it had freed him from the hatred that still chained Menias. The simple fact that love could conquer hate gave Ustarte hope.

'Do we go?' asked the golden-eyed Prial.

'Not yet.'

'But we have failed,' said Menias, the shortest and heaviest of the three. 'We should go home, find others who have survived, and continue the fight.'

Ustarte returned to the table, her heavy red silk gown rustling as she moved. The dark-eyed, slender Corvidal rose and drew back her chair. She glanced into his gentle face and smiled her thanks as she sat down. How could she tell Menias that none of the others had survived, that she had felt their death even from beyond the gateway. 'I cannot just leave these people to the fate awaiting them.'

They sat in silence once more. Then Prial spoke. 'The gateways are opening. The killers in the mist have already been seen. The *Kriaz-nor* will follow soon. The puny weapons of this world will not stop them, Ustarte. I have no wish to view the horrors to come.'

'And yet the people of this world defeated them three thousand years ago,' she said.

'They had greater weapons then,' said Menias, his voice deep and low.

She felt the frustration in him, and the anger. 'Where did they gain the knowledge for such weapons?' she countered. 'And where are those weapons now?'

'How can we know?' put in Corvidal. 'The legends speak of fantastic gods, demons and heroes. There is no history of that period in this world. Only fable.'

'And yet there are clues,' said Ustarte. 'All the legends speak of a war among the gods. That suggests to me that there was discord in Kuan-Hador, and that at least some of them sided with humanity. How else could they have created the swords of light? How else could they have won? Yes, we have failed in our attempt to prevent the opening of the gates, and we have failed so far in our search to discover what happened to the weapons humanity used to win the first war. However, we must go on.'

'It is too late for this world, Ustarte,' said Prial. 'I say we should use the last of the power to open a gateway.'

Ustarte considered his words, then shook her head. 'What power remains in me I will use to aid those who will fight the enemy. I will not run.'

'And who will fight?' asked Menias. 'Who will stand against the *Kriaz-nor*? The Duke and his soldiers? They will be cut down – or worse. They will be captured and Joined. Other nobles will be seduced by promises of riches or extended life, or power within the new order. Humans are so easily corrupted.'

'I think the Grey Man will fight,' she said.

'One human?' asked the astonished Menias. 'We risk our lives because of your faith in one human?'

'There will be more than one,' she said. 'There is another clue that links the legends. All the stories speak of the return of the heroes. They die, and yet people believe they will come again when the need is upon the land. It is my belief that those who aided humanity subtly Joined the heroes they used, so that when the evil returned their descendants would have the power to combat it.'

'With respect, Great One,' said Corvidal, 'that is a hope not a belief. There is not a shred of true evidence to substantiate such a hypothesis.'

'It is more than a hope, Corvidal. We know the power of Joining for that is how we exist. We also know that *our* rulers ensure that no Joining can ever sire – or bear – children. They dare not risk creating beings who could decide their own destiny. But I think this is what the Ancients did, enhancing their human allies and allowing the talents to be passed from generation to generation. We see it around us even now. Nadir shamen who can meld man and wolf into fearsome creatures. Source Priests whose spirits can soar and whose powers can heal terrible diseases. We know from our studies that before the coming of the Ancients mankind had few of these gifts. The Ancients imbued certain members of the human race with them. The Ancients told their allies that, in times to come, if the evil returned, these powers would flower again. Hence the legends of the return of kings and heroes. I sense it in the Grey Man.'

'He is merely a killer,' said Prial dismissively.

'He is more than that. There is a nobility of spirit in him, and a power not found in ordinary men.'

'I am not convinced,' said Prial. 'I stand with Corvidal on this issue. You are risking our lives on a forlorn hope.'

Seeing that they were all in agreement she bowed her head. 'I will open a gateway for you all to leave,' she said, sadly.

'And yet you will stay?' asked Corvidal softly.

'I will.'

'Then I will stay with you, Great One.'

Menias and Prial glanced at one another. Then Prial spoke. 'I will stay until the arrival of the *Kriaz-nor*. But I have no wish to throw away my life needlessly.'

'And you, Menias?' asked the priestess.

He shrugged his powerful shoulders. 'Where you are, Great One, there shall I be.'

Yu Yu Liang cleared his throat and spat into the sea. He was miserable. It seemed to him that his quest to become a hero was not all he had anticipated. As a ditch-digger he received a small amount of coin at the end of the week, which he would use on food, alcohol, lodging and pleasure-women. There was always enough food, never enough women and far too much alcohol. But, looking back, it had not been as unpleasant a life as it had seemed while he was living it.

Picking up a flat rock, Yu Yu threw it far out over the waves. It struck once, skimmed for another twenty feet, then disappeared below the surface.

He sighed. Now he had a sharp sword, no money, no women, and was sitting in the sunshine of a foreign land wondering why he had travelled this far. He had not intended to leave the lands of the Chiatze. His first thought had been to strike out for the mountains to the west and join a band of robbers. Then he had come upon the battlefield, and the dead *Rajnee*. He recalled the moment when he had first seen the sword. It was jutting from the earth just behind a bush. Sunlight had glanced from the blade as Yu Yu was robbing the corpse. The *Rajnee* was carrying no coin, and Yu Yu had pushed himself to his feet and walked to the sword. It was quite beautiful, the blade gleaming, the long, two-handed hilt wondrously fashioned and leatherbound. The pommel was of silver, embossed with a mountain flower. Reaching out, Yu Yu drew the sword from the earth.

He then forgot his original purpose and decided to head north-east, filled with a desire to see foreign lands. It was most peculiar, and sitting in the sunshine of the Bay of Carlis he could not, for the life of him, remember just why he had thought it was such a fine idea.

Two days later something even more mysterious occurred. He came upon a merchant who was travelling in a cart with two pretty daughters and a retarded son. The wheel had come off the cart and the group were sitting by the roadside. In his new life as a robber and an outlaw Yu Yu

103

should have stolen the man's gold, ravished his daughters and left the scene richer and more relaxed. Indeed this had been his plan, and he had marched forward, adopting what he considered to be a menacing expression. Then, to show his intent, he grasped the hilt of the sword, ready to draw it and terrify his victims.

An hour later he had repaired the cart, and escorted the merchant to his home village some six miles to the east. For this he received a fine meal, a kiss on the cheek from both daughters, and a small sack of supplies from the merchant's wife. You are too stupid to be a robber, he had told himself, as he resumed his journey.

And now that stupidity had brought him to Kydor, a land where men bearing Chiatze features stood out like . . . like . . . he struggled for a simile, but could only come up with 'warts on a whore's arse'. This was not entirely pleasing and he stopped thinking of similes. However, the point was a good one. How could a Chiatze warrior become a robber in a land where he would be instantly identified wherever he went? It was a nonsense.

At that moment a young, blond-haired woman emerged on to the small beach. To Yu Yu's surprise she ignored him and began to remove her dress and undergarments. Once naked she ran across the sand and dived into the water. Coming to the surface she swam in long, easy strokes, curving round to approach Yu Yu's position. Treading water, she threw back her head, and swept her hands through her wet hair. 'Why are you not swimming?' she called out to him. 'Are you not hot sitting there in wolf fur?'

Yu Yu admitted that he was. She laughed and swung away, swimming out into deeper water.

As swiftly as he could Yu Yu struggled out of his clothes and hurled himself into the sea, landing on his belly, which was painful. Not, however, as unpleasant as what followed. He sank like a stone. Thrashing his arms wildly, he fought for the surface. His head broke clear and he sucked in a great gulp of air. For a moment he bobbed in the water, but then he breathed out and disappeared once more beneath the cold water.

Panic swept through him. Something grabbed his hair, hauling him up. He struggled wildly, and broke through the surface once more.

'Take a deep breath and hold it,' the woman ordered him. Yu Yu did so, and bobbed alongside her. 'It is the air in your lungs that lets you float.'

Reassured by her presence, Yu Yu relaxed a little. What she said was true. As long as he held air in his chest he floated.

'Now lean back,' she said. 'I will support you.' As she floated alongside him he felt her arms below his spine and he gratefully dropped back into them. Glancing to his right he found himself staring at a pair of perfect breasts. Air whooshed from his lungs and he sank. Her arms pushed him back to the surface and he spluttered for a while. 'What kind of an idiot leaps into the sea when he cannot swim?' she asked.

'I am Yu Yu Liang,' he managed to say, between great gulps of air.

'Well, let me teach you, Yu Yu Liang,' she said.

The next few minutes were a joy as she taught him a rudimentary stroke that allowed him to pull himself through the water. The sun was warm upon his back, the water cool upon his body. Finally she bade him make his way to the shallow water close to the beach. Then he watched as she waded back to where she had laid her clothes. Yu Yu followed her.

She climbed up the rocks to where a small waterfall cascaded down to the beach and washed the salt from her body. Yu Yu gazed on her beauty, almost awestruck. Then he scrambled up and also washed himself. They returned to the beach and the woman sat down on a rock, to let her body dry in the sunshine.

'You came in with the lord Matze Chai,' she said.

'I am . . . bodyguard,' said Yu Yu. The excitement caused by her nakedness made Yu Yu feel light-headed. His grasp of the round-eye tongue, feeble at best, came close to deserting him.

'I hope you fight better than you swim,' she said.

'I am great fighter. I have fought demons. I fear nothing.'

'My name is Norda,' she said. 'I work in the palace. All the servants have heard the stories of the demons in the mist. Is it true? Or were they merely robbers?'

'Demons, yes,' said Yu Yu. 'I cut arm from one and it burn. Then . . . gone. Nothing left. I did this.'

'Truly?' she asked him.

Yu Yu sighed. 'No. Kysumu cut arm. But I would have if closer.'

'I like you, Yu Yu Liang,' she said, with a smile. Rising to her feet, she dressed and wandered away back up the rocks to the path.

'I like you too,' he called. She turned and waved, then was gone.

Yu Yu sat for a while, then realized he was growing hungry. Putting on his clothes he thrust his scabbarded sword into his belt and walked back up the hill. Perhaps, he thought, life in Kydor will not be so unpleasant.

Kysumu was sitting on the balcony of their room. He was sketching the outline of the cliffs and town across the bay. He glanced up as Yu Yu entered. 'I've had a great time,' said Yu Yu. 'I swam with a girl. She was beautiful, with golden hair and breasts like melons. Beautiful breasts. I am a great swimmer.'

'I saw,' said Kysumu. 'However, if you wish to be a *Rajnee* you must put aside carnal desires, and concentrate on the spiritual, the journey of the soul towards true humility.'

Yu Yu thought about this, then decided Kysumu was making a joke. He didn't understand it, but laughed out of politeness. 'I am hungry,' he said.

Elphons, Duke of Kydor, angled his grey charger down the slope towards the grasslands of the Eiden Plain. Behind him came his aides and his personal bodyguard of forty lancers. At fifty-one Elphons had found the long journey from the capital tiring. A man of great physical strength, the Duke had lately been plagued by sharp pains in his joints, most especially in the elbows, ankles and knees, which were now swollen and tender. He had hoped that the journey from the damp and cold of the capital to the warmer climes around Carlis would relieve the problem, but so far there had been little change. He was also experiencing difficulty at times with his breathing.

He glanced back at the convoy of five heavy wagons, the first carrying his wife and her three ladies-in-waiting. His fifteen-year-old son, Niallad, was riding alongside the convoy, the sun glinting on his new armour. Elphons sighed and heeled his horse onward.

The weather had been clement during their mountain passage, but as they made their way slowly down towards the plain the temperature rose. At first it was a pleasant warmth, after the cold mountain winds, but now it was becoming intolerable. Sweat trickled down the Duke's broad face. He lifted his gold-embossed iron helm from his head and pushed back his hood of silver mail rings, exposing thick, unruly grey hair.

The slim, balding aide, Lares, rode alongside the Duke. 'Uncommonly hot, sire,' he said, pulling the stopper from his leather canteen and pouring water on to a linen handkerchief. This he passed to Elphons, who wiped it over his face and grey-streaked beard.

Instantly the hot breeze felt cool against his skin. Unclipping his heavy red cloak he passed it to Lares.

Far below, Elphons saw the wagons of the merchant convoy enter the deep woods bordering the long Lake of Cepharis. His mood soured. They had first caught sight of the convoy earlier that morning, as a dustcloud on the horizon. Slowly they had gained on it, and were now a mere half-mile behind them. Elphons had been looking forward to arriving at the lake, divesting himself of his armour and swimming in the cool water, and did not relish the thought of sharing it with two score wagoners and their families. As always the young Lares was in tune with his master's thoughts. 'I could ride down and get them to move on, sire,' he said.

It was a tempting thought, but Elphons pushed it aside. The wagoners would be no less hot than he, and the lake was common ground. It would be enough for the Duke and his retainers to ride close and wait patiently. The wagoners would get the message and move on more swiftly. Even so, it meant that before the day was over the Duke and his retainers would be eating dust thrown up by the convoy.

Elphons patted the sleek neck of his charger. 'You are tired, Osir,' he said to the horse, 'and I fear I am not as light as once I was.' The horse snorted and tossed its head.

The Duke touched heels to the animal's flanks and began once more the long descent. A solitary cloud drifted momentarily between the sun and the land and Elphons enjoyed a few seconds of relief from the heat.

Then it was gone. With the prospect of the lake looming, Elphons drained the last of the water from his canteen, and swung in the saddle to watch his wagons making their slow and careful descent. There was scree upon the road and if not handled with skill a wagon could slide off and smash into shards on the rocky slope.

His wife, the silver-haired Aldania, waved at him, and he grinned back. As she smiled she looked young again, he thought, and infinitely desirable. Twenty-two years they had been wed, and he still marvelled at his luck in winning her. The only daughter of Orien, the last but one king of the Drenai, she had fled her own lands during the war against Vagria. Elphons had been merely a knight at that time, and had met her in the Gothir capital of Gulgothir. Under any normal circumstances a romance between a princess and a knight would have been short-lived, but with her brother King Niallad slain by an assassin, and the Drenai empire in ruins, there were few suitors for her hand. And after the war, when the Drenai declared for a republic, she was even less sought-after. The new ruler, the fat giant Karnak, made it clear that Aldania would not be welcome back home. So Elphons had won her heart and her hand, bringing her to Kydor and enjoying twenty-two years of great joy.

Thoughts of his good fortune made him forget burning heat and painful joints, and he rode for some time lost in the memories of their years together. She was everything he could have wished for: a friend, a lover, and a wise adviser in times of crisis. There was only one area in which he could offer any criticism. The raising of their son. It was the only subject on which they rowed. She doted on Niallad, and would hear no words said against him.

Elphons loved the boy, but he worried for him. He was too fearful. The Duke twisted in the saddle and glanced back. Niallad waved at him. Elphons smiled and returned the wave. If I could turn back the years, thought the Duke, I would throttle that damned story-teller. Niallad had been around six years of age when he had learned the full story of the death of his uncle, the Drenai king. He had suffered nightmares for months, believing that the evil Waylander was hunting him. For most of the summer the boy had taken to creeping into his parents' bedroom and climbing into bed between them.

Elphons had finally summoned the Drenai ambassador, a pleasant man with a large family of his own. He had sat with Niallad and explained how the monstrous Waylander had been hunted down and how his head had been cut off. The head had been brought to Drenan, where, stripped of skin, it had been displayed in the museum, alongside the assassin's infamous crossbow.

For a while the boy's nightmares ceased. But then news had come of the theft of the crossbow, and the murder of Karnak, the Drenai ruler.

Even now, nine years later, Niallad would not travel without bodyguards. He hated crowds and would avoid large gatherings when he could. On state occasions, when Elphons forced him to attend, he would stay close to his father, eyes wide with fear, sweat upon his face. No one mentioned it, of course, but all saw it.

Elphons returned his attention to the trail. He was almost at the foot of the slope. Shading his eyes he stared ahead at the wooded lake a quarter of a mile ahead. There was no one swimming. How curious, he thought. They must have pushed on. Hardy men, these wagoners. And yet they had women and children with them. One would have thought they would have appreciated a cooling swim. Perhaps they realized the Duke was close behind and were nervous about stopping. He hoped this was not the reason.

Lares moved alongside him and waved the troop of twenty soldiers forward. They cantered past the Duke and rode ahead to scout the woods.

Sadly such precautions were necessary. There had been three attempts on the Duke's life in the last two years. Such was the Angostin way. A man held power only as long as his strength and his guile held out. And his luck, thought Elphons. The four major Houses of Kydor were involved in an uneasy truce, but disputes broke out often, and battles were fought. Only last year Lord Panagyn of House Rishell had waged a short and bloody war against Lord Ruall of House Loras, and Lord Aric of House Kilraith. There were three battles, all indecisive, but Panagyn had lost an eye in the third, while Ruall's two brothers were both killed in the second. Lord Shastar, of the smaller House Bakard, had now broken his treaty with Panagyn and allied himself with Aric and Ruall, which suggested a new war was looming. This was why, Elphons believed, Panagyn had sent assassins against him. Angostin law stated that the Duke's forces could not be used in disputes between Houses. However, if the Duke was dead, his three thousand soldiers would likely join Panagyn. The man, though a brute, was a fighting soldier, and highly regarded by the troops. With them he could win a civil war and make himself Duke.

Sooner or later I will have to kill Panagyn, he thought, for if he ever slays me he will see my son murdered on the same day. Elphons found the fear of such an outcome weighed heavily upon him. Niallad was not ready to rule. Perhaps he never would be. The thought made him shiver. He looked up at the sky. 'Just give me five more years,' he prayed to the Source. In that time Niallad *might* change.

The Duke drew rein as his cavalrymen fanned out and entered the wood. Within moments they were galloping their mounts away from the trees and back to the convoy. The captain, a young man named Korsa, dragged his mount to a halt before him. 'There has been a massacre, my lord,' he said, forgetting to salute.

Elphons stared hard into the young man's ashen face. 'Massacre? What are you talking about?'

'They are all dead, sire. Butchered!'

Elphons heeled the charger into a run, his forty lancers swinging their mounts and following him.

The wagons were all drawn up within the trees some fifty feet from the water's edge, but there were no horses. Blood was everywhere, splashed against tree-trunks, pooling on the earth. Elphons drew his longsword and gazed around the scene. Lares and Korsa dismounted, while the other cavalrymen, weapons in their hands, sat nervously awaiting a command.

A cold winter wind blew across the lake. Elphons shivered. Then he climbed down from his mount and walked to the water's edge. Amazingly there was ice upon the water. It was melting fast. He scooped some into his hand. The mud beneath his feet crunched as he moved. Sheathing his sword he walked back to where Lares and Korsa were examining the traces of an overturned wagon. Blood was smeared upon the smashed wood, and a blood trail, like the crimson slime of a giant worm, could be seen leading away from the wagons and deeper into the trees. Several bushes had been uprooted.

Elphons turned to one of the soldiers. 'Ride out and keep the wagons back from here,' he said. Gratefully the man swung his horse and rode away.

Melting ice was everywhere. The Duke scanned the ground. It was badly churned, but he found a clear imprint just beyond the wagon. It was like the mark of a bear, only longer and thinner: four-toed and taloned.

In the space of a few moments something had descended upon forty wagoners and their families, killed them and their horses and dragged them away into the woods. It couldn't have happened without a sound. There must have been screams of terror and pain. Yet, only a few hundred yards away, Elphons had heard nothing. And how could ice form in this cloying heat?

Elphons followed the blood trails for a little way. Dead birds littered the ground, frost upon their feathers.

Lares crossed the blood-covered ground. The young man was trembling. 'What are your orders, sire?'

'If we skirt the lake to the north how long till we reach Carlis?'

'By dusk, sire.'

'Then that is what we shall do.'

'I cannot understand how we heard nothing. We had the woods in sight all the time.'

'Sorcery was used here,' said the Duke, making the Sign of the Protective Horn. 'Once my family is safe in Carlis I'll return with Aric's forces and a Source priest. Whatever evil is here will be destroyed. I swear it.'

It was still early when Waylander strolled into the North Tower library, climbing the cast-iron spiral staircase to the Antiquities section on the third floor. The three acolytes of the priestess Ustarte were sitting at the central table, examining tomes and parchment scrolls. They did not look up as he entered.

Strange men, he thought. Despite the thick stone of the tower the heat was already rising within the chamber, and yet they were garbed in heavy grey-hooded robes, silk scarves around their necks, and each wore thin grey gloves. Waylander did not acknowledge them as he moved past, but he felt their eyes upon his back. He allowed himself a wry smile. He had never been loved by priests.

Waylander paused and scanned the shelves. More than three thousand documents were stored here, ancient skinbound volumes, fading parchments, even tablets of clay and stone. Some were beyond deciphering, but still drew scholars from as far afield as Ventria and the distant Angostin homeland.

His search would have been so much easier had the old librarian, Cashpir, not succumbed to a fever and taken to his bed. His knowledge of the library was phenomenal, and it was through him that Waylander had gathered so many of the precious tomes. He tried to recall the day he had read of the shining swords. There had been a storm raging, the sky black and heavy. He had sat where the priests were now, reading under lantern-light. For three days he had been racking his mind for any bright shard of memory.

He glanced towards the open window, and the new wooden shutters. Then it came to him.

The old shutters had been leaking, and water had splashed to the shelves close by, damaging the documents stored there. Waylander and Cashpir had moved some of the scrolls to the table. It was one of these he had been idly scanning. The area of the shelf closest to the window was still empty. Waylander walked across the chamber to the small office used by Cashpir. The place was a mess, scrolls scattered everywhere, and he could hardly see the leather-topped

111

desk beneath the mass of books and parchment. Cashpir had an amazing mind, but no talent whatsoever for organization.

Waylander walked round the desk and sat down, picking through the parchments that lay there, recalling what had pricked his original interest on the day of the storm. One of the scrolls had told of giant creatures, melded from men and beasts. Waylander himself had been hunted by just such creatures twenty years before – sent to kill him by a Nadir shaman.

He studied the scrolls, examining each one before laying it on the floor at his feet. Finally he lifted a yellowing parchment and recognized it immediately. The ink had faded badly in places and one section of the parchment had been stained by fungus. Cashpir had treated the rest with a preservative solution of his own design. Waylander took the scroll back into the main library and walked to the window. In the sunlight he read the opening lines.

Of the glory that was Kuan-Hador there are only ruins now, stark and jagged, testimony to the fruitless arrogance of man. There are no signs of the God-Kings, no shadows of the Mist Warriors cast by the harsh sunlight. The history of the city is gone from the world, as indeed are the stories of its heroes and villains. All that remains are a few contradictory oral legends, garbled tales of creatures of fire and ice, and warriors with swords of shining light who stood against demons shaped from both men and beasts.

Having visited the ruins one can understand the birth of such legends. There are fallen statues that appear to have the heads of wolves and the bodies of men. There are the remains of great arches, built, as far as one can ascertain, for no purpose. One arch, named by the Historian Ventaculus as the Hador Folly, is carved from a sheer cliff of granite. It is the most curious piece, for when one examines it one finds that the pictographic carvings upon the inner arch pillars vanish into the rock, almost as if the cliff had grown over it like moss.

I have copied separately many of the pictographs, and several of my colleagues have spent decades trying to decipher the complex language contained in them. So far complete success has eluded us. What is apparent is that Kuan-Hador was unique in the ancient world. Its methods of architecture, the skill of its artisans, are apparent nowhere else. Many of the stones still standing are black-

ened by fire, and it is likely that the city was destroyed in a great conflagration, perhaps as the result of a war with neighbouring civilizations. Few artefacts have been recovered from Kuan-Hador, though the King of Symilia has in his possession a mirror of silver that never tarnishes. This, he claims, was recovered from the site.

Waylander paused in his reading. There followed a series of descriptions of site examinations and a suggested layout of the city. Bored by the scholarly writing Waylander skimmed through the text until he came to the concluding paragraphs.

As is ever the case when a civilization falls, tales abound that it was evil. Nomads who inhabit the areas that once were the realm of Kuan-Hador talk of human sacrifice and the summoning of demons. There is no doubt that the city boasted great magickers. I suspect, from the statues and those pictographs we have been partly able to decipher, that the rulers of Kuan-Hador did indeed have some understanding of the vile art of meld-magic. It is entirely probable that more recent examples of this abhorrent practice – among the Nadir and other barbaric peoples – are legacies of Kuan-Hador.

I have listed separately some of the oral legends pertaining to the fall of Kuan-Hador. The one most told concerns the return of the shining swords. Among the nomads of the Varnii – distant relatives of the Chiatze – the shamen speak a succession of doggerel verses at season feasts. The first and last verse read:

> *But seek ye not the Men of Clay,*
> *Who buried lie in crafted night,*
> *Their shining swords are put away,*
> *Their eyes are closed against the light.*

> *Death must await these Men of Clay,*
> *Who stand in rows of ghostly white,*
> *And will until that dreadful day,*
> *When they awake to one last fight.*

A more complete translation can be found in Appendix 5. The Historian Ventaculus produced an appealing essay on the song, claiming it to be a metaphor for the death and resurrection of those of heroic virtue, a faith system not unusual among warrior peoples.

Waylander put the scroll back in its rightful place on the shelf and strolled from the library. Minutes later he emerged on to the central terrace outside the Banquet Hall. Kysumu was waiting there, standing by the balustrade and staring out over the bay and the sea beyond. As Waylander approached the little swordsman turned. He bowed deeply. Waylander returned the compliment.

'I have found little,' he told the *Rajnee*. 'There are stories of an ancient city that once ruled this land. Apparently it was destroyed by warriors with shining swords.'

'A city of demons,' said Kysumu.

'So it is said.'

'They are returning.'

'That is quite a leap of imagination,' said Waylander. 'The city fell around three thousand years ago. The scroll I examined was written a thousand years ago. One attack on a merchant and his bodyguards is too little to convince me.'

'I also discovered a scroll,' said Kysumu. 'It talked of nomads avoiding the ruins because their legends say the demons were not all slain, but had escaped through a gateway to another world, one day to return.'

'Even so, the evidence is small.'

'Perhaps,' said Kysumu. 'But when I see birds flying south I know winter is coming. They do not need to be *large* birds, Grey Man.'

Waylander smiled. 'Let us say you are correct, and the demons of Kuan-Hador are returning. What is your plan?'

'I have no plan. I will fight them. I am *Rajnee*.'

'Matze Chai tells me you believe your sword brought you here.'

'It is not a belief, Grey Man, it is a fact. And now that I am here I know it is right. How far are the ruins from the palace?'

'Less than a day's ride.'

'Will you loan me a horse?'

'I'll do better than that,' said Waylander. 'I'll take you myself.'

If one fact of life was incontrovertible for Yu Yu Liang it was that one golden ounce of good luck was invariably followed by several pounds of bad. Usually, in his experience, falling upon him from

114

a great height. Or, as his mother would say, 'When the emperor's parade passes by, the horse-turd collectors are not far behind.'

The blonde-haired Norda had left his bed only moments before, and Yu Yu was happier than he had been in months. This was despite the initial criticism offered by the woman. 'You are not in a race,' she had whispered to him, as he clung to her.

He had paused, his heart pounding wildly. 'A race?' he managed to say, between great gulps of air.

'Be slow. We have plenty of time.'

If Nashda, the crippled god of all labourers, had appeared in his room offering him immortality at that moment it could not have been sweeter. First, there was this beautiful woman lying beneath him, her golden legs around his hips. Second, there was not a queue of impatient ditch-diggers outside the door shouting for him to hurry. Third, as far as he knew, this glorious creature desired no money from him. Which was fortuitous since he had no money. And now to be told he had plenty of time . . . Could Heaven be any sweeter?

He took her advice. There were many new joys to discover, and some obstacles to overcome. Kissing a woman who still had all her teeth was surprisingly pleasant. Almost as pleasant as the fact that there was no sand-glass on the table beside the bed, swiftly trickling his time away.

If life could get better than this, Yu Yu Liang did not know how.

The first indications that there was a price to be paid for such pleasure came just after she left, when he pulled on his harsh, woollen shirt. His upper back tingled with pain from the scratches to his skin. She had also bitten his ear, which had been most pleasurable at the time, but now throbbed a little.

Even so Yu Yu was whistling a merry tune as he stepped from the room – to find himself facing three of the Grey Man's guards.

The first, a stocky man with tightly curled golden hair, was staring at him malevolently. 'You have made a bad mistake, you slant-eyed pig,' he said. 'You think you can come here and force yourself on our women?'

In Yu Yu's village there had been a Source temple, and many of the children had attended school there. They had no wish to learn the tongue of the round-eye, but the priests had supplied two meals a day, and for this it was worth putting in a little study. Yu Yu had been a quick learner, but lack of practice since then meant he needed

115

a little time to translate complicated sentences. Apparently he had committed some kind of error and was being accused of stealing a woman's one-eyed pig. He looked into the man's face and saw the hatred there, then flicked his gaze to the man on either side. Both were staring at him through narrowed eyes. 'Well, now you are going to learn a little lesson,' continued the first man. 'We're going to teach you to stick with your own kind. Understand, yellow man?'

Despite having no knowledge of the pig theft, Yu Yu understood only too well the lesson they were about to deliver.

'I said, do you understand?'

The man's hatred turned briefly to shock, and then to blank emptiness as Yu Yu's left fist cannoned into his nose. He was already unconscious as the right cross followed. The guard hit the floor, blood seeping from his nostrils. A second guard lunged forward. Yu Yu butted him full in the face then brought his knee up into the man's groin.

The guard gave a strangled cry of pain and sagged against the Chiatze. Yu Yu pushed him away and downed him with a left hook to the jaw.

'You give lessons too?' Yu Yu asked the last guard.

The man shook his head vehemently. 'I didn't want to be here,' he said. 'It wasn't my idea.'

'I don't steal pigs,' said Yu Yu, then stalked away down the corridor, his good mood evaporating. There were scores of guards in the Grey Man's palace and when next they came it would be in greater numbers. This meant, at best, a bad beating.

Yu Yu had suffered such beatings before, blows and kicks raining in on him. The last such attack, just over a year ago, had almost killed him. His left arm had been broken in three places. Several ribs had been snapped, one of which had pierced his lung. It took months to recover, months of hardship and hunger. Unable to work he had been reduced, at first, to begging for rice at the poorhouse. Finally he had journeyed back to the Source temple. Some of the priests still remembered him, and he had been welcomed warmly. They tended his broken bones, and fed him. When his strength returned he journeyed back to the site of his beating and sought out singly each of the eight men involved in the attack. And he thrashed them. The last had been the most difficult. Shi Da was six and a half feet tall, heavily muscled and supremely tough. It had been his kicks that had snapped Yu Yu's ribs. Yu Yu had given a lot of thought to challenging Shi Da. It was a matter of honour that a challenge should be made, but the timing had to be exactly right.

So Yu Yu had walked up behind him in the Chong tavern and thwacked a heavy iron bar across the back of the man's head. As he slumped forward Yu Yu struck him twice more. Shi Da had fallen to his knees, barely conscious. 'I challenge you to man-to-man combat,' said Yu Yu, in the time-honoured fashion. 'Do you accept?'

A low garbled grunt of incomprehension came from the giant.

'I shall take that as a yes,' said Yu Yu. Then he kicked Shi Da in the jaw. Shi Da had hit the floor hard, then slowly rolled to his knees. Amazingly the big man climbed to his feet. Panicked, Yu Yu had dropped the iron bar and rushed in smashing blows left and right into Shi Da's face. Shi Da landed one clumsy punch before pitching sideways to the floor.

In his relief Yu Yu felt magnanimous and only kicked the unconscious man a few times. It was a mistake. He should have knelt by him and beaten him to death. When Shi Da recovered he put out the word that he would cut Yu Yu Liang's heart from his body and feed it to his dogs.

That was the day when Yu Yu decided upon an outlaw's life in the mountains.

Now, in a foreign land, he had made more enemies. And he still did not know why. With a little more time to work on the translation Yu Yu realized that the man had called *him* a slant-eyed pig, and that the problem was, in fact, not about theft, but about making love to the blonde woman. It seemed peculiar to Yu Yu that the shape of his Chiatze eyes, or the golden colour of his skin, should preclude him from forming friendships with Kydor women. And why would he want to stick with his own kind? It was a mystery. Yu Yu had been a ditch-digger for nine years and had never met another ditch-digger he found remotely attractive.

Except for Pan Jian.

She was the only female ditch-digger he had ever known. A monstrous woman with huge arms and a flat round face that boasted several chins, two of which sported large, matching warts. One evening, when drunk and broke, he had propositioned her.

'Pay me a compliment,' she told him, 'and I'll think about it.'

Yu Yu stared at her through bleary eyes, searching for some evidence of femininity. 'You have nice ears,' he said at last.

Pan Jian had laughed. 'That will do,' she told him, and they had rutted in a ditch.

She had been dismissed two days later for arguing with the foreman. It was a short argument. He pointed out he had seen cows with smaller and more attractive arses than hers, and she had broken his jaw.

As Yu Yu climbed the stairs to the upper level he found himself remembering her fondly. Although making love to her was like clinging to the back of a greased hippo, the ride had been enjoyable, and he had discovered in Pan Jian an unexpected tenderness. Afterwards she had talked of her life, and her hopes and her dreams. It had been a gentle night, of balmy soft breezes and a bright hunter's moon. Pan Jian had spoken of finding a small place near the Great River and starting a business, cutting rushes and weaving hats and baskets. Her hands were as big as shovels and Yu Yu had great difficulty picturing her creating delicate articles from straw. But he said nothing. 'And I'd like a dog,' she said. 'One of those small dogs that the magistrate has with him. A white one.'

'They are very expensive,' said Yu Yu.

'But they are so pretty.' Her voice was wistful, and suddenly in the moonlight her face did not seem ugly to him at all.

'Have you ever had a dog?' he asked.

'Yes. It was a mongrel. Very friendly. Followed me everywhere. She was a lovely dog. Big brown eyes.'

'She died?'

'Yes. You remember that awful winter four years ago? The famine?'

Yu Yu had shivered. He remembered, all right. Thousands had died of starvation.

'I had to eat her,' said Pan Jian.

Yu Yu nodded sympathetically. 'How did she taste?'

'Pretty good,' said Pan Jian. 'But a bit stringy.' Lifting one enormous leg, she pointed down at her fur-edged boot. 'This was her,' she said, stroking the fur. 'I made them so I wouldn't forget her.'

Yu Yu smiled as he recalled the moment. That was always the way with women, he thought. No matter how tough they seemed they were cursed with sentimentality.

Emerging into the entrance hallway, Yu Yu saw the Grey Man and

Kysumu walking out into the sunshine. He hurried across to join them. 'Are we going somewhere?' he asked.

'Do you ride?' asked the Grey Man.

'I am a great rider,' said Yu Yu.

Kysumu stepped in. 'Have you ever ridden a horse?'

'No.'

The Grey Man laughed, but there was no mockery in the sound. 'I have a grey mare famous for her gentle and patient nature. She will teach you how to ride.'

'Where are we going?' asked Yu Yu.

'We are hunting demons,' said Kysumu.

'My day is complete,' said Yu Yu Liang.

They rode for some hours. Initially Yu Yu felt comfortable in the deep saddle. It was exhilarating being so high above the ground. Until, that is, they reached small inclines or depressions where the horses picked up the pace. Yu Yu was bounced painfully around on the saddle. The Grey Man dropped back and dismounted, adjusting Yu Yu's stirrups, which were, he said, a little high. 'It is not easy to find the rhythms of the trot,' he said, 'but it will come.'

It could not come soon enough for Yu Yu. After two hours of riding his buttocks were bruised and painful.

Instead of moving directly to the ruins the Grey Man led them along a ridge of high ground overlooking the Eiden Plain. From here an observer could make out the original lines of Kuan-Hador, depressions in the land, showing where mighty walls once stood. From this height the lines of streets could also be seen, linking the edges of ruined buildings. Further to the east, where the city had once abutted the granite cliffs, there were the remains of two round towers, one seeming to have snapped across the middle, huge stones littering the ground for two hundred feet.

The ruins covered a vast area, vanishing into the distance. 'This was once a *huge* city,' said Kysumu. 'I have never seen the like.'

'It was called Kuan-Hador,' said the Grey Man. 'According to some historians, more than two hundred thousand people lived here.'

'What happened to them?' asked Yu Yu, drawing alongside.

'No one knows,' the Grey Man told him. 'Many of the ruins show signs of fire damage, so I would guess it fell during a war.'

Kysumu half drew his sword. The steel shone in the sunlight, but not with the glittering blue radiance it had displayed during the demonic attack.

'It looks peaceful now,' said Yu Yu Liang.

The Grey Man heeled the steeldust forward and rode out on to the slope. The horses placed their hoofs warily on the scree-covered trail, moving with care. At the rear Yu Yu was growing hot, and undid the brass clasp of his wolfskin cloak, intending to place it over his saddle pommel. The wolfskin fluttered up, alarming the grey mare, who reared and leapt from the trail directly on to the steep slope below. Immediately she began to slide, dropping her haunches. 'Keep her head up!' yelled the Grey Man.

Yu Yu did his best – and the descent continued at breakneck speed. The mare fought for balance on the sliding scree, righted herself then, still panicked, began to run. Yu Yu clung on in frightened desperation as the descent continued in a cloud of dust. He was almost unseated twice as the mare lurched. Dropping the reins, Yu Yu grabbed the saddle pommel.

The grey mare slowed and stood on trembling legs, steam snorting from her nostrils. Gingerly Yu Yu patted her neck, then gathered up the reins. As the dust cleared he saw they had reached the plain. Turning in the saddle he saw the Grey Man and Kysumu high above, still picking their way down the slope. Yu Yu's heart was thudding in his chest, and he felt light-headed.

Some minutes later the Grey Man rode up. 'You should step down now and let the mare rest,' he said.

Yu Yu nodded, tried to move, and let out a grunt. 'I can't,' he said. 'My legs won't work. They seem to be stuck to saddle.'

'The muscles of your inner thigh have been overstretched,' said the Grey Man. 'It is a common problem for new riders.' He dismounted then moved alongside Yu Yu. 'Just topple and I will catch you.'

With another grunt Yu Yu leant to his left. The Grey Man took hold of his arm and eased him down. Once on flat ground Yu Yu felt a little better, but it was difficult to walk. Rubbing his tortured muscles he grinned up at the Grey Man. 'My cloak frightened her,' he said.

'She is none the worse for it,' said the Grey Man. 'But this must be a lucky day for you. If she had fallen and rolled that pommel would have ruptured your spleen.'

Kysumu rode up, carrying Yu Yu's cloak. 'Did you see my ride?' asked Yu Yu.

The grey-garbed *Rajnee* nodded. 'It was very impressive,' he said, stepping from the saddle. He half drew his sword again, gazing at the blade. It remained silver steel, with not a hint of unearthly radiance.

'Maybe they have gone,' said Yu Yu hopefully.

'We shall see,' answered Kysumu.

Having tethered the horses the Grey Man and Kysumu began to scout the ruins. Yu Yu, his thighs still throbbing, wandered to the remains of what had once been a large house, and sat down upon a ruined wall. It was hot here, and the events of the day – the love-making, the fight, and the wild ride down the slope – had sapped his energy. He yawned and glanced around for the others. The Grey Man was some way to the east, climbing over a pile of ruins. Yu Yu could not see Kysumu.

Removing his sword-belt he lay down in the shade, rolled his cloak for a pillow, and dozed.

He awoke with a start as Kysumu climbed over the low wall.

Yu Yu felt curiously disorientated. Rising to his feet he stared around the ruins. 'Where is he?' he asked.

'The Grey Man has ridden further to the east to scout the woods.'

'No, not him. The man with the golden robe.' Yu Yu walked to the wall and peered out over the plain.

'You were dreaming,' said Kysumu.

'I suppose I must have been,' agreed Yu Yu. 'He was asking me questions and I had no answers.'

Kysumu pulled the stopper from a leather water-bag and drank sparingly. Then he passed it to Yu Yu.

'No demons, then?' said Yu Yu happily.

'No, but there is something here. I can feel it.'

'Something . . . evil?' asked Yu Yu nervously.

'I cannot tell. It is like a whisper in my soul.'

Kysumu sat quietly, eyes closed. Yu Yu drank more water, then glanced up at the fading sun. It would be dusk soon, and he had no wish to be in these ruins once night had fallen.

'Why do you want to find these demons anyway?' he asked the *Rajnee*.

Kysumu's face twitched. His dark eyes opened. 'Do not disturb me when I am meditating,' he said, without anger. 'It is painful.'

Yu Yu apologized, feeling foolish.

'You were not to know,' said Kysumu. 'But to answer your question I do not *want* to find demons. I am *Rajnee*. I swore an oath to stand against evil wherever I found it. This is the way of the *Rajnee*. What we experienced in the camp of Matze Chai was evil. Of that there is no doubt. And that is why my sword brought me here.' He looked closely at Yu Yu. 'It is why you are here too.'

'I don't want to fight evil,' said Yu Yu. 'I want to be rich and happy.'

'I thought you wanted to strut through marketplaces with people pointing at you and saying your name with pride.'

'That too.'

'Such respect has to be earned, Yu Yu. Were you a good ditch-digger?'

'I was a great—'

'Yes, yes,' interrupted Kysumu. 'Now think about the question, and answer it with seriousness.'

'I was good,' said Yu Yu. 'I worked hard. My foreman praised me. When times were tough I would always be employed ahead of other men. I was not lazy.'

'You were respected as a ditch-digger?'

'I was. But I was also paid for being a ditch-digger. Who will pay me for being a hero and fighting demons?'

'The payment is greater than a mountain of gold, Yu Yu. And more beautiful than the richest gems. Yet you cannot touch it, or hold it. It swells the heart and feeds the soul.'

'It doesn't feed the body, though, does it?' said Yu Yu.

'No, it does not,' agreed Kysumu. 'But think back to how you felt when we fought the demons in the camp of Matze Chai, when the sun came up and the mist departed. You recall how your heart swelled with pride, because you had stood your ground and survived?'

'That was good,' agreed Yu Yu. 'Almost as good as making love to Norda.'

Kysumu sighed.

Yu Yu walked to the edge of the broken wall. 'I cannot see the Grey Man. Why did he go off on his own?'

'He is a solitary man,' said Kysumu. 'He works better alone.'

The sun dipped below the western ridges. 'Well, I hope he gets

122

back soon. I do not want to spend a night here.' Yu Yu picked up his cloak and shook it out, then swirled it around his shoulders. 'What is a *pria-shath*?' he asked.

Kysumu's face registered shock. 'Where did you hear that word?'

'The golden man in my dream. He asked if I was a *pria-shath*.'

'And you have never heard it before?'

Yu Yu shrugged. 'I don't think so.'

'What else did he ask?'

'I don't remember. It is all very hazy now.'

'Try to think,' said Kysumu.

Yu Yu sat down and scratched his beard. 'He asked me a lot of questions, and I didn't know the answers to any of them. There was something about the stars, but I don't recall exactly. Oh . . . and he told me his name . . . Qin someone . . .'

'Qin Chong?'

'Yes. How did you know?'

'Later. Keep thinking of the dream.'

'I told him I was a ditch-digger, and I didn't know what he was talking about. Then he said, "You are the *pria-shath*." That was when you woke me. What is a *pria-shath*?'

'A Lantern Bearer,' said Kysumu. 'He was seeking me. That must be why the sword brought me here. I shall contact this spirit myself. It means going into a trance. You must stand guard over me.'

'Guard? What happens if the demons come? You will wake, yes?'

'It depends on how deep the trance. Now do not speak again.' With that Kysumu dipped his head and closed his eyes.

The last of the sunlight blazed up from behind the mountains, then darkness descended upon the Eiden Plain.

Yu Yu sat miserably upon a broken wall, and longed for a return to the lands of the Chiatze, with a good shovel in his hands and a deep ditch waiting to be dug. He wished in that moment he had never found the *Rajnee* sword, and had stayed on to face the wrath of the giant, Shi Da.

'You have brought me nothing but trouble,' he said, glancing down at the sword in his lap.

Then he swore.

A soft blue light began to glow along the length of the blade.

CHAPTER SIX

LEAVING THE STEELDUST TETHERED CLOSE TO THE LAKE, Waylander moved cautiously among the abandoned wagons, examining the tracks. The wagons had come over the pass and been drawn up here to rest the horses. Some of the footprints in the mud were of small feet, and several had run to the water's edge. A pair of shoes and a yellow shirt had been laid on a rock, indicating that at least one youngster had been preparing for a swim. The ground was too churned for Waylander to be exactly sure of what had happened next, save that the adults had herded together, pulling back towards the lake. Blood splashes to nearby trees and large stains upon the dead grass showed what happened next. They had been slaughtered – killed by huge creatures whose taloned feet left deep impressions in the earth.

The grass itself might have proved a mystery, had Kysumu not already told him of the immense cold that accompanied the coming of the mist. It was frost-damaged by temperatures far below freezing.

Waylander moved warily across the killing ground, examining the hoofprints of riders who had come upon the scene later. Twenty, maybe thirty riders had entered the wood, and left in the same direction. All around the site were the bodies of scores of birds. He found a dead fox in the bushes to the north of the wagons. There were no marks upon it.

Venturing deeper into the woods he followed the trail of dead birds and ice-scorched grass, coming at last to what he believed to be the point of origin. It was a perfect circle, some thirty feet in diameter. Waylander walked around it, picturing as best he could what must have happened here. An icy mist had formed in the spot, then rolled towards the west as if driven by a fierce breeze. Everything in its path had died, including the wagoners and their families.

124

But where then were the remains of the bodies, the discarded bones, the shredded clothing?

Backtracking towards the wagons, he stopped and examined an area where bushes had been crushed, or torn from the ground. Blood had seeped into the earth. This was where one of the dead horses had been dragged. Waylander found more deep imprints of taloned feet close by. One creature had killed the horse and torn it from its traces, pulling it deeper into the woods. The blood trail stopped suddenly. Waylander squatted down, his fingers tracing the indented earth. The horse had been dragged to this point, and then had lost all bodyweight. Yet it had not been devoured here. Even if the demon had been ten feet tall it could not have consumed an entire horse. And there were no signs that others of the creatures had gathered around to share in a feast. There were no split and discarded bones, no guts or offal.

Waylander rose and re-examined the surrounding area. The tracks of taloned feet just beyond this point were all heading in one direction, towards the lake. The demons, having slaughtered the wagoners and their horses, had returned to where he now stood – and vanished. As incredible as it seemed, there was no other explanation. They had returned from wherever they had come, taking the bodies with them.

The light was beginning to fail. Waylander returned to the steeldust and stepped into the saddle.

What had caused the demons to materialize in the first place? Surely it could not have been chance that they had happened upon a convoy. As far as he knew, there had been two attacks, one upon Matze Chai and his men, the second upon these unfortunate wagoners. Both parties contained large numbers of men and horses.

Or, looked at from another viewpoint, a great deal of food.

Waylander headed the steeldust away from the woods, and began the long ride around the lake. In the years he had dwelt in Kydor there had been no such attacks. Why now?

The sun was setting behind the mountains as he skirted the lake. A feeling of unease grew within him as he headed towards the distant ruins. Lifting his crossbow he slid two bolts into place.

When the sword began to shine Yu Yu Liang had been frightened. Now, an hour later, he would give anything he possessed to be merely frightened. Clouds had obscured the moon and stars and the only light came from the blade in his hands. From beyond the ruined walls, and all around him, he could hear stealthy sounds. Sweat dripped into Yu Yu's eyes as he strained to see beyond the jagged stonework. Twice he had tried to wake Kysumu, the second time shaking him roughly. It was like trying to rouse the dead.

Yu Yu's mouth was dry. He heard a scratching upon the stony ground to his left and swung towards it, raising his sword high. As the light shone he saw a dark shadow disappear behind the rocks. A low growl came from somewhere close by, the sound echoing in the night air. Yu Yu was petrified now. His hands began to tremble, and he was gripping the sword hilt so powerfully that he could hardly feel his fingers. They are just wild dogs, he told himself. Scavenging for scraps. Nothing to fear.

Wild dogs that could make the *Rajnee* blade shine?

With a trembling hand he wiped sweat from his eyes and glanced back towards the horses. They were tethered within the ruin. The grey mare was also shivering with terror, her eyes wide, her ears flat back against her skull. Kysumu's bay gelding was pawing the ground nervously. From here Yu Yu could just make out the line of hills, and the slope he had ridden down only a few hours before. If he was to run to the mare and clamber into the saddle he could make that ride again, and be clear of these ruins within moments.

The thought was like cool water to a man dying of thirst.

He flicked a glance to the seated Kysumu. His face, as ever, was calm. Yu Yu swore loudly, feeling his anger rise. 'Only an idiot goes seeking demons,' he said, his voice sounding shrill.

High above him the clouds parted briefly, and moonlight bathed the ghostly city of Kuan-Hador. In that sudden light Yu Yu saw several dark shapes scatter to hide among the rocks. As he tried to focus upon them the clouds gathered once more. Yu Yu licked his lips and backed across the ruin to stand alongside Kysumu.

'Wake up!' he shouted, nudging the man with his foot.

The moon shone once more. Again the dark shapes scattered. But they were closer now. Yu Yu rubbed his sweating palms on the sides of his leggings and took up his sword once more, swinging it left and right to loosen the muscles of his shoulders. 'I am Yu Yu Liang!' he shouted. 'I am a great swordsman and I fear nothing!'

'*I can taste your fear,*' came a sibilant voice. Yu Yu leapt backwards, catching his leg on the low wall and falling over it. He scrambled to his feet.

126

At that moment a huge black form came hurtling towards him, its great jaws open, long fangs snapping for his face. Yu Yu swung the sword. It slashed into the beast's neck, slicing through flesh and bone and exiting in a bloody spray. The creature's dead body cannoned into him, hurling him from his feet. Yu Yu hit the ground hard, rolled to his knees, then surged to his feet. Smoke began to ooze from the carcass alongside him, and a terrible stench filled the air.

Five more of the beasts came padding towards the ruin, clambering over the broken stones, and forming a circle around him. Yu Yu saw that they were hounds, but of a kind he had never seen before. Their shoulders were bunched with muscle, their heads huge. Their eyes were upon him, and he sensed a feral intelligence within their baleful gaze.

To his left the grey mare suddenly reared, dragged her reins loose of the rock and leapt over the wall. The bay gelding followed her lead and the two horses galloped away towards the hills. The huge hounds ignored them.

The voice came again, and he realized it was somehow speaking inside his head. '*Your order has fallen a long way since the Great Battle. My brothers will be pleased to hear of your decline. The mighty* Riaj-nor, *who once were lions, are now frightened monkeys with bright swords.*'

'You show yourself,' said Yu Yu, 'and this monkey will cut your poxy head from your poxy shoulders.'

'*You cannot see me? Better and better.*'

'No, but *I* can see you, creature of darkness,' came the voice of Kysumu. The little *Rajnee* stepped up alongside Yu Yu. 'Cloaked in shadow you stand just out of harm's way.' Yu Yu glanced at Kysumu and saw that he was staring towards the eastern wall. He squinted, trying to make out a figure there, but he could see nothing.

The demon hounds began to move. Kysumu had still not drawn his sword.

'*I see there are still lions in this world. But lions can also die.*'

The hounds rushed in. Kysumu's blade flashed left and right. Two of the beasts fell, writhing upon the stones. A third struck Yu Yu, fangs closing upon his shoulder. With a cry of pain Yu Yu rammed his sword deep into the beast's belly. In its agony the hound opened its jaws, letting out a ferocious howl. Yu Yu tore the blade clear and brought it down upon the hound's skull. The sword clove through

127

bone and wedged itself. Desperately Yu Yu tried to haul it clear. The last two beasts rushed at him. Kysumu's sword sliced through the neck of the first, but the second leapt for Yu Yu's throat.

In that instant a black bolt materialized in the creature's skull, a second lancing through its neck. The hound fell at Yu Yu's feet. Freeing his sword Yu Yu swung round to see the Grey Man upon his steeldust gelding, a small crossbow in his hand.

'Time to go,' said the Grey Man softly, pointing towards the east.

A thick mist was moving across the ancient city, a wall of fog rolling slowly towards them. The Grey Man swung the gelding and galloped away. Yu Yu and Kysumu followed him. The pain in Yu Yu's shoulder was intense now, and he could feel blood flowing down his left arm. Even so he ran swiftly.

Far ahead he saw the Grey Man still riding away. 'A pox on you, bastard!' he shouted.

Glancing back, he saw that the wall of mist was closer, moving faster than he could run. Kysumu also glanced back. Yu Yu staggered and almost fell. Kysumu dropped back to take his arm. 'Just a little further,' said Kysumu.

'We . . . can't . . . outrun it.'

Kysumu said nothing, and the two men moved on in the darkness. Yu Yu heard hoofbeats and looked up to see the Grey Man riding back towards them, leading the grey mare and the bay gelding. Kysumu helped Yu Yu into the saddle, then ran to his own mount.

The mist was very close now, and Yu Yu could hear bestial sounds emanating from it.

The grey mare needed no urging and took off at speed, Yu Yu clinging to the saddle pommel. She was panting heavily by the time they reached the slope, but panic gave her greater strength and she fought her way up the steep incline.

A little ahead the Grey Man swung the steeldust, gazing back down towards the plain.

The mist was swirling at the foot of the slope – but not advancing. Yu Yu swayed in the saddle. He felt Kysumu's hand upon his arm, then passed into darkness.

The tall, blue-garbed surgeon, Mendyr Syn, replaced the poultice on the shoulder of the unconscious man and sighed. 'I have never seen a wound reacting like this,' he told Waylander. 'It is a simple bite, yet the flesh is peeling back rather than sealing itself. It is worse now than when you brought him in.'

'I can see that,' said Waylander. 'What can you do?'

The middle-aged man shrugged, then moved to a wash-basin and began to scrub his hands. 'I have bathed it in *lorassium*, which is usually effective against any infection, but the blood does not clot. In fact, were it not impossible, I would say that whatever is in the wound is eating away at the flesh.'

'He is dying, then?'

'I believe he is. His heart is labouring. He is losing body heat. He will not last the night. By rights he should be dead already, but he is a tough man.' Wiping his hands on a clean towel, he glanced down at the grey-faced Yu Yu Liang. 'You say it was a hound that bit him?'

'Yes.'

'I hope it was killed.'

'It was.'

'I can only assume there was some kind of poison in the bite. Perhaps it had eaten something and some rancid meat was caught between its teeth.' Pinching the bridge of his long nose, the surgeon sat down beside the dying man. 'I can do nothing for him,' he said, exasperation in his voice.

'I'll sit with him,' said Waylander. 'You should get some rest. You look exhausted.'

Mendyr Syn nodded. He glanced up at Waylander. 'I am sorry,' he said. 'You have been most kind to me in my research and my one chance to repay you is ending in failure.'

'You do not need to repay me. You have helped many who needed it.'

As the surgeon rose the door opened and the shaven-headed priestess, Ustarte, entered the room, followed by Kysumu. She dipped her head towards Waylander, and then to Mendyr Syn. 'Please pardon my intrusion,' she said, looking into the surgeon's pale blue eyes. 'I thought I might be of some assistance. However, I do not wish to offend.'

'I am not an arrogant man, Lady,' said Mendyr Syn. 'If there is anything you can do for this man I would be grateful.'

'That is most gracious,' she said, moving past him to the bedside. Her gloved hand lifted the poultice clear and she examined the festering wound. 'I will need a metal dish,' she said, 'and more light.'

Mendyr Syn left the room, returning with a copper bowl and a second lantern, which he placed by the bedside. 'It may be too late to save him,' she continued. 'Much will depend on the power of his body and the strength of his spirit.'

Dipping her hand into a pocket at the front of her red silk robe, Ustarte drew forth a gold-rimmed circle of blue crystal some three inches in diameter. 'Bring a chair and sit beside me,' she told Mendyr Syn. The surgeon did so. Ustarte leant across him, placing her hand over the copper bowl. Flames sprang up within it, burning without fuel. Then she handed the blue crystal to Mendyr Syn. 'Look upon the wound through this,' she said.

Mendyr Syn held the crystal to his eye – then jerked back. 'By Missael!' he whispered. 'What magic is this?'

'The worst kind,' she told him. 'He has been bitten by a *Kraloth*. This is the result.'

Waylander stepped forward. 'May I see?' he asked. Mendyr Syn gave him the crystal. He leant over the wound, and lifted the crystal. Scores of luminous maggots were devouring the flesh, their bodies swelling as they fed. Ustarte drew a long, sharp pin from the sleeve of her robe, offering it to Mendyr Syn. 'Use this,' she said. 'Pierce the centre of each maggot then drop them into the fire.' With that she rose from her chair and turned to Waylander. 'The merest scratch inflicted by the teeth or talons of a *Kraloth* is generally fatal. Tiny eggs are deposited in the wound, and these swiftly become the maggots you saw.'

'And the removal of the maggots will give him a chance?' asked Waylander.

'It is a beginning,' she said. 'When the wound is clean I will show Mendyr Syn how to prepare a new poultice. This will destroy any eggs still present in the bite. You should know, however, that it is possible that some of the maggots may have moved deeper within his body, devouring his flesh from within. He may awake, or he may not. If he does he may be blind – or insane.'

'It seems that you know a great deal about the enemy we faced,' he said softly.

'Too much and too little,' she told him. 'We will speak after I have aided Mendyr Syn.'

'We will be outside, upon the terrace,' said Waylander. Bowing to the priestess, he spun on his heel and left the room.

Kysumu followed him and the two men walked along a wide corridor

130

leading to a terraced flower garden overlooking the bay. The night was clear, and the first hint of a new dawn tinged the sky. Waylander wandered to the marble balustrade and stared out over the gleaming water. 'What did you learn from your trance?' he asked Kysumu.

'Nothing,' admitted the *Rajnee*.

'Yet you are convinced a spirit of a dead *Rajnee* came to your friend?'

'Yes.'

'It makes no sense to me,' said Waylander. 'Why would a dead *Rajnee* contact a labourer yet not appear to one of his own?'

'That is a question I have pondered upon,' admitted Kysumu.

Waylander glanced at the little swordsman. 'And this troubles you?'

'Of course. I also feel great shame for putting Yu Yu in such danger.'

'He chose to stand his ground,' said Waylander. 'He could have run.'

'Indeed. It amazes me that he did not.'

'Would you have run?' asked Waylander, quietly.

'No. But, then, I am *Rajnee*.'

'Tonight I saw a frightened man, with a shining sword, battling demons to protect a friend. What would you call him?'

Kysumu smiled, then offered a deep bow. 'I would say he has a *Rajnee* heart,' he said simply.

The two men sat together in silence for another hour, each lost in his own thoughts. Slowly the sky lightened, and birdsong filled the air. Waylander leant back in his seat, weariness heavy upon him. He closed his eyes and dozed. Immediately he fell into dreams, swirling colours that drew him down.

He awoke with a start as the red-robed priestess moved out on to the terrace. 'Is he dead?' he asked.

'No, he will recover, I think.'

'Then you found all the . . . eggs?'

'I had help,' she said, seating herself alongside him. 'His soul was being guarded, and power flowed from within him.'

'Qin Chong,' said Kysumu softly.

Ustarte glanced across at him. 'I do not know the name of the spirit. I could not commune with him.'

'It was Qin Chong,' said Kysumu. 'In legend he is named as the

131

first of the *Rajnee*. He appeared to Yu Yu in the ruins. But not to me,' he added wistfully.

'Nor me,' she said. 'What can you tell me of him?'

'Very little. His deeds are lost among fables, oral tales expanded upon or invented. Depending which story you read, he fought dragons, evil gods, giant worms beneath the earth. He had a sword of fire called *Pien'chi*, and he was known as the Potter.'

'Do the legends say how he died?'

'Yes, in a dozen different ways, by fire, by sword, dragged down into the sea. One story has him walking down into the underworld to rescue his love, and never returning. Another even has him sprouting wings and soaring to the heavens. One has the gods appearing at his death and turning him into a mountain to watch over his people.'

Ustarte fell silent. 'Perhaps Yu Yu can tell us more when he wakes.'

'I would like to hear more of these *Kraloth*,' said Waylander. 'What are they?'

'They are meld-hounds,' Ustarte told him. 'Artificial creations born of dark magic. They are very powerful, and ordinary weapons cannot harm them . . .' she looked into his eyes and gave a wan smile '. . . unless they pierce the skull or the upper neck. As you know, their bite brings a painful death. They are led by a *Bezha* – a Houndmaster.'

'I caught a glimpse of him,' said Kysumu, 'but only the eyes.'

'He would have been wearing the robe of night,' Ustarte told him. 'It is true-black and reflects no light. The eye, therefore, cannot see it.'

'Why are they here?' asked Waylander.

'They are the advance guard of two terrible enemies. My followers and I had hoped to prevent their coming. We failed.'

'What enemies?' put in Kysumu.

'Anharat's demons – and the sorcerers of Kuan-Hador.'

'I have read the legends of Anharat,' said Kysumu. 'The Lord of Demons. I recall he was cast from the world after a war. I believe he had a brother who aided humankind.'

'The brother was Emsharas,' said Ustarte, 'and it is true that he sided with humanity. Great were the heroes who fought against Anharat. Mighty men, men of principle and courage. These were the men of Kuan-Hador.'

'I do not understand,' put in Kysumu. 'If these men were heroes, why do we fear their return?'

'Man never learns lessons from the past,' she said. 'It is his curse.

My people and I have been trying to discover some evidence of the Great War. What we have found is that there was not one war but two. The first – let us call it the Demon War – saw great horror and devastation. Only when Emsharas aided the humans did the tide begin to turn. But that aid carried within it the seeds of Kuan-Hador's downfall. In order to defeat the enemy the rebel demon lord, Emsharas, gave the lords of Kuan-Hador instruction in the most arcane secrets of meld-magic. Warriors were enhanced, blended with the power of beasts; panthers, lions, wolves and bears. And they won. Anharat's demon legions were expelled from the world. Kuan-Hador was mankind's saviour.'

'How then did they become evil?' asked Kysumu.

'By taking one small step at a time towards the dark,' she answered. 'For a little while the world knew peace and tranquillity, under the city's benevolent rule. The people of Kuan-Hador were proud of what they had achieved. Yet it had cost them greatly. They asked other nations to help bear that cost, and huge amounts of gold and silver were despatched to the city. The following year they asked for more. Several nations refused. The proud lords of Kuan-Hador decided that this refusal was an affront to the world's saviours, and sent their armies to plunder those nations. Kuan-Hador had moved from benevolent rule to tyranny. They had saved mankind, therefore – so they believed – they had earned the right to rule. Nations that rose against them were considered treacherous, and were crushed mercilessly by the *Kriaz-nor*, the meld-legions. This was the beginning of the second war – what is now termed the Great War. At first it was man against man. Kuan-Hador was powerful, yet it was but a city state and its resources were finite. By this time Emsharas was gone from the world, but his descendants aided the rebels. Slowly they began to force back the *Kriaz-nor* legions. In desperation the rulers of Kuan-Hador allied themselves with Anharat, opening portals to allow his demon warriors to return to the world.' She fell silent and stood staring out over the bay.

'Yet they were still defeated,' said Kysumu.

'Yes, they were,' she said softly. 'The rebels created their own legions – the *Riaj-nor*, men of noble hearts and great courage, wielding weapons of power. The *Rajnee* are the last embers of that fine order, and it seems, Kysumu, that of them all only you have been drawn here. Where once were legions there is now only a single warrior and a

133

wounded labourer.' She sighed, then continued her tale. 'The Great War ended here, the survivors of Kuan-Hador retreating through a portal to another world. The city was destroyed by fire, and a sorcerer – or, perhaps, a group of sorcerers – laid powerful spells upon the portal, sealing it against the return of the enemy. These spells have endured the passing of the centuries. Now they are fading. The gateway will soon open fully, allowing legions of *Kriaz-nor* to invade this land. At the moment it is merely flickering, and only a few can cross. The sorcerers who once protected it are long dead, as are the original *Riaj-nor*. There is now no power in this world to defeat them if they come in force, which is why I had hoped to replicate the original spell and cast it once more. But there are no clues to be found. There are riddles, verses and garbled legends, none of which is helpful. My last hope now rests with Yu Yu and the spirit of Qin Chong.' She swung to Kysumu. 'It seems that the *Rajnee* swords retain their magic. Why, then, are more of your comrades not here to fight?'

'Few now hold fully to the old ways,' he said, sadly. 'Most *Rajnee* are now merely bodyguards, seeking to earn riches. They will not heed the call of the swords, nor journey to foreign lands.'

'And what of you, Grey Man?' she asked. 'Will you fight the demon lords?'

'Why should I?' he countered, his voice edged with bitterness. 'It is just another war – just another group of greedy men seeking to take what does not belong to them. And they will hold it for just so long as they are strong enough to resist the next group of greedy men who desire to take it from them.'

'This one is different,' she said softly. 'If they win, the world will know the nature of true terror. Children dragged from their mothers' arms to be melded into beasts, or have their organs removed in order to prolong the lives of the rulers. Thousands butchered in the name of arcane science. Magic of the most horrific kind will become commonplace.'

When Waylander spoke his voice was cold. 'During the Vagrian Wars babes were torn from their mothers' arms to have their heads smashed against walls of stone. Children were slaughtered and men slain in their thousands. Women were raped and mutilated. This was done by men. A grieving mother would not care whether her babe was destroyed by magic or by might. No, I have had my fill of wars, Lady.'

'Then think of it as a battle against evil,' she said.

'Look at me,' he said. 'Do I have a shining sword? You know my

134

life, Lady. Does it seem to you that I have been a warrior of the light?'

'No,' she told him, 'you have also walked the path of evil, which gives you greater understanding of its nature. Yet you overcame it. You fought the darkness, and gave the Drenai people hope by recovering the Armour of Bronze. Now a greater evil looms.'

'How is it that you know so much about this evil?' he asked her.

'Because I was born of it,' she said. Her gloved hands moved to her high collar, pulling loose the hooks that held it. With a sudden wrench she opened the silken robe, letting it drop to the terrace. The morning sunlight shone upon her slim body, highlighting the striped fur of gold and black that covered her skin. Both men stood very still as she peeled off one of her gloves and raised the hand high. The fur ended at her wrists, but her fingers seemed unnatural and oddly shortened. She flexed the hand and long silver claws emerged from sheaths at her fingertips. 'I am a Joining, Grey Man. A failed experiment. It was intended that I should be a new form of *Kraloth* – a killing machine of great strength and speed. Instead the magic, which created this monstrosity of a body, also enhanced my mind. You are looking upon the future of mankind. Do you find it beautiful?'

Waylander said nothing, for there was nothing to say. Her face was human, and indescribably beautiful, but her body was feline, the joints crooked.

Kysumu stepped up behind the naked priestess, and raised her robe from the floor. Ustarte smiled her thanks and drew the garment around her. 'My followers and I came through the gateway. Six were killed in the attempt. We came to save this world. Will you help us?'

'I am not a general, Lady. I am an assassin. I have no armies. You want me to ride out alone against a horde of demons? For what? Honour and a swift death?'

'You would not be alone,' said Kysumu softly.

'I am always alone,' said Waylander. With that he strolled from the terrace.

He stared hard at the armour. It shone brightly in the lantern-light as if crafted from moonlight. The winged helm was gleaming, and he could see his reflection in the closed visor. The chainmail attached to the nape was impossibly delicate, light glittering from it as if from a hundred diamonds. The cuirass was beautifully fashioned, and engraved with runes he could not read.

135

'It would look fine upon you, sir,' said the armourer, his voice echoing in the high, domed hall.

'I do not want it,' said Waylander, swinging away and walking down a long, crooked corridor. He turned left then right, pushing open a door and stepping into another hall.

'Try it on,' said the armourer, removing the bright helm from its place on the armour tree and offering it to him.

Waylander did not reply. Angry now, he turned on his heel, moved back through the doorway and stood in the shadowed corridor. Then he walked on. Everywhere there were turnings and soon he lost all sense of direction. He came upon a set of stairs, and climbed and climbed. At the top, exhausted, he sat down. A doorway faced him, but he was reluctant to enter. He knew instinctively what he would find. And yet there was nowhere else to go. With a deep sigh he pushed open the door and gazed upon the armour tree.

'Why do you not want it?' asked the armourer.

'Because I am not worthy to wear it,' he told the man.

'No one is,' said the armourer.

The scene faded, and Waylander found himself seated beside a fast-flowing stream. The sky was bright and blue, the water fresh and cool. Cupping his hands he drank from the stream then sat back, leaning his shoulders against the trunk of a weeping willow, whose branches trailed all around him. It was peaceful here, and he wished he could stay for ever.

'Evil carries a price,' said a voice.

He glanced to his right. Just beyond the trailing branches stood a cold-eyed man. There was blood upon his face and his hands. He knelt by the stream to wash. But instead of the blood being cleansed the entire stream turned crimson, and began to bubble and steam. The willow branches darkened, the leaves falling away. The tree groaned. Waylander moved away from it, and the bark split, disgorging hordes of insects, which crawled over the dead wood.

'Why are you doing this?' Waylander asked the man.

'It is my nature,' he answered.

'Evil carries a price,' said Waylander, stepping forward. A knife appeared in his hand and he sliced it through the man's throat in one smooth motion. Blood sprayed from the wound, and the man fell back. The body disappeared. Waylander stood very still. His hands *were drenched in blood. He moved to the stream to wash them, and the stream turned crimson and began to bubble and hiss.*

'Why are you doing this?' asked a voice.

Surprised, Waylander turned, and saw a man beside the dying willow.

'It is my nature,' he told him – as the gleaming knife appeared in the newcomer's hand . . .

He awoke with a start. Pushing himself from the chair he walked out into the sunlight. He had slept for less than two hours, and he felt disoriented. Strolling down to the beach he found Omri waiting there, fresh white towels folded nearby, a pitcher of cool water and a goblet ready on the small wooden table.

'You look dreadful, sir,' said the white-haired servant. 'Perhaps you should forgo your swim and have some breakfast.'

Waylander stripped off his clothing. Wading into the cool water he flung himself forward and began to swim. His head cleared, but he couldn't shake himself from the mood the dreams had left. Turning, he headed back for the beach with long, easy strokes, then walked up to the waterfall and cleansed the salt and sand from his body.

Omri handed him a towel. 'I brought fresh clothes while you were swimming, sir,' he said.

Waylander towelled himself dry, then pulled on a shirt of soft white silk, and a pair of thin leather leggings. 'Thank you, my friend,' he said. Omri smiled, then poured a goblet of water, which Waylander drank.

Norda came running down the steps, curtsying to the Grey Man. 'There is a large party of horsemen coming up the hill, sir,' she said. 'There are knights and lancers and bowmen. Lord Aric is at the head. Emrin thinks the Duke is riding with them.'

'Thank you, Norda,' said Omri. 'We shall be there presently.'

The girl curtsied once more, then ran back up the steps. Omri glanced at his employer. 'Are we in some trouble, sir?' he enquired.

'Let us find out,' said Waylander, tugging on his boots.

'Might I suggest a shave first, sir?' offered Omri.

Waylander rubbed a hand over the black and silver bristles on his chin. 'Doesn't pay to keep a duke waiting,' he said, with a smile.

The two men strolled up the terrace steps side by side. 'Mendyr Syn said to tell you that the Chiatze warrior is sleeping more easily now. His heartbeat has steadied, and the wound is healing.'

'Good. He is a brave man.'

137

'Might I enquire how he came by the wound?' asked Omri.

Waylander glanced at the man, and saw the fear in his eyes. 'He was bitten by a large hound.'

'I see. The servants are all talking about a massacre in the woods by the lake. Apparently the Duke came upon the scene, and is now leading a company of soldiers to investigate.'

'Is that all the servants are saying?' asked Waylander, as they mounted the steps.

'No, sir. They are saying that there are demons abroad in the land. Is it true?'

'Yes,' said Waylander. 'It is true.'

Omri held his hand over his chest, made the Sign of the Protective Horn, and asked no more questions.

'Have you ever met the Duke?' Waylander asked Omri.

'Yes, sir. Three times.'

'Tell me of him.'

'He is a powerful man, both in mind and in body. He is a good ruler, fair and not capricious. He was originally of House Kilraith, but once he became Duke he renounced, as is the custom, all claims to leadership of Kilraith, the title passing to Aric. He is married to a Drenai princess and has several children, but only one son. The marriage is said to be happy.'

'A long time since I heard the words *Drenai princess*,' said Waylander. 'There are no kings in Drenan now.'

'No, sir, not now,' agreed Omri. 'The Duke's wife, Aldania, was the sister of King Niallad. He was murdered by a foul assassin just before the Vagrian War. After the war, so the story goes, the despot Karnak refused to allow her to come home. He forfeited all her estates and monies and issued a decree of banishment. So she married Elphons and came to Kydor.'

They reached the entrance hall. Beyond the double doors, Waylander could see horses and men waiting in the sunshine. Ordering Omri to organize refreshments for the riders, he walked into the long reception room. Lord Aric was there, wearing breastplate and helm. The black-bearded magicker Eldicar Manushan was standing by the far wall, his blond page beside him. A youth, dressed in dark riding clothes, and wearing a chainmail shoulder guard, was standing close by. His face was familiar, thought Waylander. He felt a small knot of tension form in his belly as he realized why. This was the grandson of

138

Orien, and the nephew of Niallad, the Drenai king. For a moment only, Waylander saw again the tortured features of the dying monarch. Pushing the memory away he focused on the heavy-set man sprawled in the wide leather chair. The Duke was powerfully built, with great breadth of shoulder and massive forearms. He glanced up at Waylander, his cold eyes locking to the Grey Man's dark gaze.

Waylander offered the seated man a bow. 'Good morning, my lord, and welcome to my home.'

The Duke nodded curtly, and beckoned Waylander to the seat opposite.

'The day before yesterday,' said the Duke, 'some forty wagoners and their families were murdered less than two hours' ride from here.'

'I know,' said Waylander. 'I rode over the ground late yesterday.'

'Then you will also know that the killers were . . . shall we say? . . . not of this world?'

Waylander nodded. 'They were demons. There were some thirty of them. They move upright and the distance between the tracks suggests that the smallest is around eight feet tall.'

'It is my intention to find their lair and destroy them,' said the Duke.

'You will not find it, my lord.'

'And why is that?'

'I followed the tracks. The demons appeared in a circle some two hundred paces from the wagons. They disappeared in another circle, taking the bodies with them.'

'Ah,' said Eldicar Manushan, stepping forward, 'a Third Level manifestation, then. A powerful spell must have been cast in that area.'

'You have come across such . . . spells before?' asked the Duke.

'Sadly, yes, sire. They are known as portal-spells.'

'Why Third Level?' asked Waylander.

Eldicar Manushan turned towards him. 'According to the Ancients' texts, there are three levels of gateway magic. The Third Level opens on to the world of Anharat and his demons, but summons only mindless blood-feeders, such as the beast described by our host. The Second Level allows, it is said, the summoning of powerful individual demons, who can be directed against specific enemies.'

'And the First Level?' asked the Duke.

'A First Level spell would summon one of Anharat's companion demons – or even Anharat himself.'

'I understand little of magic and its uses,' snapped the Duke. 'It has always sounded like babble to me. But a Third Level spell is what brought these demons, yes?'

'Yes, sire.'

'And how was this done?'

Eldicar Manushan spread his hands. 'Once again, sire, we have only the words of the Ancients, as stored in sacred text. Many thousands of years ago man and demon co-existed on this world. The demons followed a great sorcerer god called Anharat. There was a war, which Anharat lost. He and all his followers were expelled from the earth, banished to another dimension. This very land, which now prospers under your rule, was instrumental in defeating Anharat. It was then called Kuan-Hador, and its people were versed in great magic. With the banishing of Anharat and his legions Kuan-Hador began an age of great enlightenment. However, Anharat still had followers among the more savage tribes, and these banded together to destroy Kuan-Hador, butchering its people and plunging the world into a new age of darkness and desolation.'

'Yes, yes,' said the Duke, 'I have always liked stories, but I would appreciate it if you would leap across the centuries and tell me about the demons who attacked the wagoners.'

'Of course, sire. My apologies,' said Eldicar Manushan. 'It is my belief that one of the spells used in the original battle against Kuan-Hador has been – somehow – reactivated, opening a Third Level portal. It may be that it was cast again by a sorcerer, or merely recharged by a natural event, lightning, for example, striking an altar stone where the spell was first spoken.'

'Can you reverse this spell?' asked the Duke.

'If we can find the source of it, my lord, I believe that I can.'

The Duke returned his attention to Waylander. 'I am told that a party of your friends was attacked recently by these demons, but that two of the party had magical blades which held the beasts at bay. Is this true?'

'That is my understanding,' said Waylander.

'I would like to see these men.'

'One is severely wounded, my lord,' Waylander told him. 'I will send for the other.' A servant was despatched, and some minutes later Kysumu entered the room. He bowed low to the Duke, and also to Waylander, then stood silently, his face impassive.

'It would be a great help, my lord,' said Eldicar Manushan, 'were I

140

able to examine the sword. I could then, perhaps, identify which spells were cast upon the blade.'

'Give him your sword,' ordered the Duke.

'No man touches a *Rajnee* blade,' said Kysumu softly, 'save the one for whom it was forged.'

'Yes, yes,' said the Duke, 'I am also a great believer in tradition. But these are extraordinary circumstances. Hand it over.'

'I cannot,' said Kysumu.

'This is senseless,' said the Duke, without raising his voice. 'I can call fifty men to this room. Then they will take the sword from you.'

'Many will die,' said Kysumu calmly.

'You threaten me?' said the Duke, leaning forward in his chair.

Waylander rose and moved to stand before Kysumu. 'I have always found,' he said, 'in circumstances like these, that there is a subtle difference between a threat and a promise. I have read of these *Rajnee* blades. They are linked to the warriors who hold them. When a warrior dies his blade shatters and turns black. Perhaps the same would happen if he allowed Eldicar Manushan to take it from him. If that proves to be the case then we will have lost one of only two weapons proved to be of use against the demons.'

The Duke rose from his chair and stepped close to the small swordsman. 'Do you believe that your blade would become useless if handled by another?'

'It is more than belief,' said Kysumu. 'It is knowledge. I have seen it. Three years ago a *Rajnee* surrendered to an opponent and offered his sword. The blade splintered as soon as the opponent took hold of the hilt.'

'If this is true,' said Lord Aric suddenly, 'how is it that your companion carries such a blade? He is not *Rajnee*, nor was the blade fashioned for him.'

'The blade chose him,' said Kysumu.

Aric laughed. 'Then it must be a more fickle blade. Let us send for that and Eldicar Manushan can examine it.'

'No,' said Kysumu. 'The sword now belongs to Yu Yu Liang. He is my pupil, and, since he is still unconscious, I speak for him. The blade will not be examined or touched by anyone.'

'This is getting us nowhere,' said the Duke. 'I have no wish to use force here.' He looked at Kysumu. 'And I certainly have no desire to bring about either the death of a brave man or the destruction of such a powerful weapon. We are riding out to locate the source of the demon magic. Will you come with us, and aid us with your sword?'

'Of course.'

The Duke turned to Waylander. 'I would be obliged if you would offer hospitality to my son, Niallad, and his guards.'

The sound of the name struck Waylander like a dagger blade, but his face remained calm, and he bowed. 'It will be my pleasure, my lord.'

'But, Father, I want to ride with you,' said the youth.

'It would be folly to risk both myself and my heir,' said the Duke softly. 'We do not yet know the nature of the enemy. No, my son, you will remain here. Gaspir and Naren will stay with you. You will be safe.' The youth bowed, his expression downcast.

Eldicar Manushan approached him. 'Perhaps you would be kind enough to look after my page, Beric,' he asked. 'He is a good boy, but he becomes nervous when we are apart.'

Niallad looked down at the golden-haired page, and smiled ruefully. 'Do you swim, Beric?' he asked.

'No, sir,' answered the boy. 'But I like to sit by the water.'

'Then we will go to the beach while our elders and betters perform their manly tasks.' The sarcasm hung heavily in the air, and Waylander saw the Duke flush with embarrassment.

'Time to be on our way,' said the Duke.

As the men filed from the room Eldicar Manushan paused before Waylander.

'The *Rajnee* was bitten, I understand. How is the wound?'

'Healing.'

'Strange. Such wounds are usually fatal. You must have a highly skilled surgeon.'

'I do. He found translucent worms in the bite. Most unusual.'

'A clever man. Is he a mystic also?'

'I do not believe that he is. He used an ancient artefact, a blue crystal. With this he could see the infestation.'

'Ah! I have heard of such . . . artefacts. Very rare.'

'So I understand.'

Eldicar Manushan stood silently for a moment. 'Lord Aric informs me that there is a priestess currently in residence at the palace. She is said to have the gift of far-sight. I would very much like to meet her.'

'Sadly she left yesterday,' said Waylander. 'I believe she is returning to Chiatze lands.'

142

'How disappointing.'

'Are there sharks, Uncle?' asked the blond page, tugging at Eldicar Manushan's robe. Waylander gazed down at the boy's upturned face, and saw the love and trust the child had for the magicker.

Eldicar Manushan knelt by the boy. 'Sharks, Beric?'

'In the bay. Niallad is planning to swim.'

'No, there are no sharks.' The boy smiled happily and Eldicar drew him into a brief hug.

'I already told him that,' said Niallad, moving across the room. 'They prefer cooler, deeper water.'

Two soldiers entered the room, tough men with grim faces. Niallad grinned as he saw them. 'These are my bodyguards, Gaspir and Naren,' he said. 'There are no finer fighters in all of Kydor.'

'Is your life in danger?' asked Waylander.

'Always,' said Niallad. 'It is the curse of my family to be hunted by assassins. My uncle was the king of the Drenai. Did you know that?' Waylander nodded. 'He was killed by a cowardly traitor,' continued the young man. 'Shot through the back while he was praying.'

'Praying can be a perilous business,' said Eldicar Manushan.

The youth looked at him quizzically. 'Murder should not be the subject of jests, sir,' he said.

'I was not jesting, young man,' answered Eldicar Manushan. With a bow he turned and left the room.

Niallad watched him go. 'I will not be assassinated,' he told Waylander. 'Gaspir and Naren will see to that.'

'We will indeed, young sir,' said Gaspir, the taller of the men. He turned to Waylander. 'Which is the safest beach?' he asked.

'I shall have my manservant, Omri, show you,' said Waylander. 'And I will have fresh towels and cool drinks served there.'

'Most kind,' said Gaspir.

'When will Uncle Eldicar be back?' asked the blond page.

'I do not know, boy,' Waylander told him, 'but it might be after dark.'

'Where shall I stay? I do not like the dark.'

'I shall have a room prepared for you that shines with light, and someone to sit with you until he returns.'

'Could it be Keeva?' asked the youngster. 'I like her.'

'It shall be Keeva,' Waylander promised.

CHAPTER SEVEN

WAYLANDER WATCHED THE DUKE AND HIS SOLDIERS RIDE AWAY from the palace, then moved back out on to the terrace. The sunshine was bright against his tired eyes, but the breeze from the bay felt good upon his face. Omri joined him there and Waylander gave him various instructions. The white-haired manservant bowed and walked away.

Waylander continued down the steps, past the waterfall, across the rock garden and on to his spartan accommodation. The door was open. He moved to the porch then closed his eyes. He felt calm, and sensed no danger. Pushing the door further open, he stepped inside. The priestess Ustarte was seated by the hearth, her gloved hands folded on her lap, her high-collared red silk robe buttoned to the chin. She rose as he entered. 'I am sorry for the impertinence of entering your home-place,' she said, bowing her head.

'You are welcome here, Lady.'

'Why did you tell Eldicar Manushan that I had left?'

'You know why.'

'Yes,' she admitted. 'But how did you know he was the enemy?'

Moving past her, he poured himself a goblet of water. 'Tell me of him,' he said, ignoring her question.

'I do not know him, though I know his masters. He is an *Ipsissimus* – a sorcerer of great power. I have felt the emanations of his power for some time now. He has crossed the gateway for two reasons. First, in order to establish allies in this world, and, second, to break the Great Spell, which prevents their armies from crossing over.'

144

'Is he a king of some kind?'

'No, merely a servant of the Council of Seven. Believe me, that makes him more powerful than many kings of your world. Are you aware that he knew you were lying?'

'Of course.'

'Then why did you do it?'

Waylander ignored the question. 'Are you strong enough to withstand his power?'

'No. Not directly.'

'Then you and your companions should leave the palace. Find somewhere to hide – or return whence you came.'

'I cannot leave now.'

Waylander lifted the water jug and left the building, hurling the stale liquid to the flower garden and refilling the jug from the waterfall. Returning to the main room, he offered the priestess a drink. She shook her head and he filled his own goblet. 'What is it that Eldicar Manushan can offer to potential allies here?' he asked.

'Have you looked closely at Aric?'

'He seems fitter and leaner.'

'Younger?'

'I see,' said Waylander. 'Is it real, or an illusion?'

'It is real, Grey Man. Some servant of Aric's will have died perhaps to supply it, but it is real. The Seven long ago mastered the art of enhancement and regeneration, just as they mastered the vileness of Joining.'

'If I killed this magicker, would it aid you in keeping the gateway sealed?'

'Perhaps. But you cannot kill him.'

'There is no one I cannot kill, Lady. That is my curse.'

'I know of your talent, Grey Man. But I mean what I say: Eldicar Manushan cannot be killed. You could put a bolt through his heart, or cut off his head and he would not die. Slice off his arm and another will grow. The Seven and their servants are immortal and virtually invulnerable.'

'Virtually?'

'The use of spells is dangerous. The summoning of Third Level demons carries few perils. Once made flesh they exist merely to feed. But the summoning of specific demons of the First and Second Level carries great danger. Such a demon must have a death. If it cannot

145

succeed against the intended victim, then it will turn against the sorcerer who summoned it. If Eldicar Manushan was to summon a First Level demon, and that demon was thwarted, then Eldicar would be dragged back into the realm of Anharat and torn to pieces.'

'That seems a good weakness to exploit,' said Waylander.

'It would be. But that is why Eldicar Manushan has the boy with him. He is his *loachai*, his familiar. Eldicar Manushan casts his spells *through* the child. If anything were to go wrong the child would be slain.'

Waylander swore softly. Crossing the room, he sat down in the hide chair beside the hearth. Weariness lay heavy upon him. Ustarte sat opposite him.

'Can he read minds as well as you?' he asked her.

'I do not believe so.'

'Yet he knew I was lying about your departure?'

She nodded. 'He would have sensed it. As I said, he is an *Ipsissimus* and his power is very great. But it is finite. He can summon demons, create illusions, enhance youth and strength. He can regenerate himself if wounded.' She looked at him closely. 'I sense your confusion,' she said softly. 'What is it?'

'The boy,' said Waylander. 'He obviously loves his uncle. In turn Eldicar Manushan seems fond of him. It is hard to believe the boy is merely a tool.'

'And because of this you doubt whether the *Ipsissimus* can be truly evil? I do understand that, Grey Man. You humans are wonderful creatures. You can show compassion and love that is awe-inspiring, and hatred of such power and vileness it could darken the sun itself. What you find hard to accept is that such extremes are in each and every one of you. You gaze upon the works of evil men and you tell yourselves that they *must* be monsters, inhuman and different. Because to accept that they are just like you would threaten the foundations of your existence. Can you not see that you are an example of this, Grey Man? In your hatred and your lust for vengeance you became what you hunted; savage and uncaring, callous and indifferent to suffering. How much further might you have travelled had you not met the priest Dardalion, and been touched by his purity of soul? Eldicar Manushan is not a monster. He is a man. He can laugh and know joy. He can hug a child and feel the warmth of human love. And he can order the death of thousands

146

without regret. He can torture and kill, and rape and maim. It will not touch him.

'Yes, he may love the boy, but he loves power more. The spells of Eldicar Manushan are great, but when cast through a *loachai* they become enhanced. The boy is a vessel, a source of untapped spiritual energy.'

'You are sure of this?'

'I sense both their energies, the *Ipsissimus* and the *loachai*. When joined together they are terrifyingly strong.' She rose from the chair. 'And now you must ride with the Duke, Grey Man,' she said.

'I think I will stay here and sleep for a while,' he told her. 'There must be a hundred men with the Duke. He has no need of me.'

'No, but Kysumu has. Eldicar Manushan will fear the shining sword. He will see the *Rajnee* dead if he can. Kysumu needs you, Waylander.'

'This is not my fight,' he said, though he knew, even as he spoke, that he could not leave Kysumu to his fate.

'Yes, it is, Waylander. It always was,' she said, moving away towards the door.

'What does that mean?' he asked her.

'This is a time for heroes,' she said softly. 'Even shadow warriors once touched by evil.'

He watched her cross the threshold and draw the door closed behind her. With a soft curse he pushed himself to his feet and walked through to his armoury. From a chest at the rear of the room he removed a heavy linen sack. Placing it on a worktop he opened it, drawing forth a black leather shoulder-guard, reinforced by black mail rings. Returning to the chest he lifted two other wrapped items, followed by a sword-belt hung with two empty scabbards. Carefully he unwrapped the shortswords. Each had a round fist-guard of black iron beneath claw-shaped dark quillons. The bright blades gleamed with oil. Taking up a soft cloth he wiped them clean, careful to avoid the razor-sharp edges. Buckling the sword belt to his lean waist he slipped the swords into the scabbards.

His baldric, hung with throwing knives, was looped over the back of a chair. Fetching it, he removed each of the six diamond-shaped blades and honed them before slipping them back into place. Donning the chainmail shoulder-guard, he slipped the baldric over his

147

head. Lastly he took up his small, double-winged crossbow and a quiver of twenty bolts.

He strode from his rooms, climbing the steps to the upper buildings and the stable.

Will you ever learn? he asked himself.

Yu Yu Liang awoke to see sunshine streaming through a high-arched window. It was bright upon the white coverlet of his bed. He sighed, and felt a pang of deep regret. His shoulder was painful, though he could not remember why, but the sharpness of it meant he was back in the world of the flesh. Sadness filled his mind, as the feel of the sun and the whisper of a sea breeze leeched away the exquisite harmony he had come to value so highly. A figure loomed over him, the face thin and ascetic, the nose long and curved. 'How are you feeling?' asked the man. The noise was yet another intrusion, and Yu Yu felt the joy of the past years with Qin Chong slipping away. The question was asked again.

'I am flesh again,' responded Yu Yu. 'It saddens me.'

'Flesh? I was talking about your wound, young man.'

'My wound?'

'In your shoulder. You were bitten. The Gentleman and your Chiatze companion brought you. You have been injured, young man. You have been unconscious for around fourteen hours.'

'Hours?' Yu Yu closed his eyes. It was incomprehensible. On his journeys he had seen the birth of worlds, and the fall of stars; great empires rising from the mists of savagery before being swallowed by the oceans. He became aware of a dull, throbbing pain in his left shoulder. 'Why am I back?' he asked.

The man looked concerned. 'You were bitten last night by a demon beast,' he said slowly. 'But the wound is clean now. You are recovering well. I am Mendyr Syn, the surgeon. And you are resting in the palace of Dakeyras, the Gentleman.'

Bitten last night.

Yu Yu groaned as he struggled to sit. Instantly Mendyr Syn's hands came down on his good shoulder. 'Lie still. You will break the stitches.'

'No. I must sit up,' muttered Yu Yu.

Mendyr Syn transferred his grip to Yu Yu's right biceps, assisting him. 'This is not wise, young man. You are very weak.' The surgeon adjusted the pillows behind the wounded man and Yu Yu sagged back to them.

'Where is Kysumu?'

'He has gone with the Duke and his men. He will be back shortly, I don't doubt. How does the wound feel?'

'Painful.'

Mendyr Syn filled a goblet with cool water and held it to Yu Yu's lips. It tasted divine as it slipped down his parched throat. Resting his head back against the pillow he closed his eyes once more and drifted into a dreamless sleep. When he awoke the sunshine no longer lit the bed, but was shining brightly against the far wall.

The room was empty and Yu Yu was thirsty again. Pushing back the covers, he tried to swing his legs from the bed.

'Stay where you are, yellow man,' said a voice. 'You are in no condition to get up.'

Another figure loomed over him. He looked up into the man's face, noting the swollen nose and the two discoloured eyes. It was the golden-haired guard sergeant who had accosted him so many years ago. It was all so confusing. 'What is it you need?' asked the man.

'Some water,' said Yu Yu. The sergeant filled a goblet and sat on the bed, offering it to Yu Yu, who took it with his right hand and drank deeply. 'Thank you.' He struggled to think. So many scenes were whirling inside his head – like a bag of pearls without a string. Closing his eyes he began slowly and carefully to thread the thoughts. He had left the lands of the Chiatze after thrashing Shi Da. Then he had met the robbers, and later Kysumu. Together they had come . . . For a moment he drifted. Then he recalled the palace and the mysterious Grey Man. His eyes flared open. 'Where is my sword?'

'You won't need a sword for a while,' said the sergeant. 'But it is there by the wall.'

'Pass it to me, please.'

'Of course.'

'Touch only scabbard,' warned Yu Yu. The guard hefted the weapon and laid it by Yu Yu's side. Then he returned to his chair by the door. 'Why are you here?' asked Yu Yu.

'The Gentleman ordered me to guard you.' He smiled. 'He obviously thinks you have enemies.'

'Are you one of them?'

The man sighed. 'Yes, I am. I'll be honest. I don't like you, yellow

149

man. But I take my pay from the Gentleman. He treats me well, and in return I obey his orders. Fully. I don't much care if you live or die, but not one of your – other – enemies will reach you while I live.'

Yu Yu smiled. 'May you live long,' he said.

'Is it true you were attacked by demon hounds?'

The jagged memories filtered back, the ruins and the moonlight, the black hounds moving stealthily through the shadows. 'Yes, true.'

'What were they like?'

'Make wolves look like piglets,' answered Yu Yu, with an involuntary shudder.

'You were frightened?'

'Big fear. How is your nose?'

'Painful.' The man shrugged. 'I should have remembered my father's advice: if you're going to fight then fight. Don't talk. You hit hard, yellow man.'

'My name is Yu Yu.'

'I am Emrin.'

'Pleased for to meet with you,' said Yu Yu.

'Don't be too pleased. It is my intention to pay you back just as soon as you are fit and strong.'

Yu Yu smiled, then slept again. When he awoke there was no sunlight. Emrin had lit a lantern and hung it by the far wall. The soldier was dozing in his chair. Yu Yu was hungry and looked around the room for something to eat. There was nothing. Carefully he swung his legs over the side of the bed and, using his scabbarded sword as a support, pushed himself to his feet. His legs were a little unsteady.

Emrin woke. 'What do you think you are doing?' he asked.

'I am going to find food,' said Yu Yu.

'The kitchen is two floors down. You'd never make it. Wait for a while. One of the girls will be bringing supper in an hour or so.'

'I don't like lying here,' said Yu Yu. 'I don't like being . . . weak.' Suddenly his legs gave way and he slumped back down to the bed. He swore in Chiatze.

'All right,' said Emrin. 'I'll assist you. But you can't go wandering about the palace naked.' Striding across the room he gathered up Yu Yu's clothes and tossed them to the bed. Yu Yu managed to pull on his leggings and Emrin helped him into his wolfskin boots. There was no way Yu Yu could lift his injured left arm to put on his shirt, so, bare-chested and supported by Emrin, he made his way to the door.

'You are heavier than you look, yellow man,' said Emrin.

'And you not as strong as you look, Broken Nose,' countered Yu Yu.

Emrin chuckled and pulled open the door. Slowly they made their way down the corridor towards the stairs.

A few minutes after they had gone a small globe of bright light materialized outside the door to Yu Yu's room. Cold air emanated from it. A layer of frost covered the carpet. The globe swelled, forming a white, icy mist that swirled and grew until it reached from floor to ceiling. A shuffling sound emanated from the mist, and two enormous creatures stepped clear of it. They were bone-white and hairless. One ducked its head and entered the room, its massive arm lashing out at the bed. The frame split as the bed crashed into the far wall. The second lowered its head, its small red eyes staring malevolently down the corridor. A third beast slithered from the mist, a scaled white serpent with a long flat head. The head swayed from side to side just above the carpet, snuffling air through four slitted nostrils. Then it began an undulating glide along the corridor towards the stairs.

The mist rolled back across the other beasts.

And flowed along the corridor, following the serpent.

The kitchen was some fifty feet long and twenty wide, boasting several large, stone-dressed iron ovens. Shelves lined the north wall, upon which were placed stacks of plates, jugs and cups. There were five huge, and splendidly crafted, glass-fronted cabinets containing engraved crystal goblets and dishes. Below the shelves were cupboards filled with cooking utensils and cutlery. There were two main doors, one set against the eastern wall, leading to the stairs and the South Tower, the other opening on to a broad winding staircase that emerged on to the main banqueting hall.

There were no windows, and despite a hidden series of chimneys that carried away much of the heat from the ovens, the kitchen could become intolerably warm when large amounts of cooked food were being prepared and a score of servants were scurrying around.

Even now, with the servants abed and only two lanterns burning, it still retained some of the heat produced in the preparing of the

151

evening meals some two hours before. Keeva moved to a drawer and took out a knife, then opened the pantry door and removed a round crusty loaf, a slab of honey-roasted ham, and a dish of butter, which she placed on the long, marble-topped table.

'That is a *meat* knife,' said Norda, with a laugh. 'Do you know nothing, farm girl?'

Keeva pushed out her tongue at her, and continued clumsily to carve slices from the loaf. 'A knife is a knife,' she said. 'If it is sharp it will cut bread.'

Norda rolled her eyes in mock horror. 'There are fish knives, bread knives, meat knives, carving knives, shell knives, fruit knives, cheese knives. You'll have to learn them, you know, if you are ever to wait table at the Gentleman's banquets.'

Keeva ignored her, lifted the top from the butter dish and smeared a slab over her bread.

'Oh, yes,' said Norda, 'and there are butter knives.'

'What a complete waste of metal,' mocked Keeva.

Norda laughed again. 'Knives are like men: each has a different purpose. Some are great hunters, some are great lovers.'

'Ssh! Not in front of the boy!'

Norda laughed again. 'He is asleep. It is so like children. First they want to play, then they get hungry, and by the time you've brought them to the kitchen and prepared some food they are fast asleep and you are left with a mountain of bread.' The women gazed at the small blond boy, asleep on the bench, his head resting on his arm. 'So sweet,' whispered Norda. 'One day he'll be a ladies' man. You can tell. Those baby-blue eyes will melt the hardest heart. They'll be slipping out of their dresses faster than you can say *knife*.'

'Maybe he won't be like that,' said Keeva. 'Maybe he'll fall in love with one woman, get married and have a fine family.'

'True,' agreed Norda. 'He might turn out dull.'

'Oh, you are incorrigible!' Keeva cut some cold ham, placed it between two slices of buttered bread and took a huge bite.

'That's disgusting!' cried Norda. 'And now you've got butter on your chin.'

Keeva wiped her chin with her arm, then licked the butter from it. 'Too good to waste,' she said, laughing at Norda's expression of disgust. 'Now show me these wondrous knives.'

The blonde woman moved to a pine drawer and gathered up two

152

handfuls of bone-handled blades. These she arranged on the table before Keeva. They ranged in size from about eight inches long and fearsomely sharp to two inches with rounded tips. One was curved like a tulwar, ending in two prongs. 'What is that?' she asked.

'It is for cheese. First you cut a chunk, then you reverse the blade and pierce it with the prongs.'

'They are very beautiful,' said Keeva, examining the ornately carved bone handles.

The door at the far end of the kitchen was pushed open and Keeva saw Emrin enter. He was supporting Yu Yu Liang. The Chiatze's face was grey with exhaustion, but he gave a wide smile when he saw Norda. Emrin was not so pleased, his handsome mouth becoming a grim line.

'Ah, my day brightens!' said Yu Yu. 'Two beautiful women – and some food!' Emrin released his arm and Yu Yu tottered, holding his balance only by leaning on his scabbarded sword. Emrin stomped to the long table, drew his hunting knife and sliced himself several pieces of meat. Norda ran to Yu Yu's side and helped him to the table.

'My two favourite men,' she said.

'You have too many favourites,' barked Emrin.

Norda turned to Keeva and gave a wink. 'He fought for me, you know. Isn't that gallant?'

'I didn't fight for you,' snapped Emrin. 'I fought *because* of you. There is a difference.'

'And doesn't he look handsome with his war wounds?' continued Norda. 'Those dark brooding eyes, that big, swollen nose.'

'Stop it, Norda!' ordered Keeva. She moved round the table and took Emrin's arm. 'I, for one, am proud of you.'

'For what?' asked Norda. 'For ramming his nose into Yu Yu's fist?'

'Oh shut up!' said Keeva. 'He has spent today guarding Yu Yu, and has even now helped him down to the kitchen. It takes a man to be able to put aside his anger for the sake of duty.'

'Aye, he is good man,' said Yu Yu. 'I like him. Everybody like him. Now can we eat?'

'You are shivering!' said Norda, moving round behind Yu Yu. 'You shouldn't be up, you foolish man!' A cold breeze filtered through the far doorway. Keeva ran to the door, pushing it shut

153

and dropping the latch, while Norda fetched a blanket, which she draped over Yu Yu's shoulders.

'I had not realized it gets so cool in here,' said Emrin. But the women ignored him and continued to fuss over the wounded man, preparing him food and a goblet of peach juice.

Emrin wandered away from the table. He could hear sounds on the stairs beyond the second door. He strolled towards it. It opened just as he reached it. The elderly Omri entered, followed by two warriors and a young man. Omri nodded towards Emrin then called out to Keeva to bring some food for Niallad and his bodyguards.

The Duke's son halted by the sleeping child, and grinned down at him. 'I think we tired him out at the beach,' he said.

Keeva carved a dozen thick slices of cold ham, divided it on to three platters and offered it to the newcomers, who sat at the table and began to eat. The young noble thanked her, but the two guards merely tore into the meat. One of them, the taller of the two, a heavily bearded man with deep-set brown eyes, glanced at Yu Yu's sword, resting on the table top. The hilt was black and unadorned, as was the lacquered wooden scabbard. 'Doesn't look anything special to me,' he said, reaching out towards it.

'Don't touch it,' said Yu Yu.

'Or what?' snapped the man aggressively, his hand still moving.

'Do as he says, Gaspir,' ordered the young noble. 'It is his blade, after all.'

'Yes, sir,' said Gaspir, casting a malevolent glance at Yu Yu. 'It is all rubbish anyway. Magic swords!'

The boy Beric awoke and sat up. He blinked and stretched – then suddenly screamed. Keeva followed his gaze. A white mist was swirling under the far door. Yu Yu saw it, and muttered a curse. He groaned as he reached for his sword, dragging it from the scabbard. The blade was glowing with a shimmering blue light. Yu Yu tried to stand, but fell against the table.

'What is going on?' shouted Omri, his face grey with fear.

'Demons . . . are here,' said Yu Yu, levering himself up. Blood began to soak through the bandage on his shoulder.

Omri backed away from the mist, towards the door through which he had entered only moments before. Emrin saw that the old man was trembling uncontrollably. 'Steady, my friend,' he whispered.

'Must get out,' said Omri.

The mist was rising steadily now, the temperature dropping fast. Gaspir and Naren also moved back from the table, blades in hand. Keeva reached out and hefted a long carving knife, balancing it in her hand.

'We have to run!' cried Omri, his voice quavering. Emrin swung towards him. The old man turned and moved towards the other door. Emrin was about to follow him when he saw a faint, swirling mist seeping beneath the frame. Omri was almost at the door. The guard sergeant shouted after him: 'Don't, Omri! The mist . . .'

He was too late. Omri yanked at the latch. As the door swung inward white mist enveloped the old man. A massive taloned arm slashed out, crunching through bone and sending a bloody spray across the dining table. A second blow smashed Omri's skull to shards.

Emrin hurled himself at the door, slamming it shut and dropping the latch – even as Omri's lifeless body hit the floor. There was a thundering crash, and a panel on the door split. Emrin drew his own sword and backed away towards the centre of the room.

Another crash came from the second door. Yu Yu staggered forward, then fell. Emrin grabbed his arm, hauling him to his feet. The page, Beric, had ceased his screaming, and was now cowering on the bench. Keeva ran to him. She reached out for him, but he squirmed away and ran back to where the others waited. The youth, Niallad, drew his dagger, then placed his hand on the little boy's shoulder. 'Be brave, Beric. We will protect you,' he said, but his voice was fearful, his hands trembling. The page crouched down and crept under the table. Norda was already there, her hands over her face.

Icy mist swirled across the stone floor. The right-hand door gave way and a wall of mist swept across the room. Yu Yu's sword came up. Blue lightning lanced through the mist, leaping and crackling. A terrible cry of pain came from within the icy fog.

'Lift up your sword!' Yu Yu told Emrin. The guard sergeant did so, and Yu Yu touched his own blade to it. Instantly blue fire flowed from one weapon to the other. 'You too!' Yu Yu ordered Gaspir and Naren. Their blades also began to flicker. 'It will not last long,' said Yu Yu. 'Attack now!'

For a moment only they hesitated, then Emrin charged the mist, swinging his sword into it. Lightning crackled – and the mist retreated further. Gaspir and Naren joined him. A huge white form

155

leapt from the mist, cannoning into the black-bearded Gaspir, who was hurled from his feet. Naren panicked and tried to run. As the bodyguard turned the beast swung its arm. Keeva saw Naren arch backwards, talons punching through his back and exiting from his chest. Blood exploded from the dying man's mouth. Emrin ran in, slamming his sword into the beast's belly, and ripping the blade up through its chest. It let out a bellow of pain and hurled Naren's body away. Then it turned on Emrin. Keeva lifted her arm and hurled the carving knife across the room. As the beast loomed over Emrin the blade slashed into its eye socket, plunging deep. At that moment Yu Yu Liang staggered forward and swung the *Rajnee* sword. It sliced deep into the hairless white neck, cutting through muscle and bone. The great beast toppled sideways, striking the table and overturning it.

The mist shrank back, sliding across the floor and vanishing under the far doorway.

The temperature in the room began to rise. Gaspir pushed himself to his feet and gathered up his sword. It was no longer gleaming. A faint and fading blue light still shone on Yu Yu's blade. Yu Yu had fallen to his knees and was breathing heavily. The wound in his shoulder had opened up badly. Blood had soaked through the bandage and was flowing over his bare chest. Emrin moved to his side. 'Hold on, yellow man,' he said softly. 'Let me get you to a chair.'

Yu Yu had no strength left and he sagged against Emrin. Keeva and Norda helped the sergeant to lift him and seat him at the table.

'Are those things gone?' asked Niallad, gazing at the dark stair-wells.

'The sword isn't shining,' said Keeva. 'I think they have. But they may be back.'

The young noble looked at her and forced a smile. 'That was a magnificent throw,' he said. 'I've rarely seen a carving knife put to better use.'

Keeva said nothing. She was staring down at the lifeless body of the old man, Omri. A kind and gentle man, he deserved better than to die this way.

'What do we do now?' asked Gaspir. 'Do we leave or stay?'

'We stay . . . for a while,' said Yu Yu. 'Here we can defend. Only . . . two entrances.'

'I agree,' said Gaspir. 'In fact, I can't think of anything that would make me climb either of those stairwells.'

Even as he spoke a distant scream echoed eerily. Then another.

'People are dying up there,' said Emrin. 'We should help them!'

'My job is to guard the Duke's son,' said Gaspir. 'But if you want to charge up those stairs feel free to do so.' The black-bearded bodyguard glanced down at the near-unconscious Yu Yu. 'Though without the magic of his sword I doubt you'll last ten heartbeats.'

'I have to go,' said Emrin. He started to head towards the door.

'Don't!' called out Keeva.

'It is what I am paid for! I am the guard sergeant!'

Keeva moved round the table. 'Listen to me, Emrin. You are a brave man. We've all seen that. But with Yu Yu so badly hurt there is no way we could hold them off without you. You must stay here. The Grey Man told you to protect Yu Yu. You can't do that from upstairs.'

More screams sounded from above. Emrin stared at the shadowed doorway. 'Trust me,' whispered Keeva, taking his arm. His face had a haunted look as the screams continued from the floors above. 'You cannot help them,' she said. Then she turned towards Gaspir. 'We need to barricade the doors. Overturn the far cabinets and push them against the door. Emrin and I will block this one.'

'I don't take orders from serving wenches,' snapped Gaspir.

'It was not an order,' Keeva told him, masking her anger, 'and I apologize if it sounded like one. But the doors need to be blocked, and it will take a strong man to move those cabinets.'

'Do as she says,' put in Niallad. 'I'll help you.'

'You'd better be quick,' warned Keeva. 'Yu Yu's sword is beginning to shine again.'

CHAPTER EIGHT

CHARDYN, THE SOURCE PRIEST, WAS RENOWNED FOR HIS BLISTERING sermons. His charismatic personality and powerful booming voice could fill any hall and bring a host of converts to the Source. As an orator he was without peer, and would, in any just world, have been promoted to abbot many years before. Yet despite his awesome skill one small impediment had stunted his career, one tiny irrelevance used against him by men with small minds.

He didn't believe in the Source.

Once he had, two decades ago, when, full of youth and fire, he had chosen the path of priesthood. Oh, he had believed then. His faith had been strong through war and disease, through poverty and famine. And when his mother had fallen ill he had journeyed home knowing that through his prayers the Source would heal her. He had arrived at the family estate, rushed to her bedside, and called upon the Source to bless His servant and touch his mother with His healing hand. Then he had ordered a celebration feast to be prepared for that night, when they would all give thanks for the coming miracle.

His mother had died just before dusk, in appalling pain and coughing up blood. Chardyn had sat with her, staring at her dead face. Then he had walked downstairs, where the servants were setting fine silver cutlery at the celebration table. In a sudden burst of fury Chardyn had overturned the tables, scattering dishes and plates. The servants had fled his anger.

He had run out into the night, and screamed his rage at the stars.

Chardyn stayed for the funeral, and even made the Soul Journey prayer at the graveside, when his mother's body was laid alongside that of her husband, and the two children who had died in infancy. Then he had journeyed to the Nicolan monastery, where his old teacher, Parali, was the abbot. The old man had welcomed him with a hug, and a kiss upon the cheek.

'I grieve for your loss, my boy,' he said.

'I called upon the Source and He did not answer me.'

'Sometimes He does not. Or if He does He answers in a way we do not like. But, then, we are His servants, not He ours.'

'I no longer believe in Him,' admitted Chardyn.

'You have seen death before,' Parali reminded him. 'You have watched babes die. You have buried children and their parents. How is it that your faith remained strong during these dread times?'

'She was my mother. He should have saved her.'

'We are born, we live a brief time, and then we die,' said Parali. 'That is the way of life. I knew your mother well. She was a fine woman and, it is my belief, she now resides in Paradise. Be grateful for her life, and her love.'

'Grateful?' stormed Chardyn. 'I organized a celebration feast to give thanks to the Source for her recovery. I was made to look like an idiot. Well, I will be an idiot no longer. If the Source exists then I curse Him, and want no more to do with Him.'

'You will leave the priesthood?'

'Yes.'

'Then I pray you will find peace and joy.'

Chardyn had spent a year working on a farm. It was backbreaking toil for little reward, and he came to miss the small luxuries he had taken for granted as a priest, the comfort of life in a temple, the abundance of food, the times of quiet meditation.

One night, after a day of cutting and binding straw for the winter feed, Chardyn had been sitting with the other workers around the Feast Fire, listening to them talk. They were simple folk, and before they ate the roasted meat they gave thanks to the Source for the plentiful harvest. The previous year, following a failed crop, they had given thanks to the Source for their lives. In that moment Chardyn had realized that religion was what crooked gamblers dubbed a 'no lose proposition'. In times of plenty thank the Source, in times of famine thank the Source. When someone survived a plague it was down to divine intervention. When someone died of the plague they had been taken to glory. Praise the Source! Faith, it seemed, regardless of its obvious cosmic stupidity, brought happiness and contentment. Why then should Chardyn labour on a farm when he could be adding to the happiness and contentment of the world by preaching the faith? It would certainly add massively to his own happiness and contentment to be living once more in a fine house and attended by skilled servants.

So he had donned the blue robes and journeyed across Kydor, taking up a position at the small temple in the centre of Carlis. Within weeks his sermons had trebled the congregation. Two years later, the coffers swelled by donations, a new temple had been designed, twice the size of the old. Three years after that even this imposing building struggled to contain the masses who came to hear Chardyn.

The adulation of the congregation was in sharp contrast to the low regard in which the church authorities held him. Parali had seen to that. Yet it did not rankle unduly. Chardyn now lived in a large house, with many servants. He had also managed to put away a sizeable sum to indulge his taste for fine foods, expensive wines and soft women.

Indeed, he was as content as a man could be. Or, rather, he had been until this morning, when riders from the Duke had arrived demanding his presence on an expedition to exorcize demons from the ancient ruins in the valley. Chardyn had no experience of demons. Nor did he wish to acquire any. However, it would not be wise to refuse the Duke's summons, so he had swiftly gathered several scrolls dealing with the subject of exorcism and had joined the riders.

The sun was unbearably hot as the company rode down the hillside towards the valley. Up ahead Chardyn could see the Duke and his aides, riding with Lord Aric and the magicker Eldicar Manushan. Behind them came fifty bowmen, twenty heavily armoured lancers, and fifty cavalrymen armed with long sabres.

Once they reached flat ground Chardyn pulled the first of the scrolls from his saddlebag and began to peruse it, trying to memorize the incantations. It was far too complex and he put it away. The second scroll involved the use of holy water, of which he had none, so this, too, was thrust back into the saddlebag. The third spoke of the laying on of hands to remove demonic possession from someone suffering fits. Chardyn resisted the temptation to swear, screwed up the scroll and threw it to the ground.

He rode on, listening to the talk of the men around him. They were nervous and frightened – emotions he began to share as they spoke of the massacred wagoners, and of the attack upon the Grey Man and his Chiatze companions.

A lancer rode alongside him. 'I am glad you are with us, sir,' he said. 'I have heard you speak. You are blessed by the Source and a true holy man.'

'Thank you, my son,' said Chardyn.

The lancer removed his silver helm and bowed his head. Chardyn leant over, placing his hand on the man's hair. 'May the Source bless you and keep you from all harm.' Other soldiers began bunching around the priest, but he waved them away. 'Come, come, my friends, wait until we have reached our destination.' He smiled at them, exuding a bonhomie and confidence he did not feel.

Chardyn had never before visited the ruins of Kuan-Hador and was surprised by the vast distance they covered. The Duke led the riders deep into the ruins, then dismounted. The soldiers followed his lead. A picket line was set up, the horses tethered. Then the bowmen were ordered to take up positions on the camp's perimeter. Chardyn moved across to where the Duke was conversing with Aric, Eldicar Manushan, and a short, slender Chiatze warrior wearing a long grey robe. 'This is where the last attack took place,' said the Duke, removing his helm and running his fingers through his thick black and grey hair. 'Can you sense any evil here?' he asked Chardyn.

The priest shook his head. 'It seems merely a warm day, my lord.'

'What of you, magicker? Do you sense anything?'

'Sensing evil is not my forte, my lord,' said Eldicar Manushan, glancing at Chardyn, who met his eyes and saw amusement there. Something akin to mockery, he thought. Eldicar Manushan swung to the little Chiatze warrior. 'Does your blade shine?' he asked.

The man half drew his sword, then thrust it back into the black scabbard. 'No. Not yet.'

'Perhaps you should move around the ruins,' said the magicker. 'See if the evil is present elsewhere.'

'Let him stay close for the time being,' said the Duke. 'I do not know how swiftly the mist can appear, but I do know the creatures within it killed the wagoners in a matter of heartbeats.'

Eldicar Manushan bowed. 'As you wish, sire.'

The sound of a galloping horse came to them. Chardyn turned and saw the Grey Man riding his mount across the valley. He heard Lord

Aric curse softly, and noted that the amused look had vanished from Eldicar Manushan's face. Chardyn felt his own good-humour rise. He had once gone to the Grey Man for a contribution to the new temple, and had received a thousand gold pieces – without even a request for the Grey Man's name to be added to the roll of honour, or the altar table to be named after him. 'The Source will bless you, sir,' Chardyn had told him.

'Let us hope not,' said the Grey Man. 'Those of my friends He has blessed so far are all dead.'

'You are not a believer, sir?'

'The sun will still rise whether I believe or not.'

'Why, then, are you giving us a thousand gold pieces?'

'I like your sermons, priest. They are lively and thought-provoking, and they encourage people to love one another and to be kind and compassionate. Whether the Source exists or not, these are values to be cherished.'

'Indeed so, sir. Then why not make it two thousand?'

The Grey Man had smiled. 'Why not five hundred?'

Chardyn had chuckled then. 'The thousand is ample, sir. I was but jesting.'

The Grey Man dismounted, tethered his horse, and strolled across to the little group. He moved, Chardyn noted, with an easy grace that spoke of confidence and power. He was wearing a dark chainmail shoulder-guard over a black leather shirt, leggings and boots. Two shortswords were strapped to his waist, and over his shoulder was slung a small double-winged crossbow. There was not a glint of shining metal upon him, and even the chainmail had been dyed black. Though Chardyn had chosen the priesthood he had been raised in a military family. No soldier, in his experience, would pay extra to have his armour dulled. Most wanted to stand out, to shine in battle. The Grey Man's garb achieved the exact opposite. Chardyn flicked a glance at the steeldust gelding. The stirrups and bridle, and even the straps on the saddlebags, were dulled. Interesting, he thought.

The Grey Man nodded towards Chardyn, and gave a courteous bow to the Duke.

'Your company was not requested,' said the Duke, 'but I thank you for taking the trouble to join us.'

If the Grey Man registered the mild rebuke he did not show it. He glanced at the screen of archers. 'If the mist appears it will swamp

162

them,' he said. 'They will need to be more closely grouped. They also need to be told to shoot swiftly at first sight of a black hound. Their bite carries vile poison.'

'My men are well trained,' said Lord Aric. 'They can look after themselves.'

The Grey Man shrugged. 'So be it.' Tapping the Chiatze warrior on the arm, he led him deeper into the ruins, where they sat in close conversation.

'He is an arrogant man,' snapped Aric.

'With much to be arrogant about,' put in Chardyn.

'What does *that* mean?' asked Aric.

'Exactly what it says, my lord. He is a man of power – and not just due to his wealth. You can see it in his every movement and gesture. He is, as my father would have said, a man of dangerous ashes.'

The Duke laughed. 'It is a long time since I heard that phrase. But I tend to agree.'

'I have never heard it at all, sire,' said Aric. 'It sounds meaningless.'

'It's from an old tale,' said the Duke. 'There was an outlaw named Karinal Bezan. A deadly man who killed a great many people, most of them in one-on-one combat. He was arrested and sentenced to be burnt at the stake. When the executioner stepped forward and applied the torch to the tinder Karinal managed to get one hand free. He grabbed the man and dragged him into the flames and they died together, the man screaming and Karinal's laughter ringing above the roar of the blaze. Some time after that the phrase "You can burn him – but walk wide around the ashes" came into use to describe a certain kind of man. Our friend is just such a man. With that in mind, I suggest you move your men closer to the camp and pass on his warnings about the black hounds.'

'Yes, sire,' said Aric, struggling to control his anger.

The Duke rose and stretched. 'And you, sir,' he said to Chardyn, 'should walk among the men and offer them the blessing of the Source. They are far too nervous, and it will stiffen their resolve.'

And who will stiffen mine? thought Chardyn.

Kysumu listened quietly as Waylander told him of his conversation with the priestess. The *Rajnee* tapped the black hilt of his sword. 'There is no proof that he is the enemy. If there was I would slay him.'

163

'Ustarte says he cannot be killed.'

'You believe that?'

Waylander shrugged. 'I find it hard to believe he could survive a bolt through his heart, but then he is a magicker, and such powers are beyond my understanding.'

Kysumu glanced round at the archers, taking up fresh positions. 'If the mist comes, many will die here,' he said softly. Waylander nodded, and watched as the priest, Chardyn, strolled among the men, administering blessings. 'You think Eldicar Manushan plans to kill us all?'

'I don't know what he plans,' said Waylander. 'But Ustarte says he is looking for allies, so perhaps not.'

Kysumu looked into Waylander's dark eyes. 'Why are you here, Grey Man?' he asked.

'I have to be somewhere.'

'That is true.'

'And what of you, *Rajnee*? What makes you desire to fight demons?'

'I have no desire any longer to fight anything,' said Kysumu. 'When I was young I wanted to be a great swordsman. I wanted fame and riches.' He gave a brief smile. 'I was like Yu Yu. I wanted people to bow down before me as I passed.'

'But not now?'

'Such are the thoughts of the young. Pride is everything, status must be fought for. It is all empty and meaningless. It is ephemeral. Like the leaf on the oak tree. "Look at me, I am the greenest leaf, the biggest leaf, the finest leaf. None of the other leaves has my majesty." Yet autumn beckons, and winter mocks all the leaves, the great and the green, the small and the stunted.'

'I understand that,' said Waylander, 'but it is also an argument against waiting here to fight demons. What difference will it make if we fight or we run, if we win or we lose?'

'Fame is fleeting,' said Kysumu, 'but love and hate are eternal. I may be but a small leaf in the wind of history, but I will stand against evil wherever I find it, no matter the cost. The demon I slay will not descend upon the home of a farmer and murder his family. The bandit who falls beneath my sword will never again rape or kill or plunder. If my death saves a single soul from pain and anguish then it is a price worth paying.'

Chardyn clambered across the broken rocks and approached them. 'Would you like a blessing?' he asked. Waylander shook his head, but Kysumu rose and bowed. Chardyn laid his hand upon the *Rajnee*'s head. 'May the Source cherish you and keep you from all harm,' he whispered. Kysumu thanked him, and sat down once more. 'May I join you?' asked Chardyn. Waylander gestured for him to sit. 'You think the demons will come?' the priest enquired.

'Do you have a spell ready if they do?' asked Waylander.

Chardyn leant forward. 'No,' he admitted, with a wry smile. 'My knowledge of demons and exorcism is – shall we say? – severely limited.'

'I admire your honesty,' said Waylander. 'However, if you can't fight them you should leave. If they come it will be no place for an unarmed man.'

'I cannot leave,' said Chardyn, 'though I would dearly love to follow that advice. My presence helps the men.' He smiled, but Waylander saw the fear in his eyes. 'And perhaps – if the demons do come – I can hurl one of my sermons at them.'

'If the mist comes stay close to us, priest,' said Waylander.

'Now *that* is advice I will take.'

They sat in silence for a while, then Eldicar Manushan strolled over to them. He halted before Waylander. 'Will you walk with me?' he asked.

'Why not?' replied Waylander, rising smoothly. The magicker picked his way through the broken rocks until they were a little way from the others.

'I think you have misread me,' said Eldicar Manushan. 'I am not evil, nor do I seek to do you harm.'

'I am glad you have told me,' said Waylander. 'It will save me so many sleepless nights of worry.'

Eldicar Manushan laughed with genuine good humour. 'I like you, Grey Man. Truly. And there is no need for us to be enemies. I can offer you your deepest desires. It is within my power.'

'I think not,' said Waylander. 'I have no desire to be young again.'

The magicker seemed momentarily puzzled. 'Normally I would find that hard to believe,' he said at last. 'Though not in this instance. Are you so unhappy with life that you yearn to see an end to it?'

'Why do you desire my friendship?' countered Waylander.

'Look about you,' said Eldicar, gesturing towards the soldiers. 'Frightened men, small men, malleable men, the world is made up of such men as these. They live to be conquered and ruled. Look at them cowering behind ancient stones, praying that their insignificant lives will be allowed to continue past this night. If they were animals they would be sheep. You, on the other hand, are a predator, a superior being.'

'Like yourself?' asked Waylander.

'I have always loathed false modesty, so, yes, like myself. You are rich, and therefore powerful in this world. You could be useful to Kuan-Hador.'

Waylander laughed softly, and gazed around at the broken stones. '*This*,' he said, 'is Kuan-Hador.'

'It was destroyed *here*,' said Eldicar Manushan. 'This is merely one reality. Kuan-Hador is eternal. And she will prevail. This world was once ours. It will be again. When that happens it would be preferable for you to be our friend, Dakeyras.'

'*If* that happens,' said Waylander.

'It will happen. It will be bloody and many will die. But it will happen.'

'I think this is the point where you tell me what happens if I decide not to be your friend,' observed Waylander.

Eldicar Manushan shook his head. 'You do not need to hear threats from me, Grey Man. As I said, you are a predator. You are also highly intelligent. I merely ask you to consider my offer of friendship.'

Clasping his hands behind his back, Eldicar Manushan walked back to the Duke and his officers.

The afternoon was hot and clammy, heavy rainclouds obscuring the sun. Elphons, Duke of Kydor, struggled to appear relaxed. A little way to the west the Grey Man was stretched out on the ground, apparently asleep. The little Chiatze swordsman was sitting cross-legged nearby, eyes closed. The priest Chardyn was restlessly pacing back and forth, occasionally stopping to peer out over the ruins.

The men seemed a little more at ease, though Elphons knew their mood was fragile at best. Like himself, they had never fought demons.

'Will our swords cut demon flesh?' he had asked Eldicar Manushan.

166

The magicker spread his hands. 'It is said that the skin of a demon is like toughened leather, my lord. But, then, there are many kinds of demon.'

'You think they will come?'

'If they do it will be after dusk,' said Eldicar Manushan.

The Duke pushed himself to his feet and approached the priest, Chardyn, who was pacing to and fro. The man looked frightened, he thought, which was not an encouraging sign. Priests should always be serene. 'I hear you have filled the new temple with worshippers,' said the Duke. 'I must attend one of your services.'

'Most kind, my lord. But, yes, the faithful grow ever more powerful in Carlis.'

'Religion is a good thing,' said the Duke. 'It keeps the poor content.'

Chardyn smiled. 'You believe that is its only purpose?'

The Duke shrugged. 'Who can say? For myself I have never witnessed a miracle, nor has the Source ever spoken to me. But I am a soldier, first and foremost. I tend to believe what I can see and touch. I have little time for faith.'

'You have never prayed?'

The Duke chuckled. 'Once I was surrounded by Zharn tribesmen and my sword broke. I said a prayer then, I can tell you.'

'It was obviously answered, for here you stand.'

'I leapt at them and rammed the broken blade through the throat of the first man. As the others closed in, my men regrouped and scattered them. So tell me of your faith. From where does it spring?'

Chardyn looked away. 'I realized the truth about the Source many years ago,' he said softly. 'Nothing I have learnt since has changed my mind.'

'It must be comforting to have faith at times like this,' said the Duke. He glanced down and saw that the Grey Man was awake. 'Only an old soldier would be able to sleep before a battle,' he said, with a smile.

The Grey Man moved to his feet. 'If they come it won't be a *long* battle,' he said.

The Duke nodded. 'You mean the ice? I saw the dead birds in the woods. Frozen to death. I am hoping our archers will strike many down before they reach us. Then – if the Source is with us,' he added, with a glance at Chardyn, 'we can finish the rest with swords.'

167

'Always good to have a plan,' said the Grey Man.

'You disagree?'

The Grey Man shrugged. 'The tracks I saw were of creatures far bigger than bears. Forget demons, my lord. If twenty bears were to rush this camp how many would be brought down by your archers? And how many would be killed by your swordsmen?'

'I take your point, sir, but you must understand mine. I am the lord of these lands. It is my duty to protect its citizens. I have no choice but to face this evil, and hope that strength and courage will hold the day.'

The Grey Man turned towards the western peaks. 'We'll know soon enough,' he said, as the sun began to sink below the mountain-tops.

As darkness fell upon the valley a small bright spark flickered behind a half-shattered column of stone. Dust swirled around it, and moisture from the air was drawn to it. Slowly it took shape, as the molecules of earth, air and water melded to the spark of fire. A form began to materialize, tall and thin, naked under the new moonlight. The skin, at first speckled, became scaled and grey. Arms stretched from the form, and a flowing hooded robe of darkness cloaked it. The thin lipless mouth opened, dragging in air, filling the new lungs.

Niaharzz became aware, aware of the warm air around him, the soft earth beneath his feet, the silken robe upon the naked grey skin of his shoulders. The membrane over his eyes slid back and he blinked. For a moment he could not move, for the exquisite joy of material existence was strong upon him, causing his limbs to tremble.

When at last he felt confident of movement he stretched his legs and stepped to the edge of the stone column, peering round it. Some thirty paces to the east he could see the humans. Lifting his head, he tasted the air in his nostrils. The scent of flesh caused his belly to tighten, but the heady aroma of fear among these pale, pink creatures made him shudder with desire. Instinctively his mouth opened, exposing pointed fangs. Memories of a glorious past flooded him, trembling females exuding the dizzying perfume of terror, young-lings, their soft bones yielding sweet marrow.

Niaharzz quelled his hunger and leant back against the stone.

Once he had been a god, stalking the earth and feeding where he chose. Now he was a servant, fed only when his masters allowed it.

168

And as long as they controlled the gateways he would remain a slave to their ambitions.

Still, food was food. . . .

Niaharzz flipped his hood of darkness over his head, drawing it like a veil over his face. Then he moved to the far side of the rock and sought out the warrior with the bright sword of death. He was sitting on a stone, the vile weapon in his hands. Another human stood close by, tall and garbed in black. Niaharzz watched him. This one was dangerous too. He could feel it – though he sensed no magic emanating from him.

Take no risks, he told himself. In spirit form Niaharzz was immortal, but clothed in flesh he could die like any of these primitive creatures. Stay away from the sword, he warned himself. Do not let them see you.

Crouching down, he extended his hand. Seven sparks leapt from his fingers, and began to dance and swirl in the shadows of the column, forming into huge *Kraloth* hounds, their massive jaws dripping venom.

Niaharzz toyed with directing them at the swordsman, but he had already seen the man destroy several of his beauties the night before. No, the Ice Giants could rend and tear the man. His *Kraloth* would sacrifice their lives to kill the humans carrying the weapons of far-death. He gestured to the hounds, and they slunk away, keeping to the shadows, moving silently ever closer to the archers.

The sword in Kysumu's lap began to glow. The *Rajnee* climbed to a rock and held the blade aloft. 'The enemy is close!' he shouted.

Men scrambled to their feet, soldiers drawing their swords and hefting their shields, archers notching arrows to bowstrings. Chardyn peered out among the shadow-haunted ruins. 'There!' he bellowed, pointing to the west.

The first of the giant black hounds charged at the archers. Shafts flew at it, most hissing by its hurtling black form. One struck it high on the back and glanced clear without marking the skin.

'Neck or head!' shouted Waylander. Six more hounds came in sight, moving at great speed. The first beast reached the broken wall behind which the archers crouched. It leapt, clearing the barrier in one bound, its curved fangs closing upon the face of a bowman. The crunching of bone that followed made Chardyn feel sick.

All was pandemonium now as the *Kraloth* leapt among the archers.

'Kill the hounds,' Waylander ordered Kysumu. 'I'll find the Houndmaster.'

Kysumu sprinted across the ruins, his sword blazing. The Grey Man vanished into the shadows.

Chardyn stood alone.

In the distance he saw a wall of mist seeping across the valley.

The smell of blood in the air caused Niaharzz to tremble with hunger. Now is not the time to feed, he told himself. Later, when the Ice Giants had finished the slaughter. Though he hoped to be able to drag at least one live victim clear of the mist before the flesh froze. Meat should slide around the mouth, its juices rich and savoury, not break into icy pieces as fangs closed upon it.

Niaharzz moved silently to the edge of the broken column and risked a glance. The small warrior with the shining sword was among the archers now, but he was hampered by the crush of bodies; men panicking and attempting to flee. Even so, he had killed two of the hounds, curse him! Offset against this more than a dozen of the archers were down, most of them dead, but two were screaming.

The sound was delicious. It was almost as good as feeding. Niaharzz filtered the raw emotions, various degrees of terror, ranging from stomach-tightening fear to bowel-loosening panic. He blinked, a sense of shock touching his soul. Amid all the fear there was an emotion subtly different. Powerful, yes, but not sweet to the senses . . . He knew he had sensed it before, thousands of years ago, when last he had walked these night-dark lands. Niaharzz focused on the emotion, separating it from those flowing from the carnage.

Then it came to him.

It was rage. But not the boiling, extravagant rage of the fighting man. No, this was cold, controlled – and close.

Niaharzz did not move.

There was a man close by. Very close! He guessed it to be the tall man he had seen standing with the swordsman. Fear touched Niaharzz. It was not an entirely unpleasant feeling, for it made him more aware of the joys of physical reality. Very, very slowly he turned his head.

170

The man was some twenty paces to the right. He was searching the shadows, and facing away from Niaharzz.

It was so long since Niaharzz had felt his fangs close upon living flesh, the warm blood running down his throat.

Keeping his night-cloak around him he drew on his power, then raised his feet from the ground, floating silently in the shadows. The man took several steps towards a jagged wall, then turned again. Now his back was towards Niaharzz.

The *Bezha* floated towards the man, his arms extending, talons sliding from his fingers.

'Time to die,' said the man softly.

Niaharzz barely had time to register the words before the man spun on his heel, right hand extended. Something dark leapt from the small weapon in his hand.

There was no time to flee the prison of flesh, no time even to cry out against the cruel injustice of such a fate.

The bolt smashed through his skull, skewering the brain . . .

The body disappeared instantly, the black cloak floating for a moment on the wind, seeming no heavier than a grass seed. Waylander reached out and grabbed it.

Back among the ruins the remaining four *Kraloth* burst into flames, their bodies dwindling until they became little more than dancing sparks above the stones. They flickered for a few heartbeats and then were gone.

The cloak in Waylander's hands felt insubstantial. It seemed to roll under his fingers like liquid. More peculiar was the weird sensation as he tried to examine it. His gaze slid away from it, focusing on the rocks, or on his wrists, but never able to fasten to the garment itself.

'The mist is coming!' shouted Chardyn.

Waylander glanced towards the west and saw the white wall rolling towards him. Swiftly he rolled the cloak, wedged it into his belt before loping back to where the frightened soldiers were bunching together.

'Archers, stand firm!' bellowed the Duke, drawing his longsword and moving among the men.

Eldicar Manushan strode out from the group and climbed to a jutting rock. The mist swept on. The magicker raised his right arm and held it aloft, palm extended towards the mist. Then he began to chant, his voice ringing out. The mist slowed. Kysumu stepped alongside Waylander, his shining sword extended. Waylander glanced down at him. The man seemed utterly calm. The priest Chardyn eased himself behind the two men.

'Shouldn't you be praying?' asked Waylander.

Chardyn forced a smile. 'Somehow this does not feel like a day for hypocrites,' he said.

The temperature began to drop as the mist came closer. Eldicar Manushan continued to chant, his voice ringing with confidence and great power. Lord Aric had also drawn his sword now and was standing alongside the Duke and his swordsmen. The surviving archers had notched arrows to their bows and were waiting tensely.

The mist slowed to a halt immediately before the magicker, but flowed on past him on both sides. Still his voice continued to chant. Then he jerked suddenly and almost lost his balance on the stone. The chant died away. Instantly the mist swept over him. Just as it did so Waylander saw a massive form descend on the magicker, a taloned arm sweeping out, ripping through Eldicar Manushan's chest. Waylander saw the magicker's right arm slashed in two and ripped from his body, just as the mist closed over him.

'So much for magic,' he said.

Kysumu leapt towards the mist. His gleaming blade touched it, and blue lightning crackled and flashed. A huge white form towered over the little *Rajnee*. Waylander sent a bolt into its eye. The massive head jerked backwards. Kysumu slashed a vicious cut through the beast's chest, then spun on his heel to flash a reverse slice through its neck as it fell.

Ice was forming on the stones now. The mist swept on. Waylander and Chardyn moved in behind Kysumu. The sounds of screaming men and crunching bone came from all around now as the ice beasts fell upon the soldiers of Kydor.

A white serpent reared up from the ground at Waylander's feet. His sword slashed down, barely breaking the skin above the flat skull. Kysumu's blade sliced through the neck. As it did so it glanced from the blade of Waylander's weapon. Instantly blue fire flowed along Waylander's sword, and the mist retreated. For a moment only, Waylander stood staring at the shining blade. 'The magic can be transferred,' he said. 'Now we have a chance!' He glanced at Kysumu. 'We must get to the Duke!' Kysumu understood instantly

172

and the two men, followed by the priest, charged into the mist towards the sounds of battle. Kysumu cut down another of the huge creatures, then clambered over a low rock wall. The Duke and several heavily armoured swordsmen were battling bravely. Kysumu leapt in, touching his blade to the Duke's longsword. Instantly the Duke's sword blazed bright. The mist fell back a little, and the Chiatze moved from warrior to warrior, charging their blades with blue magic.

The voice of Eldicar Manushan came faintly through the mist, once more chanting. Louder and louder came the chant. The mist began to shrink, pulling back from the survivors, growing smaller and smaller until it was no more than the size of a large stone.

Eldicar Manushan strode from the rocks, still maintaining his chant. He held out his right hand and the small globe of mist floated up to it. He tossed it into the air. There was a sudden clap of thunder and a brilliant white light.

And the mist was gone.

Waylander sheathed his blade and looked hard at the magicker. There was no sign of a serious wound upon him, though his right sleeve was shorn away and his tunic slashed open. There was no blood upon the ruined cloth.

The Duke stepped forward, pulling his ice-covered helm from his head and dropping it to the ground. 'Well done, magicker,' he said. 'I thought you had been killed.'

'Merely knocked from my feet, my lord.'

'Are they destroyed?'

'They will not return to this place. I have closed the portal.'

'We owe you a great debt, Eldicar,' said the Duke, clapping the man on the shoulder. He gazed around at the sprawled bodies. Thirty men had been killed, twelve others wounded. 'Damn, but it was close,' he said. The shining sword in his hands began to fade until it gleamed only as steel in the moonlight. 'My thanks to you, Chiatze,' he told Kysumu, 'though it would have been good to have known about this trick a little earlier.'

'I did not know myself,' said Kysumu.

The Duke swung away and moved among the wounded, organizing aid for them.

Waylander approached Eldicar Manushan. 'For a moment there I thought you had been killed,' he said.

'Yes, it seemed likely.'

'I thought your arm had been torn from your body, but I see it was only your sleeve.'

'I was lucky,' said Eldicar. 'As indeed were you. You killed a *Bezha*. That is no mean feat, Grey Man. How were you able to do that?'

Waylander gave a cold smile. 'One day I might show you,' he said.

Eldicar Manushan chuckled. 'Let us hope not,' he said. The smile faded. 'Perhaps we can talk later.' With a courteous bow he moved away, and began to assist Chardyn with the wounded.

Waylander stood for a moment. The temperature was rising again, but there was still ice upon the ground. He shivered and strode across to where Kysumu was standing. The little Chiatze sheathed his sword. 'Do you believe they have gone for good?' asked the *Rajnee*.

Waylander shrugged. 'They have or they haven't.'

'Did you see the magicker fall?'

'Yes.'

'He was all but torn in half.'

'I know.'

'The priestess was right then. He cannot be killed.'

'It would appear so,' agreed Waylander. Suddenly weary, he sat down on a broken wall. Lord Aric, divested now of his armour, walked over to join them. He offered Waylander a canteen of water. Waylander accepted it and drank deeply, then passed it to Kysumu, who declined it.

'I have never seen the like,' said Aric. 'I thought we were finished for certain. Without that sword of yours we would have been. My thanks to you, *Rajnee*.' Kysumu bowed. A little way to the left a man screamed in pain, the sound ebbing away and ending abruptly. Aric looked back. 'Victory has a high price,' he said.

'It usually does,' agreed Waylander, pushing himself to his feet. 'I am riding home. I shall send wagons for the wounded. Those injured by the hounds will need swift attention. Any who can ride should follow on and I will see that Mendyr Syn is waiting for them.' With that he strode across the killing ground to where the horses were tethered. Kysumu followed and they rode from the ruins.

Clouds drifted across the moon as the two riders reached the slope, and they made the climb carefully and in silence. By the time they reached higher ground the sky had cleared, but still they rode on without speaking. Waylander was lost in thought. If the demons had been summoned by Eldicar Manushan why, then, did he defeat them? And if the demons were his creatures why did they attack him? Something was missing here, and it galled Waylander that he could not fasten to it. He replayed the events in his mind: Eldicar standing on the rock, his voice booming and confident, the mist slowing and even beginning to recede. Then Eldicar had faltered, his confidence draining away, the spell evaporating. Talons had ripped into him. Only the accidental discovery of the true power of Kysumu's blade had saved the Duke and his men.

Two hours later, still having reached no conclusions, Waylander rode his horse through the last of the trees and on to the long path leading to the upper palace. It was close to dawn, and he saw more than a hundred people milling outside the double doors. Many torches and lanterns had been lit, and his guards, led by Emrin, had placed themselves between the palace and the crowd. Many of the soldiers had swords drawn.

Emrin came running from the group as the riders approached. 'What is happening?' asked Waylander.

'Demons attacked the palace, sir,' said Emrin. 'Two men are dead, but nineteen more people are missing, including the surgeon, the foreign priestess and her followers – and your friend Matze Chai. The demons came at us in the Long Kitchens, killing Omri and one of the Duke's bodyguards – Naren, I think he was called.'

'And the Duke's son?' asked Waylander.

'He is fine, sir. We killed one demon – Yu Yu and I. Then the mist withdrew into the palace. We stayed where we were for a long while. We heard many screams.' Emrin took a deep breath and looked away. 'I did not investigate.' He looked back at Waylander, awaiting censure.

'When did you leave the kitchens?'

'About an hour ago. Yu Yu's sword was not shining, so we crept up the stairs and along to the banquet hall. We saw nothing – save that there was ice upon the walls of the outer corridor. Then we made our way to the lawns here. We found what you see, most of the servants and guests had fled. There are more down on the beach – about forty.'

'You went there – through the palace?' asked Waylander.

'Yes, sir.'

'That took courage, Emrin. Did you see any sign of the mist?'

'No, sir. But I didn't stop to investigate. I ran back through the banquet hall and out on to the terrace. I didn't stop running until I reached the beach.'

'How many of Matze Chai's servants are among the missing?'

'Ten, sir, according to the captain of his guard.'

'Fetch him.'

Emrin bowed, then turned and moved back through the crowd. Waylander saw Keeva sitting close to the trees. The page-boy was asleep, his blond head resting against her shoulder.

Moments later Emrin led the Chiatze captain to Waylander. The man bowed deeply to both Waylander and Kysumu.

'Tell me of the attack,' said Waylander.

The man glanced at Kysumu and spoke rapidly in Chiatze. The *Rajnee* turned to Waylander. 'The captain regrets that his command of the Kydor language is not sufficient to describe in detail the events. He asks if you would permit me to translate for him.'

'You may tell me in your own tongue,' said Waylander in excellent Chiatze.

The captain bowed even more deeply. 'I am Liu, noble sir. It is my honour to be captain of Matze Chai's troops. It is also my great shame that I could not reach my master in his time of peril. I was sleeping, noble sir, when a scream awoke me. I rose, pulled on my robe, and opened the door to seek out the cause of the cry. At first I could see nothing, but I felt the cold immediately. I knew what it was, sir, for it attacked our camp. I buckled on my breastplate, took up my sword and tried to reach the suite of my master. But the mist was already there, filling the corridor. It came for me – and I ran, noble sir. I heard other doors opening behind me, and I heard . . . I heard . . .' He fell silent. 'I heard people being killed,' he said. 'I did not look back. I could not have saved them.'

Waylander thanked the man then unclipped the crossbow from his belt and loaded two bolts. Without a word to the others he walked towards the double doors. Emrin swore softly then followed, sword in hand. Waylander paused in the doorway and looked back at Emrin. 'Do not follow me. You are needed here,' he said. 'Send ten wagons to the old ruins, and ensure there are plenty of bandages and a good amount of fresh water. The Duke's men have also suffered losses against the demons.'

176

Waylander pushed open the doors and walked into the darkness beyond. Kysumu strolled after him.

For almost an hour the Grey Man stalked the deserted corridors, pushing open doors, striding down stairwells, through halls and storage areas. He made no attempt to move stealthily, and it seemed to Kysumu that his companion was disappointed that they found no monsters. His anger, though controlled, was apparent in every movement.

Finally they reached the Long Kitchens. The body of Omri lay in a pool of congealing blood alongside that of the bodyguard Naren. The Grey Man knelt beside the old retainer. 'You deserved better than this,' he said. Omri's face was frozen in a mask of terror, and his eyes were wide open. For a little while the Grey Man remained beside the body, then he rose. 'He was a frightened man,' he told Kysumu. 'He abhorred violence. It terrified him. But he was a deep well when it came to kindness and compassion. You'd have to ride far to find any who would speak ill of him.'

'Such men are rare,' observed Kysumu. 'You valued him. That is good.'

'Of course I valued him. There would be no civilization without men like Omri. They care, and in caring they create all that is good. It was Omri who urged me to allow Mendyr Syn to create his hospital here. Before that Omri was raising funds for two schools in Carlis. He spent his life working for the good of others. And this was his reward – to be ripped apart by some mindless beast.'

The Grey Man swore softly, then moved away to examine the room. On the panelled floor close by there was a large stain, as if oil had seeped into the wood. Around eight feet long, it was all that remained of the creature who had killed Omri. A long-bladed carving knife lay beside the stain. The blade was pitted with rust, the bone handle singed as if from fire.

The two men left the scene and climbed to the first level of the South Tower. Here were the hospital wards of Mendyr Syn. Several of the twenty beds in the first ward had been upturned, and there was blood upon the floor. The room was still cold and there were no bodies. Moving to the second level, they found even greater chaos. Blood had sprayed to the walls and ceiling. Many of the beds were smashed.

Kysumu pointed to a bed by the far window. A body was lying within it, untouched. The Grey Man moved across the panelled floor and stood by the bedside. The occupant, an elderly woman, was dead, her hands folded across her chest. Waylander examined her. Rigor mortis was well under way.

'She has been dead for more than just a few hours,' said Kysumu. 'Probably late yesterday afternoon.'

'Yes,' agreed the Grey Man, gazing around at the smashed beds and blood-smeared walls.

'I once went into the ruins of a house destroyed by an earthquake,' said Kysumu. 'Everything was smashed. But a perfect egg was sitting in a broken plate.'

'These demons are obviously not interested in the dead,' said the Grey Man, 'unless they have killed them themselves. There were more than thirty people here,' he continued, 'not counting Mendyr Syn and his three helpers. Thirty souls sent screaming to the Void.'

The third level, the medical library, showed no sign of ice damage. The door to the office of Mendyr Syn was open, many of his papers scattered upon the two desks. The Grey Man searched the room, finding Ustarte's gold-ringed blue crystal below a pile of papers. Tucking it into his pocket, he left the office and continued up the stairs to the guest suites. Here the corridor carpets were wet, the walls cold.

Opening the door to Matze Chai's suite, the Grey Man moved across the silk Chiatze rugs and through into the bedroom. The first of the dawn light was filtering through the pale blinds. For the first time since the search had begun Kysumu saw the Grey Man relax. A low chuckle sounded from him.

Matze Chai opened his eyes and yawned. He glanced at the bedside table. 'Where is my tisane?' he asked.

'It will be a little late this morning,' said the Grey Man.

'Dakeyras? What is happening?' Matze Chai sat up, his pale blue nightcap falling from his head, revealing the carefully tied net that held his lacquered hair in place.

'I am sorry to disturb your rest, my dear friend,' said the Grey Man softly, 'but we feared you were dead. The demons came to the palace last night. Many people were killed. I shall leave you now and send your servants to you.'

'Most kind,' said Matze Chai.

The Grey Man left the room.

Kysumu bowed to Matze Chai and followed him. 'His life is charmed,' observed Kysumu.

'It is a great relief to me,' said the Grey Man. 'Matze Chai is a good friend – perhaps my only friend. He is incorruptible and loyal. It would have hurt me deeply had he been among the slain.'

'Why did he survive, do you think?' asked Kysumu.

The Grey Man shrugged. 'Who can say? Matze always takes a sleeping draught. Perhaps it lowered his heart rate and they did not sense him. Or maybe, since the creatures feed on flesh, they sought out younger meat. Matze may be a fine man, but there's precious little fat on those old bones.'

'I am glad to see your mood has lifted a little,' said Kysumu.

'Not by much,' said the Grey Man. 'You go back to the lawns. Tell Emrin to fetch Matze's servants.'

'Where will you go?'

'To the North Tower.'

'We have not searched that yet. You think it safe?'

'The demons have gone. I can feel it.'

The Grey Man slipped the bolts from his crossbow, returning them to the quiver by his side. Without another word he strode off.

CHAPTER NINE

WAYLANDER KEPT MOVING UNTIL HE WAS OUT OF SIGHT OF THE *Rajnee* then sat down on a velvet-covered bench seat in the corridor. His relief at the survival of Matze Chai was overwhelming, and he could feel his hands trembling. Leaning back against the wall, he took several deep, calming breaths. The death of Mendyr Syn and Omri saddened him greatly, but he had known them for only a short while. Matze Chai had been part of his life for three decades, a solid anchor he could always rely upon. He had not, however, realized until this day how much he cared for the old man.

But with the relief came a deeper anger, a cold and terrible resentment against the arrogant cruelty of men who were willing to visit such terror on innocent victims. Ultimately, he knew, wars were never about simple issues like right and wrong. They were launched by men who lusted after power. They did not care about the victims like Omri or Mendyr Syn. They lived for fame, and all the empty, fruitless joys it brought. One man like Omri was worth ten thousand of such killers, he thought.

Having recovered his composure Waylander moved on at a lope, scaling the stairs of the North Tower two at a time. He slowed when he reached the first level. Shelves had been torn from the walls, and manuscripts, scrolls and leatherbound volumes were scattered across the floor. Kneeling, he touched his hand to the carpet. It was wet and cold. To the left were two eight-foot stains upon the floor. Dark blood was spattered around them. Ustarte's followers, it seemed, had fought well.

Treading carefully through the debris he reached the second

180

stairwell and climbed once more. As he turned a corner he saw the body of a huge, golden wolf, its belly ripped open, its golden eyes glazing. The body twitched as he approached and it tried to raise its head. Then it slumped down and died.

Climbing past the dead beast he came across two more bodies, those of the acolytes who had followed Ustarte. Waylander struggled to remember their names. Prial was one. He was lying upon his back, his chest open, ribs splayed. The other lay close by. Huge talon marks were on his back, and the lower part of his spine was jutting from his body.

Waylander stepped over them. The door to Ustarte's apartments had been torn from its hinges. He moved into the doorway and scanned the room. Furniture had been hurled against the walls, the ornate carpet was ripped in places, and there was blood upon the floor and walls. There was no sign of Ustarte. Waylander moved to the window. Upon the sill was a bloody smear. Leaning out, he looked down. Two floors below was a balcony. A patch of blood showed on the balustrade.

Retracing his steps he returned to the stairs. The body of the golden wolf had vanished. In its place lay the third of Ustarte's acolytes.

Waylander walked to the front of the palace, where Emrin was anxiously waiting.

'The palace is clear,' said Waylander. 'Tell the servants they can return to their rooms.'

'Yes, sir. Quite a few have left your service. They have gone to Carlis. Even those who remain are frightened.'

'I don't blame them. Send some men to fetch the bodies from the Long Kitchens and the North Tower library. And set the servants tasks to take their minds from their fear. Tell them all there will be an extra month's salary to compensate for the terror they have endured.'

'Yes, sir. They will be most grateful. Did you find the priestess?'

'She and her people are dead.' Waylander looked into the young man's eyes. 'With Omri gone I need someone to manage the household. That role is yours for now. Your salary is doubled.'

'Thank you, sir.'

'No need to thank me. It is an arduous duty and you will earn your pay. Have the wagons left?'

'Yes, sir. I also sent riders to the hospital in Carlis, where Mendyr

181

Syn's two assistants are working. They should be here soon to help with the wounded.'

Waylander moved across to where Yu Yu Liang was sitting with his back to a tree. Keeva was beside him, her arm still around the shoulders of the blond page. The boy looked up at Waylander and gave a nervous smile.

'Were you very frightened?' Waylander asked the boy.

'Yes, sir. Is my uncle safe?'

'He was when last I saw him.' He turned his attention to Yu Yu. 'How are you feeling?' he asked.

'Like I want to be ditch-digger again,' said Yu Yu. 'Like I could throw this puking sword in sea and go home.'

'You can do that,' said Waylander. 'You are a free man.'

'Later,' said Yu Yu, 'but first we have to find Men of Clay.'

Many of the servants were reluctant to return to the palace, but as the boldest of them moved through the doors most of the others followed. Another fifteen joined the thirty who had already quit the Grey Man's service and journeyed to Carlis.

Waylander walked out through the banquet hall and found Kysumu sitting cross-legged on the terrace stones. The *Rajnee's* arms were extended outwards, his head bowed. Waylander moved silently past him, leaving the warrior to his meditation.

The sun was high now in a clear blue sky, shining down upon the myriad colours of the flowers in the terraced gardens. The scent of roses filled the air. It made the events of the night seem like a dream. Waylander strolled down to his apartments. The door was open, and there was a crimson smear upon the frame.

Inside the priestess Ustarte lay naked in one corner. Blood from a number of wounds to her flanks, arms and legs was seeping through her striped fur. Waylander knelt beside her. She was unconscious. Stretching her out on her back he examined the wounds. They were deep. Waylander drew the blue crystal from his pocket, slowly moving it over the tears in her flesh. He could see no sign of the flesh-eating maggots. Finding his medicine bag he took from it a curved needle and began to stitch the largest of the jagged rips in her side. Her golden eyes opened and locked to his gaze. Then they closed once more. Waylander continued his work. Her fur was not soft, like that of a cat. It was wiry and thick, the muscles beneath supple and immensely strong.

182

Indeed she was far stronger than the slim form suggested. There was further evidence of this when he tried to lift her, to carry her to his bed. She weighed at least as much as two tall men. Unable to move her, Waylander fetched a pillow and some blankets and laid them on a chair close by. Then, using old cloths, he mopped up the blood around her. Wiping his hands clean, he lifted her head and slipped the pillow under it. Then he covered her with the blankets.

Having done all he could, Waylander left the building, pulled shut the door and walked to the waterfall. Stripping off his clothes he stood beneath the cold water.

Refreshed, he returned to his rooms. He found a fresh shirt and leggings, dressed and returned to the priestess. Her breathing was shallow, her face ashen. Her eyes opened and she tried to speak, the effort causing her to wince. 'Don't talk,' he said softly. 'Rest now. I will fetch you some water.' He filled a goblet, raised her head and held it to her lips. She drank a little then sank back. 'Sleep,' he said. 'Nothing will harm you.' He was aware even as he said it that he could, in truth, make no such guarantees, but the words were out before he could stop them.

He walked to the door and sat down on the step. The fishermen were out in the bay, the white sails of their boats bright in the sunlight. Waylander leaned back against the door frame.

Eldicar Manushan had been torn apart battling the demons in the ruins. He could not, surely, at the same time, have summoned more monsters to attack the palace. Waylander considered the attack. There had been three targets, Mendyr Syn, Yu Yu Liang and Ustarte. Since Yu Yu and the *Rajnee* sword had been in the hospital building, the death of the surgeon may have been merely a tragic coincidence. Anger flickered in his weary frame. Life was full of such meaningless tragedies.

His first wife Tanya and his three children had died because a group of raiders had decided to head south-east rather than south-west. Coincidentally he had chosen that day to hunt venison, rather than stay and rebuild the south pasture fence. 'You have no time for self-pity,' he said, aloud, pushing the awful scenes from his mind.

He truly did not care whether Kydor stood or fell. War was a grisly fact of life, and one that he was powerless to alter. But the enemy had brought death to *his* house, and *that* he did care about. Demons had been unleashed within the palace. Omri had been a gentle, kind man.

Talons had torn his chest open. Mendyr Syn had devoted his life to the care of others. His last moments had been to witness his patients ripped apart.

Until now this had not been Waylander's war.

Now it was.

Leaning his head back against the door frame he closed his eyes. Sunlight was warm upon his face. A soft breeze whispered against his skin. He was almost asleep when he heard soft footfalls on the steps. His dark eyes flicked open and he drew a diamond-shaped knife from its sheath.

Keeva appeared, carrying a tray of food. Waylander pushed himself to his feet, and stood blocking the doorway. 'Emrin asked me to bring you some breakfast,' she said.

'Was it you who hurled the carving knife at the beast?' he asked.

'Yes. How did you know?'

'I saw it upon the floor. Where did you aim for?'

'The eye.'

'Did you hit it?'

'Yes. It went in to the hilt.'

'Excellent.' He looked at her closely. 'I want you to do something for me,' he said.

'Of course.'

'I want it done quietly. No one must know. No one at all.'

'You can trust me, Grey Man. I owe you my life.'

'Go to the North Tower and the rooms of the priestess Ustarte. Let no one see you. Gather some of her clothes and gloves. Do not forget the gloves. Put them in a sack and bring them here.'

'She is still alive?'

Waylander stepped back into the apartments, beckoning her to follow him. Keeva paused in the doorway and gazed down on the sleeping priestess. One arm was outside the blankets. Keeva moved closer and stared down at the exposed, fur-covered limb and the sharp claws extending from the short, stubby fingers. She recoiled instantly. 'Sweet Heaven! What is she?'

'Someone who has been badly wounded,' he said softly. 'No one must know she has survived the attack. You understand?'

'Is she a demon?'

'I do not know what she is, Keeva, but I believe there is no evil in her. Will you trust me on this?'

184

'I trust you, Grey Man. Will she live?'

'I have no way of knowing. The wounds are deep, and there may be internal bleeding. But I will do what I can.'

Ustarte opened her eyes. Her vision swam, then focused on the rough wrought ceiling above her. Her mouth was dry, and she became aware of pain. It grew from a dull, throbbing ache to needles of fire in her side and back. She groaned.

Instantly a figure appeared above her. Lifting her head he held a goblet of water to her lips. She drank sparingly at first, allowing the cool liquid to ease its way down her parched throat. The swirling began in her belly and she quelled it. Must not Change now, she thought, an edge of panic seeping into her mind. Looking up into the Grey Man's face she read his thoughts instinctively. He was concerned for her. 'I will live,' she whispered. 'If I do not . . . become the beast.' She caught an image in his mind of a golden wolf, dying on the stairs of the library. Sorrow flowed over her and tears welled in her eyes. 'They died for me,' she whispered.

'Aye, they did,' he said. The tears flowed on to her cheeks and she began sobbing. She felt his hands upon her shoulders. 'Be calm, Ustarte! You will tear the stitches. There will be time for grief later.'

'They trusted me,' she said. 'I betrayed them.'

'You betrayed no one. You did not summon the demons.'

'I could have opened a portal and taken them to safety.'

'Now you are making me angry,' he said, but the hand stroking her head was still gentle. 'There is no one living who would not change some aspect of the past if they could, to avoid a hurt or a tragedy. We make mistakes. It is just the grim game of life. Your people followed you because they loved and believed in you. You were seeking to prevent a great evil. Yes, they died to protect you. And they did it willingly. It is for you to make that sacrifice worthwhile by surviving, as they wanted you to survive. You hear me?'

'I hear you, Grey Man. But we have lost. The gateway will open, and the evil of Kuan-Hador will return.'

'Maybe so – maybe not. We still live. I have had many enemies, Ustarte, powerful enemies. Some commanded nations, others armies, others demons. They are all dead and I still live. And while I live I will not accept defeat.'

Closing her eyes, she tried to flow with the pain. Ustarte felt the blanket being lifted from her. The Grey Man was studying her wounds. 'They are healing well,' he said. 'Why will this Change be dangerous for you?'

'I become larger. The stitches will tear open. If this begins to happen you must . . . kill me. I will no longer be Ustarte. And what I become will . . . slaughter you in its agony. You understand?'

'Yes. Rest now.'

For a human it would have been sound advice, but Ustarte knew that if she did not stay conscious the swirling would begin again and she would metamorphose. She lay very still. Her thoughts began to drift. Several times she almost lost the focus. She saw again the breeding pens, felt again the terrible fear she had known. The crippled girl, dragged from her home and brought underground to the ceaseless horror of the pens. Sharp knives cutting into her flesh, noxious liquids being forced down her throat. Each time she vomited more of the fluid was poured into her mouth. Spells were cast, sharper than knives, hotter than fire, colder than ice.

Then the awful day when her frail body was merged with the beast. Its terror and rage swamped her, as its molecules flowed within her human frame. The pain was indescribable, every muscle swelling and cramping. The child was swept away in a sea of blackness. But she had clung on to her individuality, despite the roaring of the beast in her mind. Sensing her presence, the beast had calmed.

Strange dreams followed. She felt herself running on all fours, her great limbs powering her across the plain at terrible speed. Then the leap to the back of the deer, her fangs closing on its neck, dragging it down, warm blood filling her mouth. She almost lost herself in the blood-memory – but she clutched the tiny spark that was Ustarte.

She remembered the day she became aware of voices. 'This new *Kraloth* does not conform, Lord. It sleeps twenty hours, and when awake seems confused. We have noted tremors in the muscles of its hind legs, and occasional spasms.'

'Kill it,' came a second voice, harsh and cold.

'Aye, Lord.'

The thought of dying flooded Ustarte with a burst of energy, and her spirit flowed up from the dark recesses of the bestial body. She felt again the pull of the flesh, the power of the muscles in her four limbs. Her eyes opened. She reared up, trying to speak. A low, guttural growl rippled from her throat. Her paws struck at the iron bars of the cage. A man in a green tunic pushed a long stick through the bars. Something sharp and bright upon the end of it stabbed into her flesh. Fire flowed into her flanks.

Instinctively she knew it was poison. How she dealt with it remained a mystery to her to this day. She could only assume that the merging had created in her an unforeseen talent, enhancing her lymphatic pathways in such a way that she could draw the poison into her system, breaking it down into component parts and subtly changing it.

She had dropped to her haunches, waiting silently until the poison was dispersed harmlessly. Now she became aware of the thoughts of the three men in the room. One was waiting to go home to his family. Another was thinking of a missed meal. The third was considering murder.

Even as she linked to the thought she felt the man close his mind to her. A golden spell lanced through the bars, flowing over her body with whips of fire. She writhed under this new pain.

So desperate was she to escape it that she fled deep within the bestial body, allowing the beast control. It raged around the cage, slashing its great paws at the bars, bending them. Still the pain increased. Ustarte tried to flee again, surging up through the body, as if trying to claw her way free of the tortured flesh.

And in that moment she found the key that would save her life.

The beast withdrew. The spirit of Ustarte swelled. The body fell to the floor of the cage, writhing and Changing.

When she awoke she was resting in a bed. Her body was no longer quite that of the beast, but neither was it human. Her shoulders and torso were covered in thick, striped fur, her fingers were tipped with retractable talons. 'You are a mystery to me, child,' said a voice. Turning her head, she saw the third man sitting beside the bed. He was wonderfully handsome, his hair golden, his eyes a summer blue. The eyes of a kindly uncle, she thought. Yet there was no kindness in him. 'But we will learn to solve it.'

Two days later she had been taken to a stockaded palace-prison high in the mountains. Here there were other mutations, man-beasts and were-creatures, the subjects of failed experiments. There was a serpent with the face of a child. It was kept in a domed cage of thin wire mesh, and fed on live rats. The creature did not speak, but at night it would make music, high and keening. The sound would tear at Ustarte's soul every night for the five years she was imprisoned in that awful place.

Unspeakable acts were committed against her body, and she in turn was trained to kill and feed. For two years she refused to kill a human. For two years Deresh Karany, the golden-haired sorcerer, subjected her to dreadful pain. Ultimately the torture broke her resistance, and she learnt to obey. Her first kill had been a young woman, her next a powerful man with only one arm. After that she learnt not to remember the faces and forms of her victims. Time and again Deresh Karany would force her to Change, and once in the bestial form she would be directed against some hapless human. Her long fangs and terrible talons would rip into the frail flesh, tearing off limbs, lapping up blood and crunching brittle bones.

She was a good *Kraloth*, obedient and trustworthy. Not once – in either of her forms – did she turn on her jailers. Not even a growl. Her obedience was instantaneous. And day by day they grew more complacent about her. They thought they had her beaten. She could read it in their thoughts. Never, since that first day back in the city, had she let them know of her other powers. She was careful not to betray her talent. Ustarte knew that Deresh Karany sensed them. Once he had walked towards her with a dagger in his hand. His thoughts were clear. *I am going to ram this blade into your throat.*

'Good morning, my lord,' she said.

'Good morning, Ustarte.' He sat beside her. 'I am very pleased with you.'

I am going to kill you!

'Thank you, my lord. What do you require of me?'

He had smiled and sheathed the dagger. 'The creatures in this place are unique; twin forming is so rare. How does it feel when you shift from one form to the other?'

'It is painful, Lord.'

'Which form gives you the most pleasure?'

'Neither gives me pleasure, Lord. In this, my near-human form, I derive some satisfaction from study, from the beauty of the sky. In *Kraloth* guise I glory in power and strength and the taste of flesh.'

'Yes,' he said, nodding, 'the beast has no perception of abstracts. How then do you control it?'

'I cannot fully control it, Lord. It is wild and savage. It obeys me because it knows I can deny it existence, but it constantly seeks ways to overcome me.'

'The spirit of the tiger remains alive?'

'I believe so.'

'Interesting.' He fell silent and seemed lost in thought. Then he met her gaze. 'Back in the city I sensed you reaching out and touching my mind. You recall this?'

She had waited for this moment, and knew it would be dangerous to offer a complete lie. 'Yes, Lord. It was most mysterious. It was like flowing up from a deep sleep. Suddenly I heard distant voices, though I knew they were not real sounds.'

'And this has not happened since?'

'No, Lord.'

'Let me know if it does.'

'I will, Lord.'

'You are doing well, Ustarte. We are all proud of you.'

'Thank you, Lord. That is most pleasing to me.'

One day, as she strolled in semi-human form, she saw that the small postern gate was unlocked. She stood in the doorway gazing out upon the mountain path leading to the forest. Reaching out with her mind, she sensed the watchers close by, reading their thoughts. The door had been left open for her. Concentrating, she pushed her talent further. Five more guards were hidden behind the rocks some fifty paces from the postern gate. They were armed with spears and two held a strong net.

Ustarte turned away and walked back to the main exercise area.

As the months passed they trusted her more and more. She was used to assist in the training of others like herself. Prial was brought to the prison in chains. He was in his wolf form then, snapping and biting at the guards. Ustarte reached out with her talent, feeling his rage and terror. '*Be calm,*' she whispered into his mind. '*Be patient, for our time is coming.*'

Waylander sat with the sleeping priestess for a while. Her breathing was even, but the gleam of perspiration on her face showed that her temperature was rising. Moving to the kitchen he filled a bowl with cool water and returned to her side. Taking a cloth he placed it in the water, squeezed out the excess liquid and laid it on her brow. She stirred and the golden eyes opened. 'Feels good,' she whispered. Gently he dabbed the cloth to her cheeks. She slept again.

Waylander rose from the floor and stretched. Then he stood very still and listened. Walking swiftly to the window he drew the shutters closed, then stepped out through the door and into the sunshine, pulling closed the door behind him.

Eldicar Manushan and the page, Beric, were crossing the terrace garden and walking along the path to his apartments. The magicker was wearing a pale blue tunic shirt of glimmering silk. His legs were bare, and he wore no boots or shoes. His page was clad only in a loincloth, and he was carrying towels across his shoulder.

'Good day to you, Dakeyras,' said the magicker, with a broad smile.

'And to you. Where are you heading?'

'To the beach. Beric has become fond of it.'

The blond page looked up at his uncle and grinned. 'The water is very cold,' he said.

'You have taken a wrong turn,' said Waylander. 'Go back to the tall yellow rose and turn right. The steps there will take you to the sea.'

Eldicar Manushan glanced at the rough-cut walls of Waylander's apartments. 'I understand you live here,' he said. 'You are a most curious man. You build a palace of great style and beauty and yet live in little more than a cave on a cliff wall. Why is that?'

'I sometimes ask myself the same question,' said Waylander.

'Can we go to the sea now, Uncle?' put in the boy. 'It is getting very hot.'

'You go down, Beric. I will join you presently.'

'Don't be long,' said the child, running back down the path.

'The young have such energy,' observed Eldicar Manushan, moving into the shade of a flowering tree and seating himself on a rock.

'And innocence,' added Waylander.

'Yes. It is always a cause of sadness when it passes. I did not take a wrong turn, Dakeyras. I wanted to speak with you.'

'I am here. Speak.'

'I am sorry for the death of your people. It was not my doing.'

'Just an unfortunate coincidence,' said Waylander.

Eldicar sighed. 'I will not lie to you. My people have formed an alliance with . . . another powerful group. Such is the way of war. What I am saying is that I did not bring the beasts to your palace.'

'What is it you seek here?' asked Waylander. 'This is not rich land.'

'Perhaps not. But it is ours. It was once ruled by my people. We were temporarily defeated by force of arms. We retreated. Now we are coming back. There is nothing overtly evil in this. It is just human. We want what is ours by right, and are willing to fight for it. The question for you is, is this your fight? You are not a native of Kydor. You have a fine palace, servants and the freedom only riches can supply. That will not change. You are a strong and deadly man, but whether for us or against us you can make no discernible difference to the outcome.'

'Then why concern yourself with my friendship?'

'Partly because I like you,' the magicker smiled, 'and partly because you killed the *Bezha*. Not many men could have done that. Our cause is not unjust, Dakeyras. This *was* our land, and it is the way of man to fight for what he believes is just. You agree?'

Waylander shrugged. 'It is said that this land was once below the sea. Does the sea own it? Men hold what they are strong enough to hold. If you can take this land, then take it. But I will think on what you have said.'

'Don't take too long,' advised Eldicar Manushan. He turned to follow his page to the beach, then swung back. 'Did you find the body of the priestess?'

'I found the body of a creature not human,' said Waylander.

Eldicar Manushan stood silently for a moment. 'She was a Joining. A failed experiment, full of bitterness and hatred. My own lord, Deresh Karany, invested much time and passion in her training. She betrayed him.'

'And he sent the demons?'

Eldicar spread his hands. 'I am only a servant. I do not know all my master's plans.' He strolled away.

Waylander sat for some time outside the apartments. He was a hunter, trained to follow his prey and kill it. This situation was far more subtle, and infinitely more dangerous.

Added to which there was another player in the game, who had not yet shown himself.

Who was Deresh Karany?

During the next three days life in the palace began to return to a semblance of normality. The servants were still nervous, and many purchased ward-charms from stallholders in Carlis, hanging them upon the doors of their rooms, or around their necks. The temple was filled daily with new converts, all anxious to be blessed by Chardyn and the three other priests.

Chardyn himself spent hours every day poring over scrolls and learning, as best he could, the ancient spells said to be useful against demonic possession and manifestation. He also removed an ornate box, hidden below the altar. From this he took two items: a golden ring with a carved carnelian stone at the centre, and a talismanic necklet, both said to have been blessed by the great Dardalion, first Abbot of the Thirty. 'You are a hypocrite,' he told himself, as he looped the necklet over his head.

In the palace hospital many of the wounded soldiers died in agony, despite the use of the crystal supplied to the two surgeons by Waylander. Neither of the men was as skilled as Mendyr Syn. But others survived. They were visited daily by the Duke, and offered encouragement. The crippled were assured they would receive good pensions and parcels of land back near the capital.

Little was seen of Waylander during this time, and all callers to the palace were greeted by Emrin, who informed them that the Gentleman was not in residence.

In the Winter Palace, on the far side of the bay, the Duke began preparations for the celebration feast. The lords of Kydor, Panagyn of House Rishell, Ruall of House Loras, and Shastar of House Bakard, all arrived in Carlis and were given sumptuous suites in three of the towers. Lord Aric, of House Kilraith, occupied the fourth tower. Invitations to the feast were sent to all the heads of the minor noble families, and a handful of wealthy merchants, including the Grey Man.

There was great excitement among the invited, for those who had already seen the wondrous talents of Eldicar Manushan had spread the word. And the magicker had promised a night to remember for all the guests.

A little to the west of the Grey Man's apartments was a sheltered ledge, hidden from the palace above by a jutting overhang. Here there were several bench seats, created from split logs, surrounding the sanded stump of a huge tree. The Grey Man was stretched out on one of the benches. To his right sat Ustarte the priestess, dressed now in a green robe of silk. Her face was still grey and her eyes reflected both weariness and pain. On the bench opposite sat Yu Yu Liang and Kysumu.

Yu Yu's shoulder was healing fast, but he found himself wishing he was back in his hospital bed. Ustarte had tried to question him about his experiences with the spirits of the original *Riaj-nor*. Yu Yu found it hard now to remember all that he had been told. Much of it was beyond him anyway, and he hadn't understood it even when it was being relayed to him by the spirit of Qin Chong. There was a feeling of tension in the air. The Grey Man was stretched out on his side, resting on one elbow, but his face was stern, his eyes locked to Yu Yu's face. It was most disconcerting. The priestess was disappointed, and only Kysumu seemed relaxed and at ease. Yu Yu guessed this was merely an outward show.

'I am sorry,' he said in Chiatze. 'I remember the tall man coming to me. I remember he called me *pria-shath*, which Kysumu said means Lantern Bearer. Then he took my hand and we flew. High through clouds and under stars. And all the time he was talking to me. I thought I was remembering it, but when I awoke it started slipping away. Sometimes things come back to me – like when I remembered about how the magic of the swords could be passed on. But most of it is gone.'

The Grey Man swung his legs to the ground and sat up. 'When I spoke to you in the grounds of the palace,' he said, 'you told me we had to find the Men of Clay. You remember?'

'Yes, the Men of Clay. I remember that.'

'Who are they?'

'They wait in the Dome. That's what he told me. They wait for the Lantern Bearer.'

'And where is the Dome?'

'I don't know. I can't think any more.' Yu Yu was feeling agitated now.

Kysumu laid a hand on his arm. 'Stay calm, Yu Yu. All will be well.'

'I don't see how,' muttered Yu Yu. 'I am an idiot.'

'You are the Chosen, the *pria-shath*. That is why you were drawn here,' said Kysumu. 'So sit calmly and let us continue to seek the truth. You agree?'

Yu Yu leant back and closed his eyes. 'Yes, I agree. But my mind is emptying. I can feel it all washing away.'

193

'It will come back. Qin Chong told you that you must find the Men of Clay, who live in a place called the Dome. He said these Men of Clay were waiting for the Lantern Bearer. Did you see the Men of Clay in your travels with Qin Chong?'

'Yes! Yes, I did. It was after a great battle. There were thousands of warriors – men like you, Kysumu, in robes, some of grey, some white and some crimson. They knelt and prayed on the battlefield and then they drew lots. Certain of the warriors then moved away from the others. They walked into the hills. Qin Chong was with them. He was with them *and* with me, if you take my meaning. And he said, "These are the Men of Clay."'

'This is good,' said Kysumu. 'What else did Qin Chong say to you?'

'He said I must find them. At the Dome. Then we floated again, over hills and valleys, and across a bay, and we sat in a little wood, and he told me of his life, and asked about mine. I told him I dug ditches and foundations, and he said that was an honourable occupation. Which, of course, it is, for without foundations you couldn't—'

'Yes, yes,' said Kysumu, allowing his irritation to show. 'But let us return to the Men of Clay. Did he mention them again?'

'No, I don't think so.'

The Grey Man leant forward. 'When they drew lots how many men moved away into the hills with Qin Chong?'

'Several hundred, I would think,' said Yu Yu.

'And the black man,' said Ustarte.

Yu Yu blinked in surprise and stared at the ailing priestess. 'Yes, how did you know? I had almost forgotten myself.'

'My wounds have sapped my powers – but not completely,' she said. 'Tell us of him.'

'He was a wizard, I think. His skin was very dark. He was tall and well built. He wore a blue robe, and carried a long white staff, curved at the top. At least I think he was a wizard. He was related to someone famous. Grandson, or great grandson. Something like that.'

'Emsharas,' put in Ustarte.

'That's it!' said Yu Yu. 'Grandson of Emsharas, who was also a wizard.'

'Far more than a wizard,' said Ustarte. 'He was a lord of demons. According to legend, he rebelled against his brother, Anharat, and aided the humans of Kuan-Hador in the first Demon War. Through his power the warriors of Kuan-Hador defeated the demons, casting them from this dimension. That was in the days when Kuan-Hador was a symbol of purity and courage. When Kuan-Hador fell into evil ways and a second war broke out, the few descendants of Emsharas took arms against the empire. There were many battles. Nothing is known of the fate of Emsharas's descendants.'

'We seem to be no closer to an answer,' said Kysumu.

'I think that we are,' observed the Grey Man. He turned to Yu Yu. 'The last battle you saw was at the city of Kuan-Hador?'

'Yes.'

'In which direction did the Men of Clay walk?'

'South . . . south-west, maybe. A southerly direction anyway.'

'That area is mostly forest now,' said the Grey Man. 'It covers a vast area on the way to Qumtar. Do you remember any landmarks?'

Yu Yu shook his head. 'Just a lot of hills.'

'We must travel there,' said the Grey Man. To his right Ustarte gave a low moan. Her head sagged back against the headrest of the bench. The Grey Man moved swiftly to her side. 'Help me with her,' he told Kysumu. Together, and with great effort, they lifted the priestess, carrying her back to the apartments and laying her on the bed.

Her golden eyes opened. 'I . . . need a little . . . rest,' she whispered.

The men left her and returned to where Yu Yu waited. 'How is your wound?' the Grey Man asked him.

'Better.'

'Can you ride?'

'Of course. I am a great rider.'

'You and Kysumu should head back to the ruins, then strike out towards the south.'

'What are we looking for?' asked Yu Yu.

'Anything that looks familiar to you. The Men of Clay walked away from the battlefield. Did they walk far? More than a day, for example? Did they make camp?'

'No, I don't think so. I think the hills were close to the burning city.'

'Then you must find those hills. I will join you in a day or two.'

Kysumu stepped in close to the Grey Man. 'What if the demons come back? You will not have our swords to protect you.'

'One concern at a time, my friend,' said the Grey Man. 'Emrin will see that you have two good mounts and a week's supplies. Tell no one where you are heading.'

Lord Aric of House Kilraith stepped past the two guards at the door, and led Eldicar Manushan through to the rear apartments, where a third guard politely relieved Aric of his ruby-pommelled dagger. Lord Panagyn of House Rishell was lounging in an armchair, his booted feet resting on a glass table-top. A big, ugly man, with iron-grey hair and a large bulbous nose, his face was given a hint of glamour by the silver patch he wore over his left eye.

'Greetings, cousin,' said Aric amiably. 'I trust you are comfortable?'

'As comfortable as any man sitting in the fortress of his enemy.'

'Always so suspicious, cousin. You will not die here. Allow me to introduce my friend, Eldicar Manushan.'

The broad-shouldered magicker bowed. 'A pleasure, my lord.'

'So far the pleasure is all yours,' grunted Panagyn, swinging his legs from the table. 'If you are looking for an alliance with House Rishell, Aric, you can forget it. You were behind the treacherous turncoat Shastar. Had he not switched sides I would have killed Ruall, as I killed his brothers.'

'Indeed so,' said Aric. 'And you are quite right. I did convince Shastar to change sides.'

'You admit it, you dog!'

'Yes, I do.' Aric sat down opposite the astonished man. 'But all that is in the past. There are far greater prizes in our grasp now. We have battled one another to gain control of larger areas of Kydor. Larger areas of a tiny nation. But suppose for a moment we could conquer the lands of the Chiatze, and the Gothir. And beyond. Drenan, Vagria, Lentria. Suppose that we could be kings of great empires.'

Panagyn chuckled, the sound rich with mockery. 'Oh, yes, cousin,' he said. 'And we could fly over our empires on the backs of winged pigs. I do believe I saw a feathered pig swooping past my window as I arrived.'

'I don't blame you for your cynicism, Panagyn,' said Aric. 'I will even give you another opportunity for jest. Not only can we rule these empires, but we will never die. We will be immortal like gods.'

He fell silent for a moment, then smiled. 'You wish to make another jest?'

'No – but I would appreciate you offering me a taste of the narcotic you have obviously been imbibing.'

Aric laughed. 'How is your eye?'

'It hurts, Aric. How do you think it feels? An arrow cut through it, and I had to pluck out both shaft and orb.'

'Then perhaps a small demonstration would aid our negotiation,' said Aric. He turned to Eldicar Manushan. The magicker raised his hand. From the tip of his index finger a blue flame leapt into the air, closing in on itself and swirling, like a tiny, glowing ball.

'What is this?' asked Panagyn. Suddenly the ball sped across the room, flowing through the silver eye-patch. Panagyn fell back with a groan. He swore loudly and scrabbled for his dagger.

'No need for that,' said Eldicar Manushan. 'Stay calm and wait for the pain to pass. The result will surprise you, my lord. The pain should be receding now. What do you feel?'

'An itching in the socket,' muttered Panagyn. 'It feels like something is lodged there.'

'As indeed something is,' said Eldicar. 'Remove your eye-patch.' Panagyn did so. The socket had been stitched tight. Eldicar Manushan touched his finger to the sealed lids. The skin peeled back, the muscles of the lids swelling with new life. 'Open your eye,' ordered the magicker.

Panagyn obeyed him. 'Sweet Heaven!' he whispered. 'I have my sight. It is a miracle.'

'No, merely magic,' said Eldicar, looking at him closely. 'And I didn't quite get the colour right. The iris is a deeper blue in your right eye.'

'Gods, man, I care nothing for the colour,' said Panagyn. 'To be free of pain – and to have two good eyes.' Rising from his chair, he walked to the balcony and stared out over the bay. He swung back to the two men. 'How have you done this?'

'It would take rather an age to explain, my lord. But essentially your body regenerated itself. Eyes are really quite simple. Bones take a little more expertise. Had you, for example, lost an arm it would have taken several weeks – and more than two dozen spells – to regrow. Now, if you will, my lord, take a close look at your cousin.'

'Good to be able to take a *close* look at anything,' said Panagyn. 'What am I looking for?'

'Does he seem well to you?'

'You mean apart from dyeing his hair and beard?'

'It is not dye,' said Eldicar Manushan. 'I have given him back some ten years or so. He is now a man in his early thirties, and could remain so for several hundred years. Perhaps more.'

'By the gods, he does seem younger,' whispered Panagyn. 'And you could do this for me?'

'Of course.'

'And what do you require in return? The soul of my first-born?' Panagyn forced a laugh, but his eyes showed no humour.

'I am not a demon, Lord Panagyn. I am a man, just as you are. What I require is your friendship, and your loyalty.'

'And this will make me a king?'

'In time. I have an army waiting to enter this land. I do not wish them to have to fight as soon as they arrive. Far better to enter a land that is friendly, that will be a base for expansion. You have upwards of three thousand fighting men. Aric can summon close to four thousand. I do not wish for a battle so early.'

'Where is this army coming from?' asked Panagyn. 'The lands of the Chiatze?'

'No. A gateway will open not thirty miles from here. One thousand of my men will pass through it. It will take time to bring the whole army through. Perhaps a year. Perhaps a little more. But once our base here is established we will conquer the lands of the Chiatze, and beyond. The ancient realm will be restored. And you will be rewarded beyond any dream you can envisage.'

'And what of the others, the Duke, Shastar and Ruall?' asked Panagyn. 'Are they to be included in our venture?'

'Sadly, no,' said Eldicar Manushan. 'The Duke is a man with no understanding of avarice, and no desire for conquest. Shastar and Ruall are loyal to him, and will follow where he leads. No, initially the land of Kydor will be shared between you and your cousin.'

'They are to die, then?' said Panagyn.

'Indeed. Does that trouble you, my lord?'

'Everybody dies,' replied Panagyn, with a smile.

'Not everybody,' observed Aric.

In the nights that followed the attack on the palace many of the servants found difficulty in sleeping. Alone in their rooms as night fell, they would light lanterns and recite prayers. If sleep did come it was light, the merest sound of wind against the window-frames enough to have them wake in a cold sweat. Not so for Keeva, who slept more deeply than she had in years. Deep, dreamless sleep, from which she awoke feeling refreshed and invigorated.

And she knew why. When the demons had come she had not cowered in a corner, but taken up a weapon and used it. Yes, she had been afraid, but the fear had not overcome her. She remembered her uncle, and pictured his face as they sat on the riverbank. 'You'll hear people say that pride is a sin. Ignore them. Pride is vital. Not excessive pride, mind you. That is merely arrogant stupidity. No, being proud of yourself is what counts. Do nothing that is mean and spiteful, petty or cruel. And never give way to evil, no matter what the cost. Be proud, girl. Stand tall.'

'Is that how you have lived your life, Uncle?'

'No. That's why I know how important it is.'

Keeva smiled at the memory, as she sat by the bed of the priestess. Ustarte was sleeping peacefully. Keeva heard the Grey Man enter and glanced up at him. He was dressed all in black, the clothes very fine. He beckoned to her and she followed him into the weapons room. 'Ustarte is in danger,' he said.

'She seems to be recovering well.'

'Not from her wounds. She has enemies. Soon they will come for her.' He paused, his dark eyes locking to her gaze.

'What do you want me to do?' she asked.

'What do you want to do?' he countered.

'I don't understand you.'

'You have a choice of two paths, Keeva. One carries you back up the steps to the palace and your room, the other will take you to places you may not want to go.' He gestured towards the far bench. Upon it was laid a pair of soft leather leggings and a double-shouldered hunting jerkin. Beside the clothes was a belt bearing a bone-handled knife.

'These are for me?'

'Only if you want them.'

'What are you saying, Grey Man? Speak plainly.'

'I need someone to take Ustarte from here to a place of – relative – safety. It must be someone with wit and courage, someone who will not panic when the chase begins. I am not asking you to do this,

199

Keeva. I do not have that right. If you choose to return to your room I will think none the worse of you.'

'Where is this place of safety?'

'About a day's ride from here.' He moved in closer to her. 'Give it some thought. I will be with Ustarte.'

Keeva stood alone in the weapons room. Stepping forward, she laid her hand on the hunting jerkin. The leather was soft and lightly oiled. Drawing the hunting knife from its sheath, she hefted it. It was perfectly balanced, and double-edged. Conflicting thoughts assailed her. She owed her life to the Grey Man, and the debt lay heavy upon her. Equally she loved life in the palace. Proud as she was of her part in the fight against the demons, Keeva had no wish to face any further dangers. She had been lucky in the raid upon the village. Camran could have killed her straight away. That luck had doubled with the coming of the Grey Man. But, surely, there was a limit to one person's luck? Keeva felt she would cross that limit were she to agree to escort the priestess.

'What should I do, Uncle?' she whispered.

There was no answer from the dead, but Keeva remembered his oft-repeated advice.

'*When in doubt, do what is right, girl.*'

CHAPTER TEN

WAYLANDER MOVED TO THE BEDSIDE. USTARTE'S GOLDEN EYES were open. He sat beside her. 'You were wrong to do that,' she said, her voice almost a whisper.

'I gave her a choice.'

'No, you didn't. She owes you her life. She will feel obliged to do as you ask.'

'I know, but I don't have too many choices,' he admitted.

'You could become a friend to Kuan-Hador,' she reminded him.

He shook his head. 'I would have remained neutral, but they brought death to my house and to my people. I cannot forgive that.'

'It is more than that,' she said.

He laughed then, with genuine good humour. 'I forget for a moment that you can read minds.'

'And speak with spirits,' she reminded him.

His smile faded. On the first night he had tended her Ustarte had woken and told him that the spirit of Orien, the Battle King of the Drenai, had appeared to her. It had shaken Waylander, for the same spirit had appeared to him years before, offering him the chance to redeem himself by finding the Armour of Bronze.[*]

'Has he come to you again?'

'No. He harbours no ill-will towards you. He wanted you to know that.'

'He should. I killed his son.'

'I know,' she said sadly. 'You were a different man then, and

---

[*] From the novel *Waylander* (1986)

almost beyond redemption. But the goodness in you fought back. He has forgiven you.'

'Strangely, that is harder to bear than hate,' he said.

'That is because you cannot forgive yourself.'

'Can you read the minds of spirits?' he asked her.

'No – but I liked him.'

'He was a king,' said Waylander, 'a great king. He saved the Drenai, and forged a nation. When he was old, his sight failing, he abdicated in favour of his son, Niallad.'

'I know this from your own memories,' she said. 'He hid the Armour of Bronze. You found it.'

'He asked me to. How could I refuse?'

'Some men would have. And now he has asked a second favour of you.'

'It makes no sense to me. Finding the Armour of Bronze helped the Drenai overcome a great enemy. But going to a feast? Why would a dead king care about a feast?'

'He did not say. But I think you will be in danger if you go. You know that?'

'I know.'

Keeva moved in from the weapons room. Waylander turned to see her standing in the doorway. She was wearing the dark shirt and leggings and a pair of fringed riding boots. The hunting knife was belted at her waist. Her long dark hair was pulled back from her face and tied in a pony-tail. Waylander rose from the bedside. 'The clothes fit well,' he said. Moving past her he walked to a cabinet on the far wall of the weapons room. Opening it, he withdrew a small double-winged crossbow. Calling out to Keeva he carried the weapon to a bench. Under the light of a lantern he examined the crossbow, lightly oiling the bolt grooves. As Keeva came alongside he passed the weapon to her. 'I had this made for my daughter, Miriel,' he said, 'but she preferred the more traditional hunting bow. It is considerably lighter than my own bow and the killing range is no more than fifteen paces.'

Keeva hefted the bow. It was T-shaped, when viewed either vertically or horizontally, the grip projecting down from the centre of the weapon. The rear of the crossbow was fluted back, and shaped so that it settled snugly over the wrist. There were no bronze triggers. Two black studs had been set into the grip.

Waylander handed the girl two black bolts. 'Load the lower groove first,' he advised. Keeva struggled with the action. The centre of the lower bowstring was hidden inside the mechanism. 'Let me show you,' he said.

On the underside of the bow was a catch. Waylander flicked it open and pulled it down. This engaged the lower bowstring, drawing it back into view. Slipping his fingers into the groove he cocked the weapon, then slid a bolt into place. Snapping the catch, he handed the weapon to Keeva. Extending her arm, she loosed the centre bolt into a nearby target. He watched her reload it. She still struggled with the lower section. 'Do not leave it loaded for too long,' he said, 'for it will weaken the wings. When you get time, practise loading and unloading. It will become easier.'

'I do not want it to become *easier*,' she told him. 'I will take Ustarte to this place you spoke of, but then you can have this weapon back. I told you once before I do not want to be a killer. That remains true.'

'I understand that, and I am grateful to you,' he said. 'I will be with you late tomorrow. After that you will be free of any obligation to me.'

Finding a stick of charcoal and a section of parchment he drew two diamond shapes, the first with a diagonal line across it running left to right, the second right to left. 'Skirt the ruins of Kuan-Hador to the south-west and head into the mountains. Follow the main road for around a mile. You will come to a fork in the road. Take the left fork and continue until you see a lightning-blasted tree. Ride on, keeping your eyes on the trunks of the trees you pass. Each time you see these symbols change direction according to the line through the diamond, left to right or right to left. You will come to a cliff-face. If you have followed the symbols correctly you will be close to a deep cleft in the rocks. Dismount and lead the horses into that cleft. Inside you will find a deep cave with a freshwater pool. There are supplies there, and grain for the horses.'

Keeva slipped the bolts from the crossbow and loosed the strings. 'I heard the priestess say you would be in danger at the Feast. Why go?'

'Why indeed?' he observed.

'You had best be wary.'

'I am *always* wary.'

Niallad, son of the mighty Duke Elphons, and blood heir to the vanished throne of Drenan, stood naked before a full-length mirror disliking what he saw. The slender face, with its large blue eyes and full mouth, seemed to him to be that of a girl. There was no real sign yet of facial hair. His shoulders and arms were still skinny, despite the many weeks of hard physical labour he had pushed himself to complete. His chest, also hairless, carried no flesh and his ribs could clearly be seen. He looked nothing like the powerhouse that was his father.

And the fears he carried would not go away. When surrounded by crowds he would start to sweat, his palms becoming clammy, his heart beating wildly. His dreams were always of darkness, an unfamiliar maze of corridors, and the stealthy footfalls of an assassin who was never seen.

Turning away from the mirror Niallad went to the chest beneath the window and opened it, pulling forth a grey tunic and dark leggings. Dressing, he pulled on his calf-length riding boots and strapped his dagger-belt to his waist. Then came a light tapping at the door. 'Come in,' he called.

The bodyguard, Gaspir, stepped inside. He pointed at the dagger-belt. 'No weapons, young lord,' he said. 'Your father's orders.'

'Yes, of course. A hall full of enemies and we carry no weapons.'

'Only the friends of the Duke are invited,' said Gaspir.

'Panagyn is no friend, and I do not trust Aric.'

The broad-shouldered bodyguard shrugged. 'Even if Panagyn were an enemy he would be a fool to attempt an assassination in a hall filled with the Duke's supporters. Put your mind at rest. Tonight is a celebration.'

'Are there many people here?' asked Niallad, trying not to show his fear.

'Only about a hundred so far, but they are still arriving.'

'I shall be down presently,' said Niallad. 'Is the food being served?'

'Aye, it looks enticing.'

'Then go down and eat, Gaspir. I will see you in a little while.'

The guard shook his head. 'You are in my charge, young lord. I will wait outside.'

'I thought you said there was no danger.'

The man stood his ground for a moment, then nodded. 'It will be as you say,' he replied at last, 'but I will watch for you. Do not be too long, sir.'

Alone now in the sanctuary of his rooms, Niallad felt the panic building. It was not even that he expected to be attacked. His mind knew it was entirely improbable. And yet he could not suppress the fear. His uncle had been in his own garden when the assassin, Waylander, shot him in the back. His own garden! With the king murdered, the country in a state of near-anarchy, the Vagrian army had poured across the border, burning towns and cities and butchering thousands.

Niallad sat down on the bed, closed his eyes, and took several deep, calming breaths. I will stand up, he thought, and walk slowly out on to the gallery. I will not look down at the mass of people. I will turn left and descend the stairs . . .

. . . into the heaving mass.

His heartbeat quickened once more. This time it was accompanied by anger. I will not be cowed by this fear, he promised himself. Rising, he marched across the room and pulled open the door. Immediately he heard the noise from below, the chattering, the laughter, the sounds of cutlery on dishes, all mixed together creating a discordant and vaguely threatening hum. Niallad walked to the banister rail at the edge of the gallery and looked down. At least a hundred and fifty people were already present. His father and mother were seated almost exactly below him, their chairs raised on a circular dais. Lord Aric was standing close by, as was the magicker, Eldicar Manushan, and little Beric. The boy looked up and saw him. Niallad smiled and waved. The men around the Duke also glanced up. Niallad nodded to them, and stepped back from the edge. In the far corner he saw the portly priest Chardyn talking to a group of women. And there, by the terrace arch, the Grey Man, standing alone. He was wearing a sleeveless jerkin of brushed grey silk, over a black shirt and leggings. His long black and silver hair was held back from his face by a slender black headband. He wore no ornaments or jewellery. No rings adorned his fingers. As if sensing eyes upon him, the Grey Man glanced up, saw Niallad, and raised his goblet. Niallad walked down the stairs towards him. He did not know the man well, but there was space around him, and the beckoning safety of the terrace beyond.

The bottom of the stairwell had been recently closed off by an archway and two doors. A guard stood inside the porch. He bowed as Niallad approached the door. The porchway blocked much of the sound from the hall and Niallad toyed with the thought of engaging the guard in conversation for a while, putting off the dread moment when he must step through and face the throng. But the man lifted the lock-bar and pushed open the doors. Niallad stepped through and walked across to where the Grey Man stood.

'Good evening to you, sir,' said Niallad politely. 'I trust you are enjoying my father's celebration.'

'It was courteous of him to invite me,' said the Grey Man, extending his hand. Niallad shook it.

Up close he saw that the Grey Man's clothes were not entirely free of adornment. His belt had a beautiful, and unusual, buckle of polished iron, shaped like an arrowhead. The same design had been used on the outer rim of his calf-length boots.

The sound of rasping metal from behind caused Niallad to spin round. At a nearby table a chef was sharpening his carving knife. Niallad felt panic looming. The Grey Man spoke. 'I do not like crowds,' he said softly. 'They make me uneasy.'

Niallad struggled for calm. Was the man mocking him? 'Why is that?' he heard himself say.

'Probably because I've spent too long in my own company, riding the high country. I like the peace I find there. The meaningless chatter of these events grates on my nerves. Would you like to take some air with me on the terrace?'

'Yes, of course,' said Niallad gratefully. They stepped out through the archway and on to the paved stone beyond. The night was cool, the sky clear. Niallad could smell the sea. He felt himself becoming calmer. 'I suppose,' he said, 'that such problems with crowds dissipate after a while as one becomes more accustomed to them.'

'That is mostly the way with problems of this nature,' agreed the Grey Man. 'The trick is to allow oneself to *become* accustomed.'

'I don't follow you.'

'If you were faced with a snarling dog, what would you do?'

'Stand very still,' said Niallad.

'And if it attacked?'

'If I was armed I would try to kill it. If not I would shout loudly and kick at it.'

'What would happen were you to run from it?'

'It would chase and bite me. That is the way with dogs.'

'That is also the way with fear,' said the Grey Man. 'You can't run from it. It will follow, snapping at your heels. Most fears recede if you face them down.'

A servant came out on to the terrace, bearing a tray upon which were crystal goblets filled with watered wine. Niallad took one and thanked the man, who bowed and departed. 'Rare to see a nobleman thank a servant,' said the Grey Man.

'Is that a criticism?'

'No. A compliment. Are you staying long in Carlis?'

'A few weeks only. My father wanted to meet with the lords of the four Houses. He is trying to avert another war.'

'Let us hope he succeeds.'

At that moment Gaspir strode out on to the terrace. He bowed. 'Your father is asking for you, young lord,' he said. Niallad offered his hand to the Grey Man, who shook it.

'Thank you for your company, sir,' said Niallad. The Grey Man bowed.

Niallad strolled away. Somehow the conversation with the Grey Man had settled his nerves, but his heart began to beat faster as he entered the throng. 'Face it down,' he told himself. 'It is merely a growling dog, and you are a man. You only have to be here for a while, then you can return to the sanctuary of your room.'

Niallad walked on, his expression grim and determined.

Waylander watched the youth make his way across the hall. The bodyguard Gaspir was following him closely. Elsewhere he saw Eldicar Manushan moving among the crowds, smiling and chatting to people. Waylander saw that his long robe seemed to shimmer and change colour as he moved. At first sight it was silver grey, but the folds glinted at times with subtle shades of pink and red, lemon yellow and gold. Waylander's gaze flowed over the hall. There had been changes since last he had been here. The stairwells were now closed off, and the arches leading to the library boasted heavy doors of oak. He preferred the previous style. It was more open and inviting.

A servant offered him a drink, but he refused, and strolled into the hall. He could see the boy, Niallad, talking with his father and the tall, slim Lord Ruall. The lad seemed ill at ease once more and Waylander could see the gleam of sweat upon his face.

Reaching the new door to the library, Waylander tried to open it, but it was locked from the other side. Eldicar Manushan strolled over to him. 'Your garb is most elegant, sir,' he said. 'Your lack of adornment makes most men here look like peacocks. Including me,' he added, with a grin.

'An unusual robe,' observed Waylander.

'It is my favourite,' said Eldicar. 'It is woven from the silk of a rare worm. Heat and light bring about changes in colour. In bright sunshine the robe becomes golden. It is a delightful piece.' Stepping in close, the magicker lowered his voice. 'Have you considered what we spoke about?'

'I have thought on it.'

'Will you be a friend to Kuan-Hador?'

'I think not.'

'Ah, that is a shame. But it is also a worry for another day. Enjoy your evening.' The magicker's hand tapped lightly on Waylander's back. In that moment Waylander felt a sudden chill. His senses sharpened, his heartbeat quickened. Eldicar moved away back into the crowd.

The thought came to him that he should leave this place.

Waylander walked back towards the terrace. He saw Niallad, climbing the stairs. He was moving slowly, as if at ease, but Waylander could sense the tension in him. Niallad reached the gallery, then turned to his right, entering his room. Sadness touched Waylander.

'Such a grim face for so lively an evening,' said the priest Chardyn.

'I was thinking of the past,' Waylander told him.

'Not a pleasant past, it seems.'

Waylander shrugged. 'If a man lives long enough he will gather bad memories among the good.'

'That is true, my friend. Though some are worse than others. It is worth remembering that the Source is ever forgiving.'

Waylander laughed. 'We are alone here, priest. No one else can hear us. You do not believe in the Source.'

'What makes you think that?' asked Chardyn, dropping his voice.

'You stood your ground against the demons – and that makes you a brave man, but you had no spells, no belief that your god was stronger than the evil to come. I knew a Source priest once. He had faith. I know it when I see it.'

'And you, sir?' queried Chardyn. 'Do you have faith?'

'Oh, I believe, priest. I do not want to, but I believe.'

'Then why did the Source not strike down the demons as I prayed he would?'

Waylander smiled. 'Who is to say he did not?'

'Eldicar Manushan destroyed them, and though I may not be holy myself I also know holiness when I see it.'

'You think the Source only uses good men for his purposes? I have seen differently. I knew a man once, a killer and a robber. He had, to all intents and purposes, the morals of a gutter rat. This man gave his life for me, and before that had helped to save a nation.'

Chardyn smiled. 'Who can say for certain that it was the Source who inspired him? Where were the miracles, the light in the sky, the glowing angels?'

Waylander shrugged. 'My father told me a story once, about a man who lived in a valley. A great storm rose up and the river overflowed. The valley began to flood. A horseman rode by the man's small house and said to him, "Come, ride with me, for your house will soon be under water." The man told him that he needed no help, for the Source would save him. As the waters rose the man took refuge on his roof. Two swimmers came by and called out to him, "Jump into the water. We will help you reach dry land." Again he waved them away, saying that the Source would protect him. As he sat perched on his chimney, thunder filling the sky, a boat came by. "Jump in," called the boatman. Again the man refused. Moments later the water swept him away and he drowned.'

'What is the point of this story?' asked Chardyn.

'The man's spirit appeared before the Source. The man was angry. "I believed in you," he said, "and you failed me." The Source looked at him and said, "But, my son, I sent a rider, two swimmers and a boat. What more did you want?"'

Chardyn smiled. 'I like that. I shall use it in one of my sermons.' Then he fell silent.

Within the hall Eldicar Manushan, Lord Aric and Lord Panagyn had moved to the stair doors. A guard opened them and they moved through. Elsewhere Waylander saw other guests quietly leaving the hall. Most were followers of Panagyn. His expression hardened. His heart began to beat faster and a sense of danger rose in him. Moving to the terrace doors he saw a squad of soldiers marching through the gardens.

The five-man squad climbed the steps to the terrace. Waylander took the priest by the arm and drew the surprised man out into the night. The guards ignored them, and pushed shut the heavy doors, dropping a crossbar into place before marching off.

'What are you doing?' asked Chardyn. 'How will we get back in?'

'Trust me, priest, you do not *want* to go back in.' Waylander leant in close. 'I don't often offer advice,' he said, 'but were I you I would leave this place *now*.'

'I don't understand.'

'All exits from the hall have been blocked. The stairs are sealed off. That is no longer a banqueting hall, priest. It is a killing ground.'

Without another word Waylander walked away into the night.

Reaching the western postern gate he paused and glanced back at the palace, silhouetted against the night sky. Anger flared in him, but he quelled it. Everyone in that lower hall was destined for death. They would be slaughtered like cattle.

Is that why you wanted me there, Orien? he wondered. *So that I could die for killing your son?*

He dismissed the thought even as it came to him. There had been no malice in the old king. Waylander had murdered his son, and yet the old man had given him the chance to find the Armour of Bronze and, at least in part, redeem himself for his past sins. So why had he come to Ustarte? There was no mystical armour to find, no great and perilous quest to undertake. Waylander had attended the gathering, which was all that had been asked of him.

Then why did you want me here?

Into his mind came the face of a frightened youth, a boy who feared crowds and lived in terror of assassination. Orien's grandson.

With a soft curse Waylander turned and ran back towards the palace.

Within the hall a trumpet sounded, and all conversation ceased. Lord Aric and Eldicar Manushan appeared at the North Gallery rail above the throng.

'My dear friends,' said Aric. 'Now comes a moment you have all anticipated with great relish – as indeed have I. Our friend Eldicar Manushan will entertain you with wonders beyond description.'

Thunderous applause broke out, and the magicker raised his hands.

With all the doors closed the temperature in the great room began to rise. As he had at Waylander's palace, the magicker created small swirling globes of white mist, which floated and danced above the spectators, cooling the air and bringing applause.

A huge, black-maned lion appeared in the centre of the hall, and rushed towards the revellers. Several screams sounded – followed by a rush of relieved laughter as the lion became a flock of small blue songbirds, which rose up towards the rafters. The audience clapped wildly. The birds circled the hall, then gathered together, merging into the form of a small flying dragon, with golden scales and a long snout with flaring nostrils. It swooped upon the crowd, sending out a roaring blaze of fire, which engulfed the spectators by the western wall. Once more screams were followed by laughter and applause as the victims saw that not a single scorch had blemished the beauty of their satin robes and silken jackets.

On the dais the Duke Elphons clapped politely, then reached out and took the hand of his wife, Aldania, sitting beside him. A tall, slim man to the Duke's left leant in to his lord and whispered something. Elphons smiled and nodded.

At that moment Eldicar Manushan's voice boomed, 'Dear friends, I thank you for your gracious applause, and now offer a climax to the evening's entertainment, which I am sure will make what has gone before seem trivial in the extreme.'

Dark plumes of smoke began to form in the centre of the hall, twisting and snaking, braiding together like copulating serpents. The braid broke in a dozen places, and huge dark hounds leapt out, snarling, their massive fangs dripping venom. The last of the smoke floated close to the seats of the Duke and his lady. It rose up before them, forming a dark doorway, through which stepped a swordsman. He wore an ornate helm, created from layered strips of black metal, and a black silk, ankle-length tunic, split at the waist. He carried two swords, long and curved, the blades so dark they seemed to have been carved from the night sky. A third sword, scabbarded, was thrust into the black silk sash around his waist.

Stepping forward he bowed to the Duke – then flung one of his swords into the air. The second followed it. Swiftly he drew the third, and this, too, he sent spinning into the air, just as the first blade returned to his hand. He began to leap and twirl, while juggling the blades. Meanwhile the twelve black hounds moved stealthily towards the spectators.

211

Faster and faster the swordsman spun the blades.

What happened next was so swift that few registered the act. The swordsman's hand flicked out. One of the swords flew straight into the chest of Lord Ruall. Instantly the second lanced through the throat of Elphons, Duke of Kydor. The third plunged through the heart of Lady Aldania.

For a moment only, there was silence in the hall.

Then the first of the hounds leapt, its great fangs ripping out the throat of a reveller.

'Enjoy a taste of true magic!' bellowed Lord Aric.

More smoke billowed, and a score of *Kraloth* rushed from it. The crowd panicked and tried to beat their way through the barred doors. Again the smoke came. Now there were some fifty demonic hounds.

They rushed into the crowd, their long fangs ripping and tearing at the silk- and satin-clad nobles. Aric watched from the gallery, his eyes gleaming. It was incredible! He saw one young man run across the hall and try to jump to the stair rail. A *Kraloth* leapt at him, jaws closing on his leg. The noble clung desperately to the rail. The *Kraloth* fell back to the hall floor, taking the lower part of the man's leg with him. Aric tapped Lord Panagyn on the shoulder, pointing out the scene. Blood gouting from the severed limb, the noble had almost managed to haul himself on to the stairs. Aric gestured to the bodyguard Gaspir, who was standing close by. The man ran along the gallery, and down the stairs. Just as the noble believed he had reached safety Gaspir came alongside. The young man reached out to Gaspir, seeking help. The black-bearded bodyguard grabbed him, tipping him back into the hall. As his body struck the floor a *Kraloth* leapt upon him, ripping away his face.

All across the hall there were similar scenes. Aric gloried in them. He swung to make a comment to Eldicar Manushan, and saw that the magicker had withdrawn from the gallery rail and was sitting on a bench with his page. He seemed lost in thought.

Aric stared down at the dead Duke. His one complaint was that the man had died too swiftly. Pompous bastard! He should have been made to watch all his followers scream and die.

At that moment Aric saw movement on the East Gallery. The youth, Niallad, had emerged from his room and was standing at the rail, staring in horror at the blood-letting below.

Aric looked around for Gaspir. The bodyguard was standing with one of Panagyn's men. They, too, had seen the boy. Gaspir glanced towards Aric for confirmation. Aric nodded. Gaspir drew his dagger.

Niallad's mind reeled at the sights before him. The sound of screaming filled his ears. The hall was awash with blood and corpses. A severed arm was draped over one of the food tables, dripping gore on to bone-white plates. Huge black hounds were leaping on the terrified survivors. Niallad saw a man hammering at one of the doors, shouting to be let out. One hound leapt upon his back, massive teeth crunching down on his skull.

Niallad gazed down and saw his parents, slain where they sat. A black-garbed swordsman approached his father's body, reached out, then pulled a sword from his father's body. The corpse of Duke Elphons toppled sideways.

'Murderer!' screamed Niallad. The warrior looked up, then transferred his gaze to Eldicar Manushan, who was now leaning on the North Gallery banister rail, watching the carnage below. Beside him stood Lords Aric and Panagyn.

Niallad could not, at that moment, comprehend why these men were standing idly by. He felt giddy and sick and began to lose all sense of reality. Then he saw Gaspir and another man moving towards him.

'They have killed my father, Gaspir,' he said.

'They have killed you too,' said his bodyguard.

Niallad saw the knives in their hands. He backed away into his room. His legs were trembling. All his young life he had feared just such a moment as this. And now it was upon him. Curiously the terror faded away, replaced by a cold anger. His limbs ceased to tremble and he ran to his bed, where he had discarded his dagger-belt. His fingers curled around the carved ebony hilt, pulling the weapon clear. Then he swung to face the men.

'I thought you were my friend, Gaspir,' he said, and felt a surge of pride that there was no fear in his voice.

'I *was* your friend,' said Gaspir, 'but I serve Lord Aric. I will kill you swiftly, boy. I'll not throw you to the beasts.'

Gaspir stepped closer. The other man edged away to the right.

'Why are you doing this?' asked Niallad.

'There's little point in such a question,' said the Grey Man,

213

stepping through the balcony doorway. 'You might just as well ask a rat why it spreads disease. It does it because it is a rat. It knows no other way.'

The two assassins hesitated. Gaspir glanced at the Grey Man, who was standing unarmed, his thumbs resting in his belt. 'Kill the boy,' he ordered the second man, then advanced on the Grey Man. His intended victim did not back away. His right hand moved to his ornate belt buckle. In that fraction of a heartbeat Gaspir saw the arrowhead-shaped centre of the buckle slide clear. The Grey Man's hand flicked out. Blinding white light exploded in Gaspir's right eye-socket, lancing fire through his skull. He fell back.

Niallad saw the Grey Man step in swiftly, grab Gaspir's knife arm and twist it savagely. The long blade fell clear. The Grey Man caught the falling blade by the hilt, and flipped it. His arm rose and fell. There was a grunt from Niallad's left. The second assassin staggered, Gaspir's blade lodged in his neck. Even so he raised his own knife and lunged at Niallad. The youth sidestepped and, without thinking, slammed his own dagger through the man's chest, piercing the heart. He dropped without a sound.

Gaspir was on his knees groaning, one hand over the bleeding wound in his eye. The Grey Man slapped his hand away, and tore the throwing knife clear. Gaspir gave a cry of pain and fell back. The Grey Man coolly sliced his blade across Gaspir's throat. Ignoring the dying man, who continued to writhe on the floor, he walked across to Niallad.

'My parents are dead,' said Niallad.

'I know,' said the Grey Man, moving past the boy and making for the door. Gently he pushed it shut. He swung back to Niallad. 'Breathe slowly,' he said, 'and look into my eyes.'

Niallad did so. 'Now, listen to me. If you are going to survive you must understand your position. You are no longer the son of the mightiest man in the realm. You are, from this moment, an outlaw. They will hunt you and try to kill you. You are a man alone. You must learn to think like one. Strap on that dagger-belt, and follow me.'

Lord Shastar of House Bakard, his shirt torn away, blood seeping from the clawmarks on his naked back, sat huddled against the western wall, watching the black hounds ripping flesh from the bodies – some of which were still living.

214

Shastar sat very still, aware that the slightest movement could alert the creatures to his presence. Across from him he could see the bodies of the Duke and his wife, the dead Ruall lying beside them.

The black-garbed warrior who had killed them was standing silently, arms folded across his chest.

A massive hound padded across to where Shastar sat. He did not move. The beast's nostrils flared, its huge head so close to Shastar's own that he could smell the beast's foetid breath. Shastar closed his eyes, waiting for the fangs to rip away at him. Just then a dying woman close by let out a groan. The hound leapt upon her, and Shastar heard the sound of crunching bones.

Voices sounded close by. Opening his eyes he saw the magicker, Eldicar Manushan, strolling among the corpses. As he reached each hound he lightly touched it. With each touch one of the creatures disappeared, until at last the hall was eerily silent.

'Gods, what a mess,' he heard someone say. Shastar glanced to his right to see Lord Aric, picking his way across the marble floor, careful to avoid the pools of blood and severed limbs. Shastar watched, as if in a dream. He could hardly believe this was happening. How could a cultured man like Aric have been responsible for such a massacre? He had known Aric for years. They had hunted together, discussed art and poetry. There had been no indication of the monster dwelling within him.

Shastar watched as the magicker walked around the hall, staring down at the bodies. He saw him reach the East Gallery stairs. Aric moved across to the body of Duke Elphons, dragging it from the ornate, high-backed chair. The lord of House Kilraith then tore the cape from the Duke's shoulders and wiped blood from the chair before sitting down and surveying the hall. Eldicar Manushan joined him. 'There is no sign of the Grey Man,' he said.

'What? He must be here.'

At that moment a shadow fell across Shastar. He looked up to see the black-garbed warrior who had killed the Duke looming over him. The man's features were Chiatze, though his eyes were golden. He leaned in close. Shastar saw that his pupils were elongated, like those of a cat.

'This one lives,' said the warrior. Reaching down he grabbed Shastar by the arm and hauled him to his feet. The strength in the man's grip surprised Shastar. The warrior was slim and not tall, yet the heavy-set lord of House Bakard was dragged upright in an instant.

'Well, well,' said Eldicar Manushan, striding forward, 'I never cease to be surprised by the vagaries of war.' He looked into Shastar's face. 'Have you any idea of the odds against surviving an attack by so many *Kraloth*? Millions to one.' Stepping in close he looked at the wounds on Shastar's back. 'Hardly a scratch, though the wounds will still be fatal if left untreated.'

'Why have you done this?' asked Shastar.

'I can assure you it wasn't for pleasure,' said Eldicar Manushan. 'I take no joy in such enterprises. But, you see, there are only two ways to deal with potential enemies: make them allies or kill them. I just did not have the time to make so many alliances. However, since you have so luckily escaped death, I feel obliged to give you the opportunity of serving my cause. I can heal your wounds, give you back your youth, and promise you centuries of life.'

'We don't need him!' shouted Aric.

'I say who we need, mortal,' hissed Eldicar Manushan. 'What say you, Lord Shastar?'

'If an alliance with you means joining forces with a worm like Aric I'll have to decline,' said Shastar.

'You really should reconsider,' said Eldicar gently. 'Death is terribly final.'

Shastar smiled – then lunged at the magicker. His right hand curled around Eldicar Manushan's dagger, dragging it from its sheath and ramming the blade into the magicker's chest. Eldicar Manushan staggered back, then righted himself. Taking hold of the hilt he slowly pulled the weapon clear. Blood dripped from the blade. Eldicar Manushan held the dagger out before him and released it. Instead of falling to the floor it hovered in the air. 'That really hurt,' he said, aggrieved. 'But I understand your anger. Rest in peace.'

The blade spun and swept into Shastar's chest, slipping between the ribs and plunging into his heart.

Shastar grunted then fell to his knees. He too tried to pull the dagger clear, but then pitched face first to the floor. 'Such a shame,' said the magicker. 'I liked the man. He had honour and courage. Now . . . where were we? Ah, yes, the Grey Man.' He glanced up at the East Gallery. 'Your men are taking rather a long time to complete a simple task, Aric.'

Lord Aric rose from the Duke's chair and ordered two of the guards to fetch Gaspir. Moments later one of the men called from the gallery, 'My lord, Gaspir and Valik are dead. There is no sign of the boy. They must have escaped to the gardens and the beach.'

'Find them!' roared Aric.

'Good advice,' muttered Eldicar Manushan. 'It would be greatly advisable to find him – before he finds you.'

Eldicar Manushan crouched down by the body of the dead Shastar and pulled his dagger clear, wiping the blade on the dead man's leggings. Sheathing the dagger, he noted that the hem of his shimmering robe was stained with blood. With a sigh he picked his way through the corpse-strewn hall and opened the stair door. Climbing to the gallery he found Beric still sitting on the bench. Taking the boy's hand he led him back through to their own suite of rooms.

'It is time for the communion,' said Beric.

'I know.'

Eldicar sat down on a wide couch, the boy beside him. The magicker, still holding the boy's hand, closed his eyes and tried to relax. Communion did not come easily, for first he had to mask his feelings. He had not wanted this massacre, believing it unnecessary. Most of the people present would not have been a threat to the plans of Kuan-Hador. He could have engineered it so that only the Duke and his closest allies were killed. He did not want such thoughts in his mind once communion was established. Deresh Karany did not tolerate criticism.

Eldicar concentrated on thoughts of his childhood, and the small sailboat his father had built for him on the lake. Good days, when the Talent was imprecise and unskilled, and he had dreamed of becoming a healer.

He felt the first sharp tug in his mind. It was most painful, as if the flesh of his brain was being teased by a talon.

'*Not a great success, Eldicar Manushan,*' came the voice of Deresh Karany.

'*Nor yet a failure, Lord. The Duke and his allies are dead.*'

'*The Grey Man lives, as do the two sword-bearers.*'

'*I have sent eight Kriaz-nor to intercept the sword-bearers. Two squads, one led by Three-swords, the other by Striped-claw.*'

'Commune with both squads. Tell them they have three days.'

'Yes, Lord.'

'And what of the traitor, Ustarte?'

'I believe her to be alive and hidden in the palace of the Grey Man. A troop of Lord Aric's soldiers are already on their way.'

'I would appreciate her being taken alive.'

'That is the instruction they have. I would be happier if more Kriaz-nor could be sent.'

'More will come when the gateway finally collapses. Until then you must use Anharat's creatures. Tell me, why did you offer the man Shastar his life?'

'He had courage.'

'He was a potential enemy. You have a soft heart, Eldicar. Do not allow it to interfere with the orders you have been given. We are great because we obey. We do not question.'

'I understand, Lord.'

'I hope that you do. I risked my reputation to speak up for you following the débâcle at Parsha-noor. It would hurt me if you proved unworthy of my trust. When you have found the priestess commune again.'

'Yes, Lord.'

Eldicar groaned as the link was severed. 'Your nose is bleeding,' said Beric. Eldicar pulled a handkerchief from the pocket of his robe, and dabbed at it. His head was pounding.

'You should lie down,' said Beric.

'I shall,' said Eldicar, pushing himself to his feet and walking through to his bedroom.

Lying back on the satin coverlet of his bed, his head upon the soft pillow, he thought of the débâcle at Parsha-noor.

Eldicar had given the enemy an extra day to consider surrender. An extra day! They had refused, and Deresh Karany had arrived at the battlefield. He sent a First Level demon to rip out the heart of the enemy king, and a host of *Kraloth* to terrorize the city-dwellers. Oh, they had surrendered fast enough then, Eldicar recalled. When they finally opened the gates to their conquerors Deresh Karany ordered twenty-six thousand of the citizens – one in three of the city-dwellers – to be put to death. Another ten thousand had been shipped back to Kuan-Hador to be Joined.

The extra day had seen Eldicar censured before the Seven. Only the mitigating plea from Deresh Karany had saved him from impalement.

The bleeding stopped.

Eldicar closed his eyes and dreamed of sailboats.

'All in all a fine night's work,' said Lord Panagyn, peeling away the silver eye-patch and staring around the blood-drenched hall. 'Ruall, Shastar and Elphons are dead, with most of their captains and supporters.' He stared at the dead Aldania. 'Shame about the woman. I always admired her.'

Aric summoned two of his guards and ordered them to gather work parties to clear the bodies. He was not a happy man. Panagyn clapped him on the shoulder. 'Why so glum, cousin? So the boy got away. He won't get far.'

'It is not the boy who concerns me,' said Aric. 'It is the Grey Man.'

'I've heard of him. A rich merchant, and your largest creditor.' Panagyn chuckled. 'You always did love to live above your means, cousin.'

'He is a deadly man. He killed Vanis. Came into his house while it was surrounded by guards and cut his throat.'

'I heard it was suicide.'

'You heard wrong.'

'Well, you have fifty men scouring the town for him. So relax. Enjoy the victory.'

Aric stalked across the hall, past the silent, black-garbed warrior who had killed the Duke. The man was sitting quietly by the stairs, arms folded, eyes closed. He did not look up as Aric passed. Climbing the stairs, Aric moved to Niallad's room. Panagyn came in behind him. Aric knelt by the body of Gaspir. 'Stabbed through the eye, then had his throat cut,' said Panagyn.

Aric could not have cared less. He walked through to the balcony. He gazed out over the moonlit garden towards the wrought-iron gate leading to the private beach. From here he could see the blazing torches and lanterns of the searchers. There had been no boats upon the beach, which meant that the fugitives would have to swim the bay. There was no other escape route. The front of the palace had been swarming with guards.

The Grey Man had not been seen there.

'Take a look at this,' said Panagyn. Aric turned to see the Lord of

House Rishell kneeling by the second body. He pointed at the knife jutting from the man's neck. It had an ornate handle of carved ivory. 'Wasn't this Gaspir's knife?'

'Aye,' said Aric, puzzled.

Panagyn glanced back at the other body. 'So the Grey Man killed Gaspir, took away his knife and stabbed my nephew through the neck before he could kill the boy. No, that would have taken too long. He took the knife and *threw* it.' Panagyn smiled. 'I see what you mean by deadly. Have to admire skill like that, though.'

'You are taking the death of your relative very well,' snapped Aric. 'I commend the manner in which you are hiding your grief.'

Panagyn ruffled the dead man's hair. 'He was a good lad. Not very bright, though.' Rising, he moved to a nearby table and poured a goblet of wine. 'And it is hard to be sad on a night when almost all of one's enemies have been killed.'

'Well, *all* of mine are not yet dead,' said Aric.

'*All* of them never will be, cousin. That is the penalty for being a ruler.' Panagyn drained the wine. 'I think I shall take to my bed. It has been a long – and rewarding – night. You should get some rest. There is much to do tomorrow.'

'I will rest – when they have found the Grey Man,' said Aric.

Back in the hall the bodies were being cleared away. Aric descended the stairs and walked out into the night. A line of men bearing torches was climbing up from the beach. Aric waited. His captain, a thin, hatchet-faced man named Shad, approached. He gave a brief bow. 'No sign of them on the beach, Lord. I have sent out boats to search the water, and riders to scour the opposite shoreline. We are also organizing a house-to-house search through the town.'

'They could not have made it to the White Palace in this time,' said Aric. 'Are you certain no unauthorized guest left the hall?'

'There was one, Lord. The priest Chardyn. The guards assumed his name had been mistakenly omitted from the list.'

'I don't care about the priest.'

'There was no one else, Lord. The second squad reported that there was another man with the priest when they closed the western doors. From the description it was the Grey Man. He must have walked around to the rear of the palace and scaled the wall to the boy's room.'

'That much we already know,' said Aric. 'What happened *then* is what we must find out.'

'They must have gone to the beach, Lord. The tide was in so they could not have skirted the cliffs. We will find them. It will be light soon. If they are swimming in the bay the boatmen will catch them. Do you wish for them to be taken alive?'

'No, just kill them. But bring me the heads.'

'Yes, Lord.'

Aric strode back into the palace. There was a growing stench in the hall, but it faded as he climbed the stairs. Pausing at the top, he looked down, remembering the screams and cries of the dying. The pleasure he experienced had quite surprised him. Thinking back now, he found his previous joy disconcerting. He had never seen himself as a cruel man. As a child he had even hated hunting. It was most puzzling.

Panagyn had mentioned the death of Aldania. Aric paused. He had always liked the Duke's wife. She had been most kind to him. Why, then, did he feel nothing at her passing? Not the tiniest touch of guilt or regret. You are just tired, he told himself. There is nothing wrong with you.

Aric opened the door to his apartments. It was dark inside. The servants had not lit his lanterns. He was momentarily irritated – until he recalled that the servants had been ordered to leave the hall for Eldicar's performance. After that, in the chaos that had followed the slaughter, it was not surprising that they had forgotten their duties.

Moving through the main room, he walked to the balcony and stared out once more over the gardens and the distant beach. There were many boats drawn up now on the sand, and he could see the commandeered fishing boats heading back towards their moorings. Obviously the Grey Man and the boy had not chosen to swim the bay. Where, then, were they?

In that moment he heard a whisper of sound from behind. As he turned he saw a dark figure loom out of the shadows. Something glittering and bright flashed for his face. Aric hurled himself backwards. His legs thudded against the balcony balustrade and he toppled over it, striking his head on a jutting stone.

Darkness swamped him.

Aric became aware of the taste of blood in his mouth. He tried to move, but something was pulling at his arm. He opened his eyes. His face was resting against bare earth, his left arm wedged into the branches of a flowering bush. He dragged it clear, and groaned as pain shot through his side. Lying still for a moment he gathered his thoughts.

Someone had been in his room. He had been attacked and had fallen twenty feet from the balcony. The bush had broken his fall, but it felt as if he had snapped a rib. Pushing himself to his knees he saw that blood had stained the earth beneath him. Panicked now, Aric searched for signs of a wound. A drop of blood dripped to his hand. It was coming from his face. Gingerly he lifted his fingers to his jaw. It was wet and sore. He remembered the flashing blade. It had cut him along the jawline from just below the ear all the way to the chin.

With a grunt of pain Aric levered himself to his feet and staggered along the path, emerging at the front of the palace. Two guards were standing nearby. Seeing him, they ran forward and helped him back into the palace.

Within minutes he was in his rooms once more. Eldicar Manushan came to him there and examined his wounds. 'You have two cracked ribs, and your left wrist is sprained,' he said.

'What about my face? Will it be badly scarred?'

'I shall deal with that presently. What happened?'

'I was attacked. Here, in this very room.'

Eldicar moved out on to the balcony, then returned. 'There is a narrow ledge from your balcony to that of the Duke's son,' he said. 'The Grey Man did not flee the palace. He merely climbed along to your apartments and waited for the hunt to die down.'

'He could have killed me,' whispered Aric.

'He almost did. Had that cut been a hair's breadth lower it would have opened your jugular. A formidable opponent. He hides where no one would think of looking, in the very heart of his enemy's fortress.' Eldicar sighed. 'Such a shame he would not join us.'

Aric lay quietly on the bed, feeling nauseous. Eldicar spoke again: 'You were very lucky, Aric. The enhancements to your body enabled you to react with far greater speed than the average human. That allowed you – just – to avoid your throat being cut. It also helped your body absorb the impact of the fall.'

'What else do these . . . *enhancements* do, Eldicar?'

'What do you mean?'

'I seem to have . . . changed in other ways. To have lost . . . something.'

'You have lost nothing you will need as a servant of Kuan-Hador. Now, let me seal that cut.'

As the ride progressed Keeva's tension grew. From the start she had realized this was not going to be an easy task. Most of the horses shied away from Ustarte, nostrils flaring, ears flat against their skulls. There was something about her scent that frightened them. Finally Emrin had brought out an old, sway-backed mare. She was almost blind, and allowed Ustarte to approach. Emrin lifted a saddle from a nearby rail. 'I cannot ride in the usual fashion,' said Ustarte. Emrin stood still, confused. 'My legs are . . . deformed,' she told him. His expression changed to one of embarrassment.

'Perhaps a *shabraque* would be more suitable,' he said. 'We have several, though they are not comfortable for a long ride. But you will be able to sit sideways upon old Grimtail. Will that suit, Lady?'

'You are very kind. I am sorry to put you to this trouble.'

'No trouble, I assure you.' Emrin moved to the back of the stable and returned with a leopardskin *shabraque* which he fastened around the pony's neck and belly. He swung to Keeva, who was already sitting upon a tall chestnut gelding. 'I have packed supplies for around three days, and two sacks of grain for the mounts.'

'We must be swift,' said Ustarte suddenly. 'There are riders heading up from the town.'

Emrin tried to lift Ustarte to the pony. He failed. 'Your . . . robes must be very heavy,' he said. The soldier searched around the barn, returning with a three-legged stool. Ustarte stepped on to it, then carefully sat down on the mare's back.

'Keep hold of her mane, Lady. Keeva will take the reins. And you had better carry the stool with you for when you want to mount again.'

Keeva heeled the chestnut forward. Leaning down, she took up the reins of the pony. It did not move. Emrin slapped the beast lightly on the rump and the two mounts walked out into the moonlit yard. In the distance Keeva caught sight of a troop of riders cresting a hill some half a mile away.

Now, an hour later, the two women had covered very little ground. The pony kept stopping and standing stubbornly in place for several minutes at a time, breathing heavily. Its dark flanks were already wet with sweat. Ustarte seemed untroubled. 'They are not following yet,' she said. 'They are searching the palace.'

223

'If we were being chased by a cripple with a crutch he would have overtaken us by now,' said Keeva.

'The pony is old and tired. I think I shall walk for a while.' Ustarte slipped from the mare's back. Keeva dismounted alongside her, and the two women moved off into the darkness of the trees.

They walked in silence for another hour, then Ustarte stopped. Keeva heard her sigh. She saw tears on the face of the priestess. 'What is wrong?' she asked.

'The killing has begun.'

'At the palace?'

'No, at the Duke's Feast. The *Ipsissimus* has summoned demons into the hall. The people there are being slaughtered. It is vile!'

'The Grey Man?' asked Keeva, fear swelling.

'He is not there. But he is close by.' Ustarte placed the stool she was carrying on the ground and sat down. 'He is scaling the wall behind the palace, and climbing into a room. Now he waits.'

'What of the riders who came looking for you?'

'They are gathering their mounts and preparing to follow. One of the servants said they had seen us at the stables.'

'Then we must ride. On fast horses they could be upon us in less than an hour.'

Using the stool, Ustarte mounted the pony and they set off once more. The old mare seemed to have gathered strength, and for a little while they made good time. But as they reached the scree slopes above the ruins of Kuan-Hador the beast stumbled. Ustarte climbed down and placed her ear against the pony's flanks. 'Her heart is labouring. She cannot go any further carrying me.'

'We cannot escape on foot,' said Keeva. 'There is still too far to go.'

'I know,' answered Ustarte softly.

Tossing aside the stool the priestess removed her grey gloves. Slowly she undressed, the moonlight gleaming upon the striped fur of her back and flanks. Passing the robe, gloves and soft leather shoes to Keeva she said, 'You ride on. I will meet you where the trail forks on the mountain road.'

'I cannot leave you here,' objected Keeva. 'I made a promise to the Grey Man.'

'You must,' said Ustarte. 'I will deal with the men following, and I will be at the road to meet you. Now go swiftly, for I must prepare. Go!'

224

Keeva leaned over to take the reins of the pony. 'Leave her,' said Ustarte. 'There is one more service she must provide.' Keeva was about to argue when Ustarte leapt towards the chestnut. Panicked by her scent the big gelding reared, then sprang away down the slope.

Ustarte moved to the old pony. 'I am sorry, my dear,' she said. 'You deserve better than this.' Her talons slashed through the pony's throat. Blood spurted. The mare tried to rear but Ustarte was holding the reins. As the blood pumped out through the severed artery the pony's front legs buckled. Ustarte lay down alongside her, pushing her face into the gaping wound. Swiftly she drank.

Her body writhed and twisted, muscles swelling.

Though not an expert horsewoman Keeva did not panic as the gelding raced down the slope. With one hand on the reins, the other grasping the saddle pommel, she held on grimly. The gelding, only momentarily panicked by the scent of Ustarte's fur, calmed down swiftly, and by the time they reached the first bend in the trail he was moving at a trot. Keeva gently tugged on the reins, halting the animal. She stroked the long sleek neck, and whispered soothing words, then swung in the saddle to stare back up the slope.

She was angry now. The Grey Man had asked her to see Ustarte safely away from danger, and now the priestess was going back alone to face the enemy. Keeva swung the gelding and began the long ride back to where she had last seen Ustarte.

It took some time, for the slope was steep. When finally she came upon the scene there was no sign of the beast-woman. The little pony lay dead upon the trail, her throat torn out, blood pooling on the stones. From some distance away Keeva heard a fearful roar. The gelding tensed. Keeva patted his neck. The distant roar came again, accompanied by the screams of terrified horses.

Keeva sat very still, and fear was strong upon her. A part of her wanted to ride on and aid the priestess, but the greater part desired nothing more than to flee, putting as great a distance as possible between herself and the dreadful sounds. In that moment she knew there was no *right* answer to the problem. If she rode to what she thought was Ustarte's rescue, and was captured, she would not be able to keep her promise to the Grey Man. If she followed Ustarte's orders and rode on, leaving the priestess to her fate, she would also be betraying the Grey Man's trust. Struggling for calm Keeva recalled

225

the last words Ustarte had used. '*I will deal with the men following, and I will be at the road to meet you. Now, go swiftly, for I must prepare. Go!*'

She did not say she would *try to* deal with the men, but that she *would* deal with them. Keeva gazed down at the dead pony. Ustarte had said she must prepare, and part of that preparation had been to kill the beast. Keeva dismounted and knelt by the body. Blood had spread out across the trail. Just beyond it Keeva saw a blood print on the stone. It was of a huge padded paw. Moving to it, she recognized it as that of a great cat.

All was silence now. There were no more screams in the distance, no echoes of terror.

Keeva backed away to the gelding and stepped into the saddle. She guided her mount down the slope and on to the plain, skirting the moonlit ruins of Kuan-Hador and the shimmering lake beyond.

Two hours later, with the dawn approaching, she halted at a fork on the mountain road and dismounted, leading the gelding into the trees. Tethering the horse, she walked back on to the slope and sat down on a rock. From here she could see the shadow-haunted plain below. A few clouds were drifting across the night sky, casting fast-moving shadows over the land. Keeva saw a movement on the plain, and tried to focus upon it. Something was moving at speed. A wolf, perhaps?

She had only seen it for an instant, but she knew it was no wolf. Clouds obscured the moonlight and Keeva sat quietly waiting for them to pass. She heard sounds upon the trail below her and, for a fraction of a heartbeat, saw a huge striped beast leave the path and enter the trees. The gelding whinnied in fear as the wind blew the scent of the creature across its nostrils. Keeva ran back to the horse, and lifted the small crossbow from the saddle pommel. Swiftly she loaded it.

A low growl came from the undergrowth, a rumbling, deep-throated sound that spoke of massive lungs. Keeva levelled the crossbow towards the sound. Then there was silence.

The dawn light filtered through the trees. The undergrowth parted.

And Ustarte stepped out. Blood was smeared across her face and arms. Pointing the crossbow to the ground Keeva released both bolts, then ran to Ustarte. 'Are you hurt?' she asked.

'Only my soul,' said Ustarte sadly. 'Do not fear, Keeva, the blood is not mine.'

226

Staying downwind of the frightened gelding, Ustarte made her way deeper into the trees, following the sound of running water. Keeva stayed with her, and saw there were tears on Ustarte's face. Reaching the water, the priestess crouched down and eased her crooked body into the stream. When all the blood was washed away she climbed once more to the bank. She stared down at her deformed hands and began to weep. Keeva sat beside her saying nothing.

'I wanted,' said Ustarte, at last, 'to keep this world free from the evil of Kuan-Hador. Now I have added to it. My people are dead – and I have killed.'

'They were hunting us,' said Keeva.

'They were obeying the orders of their lord. How good it would be to believe that those who died under my claws were evil men. But I felt their thoughts as I leapt among them. There were husbands there, thinking of wives and children they would never see again. Such is the nature of evil, Keeva. It corrupts us all. We cannot fight it and stay pure.'

Keeva returned to her horse and fetched Ustarte's red silk gown. She helped the priestess to dress. 'We must get to the cave,' said Keeva. Leading the gelding, Ustarte following some ten paces behind, she made her way through the trees watching for the carved signs left by the Grey Man.

They climbed for just under an hour, reaching the cliff-face and finding the cleft just as the Grey Man had described it. Inside there was a large chamber. A number of boxes had been piled there. Two lanterns were set atop the boxes. They were not needed yet, for light was streaming in from above, through a crack in the upper wall.

Keeva removed the saddle from the gelding and brushed him down. Then she fed him with the grain Emrin had supplied. At the rear of the cave, running water trickled down, forming a small pool at the base before flowing on down through a fissure in the floor. When the gelding had finished the grain she tethered him close to the pool, so that he could drink when he chose.

Ustarte had stretched herself out on the floor and was sleeping.

Keeva walked out into the morning sunlight. The trail outside was rocky scree, and she could see no sign of their passing. She sat back against the cliff-face and watched the branches of nearby oaks rustling in the breeze. A pair of wood pigeons flew by, their wings making a slapping sound. She looked up and smiled, feeling some of the tension drain from her body.

A red hawk swooped down from the skies, its long talons ripping into one of the pigeons. The wings folded and it dropped to the rocks. The hawk landed alongside the still-twitching body. Talons gripped it, the curved beak ripping into the living flesh.

Weariness flowed over Keeva, and she leant back and closed her eyes. She dozed for a while in the sunshine, and dreamt of her uncle. She was nine again, and the townspeople had dragged the old witch to a stake in the marketplace. Keeva had been out buying apples, which her uncle intended to use for a pie. She had watched the crowd baying at the witch, spitting at her and striking her with sticks. There was blood on the woman's face.

They had hauled her to the stake, tied her securely, then placed bundles of dry kindling all around her. After dousing her with oil they set fire to the kindling. Her screams were terrible.

Keeva had dropped the apples and run all the way home. Her uncle had hugged her, stroking her hair. 'She was an evil woman,' he said. 'She poisoned her entire family to gain an inheritance.'

'But they were laughing as she burned.'

'Aye, I expect they were. That's the nature of evil, Keeva. It breeds. It is born in every hateful thought, every spiteful word, every greedy deed. The crowd hated her, and in hating her they drew just a touch of evil into themselves. In some it will fade away. In others it will find a place to seed.'

The child Keeva had not understood. But she had remembered.

Keeva opened her eyes. The sun was almost at noon, and she rose and stretched.

Inside the cave Ustarte was awake, sitting quietly in the shadows.

'Are they still following?' asked Keeva.

'No, some returned to Carlis with their dead and wounded. Others are waiting at the White Palace to arrest the Grey Man. But they will come again.'

'Does the Grey Man know they are at the palace?'

'Yes.'

Keeva sighed. 'Good. Then he will avoid them.'

'No, he won't,' said Ustarte. 'He is already there. His anger is very great, but his mind is cool.' Ustarte closed her golden eyes. 'The hunters are closing in on the sword-bearers,' she said.

228

'You mean Yu Yu and his friend?'

'Yes. They are being pursued by two squads of *Kriaz-nor*, one from the south, one from the north.'

'What are *Kriaz-nor*?' asked Keeva.

'They are meld-creatures like myself. Faster, stronger and more deadly than almost any human.'

'Almost?'

Ustarte gave a wan smile. 'Nothing that walks or breathes is more deadly than the Grey Man.'

Keeva saw tears once more upon the face of the priestess. 'And that saddens you?'

'Of course. Within the darkness of the Grey Man's soul a small light flickers, all that remains of a good and kindly man. I asked him to fight for us, and fight he will. If that light goes out it will be my fault.'

'It will not go out,' said Keeva, putting her hand on Ustarte's shoulder. 'He is a hero. My uncle told me that heroes have special souls that are blessed by the Source. He was a wise man, my uncle.'

Ustarte smiled. 'I pray that your uncle was right.'

CHAPTER ELEVEN

NIALLAD SAT QUIETLY ON THE LEDGE, HIS BACK AGAINST THE cliff-face, the white surf crashing upon the rocks several hundred feet below. The Grey Man was sitting motionless beside him, his face calm, no suggestion of tension in him. They had been sitting here now for two hours. The sun had been up for some time, and Niallad's clothes were almost dry.

The events of the night before kept replaying in his mind. The death of his parents, the treachery of Gaspir, the rescue by the Grey Man. It all seemed somehow unreal. How could his father be dead? He was the strongest, most vital man in the duchy. Niallad saw again his mother lying sprawled on the floor. A dreadful emptiness assailed him and he felt tears welling. The Grey Man touched his arm. Blinking, Niallad turned his head. The Grey Man lifted a finger to his lips and shook his head. No sound. Niallad nodded and glanced up. Some ten feet above them was an overhang of rock. From beyond that they could hear the guards talking outside the Grey Man's apartments.

'This is stupid,' he heard one of the guards say. 'He's not going to come back here, is he? I mean, the place has been searched. A few weapons, some old clothes. Nothing to risk your life for.'

Niallad could not help but agree. He could not understand why they had come here. After killing Aric, the Grey Man had led Niallad to the beach. There were now several boats beached there, left by the soldiers who had been searching the bay. Niallad had helped the Grey Man push out a small boat until it bobbed upon the water. Then they had climbed in and rowed across the bay. When they reached a spot some two hundred yards from the beach below the White Palace the Grey Man had slipped into the water and begun to swim. Niallad had followed him.

Upon reaching the beach the Grey Man had gestured to Niallad to remain silent, and climbed slowly to this spot. Everything about the man until then had spoken of purpose. But once they had reached here he had just sat down, and now the hours were drifting past. Niallad had no idea what he was waiting for.

Time moved on. Niallad's left leg was cramped and he stretched it out.

'About time,' he heard a guard say. 'Thought you'd forgotten all about us.'

'Gren got to talking to a blonde serving maid. Nice piece. Very tasty.'

'Speaking of tasty, I hope there's some breakfast left.'

'Any word on the runaways?' someone asked.

'I'll say there has been. Being stuck down here you missed all the excitement, lads. One search party was attacked by a wild beast. Three dead, five wounded.'

'Our lads?'

'Only one, old Pikka. Had his head stove in. The others were from House Rishell. Word from town is that the Duke's dead and most of his people. Sorcery,' he added, dropping his voice.

'What happened to the Duke?'

'Demons, they say. Appeared in the hall. Killed everybody. The Grey Man summoned them, apparently. Shad says not to talk about it. Lord Aric's going to be the new Duke. Once they've found the body of the Duke's son.'

'The Grey Man? That's what you get when you let foreigners come in and start acting like lords.'

'He always was a weird bastard,' said another voice. 'And he almost killed Lord Aric last night. Cut him right along the jawline. Missed his throat by no more than a sparrow's dick. Shad's questioning the steward now. He's a tough lad, but I reckon you'll hear him screaming before long. Best eat your breakfast quick. I tell you there's nothing like hearing a man scream to make you lose your appetite.'

Niallad heard the first two guards moving away. The others fell silent for a few moments. Then one said, 'Reckon that Norda would be great in bed.'

231

'That's true, Gren. Until Marja finds out, and cuts off your prick.'

'Don't even joke about it!' said the other, with feeling. 'She would, you know.'

Niallad turned towards the Grey Man. But he was gone.

The youth was shocked and stared around. He had heard nothing, not a whisper of cloth against the rocks. He sat still, wondering what to do. Then he heard a grunt from above, followed by a heavy thud. Looking up, he saw the Grey Man lean over the overhang.

'Traverse to the left and climb up,' he said.

Niallad did so, hauling himself over the top. The two guards were both dead. The Grey Man was dragging one body inside the door of a crudely fashioned building. Niallad just stood there. Only moments ago these men had been talking about a pretty woman. Now they would talk to no one ever again. In that moment Niallad realized the Grey Man had been waiting for the guards to change, so that when he killed them he could be sure they would not be discovered for some time. The man was chilling! Niallad had always believed Gaspir to be one of the toughest men he had ever known. But he was merely a leaf, ripped from the tree by the fury of the Grey Man's storm. Now other leaves had fallen. Niallad could still hear the voices of the guards in his mind, ordinary men, dreaming ordinary dreams.

The Grey Man dragged the second corpse inside, then returned with a bucket of water and doused the blood on the ground. 'Come inside,' he said, his voice cool.

On leaden legs Niallad stepped across the threshold. The bodies were to the right of the door. The Grey Man pushed it closed and led Niallad into a long, dark windowless room. He lit two lanterns, hanging them on the wall, and Niallad saw that the room was hung with weapons, and targets had been placed around it, some round, as if for archery, others shaped into the forms of men.

'They think you were responsible for the massacre,' said Niallad.

'It is no surprise. Murder and lies usually go together.'

'I thought you had killed Aric.'

'So did I, boy. The rug moved under my feet as I lunged at him. Perhaps I'm getting too old for this kind of life.'

The Grey Man stripped off his silk jerkin, leggings and boots, hurling them to a nearby bench. From a chest set against one wall he drew out a leather hunting shirt, buckskin leggings and knee-length moccasins. Dressing swiftly he strapped on a sword-belt then looped

232

a baldric, with seven throwing knives, over his shoulder. He glanced back at Niallad. 'Get out of those clothes,' he said. He delved into the chest once more and produced a second shirt of dark leather, which he tossed to Niallad.

'Why did you save me?' asked Niallad.

The Grey Man stood silently for a moment. 'To pay a debt, boy,' he said at last.

'My name is Niallad. Please be so kind as to use it.'

'Very well, Niallad. Get out of those clothes and find yourself a weapon that suits you. I would suggest a shortsword, but there are several sabres. Also choose a hunting knife.'

'A debt to whom?'

The Grey Man paused. 'This is no time for questions.'

'I am the Duke's son . . .' Niallad hesitated, seeing again his father's corpse. 'I am the Duke of Kydor,' he continued, his voice trembling. 'I have seen you kill four men tonight. I want to know why I am here, and what are your intentions.'

The Grey Man moved to a bench and sat down. He rubbed a hand across his face and Niallad saw how tired he was. He was not young, and there were dark rings below his eyes. 'It was my intention,' said the Grey Man, 'to board a ship and leave this land, to find a place where there were no wars, no murders, no scheming politicians, no greed. *That* was my intention. Instead I am about to be hunted once more. Why did I save you? Because a ghost came to a friend of mine. Because you are young and I knew you feared assassination. Because I am a fool, and somewhere deep inside me there is still a semblance of honour. Take your pick. As to my intentions towards you? I have none. Now, choose a weapon and let us leave more questions until we are away from here.'

'Who was the ghost?' persisted Niallad.

'Your grandfather, Orien the Battle King.'

'Why would he come to you?'

'He didn't. As I said, he came to a friend.' The Grey Man placed his hand on Niallad's shoulder. 'I know this has been a terrible night for you but, believe me, it could get worse. We do not have the time to talk now. Later, when we are away from here, I will answer what questions you have. All right?'

The Grey Man moved away. Niallad removed his tunic and donned the shirt. It was too large, but it felt comfortable. He walked around the room, examining the weapons on display. He chose a sabre with a blued blade and a fist-guard of black-stained brass. It was beautifully balanced. Finding the scabbard and belt, he tried to put it on. But the belt was too large. 'Here,' said the Grey Man, tossing him a baldric with a scabbard ring attached. Niallad settled it into place and slipped the scabbard through the reinforced leather loop.

'What do we do now?' asked Niallad.

'We live or we die,' said the Grey Man.

Emrin's head sagged forward. Blood was dripping from his mouth. His upper body was a sea of pain. 'I don't seem to be hearing any more smart remarks,' said Shad. His fist thundered against the side of Emrin's head. The chair to which he was tied swayed and fell to the floor. 'Get him up!' ordered Shad. Rough hands grabbed him. He felt sick as he was wrenched upright.

Shad's fingers took hold of Emrin's hair, yanking his head back. 'You want to say something funny now, Emrin?' he asked. Emrin's left eye was closed, but he stared silently into Shad's hatchet face. He wanted to summon up the courage for another insult, but there was nothing left. 'You see, lads, he wasn't so tough.'

'I don't . . . know anything,' whispered Emrin. Shad's fist slammed into his face, rocking his head back.

Emrin spat out a broken tooth and sagged forward once more. Shad yanked his head back. 'I no longer care if you know anything, Emrin. I've always hated you. Did you know that? Strutting around, fine as you like, with the Grey Man's money in your pockets. Buying the pretty girls, looking down on us *common* soldiers. So you know what I'm going to do? I'm going to beat you to death. I'm going to watch you suffocate on your own blood. What do you think of that?'

'Hey, come on, Shad,' put in another soldier, 'there's no call for that.'

'You can shut your mouth! If you're that squeamish wait outside.'

Emrin's heart sank as he heard the rasp of the door latch being lifted.

'Now what shall we do first to entertain you, Emrin?' asked Shad. 'Perhaps we should cut off your fingers. Or maybe . . .' Emrin felt the touch of a dagger against his groin. For the first time he screamed, the sound echoing around the ceiling of the Oak Room.

Hurling himself back against the chair Emrin tipped it and crashed to the floor, struggling furiously with his bonds. 'Pick him up,' ordered Shad. The two remaining guards moved to the chair.

From his position on the floor Emrin saw the door open. The Grey Man stepped inside, a small double-winged crossbow in his hand.

'Cut him loose,' said the Grey Man, 'and I shall let you live.' His voice was calm and conversational. The three soldiers in the room backed away, drawing their weapons.

It was Shad who spoke first. 'Big of you,' he said. 'But that weapon only has two bolts. There are three of us.'

The Grey Man's arm extended. A bolt sliced through the air, punching into Shad's throat. He stumbled back then fell to his knees, choking on his own blood. 'Now there are two of you,' said the Grey Man. 'Cut him loose.'

The guards cast nervous glances at the dying Shad. One drew a knife and slashed through the ropes binding Emrin to the chair. Then he dropped the weapon and backed away to the wall. The other man followed his lead. The Grey Man walked past Emrin to the mortally wounded Shad. The man was weakly trying to pull the bolt from his throat. The Grey Man wrenched it clear. Blood spurted from the wound. Gagging and choking Shad rolled to the floor. His legs kicked out and he died.

Emrin forced himself to his knees and tried to stand. He staggered. The Grey Man caught him. 'Steady yourself. Take a few deep breaths. I need you to be able to ride.'

'Yes, sir,' mumbled Emrin.

A young man appeared at Emrin's side. He saw that it was the Duke's son, Niallad. 'Let me help you,' he said. Emrin leant in to him.

'Go to the stable,' said the Grey Man. 'Saddle two mounts and the steeldust. I will see you there presently.'

Supported by the youth, Emrin moved through the doorway. The body of the guard who had left the room was lying on the rug. His throat had been cut. Supported by Niallad, Emrin made it to the main doors and out into the sunlight. The fresh air helped to revive him, and by the time they reached the stables he was walking unsupported.

Norda was waiting there, with several small sacks of supplies. She ran to Emrin. 'Oh my poor dear,' she said, reaching up and stroking his bruised and swollen face.

'Not . . . so pretty, eh?'

'You look good to me,' she said, 'but you'd best be seeing to your horses. The Gentleman wants his steeldust saddled. He told me that.' She took his hand. 'Now, you listen to me, Emrin, the Gentleman is a fine man, but he has many enemies. You look after him.'

Suddenly, despite all his pain, Emrin laughed. 'Me? Look after *him*? Ah, Norda, what a thought!'

The Grey Man strode from the palace and along the gravel-covered path. Norda curtsied as she saw him. Emrin saw that his face was grim. 'Can you ride?' asked the Grey Man.

'I can, sir.'

Niallad came from the stables, leading three saddled horses, two roans and the steeldust gelding. The Grey Man stepped into the saddle and called to Norda, 'My thanks to you, girl.' Norda curtsied. 'And tell Matze Chai to return home.'

'I will, sir.'

Emrin walked to the first of the roans and hauled himself painfully into the saddle, then followed the Grey Man and the youth as they rode towards the trees.

They had been riding in silence for almost an hour when Emrin heard the youth say, 'The guards will raise the alarm. How soon before we are followed?'

'We have a little time,' answered the Grey Man.

The youth was silent for a moment. 'You killed them, didn't you?' he said at last.

'Yes, I killed them.'

'You told them you would let them live if they cut him loose. What kind of a man are you?'

Emrin winced as he heard the question.

The Grey Man did not answer it. Swinging his horse, he rode back to Emrin. 'Head west towards the forest, keeping the ruins to the south. If you see mist keep clear of it. I will catch up with you before dusk.'

'Yes, sir.' As the Grey Man rode back along the trail Emrin called, 'And thank you!' Heeling his horse, he moved up alongside the young man.

Niallad was flushed and angry. 'He has no concern for human life,' he said.

'He had concern for yours – and mine,' said Emrin. 'That'll do for mc.'

236

'You condone what he did?'

Emrin hauled on the reins and swung in the saddle to face the young noble. 'Look at me!' he said fiercely, struggling to control his anger. 'Those men were about to beat me to death. You think I care that they are dead? When I was a lad a group of us thought it would be great sport to go on a deer hunt. We had our new spears, and a couple of us had hunting bows. Seven of us, there were. We went into the mountains and soon came upon tracks. As we were closing in on our quarry we moved into some dense undergrowth. Suddenly, out of nowhere, a huge grizzly reared up. One of my friends – an idiot named Steff – loosed a shaft into it. Only two of us made it down from the mountain.'

'What has this to do with the Grey Man?' asked Niallad.

'If you anger a bear don't be surprised if it rips your guts out!' snapped Emrin.

Three-swords was hot, the sun beating down on his lacquered black hair while not a breath of breeze stirred against his ankle-length tunic of black silk. He stood quietly, his hands resting on the hilts of two curved swords, scabbarded at his sides. A third sword hung between his shoulder-blades, his ornate helm tied to the hilt. The *Kriaz-nor* scanned the clearing then moved swiftly across it and into the shadows of the trees, closely followed by his three black-garbed companions.

Once in the shade Three-swords paused, enjoying the respite from the harsh sun. His golden eyes scanned the trail. Irritation touched him. They should have been given a hunt-hound, for despite his tracking skills they had lost the trail three times so far. It was most galling. Deresh Karany had given them three days to kill the sword-bearers, and two were almost gone. If they failed to complete the task in the time allotted it was likely that one of the four would be executed. Three-swords knew he was unlikely to be the one chosen, but with Deresh Karany nothing was certain.

He glanced back at his squad. Most likely it would be Stone-four, he thought. Fresh from the Stone training pen, he had yet to earn a fighting name. He had talent, though, as his apprentice name showed. He had finished fourth of fifty in the Pen rankings for that year. Three-swords ordered his companions to remain where they were, then carefully scouted further along the deer trail that led south through the trees. The ground was hard. Three-swords moved on. He heard the sound of water trickling over rocks and moved through the undergrowth towards it. Here the ground was softer, and between two bushes he saw hoofprints, and alongside the water the deep impression left by a boot.

Calling out to his soldiers, Three-swords waited for them to join him. 'Maybe half a day, maybe less,' he said, his golden gaze focusing on the boot-print. 'Edges are drying out and crumbling.' The hulking, round-shouldered Iron-arm ambled forward. Pulling his scabbard from the black sash around his thick waist, Iron-arm dropped to his knees then bent over, sniffing at the print. Closing his eyes, he screened out the scents of his three companions. A male fox had urinated in the bushes close by, the musky smell all but masking the delicate aroma left by the humans. Opening his eyes, he looked into the grim features of his captain, Three-swords. 'One is very tired,' he said. 'The one with drying blood upon him. The other one – the *Riaj-nor* – is strong.'

'He is not *Riaj-nor*,' said Three-swords. 'Their order has died out. I am told they now have pale imitations calling themselves *Rajnee*. They have gone soft in this world. It happens.'

'Not to us,' said Stone-four.

Three-swords looked at the powerfully built young warrior. 'Until idiots start thinking that,' he said. Stone-four gave a low growl. His shoulders hunched. Three-swords stepped in close to the angry *Kriaz-nor*. 'You think you are ready to face me? You think you have the skill? Make the challenge, sheep turd! Make it – and I will take your head and eat your heart.'

For a moment it seemed that Stone-four would draw his sword. His hand hovered over the black hilt. Then he relaxed.

'Wise,' said Three-swords. 'Now you might live long enough to earn a name.'

'We should have them by nightfall,' said Iron-arm. 'If we push hard.'

'Better to reach them at midnight,' said Long-stride, the tallest of the quartet. His face was long and heavily bearded, his eyes deep-set, the pupils slitted. 'They'll be deep asleep.'

'I'd sooner kill them in combat,' said Stone-four.

'That's because you're young,' said Long-stride amiably. 'They taste better if they die relaxed. Is that not so, Three-swords?'

'Aye, it is true. Rage or fear stiffens the muscles. Don't know why. Midnight it is. We shall rest here for an hour.'

Three-swords moved away and sat by the stream. The powerful Iron-arm joined him. 'No sign of Striped-claw's squad. They must be near as close as us.'

'Maybe closer,' said Three-swords, dipping his hand into the stream and scooping water to his thin mouth.

Iron-arm dropped his voice. 'Then why agree to wait until midnight? You want Striped-claw to be first?'

Three-swords smiled. 'I do not like Striped-claw. Too much cat in him. One of these days I'll have to eat his heart. I'll wager it will taste bad.'

'So why allow him the glory of the kill?'

'All the stories talk of the great skill of the *Riaj-nor* and the deadly spell-poisons of their blades. If Striped-claw overcomes such a blade, and takes the heart of the warrior who carries it, I will be disappointed. But I shall shrug and live with it.'

'You don't think that he will?'

Three-swords thought about the question. 'Striped-claw – though a ferociously good swordsman – is foolhardy and reckless. It would neither surprise me nor break my heart to hear of him being cut down by a *Riaj-nor*.'

'You said these warriors were but pale imitations,' put in Iron-arm.

'I said that is what I have been told. I prefer to withhold judgement until I have seen for myself.'

Three-swords pulled the two scabbards from his waist sash and laid them on the ground. Then he stretched out on his side and closed his eyes.

Yes, Striped-claw would arrive first. He would rush in and engage the humans without any thought of their talents, relying on his own blistering speed and skill. With luck he would suffer hugely for it. Then his men would finish the humans and Three-swords and his squad could join them for the ritual feast. It was a good thought.

He lay quietly, allowing his body to relax.

It was good to be wandering this land. For nine years Three-swords had travelled with the army, surrounded by hundreds of fellow *Kriaz-nor*, sleeping with nine others in a crowded tent, marching in formation or attacking cities. In this land the sky seemed larger, and Three-swords found that he enjoyed the freedom his mission offered.

He dozed for a while, and then became aware that he was dreaming. He could see himself standing by a cabin, a stream running nearby, his children playing near the trees. He sat up, cursing inwardly. From where does such stupidity spring? he asked himself.

'Bad dream?' asked Iron-arm.

'No.' Three-swords pushed up the sleeve of his black silk tunic and gazed down on the fine wolf fur that covered his forearm. 'It will be good when the army comes through,' he said. 'I miss the life. Do you?'

Iron-arm shrugged. 'I don't miss Sky-dagger's snoring, or the smell of Tree-nine's feet.'

Three-swords rose and slid the two scabbards back into his sash. 'I am tired of this place,' he said. 'We will not wait until midnight.'

Kysumu tethered the horses and fed them the last of the grain. The sun was setting as he moved back into the campsite and prepared a small fire. Yu Yu was already asleep, his head resting on his cloak, his knees drawn up like a child. Kysumu gazed around at the trees, their trunks glowing in the light of the dying sun, and wished he had brought his charcoal and parchment. Instead he closed his eyes and tried for meditation. Yu Yu rolled on to his back and began to snore softly.

Kysumu sighed. For the first time in many years he felt somehow lost, adrift from his centre. Meditation would not come. An insect buzzed around his face and he brushed it away. He knew what was wrong, and the very moment that the seeds of his disquiet had been sown. Knowledge made it no easier to accept. Kysumu found himself thinking back to the years of training, but most of all his thoughts returned to the Star Lily, and the Night of Bitter Sweetness.

The Night was a mystery. All the students had heard of it, but none knew what it meant. Those *Rajnee* who had passed through it were sworn to secrecy.

Kysumu had joined the temple when he was thirteen, determined to become the greatest *Rajnee*. He had worked tirelessly, studying by day and night, absorbing the teachings, enduring the hardships. Not once did he complain of the bitter cold in the cell during winter, or the stifling heat of summer. At sixteen he had been sent to work on a poor farm for a season, to learn the life of the lowliest workers. He had toiled all season, working fifteen hours a day on arid land, rewarded with a bowl of thin soup and a hunk of bread. His bed was a straw mat beneath a lean-to. He had suffered with boils and dysentery. His teeth became loose. But he had endured.

His mentor had been pleased with him. A legend among the *Rajnee*, Mu Cheng was known as the Eye of the Storm. He had left the service of the emperor to serve ten years as a temple tutor. Every time Kysumu felt he could not go on he would think of the disdain in the eyes of Mu Cheng, and in that thought would find the courage to persevere. It was Mu Cheng who first taught Kysumu the Way of the Blade. This was the hardest of lessons, for Kysumu had spent years controlling himself, steeling his body against hardships, driving it often beyond its limits. This very control stopped him from becoming the swordsman he desired to be. In combat, Mu Cheng told him, the Way of the Blade was emptiness and surrender. Not surrender to an enemy, but the surrender of control, in order that the trained body could react instantly without thought. No fear, no anger, no imagination. The sword, said Mu Cheng, is not an extension of the man. The man must become an extension of the sword.

Two more years of strenuous physical work followed. By the end Kysumu was fast, his sword work dazzling. Mu Cheng announced himself satisfied, though pointed out there was much learning still to come.

Then came the Night of Bitter Sweetness.

Mu Cheng had taken him to a small palace in the foothills overlooking the Great River. It was a beautiful structure, with delicately fashioned towers, emblazoned with elegant statues, its walls plastered and painted red and gold, its gardens immaculate, pathways wending around shimmering fountains, beds of flowers in full bloom. The scent of roses, jasmine and honeysuckle hung in the air.

Mu Cheng led the bewildered Kysumu inside. In a large room a table had been laid, and an assortment of food was on display. The two men sat on gold-embossed chairs with satin cushions. For six years the student had dined on maize and boiled fish, hard bread and salted biscuits. On occasions he had tasted honey, but these were rare. On the table before him were pastries, cured meats, cheeses –

241

delicacies of every description. Kysumu gazed upon them. Mu Cheng produced a small phial from his pocket and poured the contents into a crystal goblet. 'Drink this,' he said. Kysumu did so. For a moment nothing happened. Then the most exquisite feeling began to seep into Kysumu's body. He began to laugh. 'What is this?' he asked.

'It is a mixture of seed oils and extracts. How do you feel?'

Mu Cheng's voice sounded strange, as if the words were floating around inside Kysumu's head, booming and fading. 'I feel . . . wonderful.'

'That is its purpose,' he heard Mu Cheng say. 'Now, eat.'

Kysumu tasted one of the pastries. It was exquisite. His body all but screamed with delight. He ate another, and another. Never in his life had he experienced such pleasure. Mu Cheng poured him a goblet of wine. As the evening progressed Kysumu almost passed out with joy. Such was his rapture that he failed to notice that Mu Cheng ate nothing, and merely drank water.

As the light began to fail two young women appeared, bringing lanterns which they hung on brass hooks. Kysumu watched them, noting the way their robes of silk clung to their bodies. They departed and another young woman entered. Her hair was black, drawn back from her face and held in place by a delicate net of silver threads. Her eyes were large and lustrous. She sat beside Kysumu, and, reaching out, pushed her fingers through his hair. At her touch he trembled and turned to look into her face. Her skin was pale and flawless, her lips red and moist. She took him by the hand and drew him to his feet.

'Go with her,' said Mu Cheng.

Kysumu followed the woman willingly, to a circular chamber and a large bed covered with satin sheets. Incense was burning, the scent heady and strong. The woman stood before him. Her hand went to a brooch at her shoulder. As she removed it her robe slipped away, as if it was made of liquid, flowing down over her body and pooling at her feet. Kysumu gazed with undisguised longing at her nakedness. She took his hands and raised them to her breasts. Kysumu moaned. His knees felt weak, his legs trembling. She drew him to the bed and undressed him. 'Who are you?' he asked huskily.

'I am the Star Lily,' she told him. These were the only words he would ever hear her say.

During the next few hours, until he fell into a contented sleep, the young *Rajnee* discovered the true meaning of ecstasy.

As the dawn was breaking Kysumu awoke to the sound of bird-song beyond the window. His body was aching, his head pounding. He sat up and groaned. The events of the night came back to him and he felt a surge of joy that swept away his headache. He looked around for the woman, but she was gone.

Rising from the bed, he dressed himself and walked through the palace until he found the scene of last night's feast.

Mu Cheng was still there. Upon the table was a goblet of water and a loaf of black bread.

'Join me for breakfast,' said Mu Cheng.

Kysumu sat. 'Will they be bringing more food?'

'This *is* our food.'

'Will the Star Lily be joining us?'

'She has gone.'

'Gone? Where?'

'Back to the world, Kysumu.'

'I do not understand.'

'You have two choices now. To be a *Rajnee* or to be a wandering warrior, selling your sword and living among men and women.'

'Why have you done this to me?'

'It is not hard, student, to forswear pleasures you have never experienced. There is no strength in that. Now you truly know all that the world can offer. The memory of this night will always be with you, dark and seductive, tugging at your resolve. In many ways this is the greatest test for a *Rajnee*. It is why it is called the Night of Bitter Sweetness.'

Mu Cheng had been right. In the years that followed Kysumu would often dream of the Star Lily and her flawless skin. Yet he had resisted the urge to find her, or to seek anyone like her. He did this in order to be the best *Rajnee* he could be.

Yet here he sat, unable to commune with the spirit of the greatest *Rajnee* to walk the earth. Instead that spirit had chosen to visit a lascivious ditch-digger with a stolen sword.

It was this that stopped Kysumu from reaching the required level of non-concentration required for meditation. The thought rankled.

Yu Yu Liang sat up and stretched, then pushed himself to his feet. To Kysumu's surprise he began to move through a series of muscle-loosening exercises.

'Where did you learn those?' asked Kysumu. Yu Yu ignored him, and continued to exercise. The *Rajnee* sat quietly as the ditch-digger began to dance through the elaborate steps of the Heron and Leopard, a series of ritualistic motions interspersed with moments of utter stillness. At the conclusion Yu Yu drew his sword and began a second series of exercises, thrusting, blocking, leaping and twirling. Kysumu's surprise turned to astonishment. As the exercise continued, Yu Yu became more and more supple, his speed increasing, until the blade moved like a blur.

Finally he stopped, sheathed the sword, and strolled across to Kysumu, squatting down before him. 'You know who I am?' asked the voice of Yu Yu Liang.

'You are Qin Chong, the first of the *Rajnee*.'

'I am.'

'I have tried to reach you. You did not hear me.'

'I heard you. But I needed all my energy to commune with the *pria-shath*. He tells me you are skilled with that blade. May the Source make that a golden truth, for the enemy is upon us.'

CHAPTER TWELVE

EVEN AS HE SPOKE, FOUR BLACK-GARBED WARRIORS STEPPED FROM the shadows, moving into the clearing, their dark, curved swords in their hands. Kysumu rose and drew his own blade.

Qin Chong, in the body of Yu Yu Liang, drifted towards the centre of the clearing, his movements unhurried, his sword arm by his side, the blade trailing on the hard-packed ground.

Kysumu relaxed his body into the Way of the Sword, the great emptiness in which there was no fear, no exultation, merely a sense of quiet harmony. The four warriors spread out. Kysumu noted the way they moved. All were perfectly in balance. Kysumu sensed great strength in them, and guessed they would be fast. He could feel their confidence.

They did not rush in, and Kysumu observed they were deferring to the largest warrior. His robe of black silk, slashed to the waist, bore a silver brooch, shaped like the claw of a lion. Perhaps it was a badge of rank among the *Kriaz-nor*, thought Kysumu. The leader moved to face Qin Chong, who still stood quietly, his blade trailing.

Then he darted forward, his speed awesome. Kysumu blinked – and almost lost the Way. No human could move that fast! The dark sword lanced at Qin Chong's face. His own blade parried it, and the two fighters spun away. The *Kriaz-nor* attacked again and again. The other three warriors stood by silently. The two swords clashed repeatedly, setting up a discordant yet almost rhythmic music in the clearing. Sparks flew from the blades. Never in his life had Kysumu seen such brilliant swordplay. It was as if the two warriors had choreographed each move, practising it for years. The blades moved faster than Kysumu's eyes could follow, glittering in the new moon-light. The fighters spun away once more. There was blood on the wolfskin jerkin worn by Qin Chong. Then the swords clashed again in a whirlwind of shrieking steel. Neither of the swordsmen had spoken, and the struggle continued with renewed ferocity. Kysumu saw blood spray from the *Kriaz-nor*'s face as Qin Chong's blade nicked the skin of his cheekbone. The *Kriaz-nor* leapt back. 'I shall be proud to eat your heart,' he said. 'You are worthy.'

Qin Chong did not reply. The *Kriaz-nor* attacked again. Qin Chong leapt to his right, the sword of Yu Yu Liang flashing in a tight arc. The *Kriaz-nor* staggered for several steps, then turned. His belly opened, his entrails spilling out. With a strangled cry he tried to make one last charge, but Qin Chong stepped in to meet him, parrying his blade and sending a vicious cut into the *Kriaz-nor*'s neck, half severing the head. The huge warrior toppled to the ground.

For a moment all was stillness. Kysumu transferred his gaze to the other three warriors. Without their leader they seemed unsure, con-fidence draining from them. Suddenly one of them screamed a battle cry and ran at Kysumu. The little *Rajnee* did not wait to meet the charge, but stepped in. The *Kriaz-nor*'s blade swept down. Kysumu sidestepped, his own sword slashing up through the sword arm. The *Kriaz-nor*'s sword flew through the air, the hand still grasping the hilt. The warrior drew a serrated dagger and leapt at the *Rajnee*, who plunged his blade deep into the *Kriaz-nor*'s chest. A grunt of surprise and pain came from the warrior. Kysumu looked into the man's slitted golden eyes and watched the light of life fade from them. Dragging clear his sword, the *Rajnee* moved to stand alongside Qin Chong. The remaining two *Kriaz-nor* faded back into the forest.

'More will join them,' said Qin Chong. 'Let us ride.'

Sheathing his blade, he ran to the horses. Kysumu followed him. Swiftly they saddled their mounts and rode from the clearing. Pushing the horses hard for several miles, they came at last to a small valley. Qin Chong cut away from the trail and dismounted. Kysumu joined him. Qin Chong led the two geldings back to the trail and slapped their rumps. Both beasts headed off towards the south. Ducking back into the trees, Qin Chong beckoned Kysumu to follow him, then ran down a wooded slope and into a fast-flowing stream. Wading along it for almost a quarter of a mile Qin Chong halted alongside an old oak. There was an overhanging branch almost ten feet above the stream. Removing his sword and scabbard Qin Chong hurled it to the bank beyond the tree, then turned to Kysumu. 'Cup your hands,' he ordered. Kysumu did so. Qin Chong placed his right foot in the cup, then launched himself upwards. His hands grabbed at the branch and he hauled himself over it. Curling his legs around the bough he hung upside down, extending his arms towards Kysumu. The *Rajnee* threw his own sword to the bank, then leapt, caught hold of Qin Chong's wrists, then drew himself up until he could reach the branch.

Once back on firm ground Qin Chong headed south-east, climbing ever higher until they reached a small cave created by a sheet of overhanging rock. Here he sat, breathing heavily. Kysumu squatted down alongside him. Blood was still seeping from a shallow wound high on Qin Chong's chest.

'The *pria-shath* was right,' said Qin Chong. 'You do know how to use your blade. It was fortunate, however, that your opponent was panicked and frightened.'

'I have never seen warriors who can move at such speed,' admitted Kysumu.

'The advantages of the meld,' Qin Chong told him.

'How was it that you could make Yu Yu's body match them?'

'In all animals muscles work in rhythmic harmony, sharing the load. A man lifts a cup to his lips. He does not use *all* his strength to do this. Only a few of the muscles in his arm will be needed. If he lifts a rock he will use more. Imagine a muscle as being, say, twenty men. If you have to raise the rock ten times then the first time two of the men will do it, the second time two more, and so on. But it is possible – though not wise – to engage all of the men at once. This is what I did, though Yu Yu will not thank me when he wakes.' He smiled. 'Ah, but I have enjoyed this last moment of the flesh, the scent of the forest, the feeling of cool air in my lungs.'

'You will feel it again, surely, when we find the Men of Clay? You will return to aid us.'

'I will not return, Kysumu. These are my last moments in the world.'

'There is so much I want to ask you.'

'There is only one question that burns in your heart, swordsman. Why were you not chosen to be the *pria-shath*?'

'Can you tell me?'

247

'Better for you to discover the truth yourself,' said Qin Chong. 'Farewell, Kysumu.'

With that he closed his eyes, and was gone.

Niallad was dreaming about his father. They were hawking in the high country close to the castle. His father's bird, the legendary Eera, had brought down three hares. Niallad's bird, young and newly trained, had flown to a nearby tree and would not come down at his call.

'You must have patience,' said his father, as they sat together. 'Bird and man never form a friendship. It is a partnership. As long as you feed him he will stay with you. He will not, however, offer you loyalty or friendship.'

'I thought he liked me. He dances whenever I come close.'

'We shall see.'

They had waited for some hours, and then the hawk had flown away, never to return.

Niallad awoke. For a heartbeat he felt warm and secure in his father's love. Then, with terrible ferocity, reality smote him and he groaned aloud. He sat up, his heart breaking. Emrin was asleep on the ground close by. The Grey Man was seated upon a rock close to the horses. He did not look round. His figure was silhouetted by the bright moon and Niallad guessed he was staring back over the moonlit plain, seeking signs of pursuit. He had rejoined them some hours before, leading them to this high, lonely place, bordering the trees. The Grey Man had said little to him.

The young man rose from his blanket and strolled to where the Grey Man sat. 'May I join you?' he asked. The Grey Man nodded. Niallad sat alongside him on the flat rock. 'I am sorry for my words earlier. It was ungrateful of me. Without you I would have been killed by a man I trusted. And Emrin would be dead.'

'You were not wrong,' said the Grey Man. 'I am a killer. Did you have a bad dream?'

'No, a good one.'

'Ah, yes. They can hurt worse than fire on the soul.'

'I cannot believe my father is dead,' said Niallad. 'I thought he would either live for ever or die swinging his great sword and cleaving his enemies.'

'When it comes, death is usually sudden,' said the Grey Man.

They sat in silence for a while. Niallad found himself calmed by the

248

Grey Man's presence. 'I trusted Gaspir,' said the boy at last. 'He had the ability to make me lose my fear. He seemed so strong. So loyal. I shall never trust anyone again.'

'Do not even think that,' warned the Grey Man. 'There are people who are worthy of trust. If you become suspicious of everyone you will never have true friends.'

'Do you have friends?'

The Grey Man looked at him and smiled. 'No. Therefore I speak from experience.'

'What do you think will happen now?'

'They'll be more careful who they send after us. Tough men, trackers, foresters.'

'Demons?' asked the boy, trying to disguise his fear.

'Aye, and demons,' agreed the Grey Man.

'We are beaten, aren't we? Panagyn and Aric have thousands of men. I have nothing. If I was to make it back to the capital I wouldn't know where to go.'

'The armies mean nothing without men to lead them,' said the Grey Man. 'When I have you in a place of safety I shall return. Then we will see.'

'You would go back to Carlis? Why?'

The Grey Man did not answer, but pointed down to the plain below. In the distance Niallad could see a line of riders. 'Wake Emrin,' ordered the Grey Man. 'It is time to be moving.'

Yu Yu groaned as he awoke. He felt as if a herd of oxen had spent the night walking across his body. With a grunt of pain he struggled up. Kysumu was at the mouth of the cave, his sword in his lap. 'I don't want to be a hero,' grumbled Yu Yu.

'You have been asleep for hours,' said Kysumu wearily. The little *Rajnee* rose and padded away from the cave. Yu Yu pushed himself to his knees and groaned again. Glancing down, he saw the fresh stitches in the new wound to his shoulder. 'Every time I fight I get hurt,' he said, though Kysumu was nowhere in sight. 'Every time. And when a great hero takes over my body *he* gets hurt. I'm tired of my body getting hurt. Once we find the Men of Clay I'm going home. I'm going to dig ditches.' He thought about it for a moment, remembering the threat to his life. 'No, first I'm going to sneak into Shi Da's house and cut his throat. *Then* I'll dig ditches.'

'You are talking to yourself,' said Kysumu, returning to the cave with a double handful of dark berries. He offered them to Yu Yu, who sat down and ate gratefully. They did no more than dent the edge of his appetite.

'Qin Chong came to me,' said Kysumu.

'I know. I was there. Here. Whatever! He was very complimentary about my strength and speed. We fought well, hey? Cut his bastard head off.'

'You fought well,' agreed Kysumu. 'But now there are six more *Kriaz-nor* closing in on us.'

'Six? That's a lot,' said Yu Yu. 'Don't know if I could kill six.'

'*You* couldn't kill one,' said Kysumu, an edge of irritation in his voice.

'I know why you are angry. Qin Chong wouldn't tell you why you weren't the *pria-shath*.'

Kysumu sighed. 'You are correct, Yu Yu. All my life I have struggled to be the perfect *Rajnee*, to be worthy of the name, and to uphold the standards set by men like Qin Chong. I could have been rich, the owner of a palace, the lord of a province. I could have wed the Star Lily.'

'The Star Lily?' queried Yu Yu.

'It is not important. I have eschewed all riches and remained a humble swordsman. What more could I have done to be worthy?'

'I don't know,' said Yu Yu. 'I haven't done any of these things. But, then, I didn't want to be the *pria-shath*.' He wandered out of the cave, seeking more berries and finding a bush some sixty paces away. They were not quite ripe, but they tasted heavenly. Yu Yu had no idea why Kysumu longed to be the *pria-shath*. What was so great about being hunted and hungry, with killers on your trail? As far as Yu Yu was concerned he wished Kysumu *had* been the *pria-shath*. Having stripped the bush Yu Yu turned – and stopped in his tracks. The cave was set into the side of a domed hill. Yu Yu stared at it, remembering his spirit journeys with Qin Chong. As fast as his bruised limbs would carry him he hurried back to the cave. 'We are here,' he told Kysumu. 'This is it! This is the hill of the Men of Clay.'

'You are sure?'

'Certain.'

The two men moved to the open air, scanning the hillside. 'How do we enter?' asked Kysumu.

'I don't know.'

Slowly they traversed the base. No trees grew upon the hillside, and there were no openings of any kind, save for the cave in which they had rested. Kysumu climbed to the top, scanning the surrounding ground. Then he returned to where Yu Yu waited.

'I can see no sign of an entrance,' said Kysumu.

They walked back to the cave and Kysumu began to examine the grey walls. They were seamless. Yu Yu waited outside. He, too, was mystified. In his dream he had seen the *Riaj-nor* walking to this hillside and vanishing inside. He did not recall there being a cave, nor indeed an overhang like the one above, jutting from the hillside like a lean-to roof.

He walked back to the berry bush and stared at the overhang and the land below it. He had been a ditch-digger and a builder for most of his adult life, and he knew a little about the movement of soil. It seemed to him then that the area around the cave mouth could have eroded, exposing the cave. Kysumu joined him. 'I can find nothing,' he said.

Yu Yu ignored him, and walked to the rock face, just to the left of the cave mouth. His body was still aching, but he reached up, found a handhold and slowly began to climb. Had he not been so bruised and weary the climb would have been easy. As it was he was grunting as he hauled himself over the lip of the overhang. 'Up here!' he called, beckoning Kysumu to follow him. The little *Rajnee* scaled the face swiftly. There was a slab of stone, some six feet high and four feet wide, set vertically into the hillside.

'It looks like a door,' said Kysumu, pushing at it. It did not budge.

Yu Yu did not answer. He was staring towards the tree line, where six warriors had emerged.

Kysumu saw them too. 'At least they don't have bows,' he muttered. 'Perhaps I can kill them as they climb.'

Yu Yu stepped towards the rock door, extending his hand. As his fingers touched the stone it shimmered. Just like a pebble falling into a pond. Tiny waves rippled out. Yu Yu stared at the ripples, then he reached out. His hand passed through the door as if through a cold fog. He gestured to Kysumu, who was watching the advancing *Kriaz-nor*. 'I have found the way in,' he said, pointing to the cold stone.

'What are you talking about?'

Yu Yu swung back – to see that the entrance was solid stone once more.

'Take my hand,' said Yu Yu.

'We have you now, little men!' shouted a *Kriaz-nor*, running forward and scrambling up towards them. Kysumu's blade swept into the air.

Yu Yu touched the stone once more, and, as the ripples began, grabbed Kysumu's arm and dragged him through the fog.

On the other side they stood in pitch darkness.

'Oh, this is wonderful!' said Yu Yu. 'What now?' Immediately a score of lanterns flared. Kysumu narrowed his eyes against the sudden glare. As his vision acclimatized he saw that they were standing in a short tunnel, leading to a vast domed hall. Releasing Yu Yu's hand, Kysumu moved to the end of the tunnel. Within the hall, standing in ranks, were several hundred dazzlingly white, full-sized clay figures. Each of the figures was of a *Riaj-nor* swordsman. They were magnificently cast and sculpted. Towards the front of the silent army three of the figures lay broken. A section of rock had fallen from the roof, shattering them. Kysumu picked up a section of a fragmented head and examined it. He had never seen such quality of workmanship. Reverently replacing it on the ground he moved through the ghostly ranks, gazing upon their faces. Such nobility. Such humanity. Kysumu was awestruck. He felt he could see modest heroism in every face. These were the great ones, who had fought a colossal evil for the benefit of mankind. Kysumu's heart swelled. He felt immensely privileged merely to gaze upon their features.

Yu Yu sat down, leaning his back against the wall and closing his eyes.

After a while Kysumu came back and sat alongside him. 'What do we do now?' he asked.

'You do as you please,' said Yu Yu. 'I need to rest.' Stretching out, he laid his head on his arm and fell asleep.

Kysumu rose. He could not take his eyes from the grim Men of Clay. Every face was different, though each wore the same armour, ornate helms that flared out to protect the neck, torso protectors that seemed to have been created from coins, perfectly round and held together by small rings. Each of the warriors was also clothed in a full-length tunic, split to the waist at front and back. Their swords were like his own, long and slightly curved. Kysumu strolled through the ranks again, wondering which of these men was Qin Chong.

The lanterns burned brightly. Kysumu examined one, and saw that

252

it carried no oil, no fuel of any kind. A globe of glass sat upon a small cup, white light radiating from its centre.

Slowly he walked around the domed hall. On one side he found hundreds of small golden items laid on a wide rocky shelf. Some were rings, others brooches or wrist bangles, scattered and piled one upon another. There were pendants, ornaments and tiny good-luck figures shaped in the form of animals, dogs, cats, even the head of a bear. Mystified, Kysumu returned to where Yu Yu slept. He did not try to wake him. Yu Yu was exhausted.

A dull thumping sound echoed through the hall. Kysumu guessed that the *Kriaz-nor* had climbed to the overhang and were seeking a way through. They will not move that rock, he thought. But sooner or later he and Yu Yu would have to leave this place and face them.

He stared once more at the Men of Clay. 'Well, we have found you, my brothers,' he said. 'But what happens now?'

Matze Chai sat quietly, waiting for the interrogation to begin. He had heard of the massacre at the Winter Palace, and knew that Waylander was now, once more, a hunted man. What he did not know was why he had been summoned to the Oak Room of Waylander's home.

The captain of his guard, young Liu, was standing at his master's right-hand side. Opposite sat the magicker Eldicar Manushan, and two men who had been introduced as Lords Aric and Panagyn. Matze instantly found himself disliking both of them. Aric had the look of a contented weasel, while Panagyn's face was flat and brutal. A slender blond-haired little boy stood beside the magicker. Despite himself Matze found himself warming to the little lad, which was most strange since he loathed children.

The silence grew. Finally Eldicar Manushan spoke. 'It is my understanding that the individual known as the Grey Man is one of your clients.'

Matze said nothing, but he held the magicker's gaze, and maintained an expression of icy disdain.

'Is it your intention to answer none of my questions?' asked the magicker.

'I was not aware that it was a question,' said Matze. 'It seemed to me a statement of fact. There is no secret concerning my visit. I organize the financial dealings of the Grey Man, as you call him, within the lands of the Chiatze.'

'My apologies, Matze Chai,' said Eldicar, with a thin smile. 'By what name do you know this man?'

'I know him as Dakeyras.'

'Where is he from?'

'Some land in the far south-west. Drenan or Vagria. It is not my business to enquire too deeply into the background of my clients. I am retained to make their finances grow. That is my talent.'

'Are you aware that your client and a vile sorceress caused the death of more than a hundred people, including the Duke and his lady?'

'If you say so,' answered Matze, pulling a perfumed handkerchief from his red silk sleeve. Delicately he dabbed it to his nose.

'We do say it, you slant-eyed horse turd,' snapped Lord Panagyn.

Matze did not look at the man, but kept his gaze firmly on the face of the magicker.

'Your client has also kidnapped the heir to the Duchy, dragged him from the palace amid the slaughter.'

'An amazingly gifted man, obviously,' said Matze. 'And yet, apparently, not very intelligent.'

'Why is that?' asked Eldicar.

'He summons demons to wipe out the Duke and all his followers, yet somehow fails to kill the two most powerful lords. Instead of slaying them – a feat he could accomplish with ease – he decides to kidnap the Duke's son and, thus burdened, rushes off into the night, leaving his enemies alive and in possession of his castle, his lands and a great deal of his wealth. Hard to imagine what he thought he was achieving. Remarkably stupid.'

'What are you insinuating?' snarled Aric.

'I would have thought that was obvious,' said Matze. 'My client, as you well know, was not responsible for the murders. He had no reason to kill the Duke, and certainly would not resort to summoning demons if he could. So stop playing stupid games. I do not care who rules this realm, or who summoned the demons. I am supremely uninterested in such matters. I am a merchant. My interests lie in commerce.'

'Very well, Matze Chai,' said Eldicar smoothly. 'Let us put aside questions of guilt and innocence. We need to find the Grey Man, and we need you to tell us all you know about him.'

'My clients require from me a great deal of discretion,' Matze told him. 'I do not gossip about their affairs.'

'I am not sure that you realize the peril of your predicament, sir,' said Eldicar, his voice hardening. 'The Grey Man is our enemy, and must be found. The more we know about him the easier the task. It would be better for you to speak freely than to have the words wrung from you. And, believe me, I have the power to tear the words from you in between screams of agony.' Eldicar smiled and leant back in his chair. 'However, let us put aside such thoughts for a moment and examine ways in which you might reconsider your position and become my friend.'

'Friendship is always welcome,' said Matze.

'You are an old man, close to death. Would you like to be young again?'

'Who would not?'

'A small demonstration then – as a gesture of good faith.' Eldicar lifted his hand. A fist-sized globe of shimmering blue smoke appeared. It sped from his fingers, flowing into the nostrils and mouth of the startled Liu. The Chiatze guard fell to his knees, choking. Blue smoke exploded from his lungs and he gasped, taking in great gulps of air. The smoke flowed around Matze Chai. The merchant tried to hold his breath, but the smoke clung to his face. At the last he inhaled. A tingling sensation seeped through his limbs. He felt his heart beat faster, his muscles swelling with new life. Energy roared within him. He felt strong again. His vision cleared, and he found he could see with greater clarity than he had for years. He turned to Liu. The young captain had regained his feet. Matze's expression hardened as he saw Liu's dark hair was showing grey at the temples.

'How does it feel, Matze Chai?' asked Eldicar Manushan.

'It feels very fine,' answered Matze coldly. 'However, it would have been good manners to ask my captain if he objected to losing some of his youth.'

'I have given you twenty years, merchant. I can give you twenty more. You can be young and virile once more. You can enjoy your wealth in a manner denied to you for decades. Are you now willing to be my friend?'

Matze took a deep breath. 'My client is unique, magicker. Some men are talented painters and sculptors, others can grow any kind of bloom, in any kind of climate. You are obviously skilled in the arcane arts. But my client is a master of only one skill, one terrible talent. He is a killer. In all my long and – thus far – remarkably uneventful life I have neither known nor heard of anyone to match him. He has fought demons, and magickers, and were-beasts. He is still here.' Matze Chai gave a thin smile. 'But then I think you already realize this. He was supposed to have died in your massacre, and he did not. Now you believe you are hunting him. It is an illusion. He is hunting you. You are already dead men. I do not desire friendship with dead men.'

Eldicar looked at him in silence. 'It is time to know pain, Matze Chai,' he said. As he spoke he raised his hand and pointed to Liu. The officer's dagger slid from its sheath, spun, and plunged through Liu's right eye socket. He fell without a sound.

Matze sat silently, his hands upon his lap as the guards moved in.

Three-swords stepped back from the rock door. Iron-arm continued to beat at the stone with the pommel of his sword. 'Enough,' said Three-swords. 'It will not budge.'

'How, then, did they pass through?'

'I do not know. But we have searched the hillside and this is the only way out. So we wait.'

The two *Kriaz-nor* climbed down to join the others. Long-stride was sitting down in the cave mouth, Stone-four beside him. The two survivors of Striped-claw's group were standing apart. Three-swords called them to him. They were both fresh from the Pens. It was stupid of Striped-claw to have chosen them for this task, but entirely predictable. Striped-claw liked to impress, and Pen-younglings were easier to impress than seasoned warriors. 'Tell me of the fight,' said Three-swords.

One of the warriors began to speak. 'Striped-claw told us to stand back while he made the kill. Then he fought the one in the wolfskin. It was very fast. The human moved like a *Kriaz-nor*. Great speed. Then Striped-claw went down. It was then that Hill-six attacked the second man. He died.'

'Then you ran?'

'Yes, sir.'

Three-swords stepped back from the pair and drew one of his swords. In one move of dazzling speed he beheaded the speaker. The second warrior turned to run, but Three-swords was upon him within a few paces, his blade slashing through the back of the *Kriaz nor*'s neck. Turning, he strolled back to Iron-arm. 'Fresh

256

meat,' he said. 'But leave the hearts. I do not want the blood of cowards flowing in my veins.'

At that moment the ground began to vibrate. Three-swords almost lost his footing.

'Earthquake!' shouted Stone-four.

A dull sound like distant thunder boomed across the clearing. A dislodged boulder rolled past them.

'It is coming from inside the hill,' said Iron-arm.

Another boulder moved, falling upon the overhang and bouncing out to crash to the ground close by. 'Back to the tree-line,' ordered Three-swords. Iron-arm ran to one of the bodies and, hauling it behind him, followed his three comrades back to the safety of the trees.

Yu Yu felt stronger when he awoke, his bruised body refreshed. Kysumu was sitting cross-legged beside him, eyes closed and deep in a meditation trance. Yu Yu sat up and stared out over the white ranks of the ghostly army.

Leaving Kysumu, he strolled among the clay figures, looking at faces, seeking out Qin Chong. But he was nowhere to be found. At last Yu Yu came upon the broken figures. Kneeling, he pieced together what he could of the heads. As he half completed the second, sadness touched him. In his hands he held the features of the *Riaj-nor* who had befriended him in his dreams. 'What do I do now?' he whispered. 'I am here.' There was no answer. Yu Yu placed the broken pieces on the ground and sat back. Kysumu should have been the *pria-shath*. He was a trained *Rajnee*.

Yu Yu moved back to Kysumu and waited for the trance to end. Within minutes Kysumu opened his eyes. 'Are you feeling stronger?' asked the swordsman.

'Yes,' answered Yu Yu miserably.

'Did Qin Chong come to you in your sleep?'

'No.'

'Do you have any idea of what to do now?'

'No, I don't!' snapped Yu Yu. 'I don't know how statues can help us.' Pushing himself to his feet he walked away from the swordsman, anxious to avoid further questioning. Yu Yu had never felt so useless. He wandered around the walls, coming at last to the ledge scattered with golden ornaments. In his mind's eye he saw the warriors lining up here, placing their trinkets upon the rock. He picked up a small golden ring, then let it drop. In his vision he had seen warriors march into the depths of the hill. Now there were only statues. Where were the warriors? Had they been covered with clay? The broken head of Qin Chong's statue had been hollow, and there were no bones or scraps of hair within it, so that seemed unlikely. What, then, was the purpose behind these statues? Yu Yu strained at the thought until his head hurt. 'You must wake the Men of Clay,' Qin Chong had told him.

'Wake up!' bellowed Yu Yu.

'What are you shouting for?' Kysumu called out.

Yu Yu did not reply. Unable to think of an answer he turned back to the ledge. His gaze fell upon a threaded rod of gold some four inches long. Beside it was a circular stand, with a hole at the centre. Yu Yu picked up the stand and inserted the rod into the hole, screwing it tight. The top of the rod was hooked, like a shepherd's crook.

'What are you doing?' asked Kysumu, coming alongside.

'Nothing,' said Yu Yu. 'Amusing myself. Something should hang from this hook.'

'We have more important matters to decide,' said Kysumu.

'I know.' Yu Yu continued to probe among the ornaments, finally finding a small golden bell with a ring at the crest. 'This is it,' he said, carefully hooking the bell to the rod. 'Pretty.'

'Yes, it is pretty,' said Kysumu, with a sigh. Yu Yu flicked the bell. A small chime sounded. The bell continued to swing, and the next chime was louder than the first. The sound began to reverberate through the domed hall, growing louder and louder. The rock wall began to vibrate, ornaments tumbling from it. Kysumu tried to say something, but Yu Yu could not hear him. Yu Yu's ears were hurting and he covered them with his hands.

Dust fell from the domed ceiling, and cracks appeared in the walls. The bell was now booming louder than thunder. Yu Yu felt sick. He staggered back from the ledge and fell to his knees. Kysumu had also covered his ears, and was squatting down, a look of intense pain upon his features.

The clay statues were trembling now. Yu Yu saw tiny cracks appear in the nearest figure, spreading out like a spider's web. And still the terrible tolling of the bell continued. Pain roared inside Yu Yu's head.

And he passed out.

CHAPTER THIRTEEN

KYSUMU ROLLED TO HIS KNEES. BLOOD WAS DRIPPING FROM HIS nose. The noise was so incredible now that it had transcended mere sound. Everything hurt, ears, eyes, fingertips, belly. Every joint pulsed with pain. Kysumu forced himself to his feet and fell against the ledge, where the bell was still vibrating. Reaching out, the swordsman closed his hand around the tiny object. Instantly the tolling ceased. Kysumu staggered, then fell. He could scarcely breathe. Dust was everywhere, like a fog. Lifting the collar of his robe, he held it over his mouth. His ears were still ringing, his hands trembling.

Only then did he see the shining lights gleaming through the cracks that criss-crossed the statues. He blinked and tried to focus. It was as if the sun itself was trapped within the clay. The cracks of light widened, clay falling away. As the dust settled Kysumu saw that most of the statues were now bathed in golden light. The domed hall blazed with brightness. Kysumu closed his eyes against it, and where, only moments before, he had covered his ears, now he held his hands over his face. He waited for a few heartbeats, then opened his fingers. Light still blazed against his closed lids, and he waited again. Finally the brilliance faded. Kysumu let fall his hands and opened his eyes.

The Men of Clay were gone. Standing in the hall were several hundred living, breathing *Riaj-nor*.

Kysumu rose and approached them. They waited in silence. He bowed deeply. 'I am Kysumu,' he said, in formal Chiatze. 'Is Qin Chong among you?'

A young man stepped forward. He was wearing a full-length tunic of silver satin, his sword thrust into a black silk sash around his

259

waist. He removed his helm and neglected to bow to Kysumu. 'Qin Chong did not survive the transformation.' Kysumu looked into the man's eyes. The pupils were black slits surrounded by gold. In that moment Kysumu felt as if he had been stabbed through the soul. His heart sank. These were not men at all. They were creatures just like the *Kriaz-nor*.

'I am Ren Tang,' said the warrior. 'Are you the *pria-shath*?'

'No,' said Kysumu, turning away. 'The bell rendered him unconscious.'

Ren Tang strode to where Yu Yu lay. Other warriors gathered in silence around him. Then Ren Tang nudged Yu Yu with his foot. 'Behold the great one, the *pria-shath*,' he said. 'We have crossed the centuries to aid a human monkey in wolfskin.' Some of the men chuckled. Kysumu knelt beside Yu Yu and saw that he, too, had bled from the nose. He rolled him on to his back. Yu Yu groaned. Kysumu hauled him to a seated position.

'I feel sick,' muttered Yu Yu. He opened his eyes, then jerked as he saw the warriors milling around. He swore loudly.

'You did it, Yu Yu,' said Kysumu. 'You brought the Men of Clay back to life.'

'It takes no great intellect to ring a bell,' sneered Ren Tang.

'I spoke with Qin Chong,' said Kysumu, his voice cold. 'He was a man of great power and strength. He also understood courtesy and the need for good manners.'

Ren Tang's feral eyes locked to Kysumu's gaze. 'First, *human*, Qin Chong was not a *man*. He was, as we are, *Riaj-nor*. Second, I care nothing for your opinions. We drew lots to see which of us would fight for you humans when the gateway spell began to fail. It is enough that we will fight for you. Do not expect more.'

'It is not important,' said Yu Yu, climbing to his feet. 'I don't care whether they treat me with respect. Qin Chong sent them here to fight. So let them fight.' He looked into Ren Tang's eyes. 'Do you know who you are supposed to fight, and where?'

'You are the *pria-shath*,' said Ren Tang, contempt in his voice. 'We await your orders.'

'Very well,' said Yu Yu. 'Why don't you take some of your fighters and go outside? There were some enemy warriors out there earlier.'

Ren Tang put on his helmet and tied it below his chin. Taking several of the warriors with him he strode down the tunnel, returning

260

moments later. 'We cannot get out,' he said. 'The stone door will not budge.'

'Is that right, Buttock Brain?' said Yu Yu. 'One simple order and already you fail.'

For a moment Ren Tang stood stock still. Then his sword flashed into the air, the point hovering over Yu Yu's throat. 'You dare insult me?'

'What insult?' snarled Yu Yu. 'You wait thousands of years and your first act is to draw your sword against the only person who can lead you out of this tomb. What animal did they join you with? A goat?'

Ren Tang snarled. The sword lanced forward. Kysumu's blade blocked it.

A low growl came from Ren Tang, and his eyes glittered in the lantern-light. 'You cannot beat me, human,' he said. 'I could cut out your heart before you could move.'

'Show me,' said Kysumu quietly.

Another warrior stepped from the ranks. 'Enough of this,' he said. 'Ren Tang, put away your sword. You too, human.' He was taller than most of the *Riaj-nor* and slightly round-shouldered. His armour was the same as that of the others – ornate helm and a torso guard of gold coins – but his ankle-length tunic was of heavy crimson silk. 'I am Song Xiu,' he said, offering a respectful bow to both Kysumu and Yu Yu. He looked at Ren Tang, who stepped back, sheathing his sword.

'Why are you so angry?' Yu Yu asked Ren Tang.

The warrior swung away from him and walked back into the ranks of the *Riaj-nor*. Song Xiu spoke for him. 'He is angry because yesterday we won a great victory. After all the years of struggle and suffering. We thought it was over, and that we would have a chance to know peace. To rest and lie in the sunshine. To send for the pleasure girls and rut and get drunk. It was a glorious day. But then the black wizard told us that the spell would one day falter, and Qin Chong asked all the *Riaj-nor* to draw lots to see which of us would leave the world we knew and enter the long sleep. Now we are here, to fight again and die for a cause that is not our own. Ren Tang is not alone in feeling angry, human. We only agreed because Qin Chong said he would lead us. But he is dead. He fought his way across two continents, facing and overcoming dangers you could not possibly imagine. Only to die from a rockfall inside a hollow hill. You expect us to be less than angry?'

Yu Yu shrugged. 'You didn't want to be here. I didn't want to be here. But we *are* here. So let's leave this place. I need to breathe fresh air.'

261

Yu Yu strode along the tunnel to the rock door and stretched out his hand. Instead of passing through it his fingers touched solid rock. 'Oh, it just gets better,' muttered Yu Yu. He kicked the stone. Cracks flowed across it. The door shivered and broke, collapsing to the overhang and falling to the trail below. Yu Yu gave a proud grin and swung to Kysumu. 'Nobody told me how to do that,' he said. 'I just did it myself! Good, hey?' Then he stepped out into the light. Kysumu followed him, then the *Riaj-nor*. The warriors milled around, turning their faces up to the sunlight. Two of them approached the body of the dead *Kriaz-nor*. One knelt down and dipped his finger in the gaping wound at the warrior's neck. Lifting his hand he licked blood from the finger. 'Recent kill,' he said. Peeling a strip of flesh from the body he put it in his mouth and chewed upon it. Then he spat it out. 'Tastes of fear,' he said.

Kysumu walked away from the group and stood staring into the distance. Yu Yu joined him. 'Are you all right, *Rajnee*?'

'Look at them, Yu Yu. All my life I have dreamt of being as great as these. And what are they? Part animal, part man – and as vile as those we fight against. I thought to find great heroes. Instead . . .' His voice tailed away.

'They are here,' said Yu Yu. 'They endured a spell that left them dead for centuries, so that they could protect a new generation. Doesn't that make them heroes?'

'How could you understand?' snapped Kysumu.

'Being a ditch-digger, you mean?'

'No, no,' said Kysumu, reaching out and gripping Yu Yu's shoulder. 'There is no dishonour in that. What I meant was that all my life I have denied myself pleasure. No fine foods, strong drink, women, gambling. I possess nothing but my robes, my sword and my sandals. I did this because I believed in the order of the *Rajnee*. My life had a noble purpose. But it has all been based on a falsehood. To win that war our ancestors merely duplicated the enemy. No honour, no holding to principles. What does that make of my life?'

'You have honour and principles,' said Yu Yu. 'You are a great man. It doesn't matter about the past. You are who you are, regardless of it. When I first began to dig trenches they told us the foundations needed to be four feet deep. When the first earthquake hit, all our new buildings crumbled. Foundations should have been six feet deep, you see. All that digging just to make an unsafe house. But it didn't make me a bad digger. I was a great digger. A legend among diggers,' he added.

At that moment Song Xiu and Ren Tang approached them. 'What are your orders, *Pria-shath*?' asked the crimson-clad Song Xiu.

'Do you know how to make the gateway stay closed?' asked Yu Yu.

'Of course. The spell was cast using the power of *Riaj-nor* blades,' said Song Xiu. 'We must assemble at the gateway and hold our swords against it.'

'That is all we have to do?' asked Yu Yu, astonished. 'Just walk up to the gateway and tap it with a sword? We could have done that!'

'It will take more than two,' said Ren Tang.

'How many?' asked Kysumu.

Song Xiu shrugged. 'Ten, twenty, all of them. I do not know. But it will all be for nothing if the gateway is fully open. We must reach it before that event, while it is still blue.'

'Blue?' queried Yu Yu.

'I watched the first spell cast,' said Song Xiu. 'It began with what appeared to be white lightning searing across the opening. Then the colour deepened, becoming at first pale blue like a winter sky, then darker. At the last it was silver, like a sword blade. Then the light faded, the silver turned to grey and we were standing before a wall of solid rock. After the Men of Clay were chosen we were told that as the spell degrades it will flow through the colours in reverse. If it reaches white the spell is finished. If we can restore it to silver the gateway will seal itself.'

'Then we'd better get started,' said Yu Yu.

Eldicar Manushan felt sick. The communion had been more painful than usual but, then, it had been prolonged almost beyond endurance. Yet it was Deresh Karany's torture of Matze Chai that had turned his stomach. The old man had been far tougher than anyone could have expected, considering his effete lifestyle. The boils sprouting on his flesh, the open, cancerous wounds had failed to break him. Blinding head pain had weakened his resolve, the fat maggots chewing upon his wounds bringing him even closer to the edge. But it was the leprosy that had sent him spinning into Deresh Karany's control. The old man was fastidious to the point of obsession. The thought of his own skin decaying and falling away had been too much for him.

263

'*It was good that you gave him those extra twenty years, Eldicar. He would not have survived the pain without the gift.*'

'*Indeed not, my lord.*'

'*You seem to be suffering.*'

'*The communion is always painful.*'

'*So do you think there is anything more to be learned from the merchant?*'

'*I believe not, my lord.*'

'*Still, it is enough. The Grey Man is an assassin once known as Waylander. It is almost amusing. Niallad has lived his whole life in fear of meeting this man, and now he is travelling with him.*'

Eldicar's head felt as if it would burst. He sagged against the cellar wall. '*You must try to be tougher, Eldicar. Take note of the wonderful display shown by the Chiatze. Very well, I will let you go.*'

Freedom from pain made Eldicar cry aloud. He sank to his knees. The cellar was cold. He sat down, resting his back against the wall. Tied to a chair close by was the unconscious Matze Chai. He was naked, his body a mass of festering sores, his skin showing the white blotches of leprosy. Maggots crawled upon his bony thighs.

I wanted to be a healer, thought Eldicar. With a sigh he pushed himself to his feet and walked to the door. He glanced back at the dying man. There was no one here, save for himself and the prisoner. No guard outside the unlocked door. Deresh Karany had evinced no further interest in the man. Turning back Eldicar moved to Matze Chai's side. Taking a deep breath he laid his hands on the merchant's blood-encrusted face. Deresh Karany's spells were powerful and destroying the leprosy was the hardest task. It was deep-rooted. Eldicar worked silently, his mind focused. First he killed the maggots and healed the boils. The merchant groaned and began to wake. Eldicar placed him in a deep sleep then continued. Concentrating all his power into his hands Eldicar pulsed life-giving energy into Matze's veins. Eyes closed, he sought out all pockets of the disease, slowly eradicating them.

Why are you doing this? he asked himself. There was no rational answer. Perhaps, he thought, it will add one fragrant lily to the rancid lake of my life. Stepping back he gazed down at the sleeping man. Matze's skin gleamed with health. 'You did not come out of this too badly, Matze Chai,' he said. 'You still have your twenty years.'

Pulling shut the door behind him, Eldicar climbed the stone stairs to the first level and moved through to the Oak Room. Beric was sitting by the far window. Lord Aric was lounging on a couch nearby. 'Where is Panagyn?' asked Eldicar.

'He is preparing to ride out in search of the Grey Man,' said Aric. 'I think he is looking forward to the hunt. Did you learn anything from the slant-eye?'

'Yes. The Grey Man is an assassin called Waylander.'

'I have heard of him,' said Aric. 'I wish you'd let me observe the torture.'

'Why?' asked Eldicar wearily.

'It would have been amusing, and I am bored.'

'I am sorry to hear that, my friend,' said Eldicar. 'Perhaps you should visit Lady Lalitia.'

'Aye, I think I will,' said Aric, his mood momentarily brightening.

The small group had made camp in a wooded hollow close to the crest of a hill overlooking the Eiden Plain. Waylander was standing alone, staring out over the ruins of Kuan-Hador. Behind him the priestess Ustarte was sleeping. Emrin and Niallad were skinning three hares Keeva had killed that morning.

'It looks so peaceful in the moonlight,' said Keeva. Waylander nodded. 'You look tired,' she added.

'I am tired.' He forced a smile. 'I am too old for this.'

'I have never understood wars,' said Keeva. 'What do they achieve?'

'Nothing of worth,' he said. 'Mostly it comes down to mortality and the fear of death.'

'Fear of death makes men kill one another? That is beyond me.'

'Not the soldiers, Keeva, the leaders, the men who desire power. The more powerful they perceive themselves to be, the more god-like they become in their own eyes. Fame then becomes a kind of immortality. The leader cannot die. His name will echo down the centuries. It is all nonsense. They die anyway and turn to dust.'

'You really *are* tired,' she said, hearing the weary contempt in his words. 'Why don't you get some rest?'

Ustarte awoke and called out to them. Waylander strolled to where the priestess was sitting. Keeva followed him. 'How are you feeling?' asked Waylander.

'Stronger,' she said, with a smile, 'and not just because of the sleep. Yu Yu Liang has found the Men of Clay.'

'And?'

'The *Riaj-nor* have returned. Already they are marching towards the gateway. Three hundred of them. When they reach it the power of their swords will seal it for another millennium.' Her smile faded. 'But it will be close. The *Ipsissimus* has been directing a dispersal spell against the gateway for days. If he succeeds, and the gateway spell is broken, no force in this world will bring it back.'

'You have magic,' said Emrin, moving in. 'Can you not . . . cast your own spell against the magicker?'

'I have very few spells, Emrin. I have a talent for far-sight and once I could move freely between worlds. That power is almost gone. I do not know why. I think it was part of the meld-magic that created me, and the magic is fading. But, no, I cannot fight the *Ipsissimus*. We must just hope that the *Riaj-nor* can save us.'

Climbing clumsily to her feet, she took Waylander by the arm. 'Come, walk with me.'

They moved away from the group. Behind them Keeva started a small fire, and she and Emrin sat quietly beside it, preparing the hares. Niallad stood up and wandered away into the woods.

'They tortured Matze Chai,' Ustarte told Waylander. 'I only saw glimpses of it. He was extraordinarily brave.'

'Glimpses?'

'There is a cloak spell over the magicker and his *loachai*. I cannot *see* events around them. But I did fasten to the thoughts of Matze Chai.'

'He is still alive?' asked Waylander softly.

'Yes, he lives. There is something else. The *loachai* then healed Matze, bringing him back from the point of death.'

'So his master could torture him again?'

'I don't think so. It was as if the cloak-spell parted for a heartbeat and I caught just a glimpse of his thoughts – more an echo of his emotions. He was saddened and sickened by the torture. His healing of Matze Chai was a tiny act of rebellion. It is mysterious. I feel there is some fact we have overlooked. Something vital. It is like a nagging thought just below the level of consciousness.'

'I have the same feeling,' said Waylander. 'It has been bothering me ever since the battle with the demons. I saw the magicker ripped apart. But just before that I saw him falter. His spell was working, the mist was receding. Then he seemed to lose all confidence. His voice stammered. The mist swept over him. I watched his arm torn from his body. Yet, moments later, his voice rang out again, and he conquered the demons.'

'An *Ipsissimus* has great power,' said Ustarte.

'Then why did he lose it for those few heartbeats? And why did he not have his *loachai* with him? Surely that goes against what you told me about a magicker and his *loachai*. The boy is supposed to be Eldicar's shield.'

'The boy was with Keeva and Yu Yu at the time,' said Ustarte. 'Perhaps when the demons attacked them Eldicar sensed his peril. That could be why he lost concentration.'

'It still makes no sense,' insisted Waylander. 'He leaves his *shield* behind, and when the *shield* is in danger *he* gets ripped apart? No. If the *loachai* had been sent against the demons, and his master was threatened, it would be understandable. You told me that the master is the one with the real power, and he directs it through his *loachai*. Therefore if the master was threatened the link to his servant could be severed, leaving the *loachai* defenceless. But that was not what happened. It was Eldicar who fought the demons.'

Ustarte considered his words. 'He cannot be the *loachai*,' said Ustarte. 'You say the boy is around eight years old? No child could summon the power of an *Ipsissimus*, no matter how gifted. Nor do I believe anyone of that age would radiate such consummate evil.'

'Beric is a fine boy,' said Niallad, moving out of the darkness. 'I like him greatly. There is no evil in him.'

'I like him too,' said Waylander, 'but something is not right here. Eldicar told me he did not summon the demons to my home. I believed him. He spoke of Deresh Karany.'

'I know this man,' said Ustarte, her voice cold. 'He is vile beyond all imaginings. But he is a grown man. I would have sensed it had there been more than one *Ipsissimus*.' She turned to Niallad. 'You must pardon my intrusion, but I am reading your thoughts, and I need to see events through your memories. Think back to the night your parents were killed.'

'I don't want to do that,' said Niallad, backing away.

'I am sorry,' said Ustarte, 'but it is vital. Please, Niallad.' The young man stood very still. He took a deep breath, and Waylander saw that he was gathering his strength. Then Niallad nodded to Ustarte and closed his eyes.

'Now I see,' whispered Ustarte. 'The boy is there. You see him. He is standing alongside the magicker.'

'Yes, I remember. What point are you making?'

'Think back. How did he seem to you?'

'He was just standing there, watching.'

'Watching the slaughter?'

'I suppose so.'

'His face shows no emotion. Not shock, not surprise, not horror?'

'He is just a child,' said Niallad. 'He probably didn't understand what was happening. He is a wonderful boy.'

Ustarte swung and looked across at Keeva and Emrin. 'All of you are smitten by the boy. Even Matze Chai, as he faced torture, could think only good thoughts of Beric. This is not natural, Grey Man,' she said. She returned her gaze to Niallad. 'Think back now over all the times you have been with Beric. I need to see the events myself.'

'It is not that often,' said Niallad. 'The first time was in the Grey Man's palace. He and I went to the beach.'

'What did you do there?'

'I swam, Beric sat on the sand.'

'He did not swim?'

Niallad smiled. 'No, I teased him about it and threatened to carry him into the water. I reached down but he grabbed on to a rock and I could not lift him.'

'I do not see a rock in your memory,' said Ustarte.

'There must have been. I almost tore my back trying to prise him away.'

Ustarte reached out and took Niallad by the arm. 'Picture his face, as well as you can. Look at it closely. I need to see it! Every detail.' She stood very still, and Waylander saw her jerk, as if stung. She backed away from Niallad, her eyes wide with fear. 'He is not a child,' she whispered. 'He has become a meld-creature.' Waylander moved alongside her.

'Tell me!' he said.

'Your suspicions were correct, Grey Man. Eldicar Manushan is the *loachai*. The one who appears as a child is Deresh Karany – the *Ipsissimus*.'

'It cannot be,' whispered Niallad. 'You are wrong!'

'No, Niallad. He is radiating a charm-spell. All who come close are deceived by it. It is fine protection. Who would suspect a golden-haired and beautiful child?'

268

Ustarte walked away, lost in fearful memories. She had crossed a gateway between worlds to escape Deresh Karany's evil. And now he was here – and all her hopes of victory seemed suddenly frail, as insubstantial as woodsmoke.

She should have known he would come. She should have guessed it would be in a different form. Deresh Karany had become obsessed with the mysterious magic of the meld. He had realized through Ustarte that the possibilities went far beyond the mere physical. The correct balance could enhance the powers of the mind. Already virtually immortal, Deresh desired more. Conducting increasingly grisly experiments on his hapless captives, he sought the key that would unlock the secrets of the meld.

Ustarte had become his passion. She shuddered at the memory. He worked on her endlessly, seeking to find the source of her ability to change form. One day he had her strapped to a table. Sharp knives opened her flesh, and Deresh removed one of her kidneys, replacing it with a spell-charged organ taken from a failed meld. The pain had been indescribable and only Ustarte's great strength had saved her from madness. As she lay in her cell recovering she felt the organ stir within her, like a living creature. Tendrils slid from it, probing along the muscles of her back and into her lungs. Ustarte had gone into a terrible spasm. Her life was being drawn from her, and in her panic she threw herself into the change. The creature within her was crushed, but one tiny tendril broke off and fled deep into Ustarte's skull, nestling against the base of her brain. There it died. Poison seeped from its corpse, hot and burning. Tiger-Ustarte roared furiously, slashing her great paws against the walls of the cell, ripping out great chunks of plaster. Then, as she had with the first poison used on her, Ustarte absorbed it into her system, breaking it down, rendering it harmless. It could no longer kill her, but it did change her.

When Ustarte awoke, back in her own form, she felt different. Faintly dizzy and nauseous she had sat upon the floor, amid the ruins of the furniture torn to shreds by her tiger self. Suddenly her mind opened, and she heard the thoughts of every man and creature within the prison. Simultaneously. The shock made her scream, but she did not hear it. Her mind was full to bursting. Resisting panic, she tried to focus, creating compartments of the mind, which she closed against the tumultuous roar. The most powerful of the thoughts would not be shut out, for they were born of agony.

269

And they were coming from Prial. Two of Deresh Karany's assistants were experimenting on him.

Anger flooded through Ustarte, and a pulsing, volcanic rage began to build. Rising from the floor she focused on the men – and reached out. The air around her seemed to shiver and part. A fraction of a heartbeat later she found herself standing alongside the torturers within one of the meld-rooms on the other side of the prison. Ustarte's talons ripped through the throat of the first man. The second tried to run, but she leapt upon his back, bearing him to the ground. His head struck the stone floor, shattering the bones of his face.

Ustarte freed Prial.

'How did you . . .?' whispered Prial. 'You . . . appeared from the air.' There was blood upon his fur, and several implements were still embedded in his flesh. Gently Ustarte eased them clear.

'We are leaving now,' said Ustarte.

'The time has come?'

'It has come.'

Closing her eyes she pulsed a message to all of the meld-creatures within the prison. Then she disappeared.

The apartments of Deresh Karany were empty, and she recalled that he had gone to the city to meet with the Council of Seven. Deresh had plans to open a gateway between worlds and invade once more an ancient realm that had defeated them so many years before.

From outside came the sound of splintering timbers and screaming men. Ustarte walked to the window and saw the creatures of the meld swarming across the exercise ground. Guards were fleeing in terror. They did not get far.

An hour later Ustarte led the one hundred and seventy prisoners out into the countryside, high into the forested mountain slopes.

'They will hunt us down,' said Prial. 'We have nowhere to go.'

His words were proved true within days, when *Kriaz-nor* troops and hunt-hounds began scouring the forest.

The escapees fought well, and for a time enjoyed some small victories. But gradually they were whittled down, and forced further into the high country. Some of the prisoners took off on their own, moving still higher into the snow, others were sent by Ustarte in groups to seek freedom to the east or the south. Disfigured and malformed as they were, she warned them to avoid the haunts of men.

On the last morning, as several hundred *Kriaz-nor* were climbing towards their camp, Ustarte gathered the remaining twenty followers around her. 'Stay close to me,' she ordered her people, 'and follow when I move.' Reaching out she pictured the gateway as she had seen it in Deresh Karany's thoughts.

The air rippled. Ustarte threw out her arms. 'Now!' she cried, just as the *Kriaz-nor* burst upon the camp. Ustarte stepped forward. Bright lights in a score of colours flickered around her. As they faded she found herself standing within a green clearing in the shadow of a line of tall cliffs. The sun was shining brightly in a clear blue sky. Only nine of her followers made it through with her. Startled *Kriaz-nor* warriors were standing close by. Ahead was a huge stone arch, cut into the cliff. Beneath the arch the rock was glowing, ripples of blue lightning flashing across it. The *Kriaz-nor* rushed at them. Ustarte leapt towards the arch. Prial, Menias, Corvidal and Sheetza, a young girl with the scaled skin of a lizard, ran with her. The others charged the *Kriaz-nor*.

Throwing out her arms, Ustarte summoned all of her power. For an instant only the rock before her faded, and through it she saw moonlight over a series of ghostly ruins. As it began to fade she, and the last of her followers, stepped through.

Behind her the gateway closed, only bare rock remaining.

Sheetza stumbled and fell. Ustarte saw that a knife was embedded in her back. The deformed girl was unconscious. Ustarte drew out the blade and threw it aside. Then she laid her hands over the wound, sealing it. Sheetza's heart was no longer beating. Concentrating her power Ustarte set the girl's blood flowing. Sheetza opened her eyes. 'I thought I was stabbed,' she said, her voice sibilant. 'But there is no pain. Are we safe now?'

'We are safe,' said Ustarte, feeling for the girl's pulse. There was none. Only Ustarte's magic kept the blood flowing. She was, in effect, already dead.

In the distance Ustarte saw a glimmering lake. The small group made their way to it. Corvidal went for a swim with Sheetza. The girl moved through the water with the grace of a dolphin. When she emerged she was laughing. She sat down at the water's edge and splashed Menias. He ran forward and grabbed her and they both fell into the water.

Ustarte moved away from them. Prial came and sat with her. 'Maybe some of the others got away,' he said.

Ustarte did not answer. She was watching Sheetza. 'I didn't know you were also a healer,' he said.

271

'I am not. Sheetza is dying. Her heart was pierced.'

'But she is swimming,' said Prial.

'When the magic fades she will pass away. A few hours. A day. I don't know.'

'Oh, Great One! Why are we so cursed? Did we commit some vile sins in a past life?'

That night Ustarte sat talking with Sheetza. The priestess could feel the magic in the girl fading. She tried to add more power to it, but to no avail. Sheetza grew sleepy and lay down. 'What will we do in this world, Great One?' asked Sheetza.

'We will save it,' answered Ustarte. 'We will thwart the foul plans of Deresh Karany.'

'Will the people here accept me?'

'When they know you they will love you, Sheetza, as we love you.' Sheetza had smiled, and fallen asleep. Some time in the night, as Ustarte lay beside her, the lizard girl finally died.

Still lost in thought, Ustarte did not notice Waylander move alongside – not until he laid his hand on her shoulder.

'I was very arrogant to believe I could stand against Deresh Karany and the Seven,' she said. 'Arrogant and stupid.'

'Rather let us say brave and unselfish,' said Waylander. 'But do not judge yourself yet. Tomorrow Emrin and Keeva will take the lad over the high passes and try to make it to the capital. Once they are safely on the road I shall put your magicker's immortality to the test.'

'You must not go against him, Grey Man.'

'I don't have a choice.'

'We all have choices. Why throw your life away needlessly? He cannot die.'

'It is not about him, Ustarte. These men have killed my people, and tortured my friend. What kind of a man would I be if I did not fight them?'

'I do not want to see you die,' she said. 'I have seen too much death already.'

'I have lived long, Ustarte. Perhaps too long. Many better men are now below ground. Death does not frighten me. But even if I were to accept what you say about the folly of hunting Deresh Karany, there is one fact I cannot ignore. Matze Chai is still their prisoner. And I do not desert my friends.'

CHAPTER FOURTEEN

LORD ARIC OF HOUSE KILRAITH LOUNGED BACK IN THE CARRIAGE AND stared idly out of the window at the houses along the Avenue of Pines. There were few people on the streets of Carlis. The massacre of the Duke and his followers had been shocking enough, but to learn that demons were responsible had terrified the population. Most stayed behind locked doors, rediscovering the delights of prayer. Several hundred families were congregated within the temple, believing its walls would keep out all evil spirits. They were hoping for an appearance from Chardyn, but the priest had wisely gone into hiding.

The carriage moved on through the deserted town.

Aric's mood was not good. As he had told Eldicar Manushan, he was bored. It was impolite of the man to have forbidden him to see the torture of the Chiatze. There was something about screams of pain that cut through the malaise Aric had been suffering for some while.

His spirits lifted a little as he thought of Lalitia, remembering the slim, red-haired girl he had discovered in the prison. She had courage and ambition, and a body she had soon learnt how to use. Those had been good days, he thought.

Aric had been lord of the Crescent then, enjoying a fine life on the taxes he received from the farmers and fishermen. But not so fine as some of the other nobles, notably Ruall, whose income was ten times that of Aric. One night, at the old Duke's palace in Masyn, Aric had taken part in a gambling tourney. He had won twenty thousand gold pieces. Ruall had been the biggest loser. From being moderately wealthy Aric had suddenly become, in his own eyes at least, rich. He had spent like a man with ten hands, and within a year had debts at

273

least the equal of the money he had won. So he gambled again, and this time lost heavily. The more he lost, the greater he gambled.

He had been saved from destitution only by the death of the old Duke and the accession of Elphons. This, in turn, allowed Aric to assume the lordship of Kilraith. With the new funds from taxes he was able at least to maintain the interest on his debts.

The arrival of the Grey Man had been his salvation. He had leased the mysterious stranger the lands of the Crescent, against ten years of taxation. It should have been enough to allow Aric freedom from debt. And it would have – had he not accepted Ruall's wager of forty thousand gold pieces on a single horse-race. Aric had been delighted for, though the two horses were evenly matched, Aric had already paid a stable-boy to feed Ruall's thoroughbred a potion that would seriously affect its stamina. The potion had worked better than expected, and the horse had died during the night. So Ruall had substituted another racing mount. Aric could not object. The new horse had beaten Aric's racer by half a length.

The memory still galled, and was made only slightly less bitter by the recollection of Ruall's death, the look of surprise as the black sword sliced into him, and the expression of dreadful agony as life fled from him.

Aric recalled the night Eldicar Manushan had appeared at his door, the beautiful child beside him. It had been almost midnight. Aric had been mildly drunk, and his head was pounding. He swore at the servant who announced the visitors, hurling his goblet at the man and missing him by a yard. The black-bearded magicker had strolled into the Long Room, bowed once, then approached the bleary-eyed noble. 'I see that you are suffering, my lord,' he said. 'Let us remove that head pain.' He had reached out and touched Aric on the brow. It was as if a cooling breeze was flowing inside Aric's head. He felt wonderful. Better than he had in years.

The boy had fallen asleep on a couch, and he and Eldicar had talked long into the night.

It was around dawn when the magicker first mentioned immortality. Aric had been sceptical. Who would not be? Eldicar leant forward and asked him if he wanted proof.

'If you can supply it, of course.'

'The servant you threw the goblet at, is he valuable to you?'

'Why do you ask?'

'Would it distress you were he to die?'

'Die? Why would he die?'

'He is not a young man. He will die when I steal what remains of his life, and give it to you,' said Eldicar.

'You are jesting, surely.'

'Not at all, Lord Aric. I can make you young and strong in a matter of minutes. But the life force I will give you must come from somewhere.'

Looking back, Aric could not remember why he had hesitated. What possible difference could the death of a servant make to the world? And yet, he recalled, he had wondered if the man had a family. Baffling. As the dawn came up, Eldicar moved to a cabinet and took a small, ornately embellished mirror. He approached Aric, holding the mirror before the nobleman's face. 'Look at yourself. See what is.' Aric saw the sagging face, the hooded eyes, all the signs of age and a life of mild debauchery. 'Now see what could be,' said Eldicar softly. The image in the mirror shimmered and changed. Aric had sighed with genuine regret as he looked upon the man he had once been, hawkishly handsome and clear-eyed. 'Is the servant important to you?' whispered Eldicar.

'No.'

An hour later the youth and vitality he had been promised had become a reality. The servant died in his bed.

'He did not have a great deal of life left,' said Eldicar. 'We will need to find someone else soon.'

Aric had been too delighted to care about such matters.

The carriage trundled on, turning right into Merchants Square. Aric saw the sign for the Starlight tavern, a brightly painted shield showing a woman's head surrounded by stars. He remembered his first meeting with Rena there. She had served him his food, and curtsied prettily. Not a very bright woman, he recalled, but she had been warm in bed, and she had loved him. He had taken her on as the housekeeper of a comfortable villa he owned just outside Carlis, on the shores of Willow Lake. She had borne him a daughter, a delightful child, curly-haired and precocious. She would perch on Aric's lap and demand stories of olden times, of fairies and magic.

The carriage slowed as it climbed the hill. The driver cracked his whip and the two horses lurched into the traces. Aric settled back into the deep horsehair-filled leather seat.

Rena had been crying about something on that final day. Aric couldn't remember what. She had taken to crying a lot in the last few months. Women, thought Aric, could be so selfish. She should have realized that, with his new youth and vigour, he would need other outlets. The plump, docile Rena had been entirely adequate for the tired, middle-aged man he had been. But she was not equipped to dance the night away in gowns of satin, or to attend the various banquets and functions that Aric now gloried in. She was, after all, merely a low-born housekeeper. Then he remembered why she had been crying. Yes, he had tried to explain this to her. She had prattled on about his promise of marriage. She should have realized that such a promise from an ageing, poverty-stricken noble should not have been held against the young and powerful man he had become. A different man had made that promise. But she did not have the wit to understand, and had begun to wail. He had warned her to be quiet. She took no notice. So he had strangled her. It was a most satisfying experience, he recalled. Looking back, he wished he had made it last a little longer.

Under different circumstances Aric would have raised the child himself, but with the need to plan for the Duke's assassination he had had no time. Anyway Eldicar Manushan had pointed out that the girl's life force would prove far more efficacious than the servant whose death had provided Aric with his first taste of immortality. 'Being of your own blood she will supply years of youth and health.'

Aric had no doubt that it was true. He had stood in the child's bedroom as she lay sleeping and felt the tremendous surge of vitality that flowed into him as she died.

The carriage came to a halt and Aric climbed out. He strode to the front door, which was opened by a large middle-aged woman. She curtsied and led him through to a beautifully furnished room. Lalitia, wearing a simple dress of green silk, was sitting beneath a lantern, reading.

'Wine for our guest,' she told the fat woman. Aric strolled across the room, kissed Lalitia's hand, then seated himself on a couch opposite her.

As he looked at her, noting the whiteness of her neck and the beautiful curve of her breasts, he found himself thinking of how it would feel to slide a dagger through that green dress. He pictured it flowering with blood. Eldicar should have let him see the Chiatze tortured. He had been thinking about the music of screams all day. And he had no more use for Lalitia. So there was no reason why he should not kill her.

'You seem in good humour, my lord,' said Lalitia.

'I am, my sweet. I feel . . . immortal.'

There was something in Aric's manner that caused a tremor of fear in Lalitia. She couldn't quite pin down the reason. He seemed relaxed, but his eyes were glittering strangely. 'It was a great relief to me that you survived the massacre,' she said. 'It must have been terrifying.'

'No,' he said. 'It was exhilarating. To see so many enemies die at one time. I wish I could do it again.'

Now the fear was really growing. 'So you will be the new Duke,' said Lalitia.

'For a while,' he said, rising and drawing his dagger.

Lalitia sat very still.

'I am so bored, Red,' he said conversationally. 'So little seems to pique my interest of late. Would you scream for me?'

'Not for you or any man,' she said. Aric moved in closer. Lalitia rolled away from him, her hand dipping down behind a satin cushion and emerging holding a thin-bladed knife.

'Ah, Red, you were always such a delight!' said Aric. 'I am not bored at all now.'

'Come any closer and you'll never be bored again,' she told him.

The door behind Lalitia opened and the Source priest Chardyn entered. Aric smiled as he saw him. 'So this is where you've been hiding, priest? Who would have thought it? My men have searched the houses of your congregation. They didn't think to check the homes of local whores.'

The burly priest stood very quietly for a moment. 'What has become of you, Aric?' he asked.

'Become of me? What a ridiculous question. I am younger, stronger and immortal.'

'Last year I visited you at Willow Lake. You seemed content. You were playing with a child, I recall.'

'My daughter. A sweet creature.'

'I was not aware you had a daughter. Where is she now?'

'She died.'

'Did you grieve?' asked Chardyn, his voice low and compelling.

277

'Grieve? I suppose that I must have.'

'Did you grieve?' asked Chardyn again.

Aric blinked. The man's voice was almost hypnotic. 'How dare you question me?' he blustered. 'You are a hunted – criminal. Yes, a traitor!'

'Why did you not grieve, Aric?'

'Stop this!' shouted the noble, stepping back.

'What have they done to you, my boy? I saw you with that child. You clearly loved her.'

'Loved?' Aric was nonplussed. He turned away, his dagger forgotten. 'Yes, I . . . seem to remember that I felt . . .'

'What did you feel?'

Aric swung back. 'I don't want to talk about this, priest. Look, leave now and I will not report that I have seen you. Just go. I need to . . . to talk with Red.'

'You need to talk with *me*, Aric,' said Chardyn. Aric stared at the powerfully built priest, and found himself looking into the man's deep, dark eyes. He could not look away. Chardyn's gaze seemed to hold him trapped. 'Tell me about the child. Why did you not grieve?'

'I . . . don't know,' admitted Aric. 'I asked Eldicar . . . on the night of the killings. I couldn't understand why I reacted in the way that I did. I felt . . . nothing. I asked if I had lost something when he gave me my – my youth.'

'What did he say?'

'He said I had lost nothing. No, that's not quite right. He said I had lost nothing that would be of value to Kuan-Hador.'

'And now you want to kill Lalitia?'

'Yes. It would amuse me.'

'Think back, Aric. Think of the man sitting with his child by that lake. Would it have amused him to kill Lalitia?'

Aric tore his gaze away from the priest and sat down, staring at the dagger in his hand. 'You are confusing me, Chardyn,' he said, and became aware of a pounding pain in his head. Placing the dagger on the table before him he began to rub his temples.

'What was your daughter's name?'

'Zarea.'

'Where is her mother?'

'She died too.'

'How did she die?'

'I strangled her. She would not stop crying, you see.'

'Did you kill your daughter too?'

'No. Eldicar did that. Her life force was very strong. It gave me greater youth and strength. Surely you can see how good I look.'

'I see far more than that,' said Chardyn.

Aric looked up and saw Lalitia staring at him, an expression of revulsion on her face. Chardyn came closer, sitting alongside Aric on the couch. 'You once told me that Aldania had been kind to you. Do you remember?'

'Yes. My mother had died and she invited me to the castle in Masyn. She sat and hugged me as I wept.'

'Why did you weep?'

'My mother had died.'

'Your daughter died. Did you weep?'

'No.'

'Do you remember how you felt when your mother died?' asked Chardyn.

Aric looked inside himself. He could *see* the man he had once been, and *watch* the tears flow. But he no longer had any inkling as to why the man was crying. It was most peculiar. 'You were right, Aric,' said Chardyn softly. 'You did lose something. Or rather Eldicar Manushan stole it from you. You have lost all understanding of humanity, compassion, kindness and love. You are no longer human. You have murdered a woman who loved you, and agreed to the killing of a child you adored. You have taken part in an unholy massacre, which saw the brutal slaying of Aldania, who was kind to you.'

'I – I am immortal now,' said Aric. 'That is what is important.'

'Yes, you are immortal. Immortal and bored. You were not bored that day by the lake. You were laughing. It was a good sound. You were happy. No one had to die to bring you amusement. Can you not see how they have tricked you? They have given you longer life, and yet removed all the emotions you needed to *enjoy* that greater life.'

Aric's head was bursting. He pressed his hands to his temples. 'Stop this, Chardyn. It is killing me! My head is on fire.'

'I want you to think of Zarea, and that day by the lake,' said Chardyn. 'I want you to hold to it, to feel her tiny arms around your neck, the sound of happy childish laughter ringing in your ears. Can you hear it, Aric? Can you?'

'I can hear it.'

279

'Just before we all went inside she was cuddling you. She said something to you. You remember?'

'Yes.'

'Say it.'

'I don't want to.'

'Say it, Aric.'

'She said, "I love you, Papa!"'

'And what did you reply?'

'I told her I loved her too.' Aric gave a groan and fell back, his eyes squeezed shut. 'I can't think . . . the pain . . . !'

'It is the spell upon you, Aric. It is fighting to stop you remembering. Do you want to remember how it felt to be human?'

'Yes!'

Chardyn opened his collar and lifted clear the golden necklet he wore. A talisman hung from it, a piece of jade in the shape of a tear-drop. Runes had been cut into the surface. 'This was blessed by the Abbot Dardalion,' said Chardyn. 'It is said to ward off spells and cure disease. I do not know, in truth, if it carries magic or is merely a trinket. But, if you are willing, I will place it around your neck.'

Aric stared at the jade. A part of him wanted to push it away, to ram his dagger into the bearded throat of the priest. Another part wanted to remember how he felt when his daughter told him she loved him. He sat very still, then he looked into Chardyn's eyes. 'Help me!' he said. Chardyn looped the necklet over Aric's head.

Nothing happened. The pain came again, almost blinding him, and he cried out. He felt Chardyn take his hand and lift it to the jade tear-drop. 'Hold to it,' said the priest. 'And think of Zarea.'

I love you, Papa!

From deep below the pain came a rush of emotion, swamping Aric's mind. He felt again his daughter's arms around his neck, her soft hair rubbing on his cheek. For a moment pure joy filled him. Then he saw himself standing by the little girl's bed, revelling in the theft of her life force. He cried out and began to sob. Lalitia and Chardyn sat silently as the nobleman wept. Slowly the sobbing faded away. Aric gave a groan and snatched up the dagger, turning the point towards his own throat.

Chardyn's hand swept up, grabbing Aric's wrist. 'No!' shouted the priest. 'Not this way, Aric! You were weak, yes, to desire such gifts.

But you did not kill your woman. Not the real you. You were under a spell. Don't you see? They used you.'

'I stood and laughed as Aldania died,' said Aric, his voice trembling. 'I joyed in the butchery. And I killed Rena and Zarea.'

'Not you, Aric,' repeated Chardyn. 'The magicker is the real evil. Put down the dagger, and help us find a way to destroy him.'

Aric relaxed and Chardyn released his hand. The lord of Kilraith rose slowly to his feet and turned to Lalitia. 'I am so sorry, Red,' he told her. 'At least I *can* apologize to you. I can never ask forgiveness from the others.' He swung to Chardyn. 'I thank you, priest, for returning to me that which was stolen from me. I cannot help you, though. The guilt is too great.' Chardyn was about to speak, but Aric held up his hand. 'I hear what you say about Eldicar, and there is truth in it. But I made the choice. I allowed him to kill a man to feed my vanity. Had I been stronger my Rena and little Zarea would still be alive. I cannot live like this.'

Moving past them he went to the door and opened it. Without a backward glance he strolled out into the night. Climbing into his carriage he bade the driver take him to Willow Lake.

Once there he dismissed the man and walked past the deserted villa and out to the moonlit shores. He sat down by the jetty, and pictured again the glorious day when he and his daughter had laughed and played in the sunshine.

Then he cut his throat.

Lord Panagyn had always believed himself immune to fear. He had fought battles and faced enemies all his adult life. Fear was for lesser men. Thus it was that he did not at first recognize the trembling in his belly, or the first tugs of panic pulling at his mind.

He ran headlong through the forest, his arms thrashing aside the overhanging vegetation, ignoring the twigs and thin branches that snapped back against his face. He stopped by a gnarled oak to catch his breath. Sweat had soaked his face, and his close-cropped iron-grey hair lay damp against his skull. Looking around he was no longer sure where he was in relation to the trail. But that did not matter now. Staying alive was all that counted. Unused to running, his legs were cramped and painful, and he sank to his haunches. His scabbard caught against a tree root, ramming the hilt of his cavalry sabre against his ribs. Panagyn grunted with pain, and shifted to his left, lifting the scabbard clear.

A cool breeze filtered through the trees. He wondered if any of his men had survived. He had seen some of them run, throwing aside their crossbows and trying to make it back to the cliffs. Surely Waylander could not have killed them all! It was not humanly possible. One man could not slay twelve skilled fighting men!

'Do not treat this man lightly,' Eldicar Manushan had warned him. 'He is a skilled killer. According to Matze Chai, he is the finest assassin this world has seen.'

'You want him brought in alive or dead?' Panagyn had asked.

'Just kill him,' said Eldicar. 'Be advised that there is a woman with him gifted with far-sight. I shall surround you and your men with a cloak-spell that will prevent her from sensing you. But this will not prevent Waylander, or any of the others, from seeing you with their eyes. You understand?'

'Of course. I am not an idiot.'

'Sadly, in my experience, that is exactly the phrase most used by idiots. As to the priestess, we would prefer her to be taken alive, but this may not be possible. She is a Joining – a were-creature. She can become a tiger. Once in that form you will have to kill her. If you can take her while in her semi-human guise, bind her wrists and ankles and blindfold her.'

'What of the others?'

'Kill them all. They are of no use.'

Panagyn had chosen his twelve men with care. They had all fought beside him in a score of battles. Cool men, hardy and tough, they would not panic or run. Equally they would think nothing of killing captives.

So where had it gone wrong? he wondered.

He had guessed rightly that Waylander would seek to escape over the high roads and had led his men in a fast ride to an area called Parsitas Rocks. There they had left the horses and scaled the towering cliff-face, emerging above the escapees. From here they moved through the forest, taking up positions on both sides of the trail and preparing their crossbows. Far below, Panagyn had seen the riders, and glimpsed the shaven-headed priestess walking just behind them. Panagyn ordered his men to shoot high, killing the riders and allowing the walking priestess to be taken alive.

Panagyn himself had crouched down alongside one of the bowmen on the left of the trail, ducking behind a thick bush. Here he waited in silence, listening for the sound of hoofbeats upon the hard-packed trail. Time drifted by. A trickle of sweat ran down Panagyn's cheek. He did not move to brush it away, wanting to risk no sound. The clip-clopping of walking horses drifted to him. He glanced at the bowman, who raised his weapon to his shoulder.

Then came a thud and a crash from the opposite side of the trail. Someone cried out. The sound was followed by a choking gurgle. Then silence. Panagyn risked a glance. One of his men came running from the bushes. Panagyn saw him swing and raise his crossbow. A small black bolt flowered from the man's brow. He staggered back, loosing his own shaft into the air. Then he fell, the body twitching for a few moments.

A man to Panagyn's right screamed and reared up, fingers scrabbling at a bolt jutting from his neck. The warrior beside Panagyn twisted, bringing his crossbow to bear. Panagyn saw something streak through the air. The crossbowman pitched to his right. Panagyn did not see where the bolt had struck him. Panicked by the unseen killer, others of Panagyn's men rose from their hiding places, shooting at shadows. Another man went down, this time with a bolt through the eye. The remaining men threw aside their bows and fled.

Lurching to his feet, Panagyn ran into the trees, his arms flailing at the undergrowth as he blundered through bushes. He scrambled up the hillside, half slid down a steep incline and kept moving until his lungs could take no more.

Now, as he sat by the tree, he started to regain a little composure. If he could just get back to the cliffs, and climb down to the horses . . .

Pushing himself to his feet he started to turn. His foot caught in a tree root and he stumbled. It saved his life. A black bolt slammed into the oak. Panagyn hurled himself to the right and darted away into the trees. He scrambled over the lip of a rise, then half slid down the slope, emerging on to the trail. Several riders were sitting motionless upon their mounts, and Panagyn saw the shaven-headed priestess close by. No one moved.

Panagyn backed away, drawing his sword.

A black-clad figure stepped into sight, long black and silver hair held back from his head by a leather headband. In his hand was a small double-winged crossbow. From the other side of the trail came four of his men. Their hands were raised. A dark-haired woman walked behind them. She, too, was carrying a small crossbow.

Panagyn switched his gaze back to Waylander. The man's face was set and grim, and Panagyn could read his own imminent death in Waylander's eyes. 'Face me like a man!' challenged Panagyn, in desperation.

'No,' said Waylander. The crossbow came up.

'Do not shoot!' ordered Niallad. Panagyn flicked a glance at the young man, who had heeled his horse forward.

'This is not some game, Niallad,' said Waylander. 'This man is a traitor who took part in the killing of your parents. He deserves to die.'

'I know that,' replied Niallad, 'but he is a lord of Kydor and should not be shot down like some common bandit. Have you no understanding of the chivalric code? He has challenged you.'

'The chivalric code?' said Waylander. 'Did he use the chivalric code when the demons came? You think he and his killers were hiding here to offer us a challenge?'

'No,' said Niallad, 'they were not. And I accept that Panagyn is a disgrace to all that nobles should hold dear. But I will not be a disgrace, or party to a disgrace. If you will not accept his challenge then let me fight him.'

Waylander gave a rueful smile. 'Very well . . . my lord, it will be as you say. I'll kill him in the time-honoured fashion.' Handing his crossbow to Niallad, the assassin moved into open space and drew one of his shortswords.

Panagyn grinned. 'Well, Waylander,' he said, 'you're good at shooting men from ambush. Let's see how you fare against an Angostin swordsman.'

CHAPTER FIFTEEN

AS HE MOVED, WAYLANDER LOOSENED THE MUSCLES OF HIS shoulders. Panagyn was a large man, and his cavalry sabre was custom-made, heavier than the standard issue and some six inches longer. He guessed that the man would attack with a sudden charge, relying on brute strength to force his opponent back. The fact that he had agreed to this duel surprised Waylander. Codes of chivalry were largely for the story-tellers and bards to sing of. Enemies should be slain with the minimum of effort. He had learnt this during close to forty years of combat and danger. The knowledge had been hard-won.

So why are you doing it? he wondered, as Panagyn also began to work on the muscles of his shoulders, swinging the sabre left and right.

Then it came to him. There *ought* to be such codes, and the world would be a lesser place if the young, like Niallad, failed to believe in them. Perhaps, given time, he could make such codes a reality within Kydor. Waylander doubted it.

You are getting old and soft, he told himself.

Panagyn charged. Instead of stepping back, Waylander leapt to meet him, blocking a savage cut and ramming his head into Panagyn's face, crushing his nose. The burly nobleman staggered back. Waylander lunged. Panagyn blocked desperately, then backed away. Waylander circled him. Panagyn dragged out a dagger and flung it at Waylander. As he ducked, the nobleman rushed in. Waylander dropped to the ground, then kicked out, catching Panagyn below the right knee, just as the man's weight was coming down

285

on it. Panagyn fell heavily. Waylander rolled to his feet and sent a slashing blow that cannoned from the top of Panagyn's head, opening his scalp. With a cry of rage and pain Panagyn charged again. This time Waylander stepped swiftly to his left, slamming the shortsword into Panagyn's belly. The blade sank deep. Waylander grabbed the hilt with both hands, tipping the sword and driving it up into Panagyn's heart. The nobleman sagged against him.

'This is for Matze Chai,' said Waylander. 'Now rot in Hell!'

Panagyn toppled to the ground. Putting his foot on the dead man's chest, Waylander tore his sword loose and cleaned the blade on Panagyn's embroidered tunic.

Stepping back, he turned towards the horses – and stopped.

Niallad was sitting very still, the crossbow pointed at Waylander. 'He called you by a name, Grey Man,' said the boy, his face pale. 'It is an old word meaning stranger or foreigner. Tell me that is all he meant. Tell me that you are not the traitor who killed my uncle.'

'Put up that weapon, boy,' said Emrin. 'He is the man who saved your life.'

'Tell me!' shouted Niallad.

'What is it you want to hear?' asked Waylander.

'I want the truth.'

'The truth? All right, I'll tell you the truth. Yes, I am Waylander the Slayer and, yes, I did kill the king. I killed him for money. It is a deed that has haunted me all my life since. There is no way to make amends when you kill the wrong man. So, if you want to use that weapon on me, do so. It is your right!'

Waylander stood very still and stared at the crossbow in the youth's hand. This was the weapon he had used to kill the king, the crossbow which had sent so many to their death. In that frozen moment of time Waylander thought how fitting it would be to be killed by this weapon, loosed by the only blood relative of the innocent king whose murder had plunged the world into chaos. He relaxed and waited.

At that moment the wind changed. Ustarte had moved closer and her scent drifted across the nostrils of Niallad's horse. It reared. Niallad was thrown back in the saddle. His hand involuntarily squeezed the bronze trigger of the crossbow. The bolt slammed into Waylander's chest. He half turned, took three faltering steps then fell to the grass close to the body of Panagyn.

286

Ustarte reached his side first, turning him and pulling the bolt clear.

'I didn't mean to shoot!' said Niallad.

Keeva and Emrin dismounted and ran towards the fallen man. Ustarte waved them back. 'Leave him to me,' said Ustarte. Putting her arms beneath the unconscious Waylander, she lifted him with ease and carried him into the forest.

When he opened his eyes he was lying on a bed of leaves. Ustarte was squatting beside him. Waylander's hand went to his chest. 'I thought he had killed me,' he said.

'He did,' Ustarte told him, her voice heavy with sadness.

Kysumu stared out over the ruins of Kuan-Hador. The sun was setting, and the plain below seemed immensely peaceful. Moving away from the warriors of the *Riaj-nor*, he squatted down and drew his sword. A great sadness was upon him. It lay like a boulder on his heart.

He remembered his teacher Mu Cheng, the Eye of the Storm, and the long years of training. Mu Cheng had tried, with great patience, to show Kysumu the secrets of the Way of the Sword, how to release control and become a living weapon. The sword, Mu Cheng had said, is not an extension of the man. The man must become the extension of the sword. No emotion, no fear, no excitement. Calm, and in harmony, the *Rajnee* did his duty, no matter the cost. Kysumu had tried. He had struggled with every fibre of his being to master the Way. His swordsmanship was beyond excellent, but it could not reach the sublime skill shown by Mu Cheng. 'It will come one day,' Mu Cheng had told him. 'And on that day you will be the perfect *Rajnee*.'

Two years later Kysumu had accepted the role of bodyguard to the merchant Lu Fang. He soon discovered why Lu Fang needed a *Rajnee* bodyguard: the man was amoral to the point of evil. His ventures included forced prostitution, slavery, and the distribution of deadly narcotics. Upon learning this, Kysumu had climbed the stairs to Lu Fang's apartments and informed him that he could no longer be his bodyguard.

Lu Fang had railed at him. 'You gave me your promise, *Rajnee*,' he said. 'And now you will leave me unprotected?'

'I will stay until noon tomorrow,' Kysumu told him. 'You will send your servants out in the morning to find other protectors. Then I leave.'

Lu Fang had cursed him, but the curses were just empty sounds to the young *Rajnee*. There was no honour to be gained in defending a man like Lu Fang. He walked from the apartments to the balcony beyond. Two hooded and masked figures were stealthily climbing the stairs. Kysumu moved to block them, his sword raised. Both men hesitated. 'Leave now,' said Kysumu, 'and you live.'

The men glanced at one another. Both carried thin-bladed daggers, but neither had a sword. They backed down the stairs, Kysumu following them. As they reached the last step they turned and ran.

Another figure moved into sight.

It was Mu Cheng.

As Kysumu stood now, overlooking the Eiden Plain, and the ghostly ruins of the ancient city, he remembered his shock at the condition of his former master. Mu Cheng's eyes had been red-rimmed, and there was stubble upon his cheeks. His robes were dirty, but the sword he held was clean. It shone brightly in the lantern-light.

'Step aside, pupil,' said Mu Cheng. 'The villain will die tonight.'

'I have told him I can no longer serve him,' said Kysumu. 'I leave him at noon tomorrow.'

'I have promised he will die tonight. Step aside.'

'I cannot, master. You know this. Until noon I am his *Rajnee*.'

'Then I cannot save you,' said Mu Cheng. The attack was incredibly swift. Kysumu barely blocked it. The two swordsmen had then engaged in a blisteringly fast series of encounters. Kysumu could never recall quite when it happened. But somewhere within that fight he had discovered the Way of the Sword. He had relinquished control. His blade moved faster and faster, casting bewildering patterns of light in the air. Mu Cheng had been forced back until, at the last, Kysumu's sword cut through his chest. The Eye of the Storm died without a word. His sword fell to the carpeted floor, the blade shattering into a hundred shards.

Kysumu stared down at the dead face of a man he had loved.

The voice of Lu Fang came from the balcony above. 'Are they dead? Are they gone?'

'They are gone,' said Kysumu, striding from the house.

Two days later Lu Fang had been stabbed to death in a market square.

Now Kysumu looked back and wondered just why he had longed to be a *Rajnee*. Around him he could hear the coarse, gutter language of the *Riaj-nor*. What a fool I have been, he thought. Everything I was taught was based on lies. I have wasted my life trying to be as great as the original heroes of legend. And now I find they are part beast, part man, and have no honour in them.

Yu Yu Liang approached, squatting down beside him. 'They will come, you think, the demons?' he asked.

'They will come.'

'You are still sad?'

Kysumu nodded.

'I've been thinking about what you said, Kysumu. I think you are wrong.'

'Wrong?' Kysumu gestured towards the warriors. 'You believe they are great and mystic heroes?'

'I don't know. But I was talking to Song Xiu, and he was saying that the meld affects the body in a number of ways. One of them is that no *Riaj-nor* can sire children.'

'What is your point, Yu Yu?' snapped Kysumu.

'Whatever you think of them they *did* defeat the enemy. But once they were all dead – of old age or whatever – who could replace them? Ordinary men did not have the strength or the speed. So the elders had to find special men. Men like you, Kysumu. It is not about a lie. It is not about trickery. It doesn't matter that the original warriors were Joinings. The order of the *Rajnee* has always been . . . pure. That is why they have inspired our people for centuries. I know I am not putting this well. I am no debater. You were raised to believe in stories about a great warrior people. Well, they are great warriors. They did fight and die for us. You were then taught to believe in the *Rajnee* code. It is a good code. You do not swear, you do not lie, you do not steal, you do not cheat. You fight for what you believe in, and never give in to evil. What is wrong with that?'

'Nothing is wrong with it, Yu Yu. It just isn't based on truth.'

Yu Yu sighed and pushed himself to his feet. Song Xiu and Ren Tang walked across to join them.

'The gateway is an hour's march from here,' said Song Xiu. 'It will be guarded. One of our scouts picked up the trail of a small group of *Kriaz-nor*. It is my belief they saw our arrival, and will have communicated it to their masters.'

289

'There are going to be demons among those ruins,' said Yu Yu. 'They will come in a mist. Big black dogs and white bear creatures and serpents.'

'We have fought them before,' said Ren Tang.

'So have I – and I'm not looking forward to doing it again,' said Yu Yu.

'And you shouldn't,' said Kysumu, his voice gentle. 'You have fulfilled your part in this, Yu Yu. You were chosen to find the Men of Clay and you have done this. But from now on other skills will be required. You should make your way back to the coast.'

'I can't leave now,' said Yu Yu.

'There is nothing more you can do. I do not mean this unkindly, but you are not a swordsman. You are not *Rajnee*. Many of us – perhaps all of us – will die upon that plain. It is what we were trained for. You have great courage, Yu Yu. But now is the time for other skills to come into play. You understand? I want you to live. I want you to . . . go home and find a wife. Have a family.'

Yu Yu was quiet. Then he shook his head. 'I may not be a swordsman,' he said, with great dignity, 'but I am the *pria-shath*. I brought these men to this place. I will lead them to the gateway.'

'Ha!' said Ren Tang. 'I like you, human.' Throwing his arm around Yu Yu's shoulder he kissed his cheek. 'You stay close to me. I'll teach you how to use that demon-sticker.'

'Time to march,' said Song Xiu.

Yu Yu Liang, the Chiatze ditch-digger, led the fighting men of the *Riaj-nor* down on to the Eiden Plain.

As they reached the ruins a mist began to form ahead of them.

Norda was quite sure she was dreaming. At first she had been frightened, but now she relaxed, wondering where the dream would take her next. She rather hoped it would involve Yu Yu Liang.

The first part of the dream had been very real. Eldicar Manushan had sent for her, and told her that Beric had need of someone to sit with him while Eldicar himself was engaged in other duties. This was no hardship, for Beric was a delightful boy. Norda had been a little surprised to hear that Beric was waiting for her in the North Tower library. It was getting late, and in Norda's experience little boys tended to dislike dark, cold places.

Norda had climbed the circular stair, and been surprised to find four dark-garbed swordsmen in the library room below the tower. She had paused, sudden fear flooding her system. Such . . . creatures as these had been the talk of the palace for days now, with their cat-like eyes and their haughty manner.

The first of them had bowed to her and offered her a sharp-toothed smile. His arm swept out, beckoning her to mount the stairs.

At this point Norda had no idea it was a dream. She climbed the stairs to the tower, and found Beric lounging on a wide couch. He was wearing only a white robe, belted at the waist. The tower room was chilly, a cold breeze whispering from the open balcony. Norda shivered. 'You must be cold,' she said to the boy.

'Yes, Norda,' he said sweetly. She was filled with the urge to hug him, and crossed the room to sit beside him. He snuggled into her. That was when she first realized that she was dreaming. Norda felt light-headed as he moved in close, and awash with feelings of love and contentment. It was really quite exquisite. She gazed down at his beautiful face, and saw that it was swelling at the temples, large blue veins pulsing across the stretching skin of his brow. His eyes grew smaller under heavy brows, the blue changing, becoming tawny gold. He seemed to be smiling, but she saw that, in reality, his lips were being dragged back across his cheeks, as his teeth grew longer and thicker, overlapping each other. His face was but inches from her own, and Norda frowned as it changed. She still felt great love for the boy, even though he was obviously a boy no longer. Norda regretted the cheese and bread she had eaten for supper, and the goblet of red wine with which she had washed it down. Cheese and wine always made her dream. But how odd that Beric should feature. Normally Norda dreamt of more potent men – men like Yu Yu Liang and Emrin. Even the Grey Man had figured in the more erotic dreams.

'You are not so pretty now, Beric,' said Norda, reaching up to stroke the pallid grey skin of his face. Her fingers brushed against his now dark hair. It was more like a pelt. His own, taloned, hand moved across her shoulder. She glanced down and saw that the skin of his arm was scaled and grey.

Something touched her leg. Norda saw that it was a long, scaled tail, with what seemed to be a claw growing from the base. She laughed.

'What is amusing, my dear?' asked the creature.

'Your tail,' she said. 'Long tails.' Then she laughed again. 'Emrin has a long tail. Yu Yu's tail is shorter and thicker. They don't have claws on them, though. I'll not drink that Lentrian wine again, that's for sure.'

'No, you won't,' said the creature.

The tail slid up over her belly, the claw pricking at the skin.

'That hurts,' said Norda, surprised. 'I've never felt pain in a dream before.'

'You never will again,' said Deresh Karany. The claw ripped into her.

Eldicar Manushan climbed the stairs and tapped lightly at the door. When he entered he gave one glance to the shapeless husk that only moments before had been a vibrant, friendly young woman. The desiccated corpse had been carelessly flung into a corner.

Deresh Karany was standing by the balcony window, staring out into the night.

Eldicar found the melded form repugnant, and realized that Deresh had let fall the charm-spell. 'Are you refreshed, Lord?' asked Eldicar.

Deresh turned slowly. His legs were twisted, the knees reversed, the feet splayed. The long tail, resting on the carpeted floor, gave him balance. His grey face twisted towards Eldicar. 'Invigorated, my friend. No more. Her essence was very powerful. It gave me a vision. Panagyn and Aric are dead. The Grey Man will be coming here. He thinks to kill us.'

'And the gateway, Lord?'

'The *Riaj-nor* are battling to reach it.' Deresh Karany moved clumsily towards the couch. His taloned feet hooked into a rug and he half slipped. 'How I loathe this form!' he hissed. 'When the gateway is open, and this land is ours, I shall find a way to reverse this . . . this foulness.'

Eldicar said nothing. Deresh Karany had become obsessed with the twin-meld, and acquiring the ability to change at will. As far as Eldicar could see, he had succeeded admirably. Deresh could assume the perfect body of a golden-haired child, or this powerful monstrosity, part lizard, part lion. This second form suited his personality perfectly.

'What are you thinking, Eldicar?' asked Deresh Karany suddenly.

'I was thinking of the problems of the meld, Lord,' replied Eldicar.

292

'You have mastered the twin forms. I don't doubt you will find a way to make the larger form more . . . attractive to the eye.'

'Aye, I will. Have you set the guards in place?'

'Yes, Lord. Three-swords and his group will be patrolling the lower access points, and Panagyn's soldiers are watching the grounds and the other entrances. If Waylander does come he will be captured or killed. But surely he is no threat to us. He cannot kill us.'

'He could kill you, Eldicar,' said Deresh. 'I might decide not to revive you. Tell me, how did it feel to have your arm ripped off by Anharat's demons?'

'It was agonizing, Lord.'

'And that, my dear Eldicar, is why I don't want Waylander to reach me. He cannot kill me, but he can cause me pain. I do not like pain.'

Except in others, thought Eldicar, remembering the sharp hurts of the many communions, and Deresh Karany's dismissive contempt of his own suffering. Deresh had always insisted upon communion, rather than conversation. He claimed that he did not want to risk being overheard. But there had been many occasions when no one had been close enough to eavesdrop. Even then Deresh had demanded communion. Some part of him revelled in the pain it caused Eldicar. How I hate you! he thought.

In that moment he felt a great warmth settle over him. He looked into the crooked features of his master and smiled. He knew it was the charm-spell, yet he was unable to resist its power. Deresh Karany was his friend. He loved Deresh Karany, and would die for him.

'Even Waylander will be unable to resist the spell,' said Eldicar. 'He will love you as I do.'

'Perhaps, but we will give him to Anharat anyway.'

'One of his demons, you mean, Lord?' Eldicar could not keep the fear from his voice.

'No. You will help me prepare for the Summoning.'

Even through the comforting warmth of the charm-spell Eldicar felt panic rising. 'Surely, Lord, we do not need Anharat to kill one mortal. Will he not be insulted by being summoned for such a small task?'

'Perhaps he will,' agreed Deresh, 'but then again even the Lord of Demons must enjoy feeding occasionally. An added advantage will be to remind Anharat who is the master and who is the servant.'

Deresh saw the growing terror in Eldicar and laughed. It was an ugly sound. 'Fear not, Eldicar, there is a good reason for using Anharat. Ustarte is with Waylander. She knows several ward spells. She will most certainly lay one upon him. Now, if I was to summon a lesser demon and her ward spell proved effective, that demon would turn on me – or, rather, on you as my *loachai*. There is no ward-spell that can turn back Anharat. Once loosed against a victim he is unstoppable.'

There was truth in that, Eldicar knew. Equally the Summoning would take a great deal of power. His heart sank as he realized what was coming.

'Pick ten of the servants,' said Deresh. 'Young ones, preferably female. Bring them here, two at a time.'

'Yes, Lord.'

As Eldicar Manushan left the tower he tried to think of lakes and sailboats.

But there was no refuge there.

Yu Yu stumbled – just as a huge white-furred creature broke through the line before him. Song Xiu leapt across his path, sending his sword slashing through the creature's neck. It roared and lashed out. Song Xiu grabbed Yu Yu, hauling him out of the demon's reach. Ren Tang and Kysumu both stabbed the beast, which fell writhing to the ground. More demons swept through the breach. Yu Yu clove his blade through the neck of a serpent. Kysumu half decapitated a black *Kraloth* hound as it leapt towards his throat.

Then the mist faded back. The *Riaj-nor* regrouped. Yu Yu glanced around. It seemed to him that they had lost around forty of their number. And they had covered barely half a mile. The *Riaj-nor* fought with a savagery Yu Yu could scarcely believe. There were no war cries, no exhortations, no screams from the wounded and dying. Merely blinding webs of dazzling blue light from the mystical blades as they ripped and tore into the flesh of the demonic army opposing them.

Kysumu had been right. This was no place for Yu Yu. He knew that now. He was merely a clumsy, slow human. Several of the *Riaj-nor* had died protecting him, and both Song Xiu and Ren Tang watched over him constantly.

'Thank you,' said Yu Yu, in the brief lull.

Ren Tang grinned at him. 'It is our duty to protect the *pria-shath*,' he said.

'I feel like a fool,' Yu Yu told him.

Song Xiu stepped in. 'You are not a fool, Yu Yu Liang. You are a brave man, and you fight well. With a touch of the meld you could be very good.'

'They are coming again,' said Kysumu.

'Then let us not keep them waiting,' said Ren Tang.

The *Riaj-nor* swept forward. The mist rolled towards and around them. Winged creatures appeared overhead, throwing barbed darts down upon the fighting men. The *Riaj-nor* drew daggers from their belts and hurled them up at the demons. They fell from the sky to be stabbed to death. One warrior tore a dart from his shoulder and leapt, grabbing a creature by the ankle. Huge black wings flapped furiously, but the combined weight bore both of them down. The *Riaj-nor* stabbed the dart through the creature's bony chest. As it died its talons ripped across the *Riaj-nor*'s throat. Blood sprayed over Yu Yu. Swinging round, he hacked off the demon's head.

Ren Tang went down. Yu Yu leapt across his fallen body, delivering a mighty blow to the chest of the bear-like beast that had downed him. The blade sank deep. The creature bellowed in pain and fell back. Ren Tang rose to his feet. There was blood on his face, and a flap of skin was hanging from his temple.

The fighting was furious now. The demons were above them and all around them. But still the *Riaj-nor* drove forward into the mass.

More than half of the Men of Clay were dead, but the demon hordes were thinning now.

Yu Yu was close to exhaustion. Ice was clinging to his wolfskin jerkin. He tripped and fell across the body of a dead *Riaj-nor*. Kysumu hauled him to his feet.

The mist parted.

A warm breeze blew across the ruins.

And the demons vanished.

Song Xiu put his arm around Yu Yu and pointed to a line of cliffs. 'There is the gateway,' he said.

Yu Yu peered through the gloom. He could see a flickering blue light against the grey stone. But it was not the light that caught his attention.

It was the two hundred black-garbed *Kriaz-nor* warriors who were moving out to form a defensive line.

Yu Yu swore. 'After all we've been through you'd think we deserved a bit of luck,' he grumbled.

'This is luck,' said Ren Tang. 'You can't feast on the hearts of demons.'

Yu Yu looked at him, but made no response. Despite the attempted lightness of his tone, Ren Tang looked bone weary. Song Xiu leant on his sword and swung to assess the remaining warriors. Yu Yu did the same. There were just over a hundred *Riaj-nor* left standing, and many were wounded.

'Can we beat them?' asked Yu Yu.

'We don't have to beat them,' said Song Xiu. 'We just have to get through them and reach the gateway.'

'We can do that, though, hey?'

'It is why we came,' said Song Xiu.

'Let's do it,' said Ren Tang. 'And then I want to find a town and a tavern and a fat-arsed woman. Maybe two.'

'Taverns or women?' asked another warrior.

'Taverns,' admitted Ren Tang. 'I'm a little too tired to want more than one woman.' Putting aside his sword, he lifted the bloody flap of skin back into place, pressing his hand against the wound.

Song Xiu moved alongside him, drawing a curved needle from a small pouch tucked into his waist sash. Swiftly he stitched the upper section of the wound. 'Well,' he said, 'if you don't want both women I'll take one.'

'Aye,' answered Ren Tang, with a quick grin. 'So let us not waste any more time. Let's sweep away these ugly vermin, then get drunk.'

'Agreed,' said Song Xiu, with a brief smile. Then he took a deep breath and swung to Yu Yu. 'I heard what your friend told you earlier. He was wrong then, but his words are right at this time. You cannot come with us on this last fight. We will not be able to protect you. And once we break through we will not be able to protect ourselves.'

'What do you mean?'

'As our swords touch the gateway they will simply cease to be. They will be absorbed by the spell that was placed there.'

'Then you will all be killed,' said Yu Yu.

'But the gateway will be closed,' pointed out the *Riaj-nor*.

'I will not stay behind,' insisted Yu Yu.

Ren Tang stepped in. 'Listen to me. Despite my hatred of them, I have to admit these *Kriaz-nor* are great fighters. We *cannot* battle them *and* look after you. Yet if you come we will be forced to try to protect you. You see the predicament? Your presence will lessen our chance of success.'

'Do not be sad, Yu Yu,' said Song Xiu. 'It was for people like you that Qin Chong and I, and the others, surrendered our humanity. It is pleasing to me that you are here. For it shows that we did not take this path in vain. Your friend Kysumu can come with us. He will represent humans in this encounter. It is what he wants. He has no true love of life. He knows no fears, as he knows no joys. That is why he can never be the hero you are. And that, my friend, is why *you* were the *pria-shath*. Without fear there can be no courage. You have fought beside us, ditch-digger, and we are proud to have known you.' He held out his hand. Yu Yu blinked back tears as he shook it. 'Now we must fulfil our destiny,' said Song Xiu.

The *Riaj-nor* formed a fighting line, Ren Tang, Song Xiu and Kysumu at the centre.

Yu Yu stood by wretchedly as they walked slowly towards the ancient enemy.

Waylander looked into Ustarte's golden eyes. 'You are telling me that I am dying? I feel fine. There is no pain.'

'And no heartbeat,' said Ustarte sadly.

Waylander sat up and felt for his pulse. She was right. There was nothing. 'I do not understand.'

'It is a talent I did not know I had until we crossed the gateway. One of my companions, a lovely child named Sheetza, was stabbed. Her heart, too, had stopped beating. I healed the wound – as I have yours – and sent a surge of my power into her blood, causing it to continue to flow through the body. She lived for some hours, but then, as the spell faded, she died. You have a few hours left, Waylander. I am sorry.'

Keeva stepped forward from where she had been standing in the shadows of the trees. 'There must be something you can do,' she said, dropping to her knees beside the Grey Man.

'How many hours?' Waylander asked.

'Ten – perhaps twelve at the most,' Ustarte told him.

'The boy must not know,' said Waylander, rising to his feet. He walked back through the trees to where Emrin and Niallad were sitting by the trail.

As Niallad saw him he scrambled to his feet. 'I did not mean to shoot,' he said.

'I know. It barely pierced the skin. Come, walk with me.'

Niallad stood very still, fear showing on his face. 'I will not harm you, Niallad. We need to talk.' Waylander led the boy to a cluster of rocks beside a fast-flowing stream, and there they sat as the sun sank below the mountains. 'Evil creeps up on a man,' said Waylander. 'He starts out on a mission he believes is just, and with every killing he darkens his soul just a little more. He lives neither in the day nor in the night. And eventually this man of twilight, this . . . Grey Man finally steps into the dark. As a young man I tried to live a decent life. Then one day I arrived home to find my family butchered. My wife, Tanya, my son, my two baby girls. I set out to hunt down the nineteen men who had taken part in the raid. It took me almost twenty years to find them all. I killed every one. I made them suffer, as Tanya had suffered. They all died in dreadful agony. I look back on the torturer I became and I barely recognize the man. His heart was stone. He turned his back on almost everything of value. I cannot tell you now why he . . . I accepted the contract to kill the king. It no longer matters why. The simple fact is that I did accept, and I did kill him. And in killing him I became as evil as the men who murdered my family. I tell you all this not to excuse myself or to ask for forgiveness. Forgiveness is not yours to give. I tell you simply because it may help you in your own life. You fear being weak. I see that fear in you. But you are not weak, Niallad. One of the men who slaughtered your parents was in your power, and you upheld the chivalric code. That is strength of a kind I never possessed. Hold to that, Niallad. Hold to the light. Keep that code in your heart with every decision you make. And when, one day, you are faced with a rival, or an enemy, make sure you do nothing that would bring you shame.'

With that Waylander rose and the two walked back to the horses. Waylander gathered up his bow and loaded it. He called the four prisoners to him. They shuffled forward uncertainly. 'You are free to go,' he said. 'If I see you again you die. Now get out of my sight.'

The four men stood for a moment, then one walked away into the forest. The others waited to see if Waylander would shoot him.

When he did not the others followed. Waylander approached Emrin. 'There should be no pursuit now,' he said. 'Their horses are far away. So take the high road and bring Niallad and Keeva to the capital. If the lad is strong enough he will win over the other nobles and become the Duke. I want you to stand beside him.'

'I will, sir. Where are you going?'

'Where you can't follow, Emrin.'

'No, but I can,' said Keeva.

Waylander turned to her. 'You told me you did not wish to become a killer. I respect that, Keeva Taliana. If you walk with me now you will have to use that bow.'

'There is no time for debate now,' said Keeva grimly. 'I shall come with you to stop the magicker. Just in case – for any reason – you are unable to do so.'

'Then let it be so,' he said. 'And now we must go. We have some hard riding to do.'

'There is no need to ride,' said Ustarte. 'Come, stand with me, and I shall take you where you wish to go.'

Waylander and Keeva moved alongside her.

Niallad called out. 'For what it is worth, Grey Man, I do forgive you. And I thank you for all you have done for me.'

Ustarte raised her hands. The air shimmered before her. Then she stepped from sight, Waylander and Keeva disappearing with her.

CHAPTER SIXTEEN

THE MASSIVE NAVE OF THE TEMPLE WAS THRONGED WITH PEOPLE; mothers holding fast to their children, husbands staying close to their loved ones. Hundreds of the citizens of Carlis had taken refuge here, workers, merchants, tanners and clerics all huddled together. A few soldiers were with them, men who had been ordered to watch for the renegade priest Chardyn.

Priests moved among the crowds, offering blessings, leading prayers.

The corpse of an elderly man lay by one of the walls, the face covered by a cloak. His heart had failed. The body was a reminder of the perils that awaited them outside. Fear was almost palpable, and conversations were held in hushed whispers. The topic was the same everywhere. Would the hallowed walls keep out the demons? Were they safe within this holy place?

A white-robed figure moved into sight, climbing the steps to the high altar. A cry went up from the crowd as they recognized Chardyn. People began to cheer. Relief swept through the crowd.

Chardyn stood in full sight of them all and spread his arms. 'My children!' he bellowed. Several soldiers moved forward. Chardyn looked down at them. 'Stand where you are!' he thundered.

Such was the power in his voice that the soldiers stopped, and glanced at one another. The crowd would tear to pieces any who tried to harm the priest. The soldiers relaxed.

'The Duke is dead,' said Chardyn, transferring his gaze to the crowd. 'He was slain by sorcery. And now demons stalk the land. You know this. You know that a magicker summoned Hell-hounds to kill and to maim. That is why you are here. But let me ask you this: do you think these walls might protect you? These walls were built by *men*.' He fell silent, his eyes scanning the silent congregation. Then he pointed at a large man standing at the centre of the throng. 'I see you, Benae Tarlin! You and your team constructed the south wall. What power do you possess that will hold back demons? What magic did you invest in these stones? What ward-spells did you cast?' He waited for an answer. The crowd swung to stare at the hulking man, who reddened and said nothing. 'The answer is none!' roared Chardyn. 'They are merely walls of stone. Cold, lifeless stone. And so, you might ask, where is the sanctuary against the evil that is outside? Where can we hide to be safe?' He paused and allowed the silence to grow.

'Where is anyone safe from evil?' he said at last. 'The answer is nowhere. You cannot run from evil. It will find you. You cannot hide from evil. It will burrow down to the deepest place in your heart and it will discover you.'

'And what of the Source?' shouted a man. 'Why does He not protect us?'

'Aye, what of the Source?' responded Chardyn. 'Where is He in our hour of need? Well, He is here, my friends. He is ready. He waits with a shield of thunder and a spear of lightning. He waits.'

'What is he waiting for?' came another shout, this time from the stone-mason Chardyn had picked out earlier.

'He is waiting for *you*, Benae Tarlin,' answered Chardyn. 'He is waiting for you, and he is waiting for me. At the palace of the Grey Man there is a magicker, a man who summons demons. He has bewitched the lords Aric and Panagyn, and arranged the massacre of many of our leading citizens. He now rules Carlis, and soon, perhaps, all of Kydor. One man. One vile and evil man. One man who believes that the murder of a group of nobles will cow and terrorize an entire population. Is he right? Of course he is. Here we are, cowering behind walls of stone. And the Source waits. He waits to see if we have the courage to believe. If we have the faith to act. Every week we assemble here and we sing songs of the Source, of His greatness and His power. Do we believe them? We do when times are good. You listen to sermons about the heroes of the Source, of the Abbot Dardalion and the Thirty, his warrior priests. My, but they make great listening, do they not? A few men who, with courage and faith, set themselves against a terrible enemy. Did they cower behind walls and ask the Source to fight for them? No, for the Source was *within* them. The Source fed their courage, their spirit, their strength. That same Source is within *us*, my friends.'

'Well, I don't feel it!' called Benae Tarlin.

'Nor can you while you hide,' Chardyn told him. 'Your son slipped down that cliff last year, and you climbed down to the ledge to rescue him. He clung to your back and you felt you did not have the strength to carry him clear. We have talked of this, Benae. You prayed for the strength to bring your son to safety. And you did so. Did you sit upon that cliff and call out for the Source to raise your boy on a magical cloud? No. You set off in faith and your faith was rewarded.

'I tell you now that the Source waits. He waits with power greater than any magicker. You want to see that power – then walk with me to the palace of the Grey Man. We will find the magicker. And we will destroy him.'

'If we march with you,' asked another man, 'do you promise the Source will be with us?'

'With us and within us,' said Chardyn. 'I pledge it upon my life.'

Three-swords was standing by the window, looking out over the bay, when he caught what seemed to be a flash of light on one of the lower terraces. He stepped out on to the balcony and peered at the area below. Two human guards were walking down the steps. They were heading in the direction from which the light came. Three-swords relaxed and went back into the library.

Iron-arm was stretched out on a long bench. Stone-four and Long-stride were sitting at the base of the stairs. There had been no screams from the upper chamber for some time. Three-swords did not like the sound of screams, especially from young females. He had little stomach for cruelty. In battle you fought an enemy and killed it. You did not set out to make it suffer. Iron-arm strolled across to join him. 'The magicker is on his way back,' said Iron-arm. Three-swords nodded. He had not yet scented the man, but Iron-arm was never wrong. Then Three-swords caught the scent. It was faintly acrid, the scent of fear.

The black-bearded magicker came up the stairs and stopped. He stared at the circular steps leading to the upper chamber. Then he moved to a seat and slumped down, rubbing his eyes. 'All is quiet out there,' he said to Three-swords.

302

The warrior knew he was merely making conversation in a bid to delay his return to Deresh Karany. 'So far,' said Three-swords.

Iron-arm rose suddenly and strode to the window. 'Blood,' he said, opening his mouth and drawing in a hiss of air over his tongue. 'Human blood.' Three-swords and Long-stride joined him instantly.

Three-swords closed his eyes and breathed in deeply. Yes. He could just taste it on the air. He turned to Eldicar Manushan. 'At least one man is bleeding heavily.'

'Two,' said Iron-arm. 'And there is something else.' His broad nostrils flared. 'It is very faint. But . . . yes . . . big cat. Lion, maybe. No. Not a lion – a meld.'

'Ustarte!' whispered Eldicar Manushan. He backed away from the window, then swung to Stone-four and Long-stride. 'Get out there. Find her. Kill anyone with her.'

'It might be better to stay together,' said Three-swords.

'This Waylander must not reach the tower,' said Eldicar Manushan. 'Do as I say.'

'Move warily,' Three-swords told Long-stride and Stone-four. 'This human is a hunter and a canny fighter. He uses a crossbow that shoots two bolts.'

The two warriors descended the staircase. Eldicar Manushan sat down. The smell of fear was strong on him now, and Three-swords joined Iron-arm at the window. 'The cat-woman is sick,' said Iron-arm, 'or weak. I cannot tell which. She is out of sight, just below those gardens. She has not moved.'

'Can you scent any humans?'

'No – only the wounded or dead. I would think they are dead, for there is no movement or sound from them.'

From where they stood they saw Long-stride and Stone-four emerge into the gardens. Stone-four was moving swiftly, but Long-stride tapped him on the shoulder, ordering him to slow down.

'They won't surprise Long-stride,' said Iron-arm. 'He's careful.'

Three-swords did not answer. He glanced back at Eldicar Manushan. Why was the man so terrified?

He strolled across to where the magicker sat. 'What is it that I do not know?' he asked.

'I don't know what you mean.'

'What is happening here, Eldicar? Why were so many women killed? Why are you so frightened?'

Eldicar licked his lips, then rose and moved in close to Three-swords. 'If the human gets through,' he whispered, 'Deresh Karany will perform the Summoning.'

'So he will use a demon to kill him. He has done this before.'

'Not any demon,' said Eldicar. 'He plans to summon Anharat himself.'

Three-swords said nothing. What was there to say? The arrogance of these humans was beyond his understanding. He saw Iron-arm looking at him quizzically, and he knew why.

He is scenting my fear now, thought Three-swords.

As the air shimmered around her Keeva felt an icy wind swirl over her body. Bright colours exploded before her eyes. Then, as if a curtain had opened, she saw the moonlit apartments of the Grey Man appear before her. The ground shifted under her feet and she half staggered. Ustarte gave out a low moan and sank to the ground. Instantly Waylander knelt by her. 'What is wrong?'

'I am . . . exhausted. It . . . takes great energy. I will be fine.' Ustarte stretched herself out. 'So . . . little power left,' she whispered. She closed her eyes. Waylander moved towards the door of his apartments, and two guards appeared on the pathway to the right. One was holding a hunting bow, an arrow notched to the string. The second carried a spear. Both men froze as they took in the scene.

Keeva raised her crossbow. 'Put down your weapons,' she said.

For a moment it seemed they would obey her, but then the bowman drew back on the string. A bolt from Waylander's weapon slammed into his chest. He grunted and fell back, his arrow slashing through the air, missing Keeva by inches. The spearman charged at Keeva. Instinctively she pressed both trigger studs on her crossbow. One bolt struck the spearman in the mouth, smashing his teeth, the second entered his skull between the eyes. His charge faltered and he dropped the spear. His hand went to his mouth. Then, as if his bones had turned to water, his body crumpled and he fell at Keeva's feet.

She looked round for the Grey Man, but he had entered the apartments. She transferred her gaze to the dead man, and felt sick. The other guard groaned. Rolling to his stomach, he tried to crawl away. Keeva crossed the ground and stood over him. 'Lie still,' she told him. 'No one is going to harm you further.'

Kneeling by his side, she put a hand to his shoulder, to help him turn on to his back. He relaxed at her touch and she looked into his eyes. He was young and beardless, with large brown eyes. Keeva smiled at him. He seemed about to say something. Then a bolt smashed into the side of his head, crunching through the temple.

Fury swept through Keeva and she swung on the Grey Man. 'Why?' she hissed.

'Look at his hand,' said Waylander.

Keeva glanced down. Moonlight shone upon the dagger blade. 'You do not know that he was going to use it,' she said.

'I did not know that he wasn't,' Waylander told her. Moving past her, he wrenched the bolt clear of the soldier's head, cleaned it on the man's tunic, and slipped it back into his quiver. 'We do not have time for lessons, Keeva Taliana,' he said. 'We are surrounded by enemies who will seek to take our lives. To hesitate is to die. Learn fast – or you will not survive the night.'

Behind them Ustarte called out weakly. Waylander knelt by her. 'There are *Kriaz-nor* within the tower. The wind is off the sea and they will scent the blood.'

'How many can you sense?' he asked.

'Four. There is something else. I cannot quite fasten to it. There has been murder done and there is a tremor in the air. Magic is being cast, but for what purpose I cannot tell.'

Waylander took her hand. 'How soon before you can walk?'

'A few moments more. My limbs are trembling. I have no strength yet.'

'Then rest,' said Waylander, rising and moving to Keeva. 'I have something for you that will give you an edge,' he said.

Ustarte called out again. 'Two *Kriaz-nor* are moving down the terrace steps.'

Long-stride moved warily. He had not yet drawn his sword. There would be time for that. For now he was using all his senses. He could smell the blood, and the sour odour of urine. The bladders of the dead had emptied. The scent of the meld-woman was also strong, and Long-stride could detect within it an unhealthy aroma. The woman was sick. Stone-four was moving too fast, and was some paces ahead now. Irritated, Long-stride caught up with him. 'Wait!' he ordered.

Stone-four obeyed him and they moved stealthily around the

corner. Some fifteen paces ahead of them, sitting upon a rock, was a dark-garbed human. In his left hand he held a double-winged crossbow. Beyond him lay the cat-woman. 'Let me kill him,' said Stone-four. 'I want to win a name!'

Long-stride nodded, and continued to sniff at the air.

Stone-four stepped towards the human. 'Your weapon looks formidable,' he said. 'Why don't you show me how formidable?'

'Come a little closer,' said the human, his voice calm.

'Surely this range is adequate,' replied Stone-four.

'Aye, it is adequate. Did you wish to draw your sword?'

'I will not need it, human. I shall remove your heart with my hands.'

The human rose. 'I am told you are very fast, and that bows are useless against you. Is this true?'

'It is true.'

'Let us find out,' said the man, his voice suddenly cold. Long-stride felt the beginning of apprehension as he heard the man's tone, but Stone-four was tensed and ready. The bow came up. Stone-four's right hand swept up, snatching the bolt from mid-air. Instantly a second bolt followed the first. Stone-four moved with lightning speed, catching this with his left hand. He grinned widely and glanced at Long-stride. 'Easy!' he said. Before Long-stride could warn his comrade the human's right hand flashed out. The throwing knife sped through the air, slamming into Stone-four's throat. The *Kriaz-nor*, his windpipe severed, took two faltering steps towards the human, then toppled face-first to the ground.

Long-stride drew his sword. 'You have any more tricks to play, human?' he asked.

'Only one,' said the man, drawing a shortsword.

'And what might that be?'

Long-stride heard a whisper of movement behind him. Spinning on his heel, he scanned the area. Nothing was there. Low bushes and rocks that could not hide a human. Then he saw something so weird that he did not at first register what it was. A crossbow suddenly extended from low to the ground. Long-stride blinked. He could not focus properly on the area around it. The weapon tilted and, in that fraction of a heartbeat, Long-stride saw a slim hand upon the weapon. Two bolts slashed towards him. His sword swept up blocking the first. The second slammed into his chest, burying itself deep into his lungs. A sword blade plunged into his back. Long-stride arched, then swung, his own sword slicing the air. But the human had not crept up behind him as he had thought. The man was still standing some fifteen paces away. He had hurled the sword! Long-stride felt all strength seeping away. Letting fall his blade, he walked stiffly to a rock and sat down heavily. 'You are very skilful, human,' he said. 'How did you make the crossbow shoot?'

'He didn't,' said a female voice.

Long-stride looked towards his left and saw a woman's head appear, floating in the air. Then an arm came into sight, sweeping upwards, as if pushing a cloak aside. Then it came to him. 'A *Bezha* cloak,' he said, slipping from the rock.

Pain roared through him as he fell, and he realized his weight had come down upon the sword jutting from his back, driving it deeper. He struggled to rise, but there was no power left in his limbs. His face was resting against a cold flagstone.

It felt surprisingly pleasant.

Waylander and Keeva helped Ustarte inside the apartments. 'I just need to rest for an hour or so,' said the priestess. 'Leave me here. Do what you have to do.'

Keeva reloaded her crossbow and walked to the doorway. 'Do you have a plan?' she asked Waylander.

He smiled at her. 'Always.'

'How are you feeling?'

The smile faded. 'I've felt better.'

She looked into his face. Dark rings showed under his eyes, and his skin was pallid, the cheeks sunken. 'I'm sorry,' she whispered. 'I don't know what else to say.'

'No one lives for ever, Keeva. Are you ready?'

'I am.'

Waylander moved out into the darkness, and ran along the path, cutting left towards the waterfall. Keeva followed him. He clambered up the rocks and entered a dark opening. He waited for her there and took her hand. 'These steps lead up into the palace,' he said. 'Once we are there I want you to make your way to the stairs underneath the library. Cover yourself with the cloak then climb the stairs until you can see into it. Do nothing more until I make my move. You understand this?'

'I understand.'

Still holding her hand he climbed the stairs. The darkness was total. At the top he paused, listening. There was no sound from beyond and he slid open the panel leading to the corridor outside the Great Hall. Lanterns had been lit here, but there was no sign of people. Waylander released her hand. 'Be lucky, Keeva,' he said, then moved away swiftly.

Keeva was suddenly fearful. All the time he had been with her she had felt somehow protected. Now alone, she found her hands trembling.

'Be strong,' she told herself, then ran along the corridor towards the library stairs.

'I cannot see them,' said Eldicar Manushan, staring out over the terraced gardens. Three-swords did not answer. He exchanged glances with Iron-arm. The huge warrior nodded. Three-swords turned away. He had always liked Long-stride. The warrior was reliable and cool under pressure. He would be hard to replace. 'What can be taking them so long?' asked Eldicar Manushan. 'Are they eating his heart, do you think?'

'They are not eating anything,' said Three-swords. 'They are dead.'

'Dead?' responded the magicker, his voice rising. 'They are *Kriaz-nor*. How can they be dead?'

'We die too, magicker. We are not invulnerable. This assassin is obviously everything you feared. Are you sure he is human, and not meld?'

Eldicar Manushan wiped sweat from his face. 'I don't know what he is, but he killed a *Bezha*. I was there. A little while ago he entered a house, surrounded by guards and killer dogs. He killed the merchant who lived there and then left. No one saw him.'

'Perhaps he knows magic,' said Iron-arm.

'I would have sensed it,' said Eldicar. 'No, he is just a man.'

'Well,' continued Iron-arm, '*just a man* has killed two *Kriaz-nor*. And now he is coming to kill you.'

'Be quiet!' stormed Eldicar, swinging round and staring out over the balcony. He gazed down at the ground some fifty feet below and watched for any sign of movement on the steps. Dark clouds obscured the moon and lightning flashed over the bay, followed some seconds later by a rolling boom of thunder. Rain began to lash down, hissing against the white walls of the palace. Eldicar could see little now, and moved to the shelter of the balcony doorway.

Back in the library Three-swords was just about to pour a goblet of water, when he paused, nostrils flaring. Iron-arm had also caught the scent. Three-swords carefully replaced the goblet on the table and turned, his golden gaze raking the room and the wrought-iron stairs leading up to it. He could see nothing, but he knew someone was close. Iron-arm moved stealthily along the wall.

Three-swords strolled casually towards the stairs, then darted forward. As he did so a crossbow appeared from thin air, and loosed a bolt. Three-swords swayed to one side. The bolt flashed by him. A second followed the first. Three-swords' arm swept up. The point of the bolt gashed the back of his hand, before careering across the library and clattering against the shelves. Three-swords leapt down the stairs, grabbing the outstretched arm. With one heave he threw the assassin back over his shoulder and into the room. The archer landed heavily. Three-swords spun and ran up the stairs. The assassin had come to his knees, although that was not what Three-swords saw. He saw a head and one arm, and a disembodied foot. Reaching out, he tore away the *Bezha* cloak with one hand, while dragging the assassin to his feet with the other. He was about to rip out the man's throat when he saw that he held a slim young woman. She kicked him, but he ignored it and turned towards Eldicar Manushan.

'This is not your Waylander,' he said. 'It is a female.'

'Well, kill her,' shouted Eldicar.

The woman drew a dagger from its sheath. Three-swords absently batted it from her hand. 'Stop struggling,' he said. 'It is beginning to annoy me.'

'What are you waiting for?' said Eldicar. 'Kill her.'

'I have already killed one woman for you, magicker. I did not relish that task, but I did it. It still sits badly with me. I am a warrior, not a woman-killer.'

'Then you do it,' Eldicar ordered Iron-arm.

'That's my captain,' said Iron-arm. 'Where he goes I follow.'

'You insolent dogs! I'll kill her myself!' Eldicar pulled his dagger from his belt and took one step away from the balcony door. At that moment something dark moved into sight behind him. A hand

309

hooked into the collar of his robe, dragging him back. His hips hit the balcony rail and his body cartwheeled over the edge. Iron-arm sprang towards the balcony. There was no one there. He glanced up.

Through the lashing rain he saw a dark figure scaling the wall, heading towards the upper balcony of the library tower.

Iron-arm looked down. Fifty feet below the magicker lay spread-eagled on the stones. Moving back into the room, Iron-arm headed for the upper stairs.

Three-swords stopped him. 'Trust me, my friend, you do not want to go up there.' He looked down at the woman in his grasp, then released her. She half fell. Three-swords saw a swelling on the side of her face, and her left eye was closing fast. 'Sit down,' he said, 'and drink some water. What is your name?'

'Keeva Taliana.'

'Well, Keeva Taliana, have your drink and gather your strength. Then, were I you, I would leave this tower.'

Eldicar Manushan lay very still. Pain threatened to engulf him, but he concentrated his powers, blocking the agony. Fighting for calm, he sent his spirit flowing through his broken body. He had landed heavily on his back, but, thankfully, his spine was not severed. His right hip was smashed, and his left leg broken in three places, his left wrist fractured. His head had missed the stone of the path, striking the soft earth of a flower-bed beside it. Otherwise his neck might have been broken. There were some internal injuries, but quietly and carefully Eldicar healed them. Occasionally the pain would burst through his defences, but he held it back and continued to direct power to his injuries, accelerating the healing. He could do little about the broken bones in such a short time, but he swelled and stiffened the muscles around them, forcing them back into position.

The rain pounded down upon him as he lay there. Lightning speared across the sky. By its light he saw Waylander scaling the wall. He had almost reached the upper balcony. Despite his broken bones Eldicar felt a wave of relief sweep over him. He would not now have to be in the room when Anharat was summoned. Even better, the Lord of Demons could not be summoned through *him*.

Carefully Eldicar rolled to his stomach and pushed himself to his knees. Sharp pain flared in his ruined hip, but the muscles around it held firm. Rising to his feet, he let out a groan as his broken leg

310

twisted, a jagged shard biting into the cramped muscles of his calf. Bending down he forced the bone back into place with his thumbs, then tightened the muscles once more.

Taking a deep breath he put weight on the injured limb. It held. Almost all of his talent had been used, and Eldicar knew he had to find a place of safety where he could rest and recoup his power. Slowly he inched his way towards the palace, entering a corridor opposite the Oak Room. It came to him then that he did not want to remain in this place. He wanted to go home. If he could just make it to the stables and saddle a horse he could ride for the gateway and never again be forced to serve monsters like Deresh Karany. Eldicar thought of the family house beside the lake, the cool breezes flowing over the snow-capped mountains.

He paused as pain swamped him.

I should never have come, he thought. This venture has ruined me. He saw again the contempt in the *Kriaz-nor*'s eyes as he called for the death of the girl, and remembered the night of horror when the *Kraloth* had ripped into the nobles of Kydor.

'I am not an evil man,' he whispered. 'The cause was just.'

He tried to hold to the teachings of his youth, about the greatness of Kuan-Hador, and its divine purpose to bring peace and civilization to all peoples. Peace and civilization? Desiccated corpses were strewn around Deresh Karany, who was summoning the Lord of Demons.

'I am going home,' said Eldicar Manushan.

He limped towards the main doors and dragged them open, stepping out into the storm-swept night.

And came face to face with an angry crowd, led by the priest Chardyn.

There were many conflicting thoughts and emotions within the Source priest Chardyn as he led the townspeople up the hill towards the White Palace. First and foremost was a terrible fear. Righteous anger had led him to make his speech at the temple, allied to an underlying belief that an army of common folk would prove a match for a few score soldiers and a magicker.

But when the march began many of the townspeople had drifted away. And when the storm came even more hung back. And so it was that Chardyn arrived at the White Palace leading a bedraggled group of around a hundred people, many of them women.

He had promised them that the Source would show His power. He had pledged a shield of thunder and a spear of lightning. Well, he had the thunder and the lightning – and with it the sheeting rain that had drenched his followers, cooling their ardour.

Very few of the people with him had weapons. They had not come to fight. They had come to witness the miracle. The stone-mason, Benae Tarlin, was carrying an iron spear, and, to his right, Lalitia was holding her dagger. Benae had asked Chardyn to bless the spear, and the priest had solemnly laid his hands upon it, and in a loud voice had intoned, 'This is a weapon of righteousness. May it blaze with the Light of the Source!' That had been back in Carlis, and the crowd had cheered mightily. What Chardyn had noticed was that the spear was old and dull, the point pitted with rust.

The small crowd crested the hill and saw the palace. 'When will we see the magic?' asked Benae Tarlin.

Chardyn did not answer. His white robes were soaked and he felt a great weariness upon him. His own anger had long since been replaced by a feeling of impending doom. All he knew was that he would enter the palace and do his best to wring the throat of Eldicar Manushan. He marched on, Lalitia beside him.

'I hope you are right about the Source,' she said.

As they came closer the doors of the palace opened, and Eldicar Manushan stepped out to meet them.

Chardyn saw him, and hesitated. Thunder rumbled above them, and Chardyn could feel the fear in the crowd swelling. Eldicar Manushan looked at him. 'What do you want here?' he called.

'I am here, in the name of the Source, to put an end to your evil,' replied Chardyn, aware that his normally powerful voice lacked conviction.

Eldicar moved out from the doorway. The crowd fell back. 'Leave here now,' boomed the magicker, 'or I shall summon demons to destroy you all!'

Benae Tarlin backed away from Chardyn. Lalitia swore and stepped in. 'Give me that!' she hissed, snatching the iron spear from the stone-mason's hand. Spinning on her heel Lalitia took two running steps towards Eldicar Manushan and launched the weapon.

The surprised magicker threw up his arm but the spear plunged into his belly. He staggered and almost fell. Then he grabbed the iron haft with both hands, dragging it clear. 'I cannot die!' he shouted.

Thunder boomed as he spoke – and a blast of lightning tore down from the sky. The iron spear in Eldicar's hand exploded in a tremendous flash of white light. The magicker's body was hurled high into the air. The force of the explosion threw Lalitia from her feet. Chardyn ran to her, helping her up. Then he walked slowly towards the charred body of Eldicar Manushan. One arm was completely gone and a part of the man's chest had been torn open. A blackened section of the iron haft had crashed through Eldicar's face and was jutting from the rear of his skull.

As Chardyn stood there he saw the body twitch. One hand opened and closed. The leg jerked. Eldicar's eyes flared open. Blood bubbled from his ruined chest, but the wound began to close.

Lalitia dropped to her knees beside the magicker and rammed her dagger into his throat, severing the jugular. Blood pumped out. Eldicar's eyes stayed open for a little while, wide and terrified. Then they closed, and all movement ceased.

Benae Tarlin moved alongside Chardyn, and then the other townspeople crowded around.

'All praise to the Source!' someone said.

'The spear of lightning,' said another.

Chardyn looked up from the charred corpse and saw people staring at him, their faces awestricken. Benae Tarlin took his hand and kissed it. Chardyn realized that the crowd were waiting for him to say something; some grand words, something memorable to match the occasion. But he had nothing to say.

He turned away from them and began the long walk back to Carlis.

Lalitia came alongside him, taking his arm. 'Well, you are a saint now, my friend,' she said. 'A man of miracles.'

'It was no miracle. He was struck by lightning in a storm,' said Chardyn. 'And I am a fraud.'

'How can you say that? You promised them the Source would strike him down. He was struck down. Why do you continue to doubt?'

Chardyn gave a sigh. 'I am a liar and a charlatan. You – though I love you dearly – are a whore and a thief. You think the Source would work his wonders through people like us?'

'Perhaps that is the real miracle,' she said.

The fingers of Waylander's left hand were cramping as he eased himself up the wall, reaching for the cracks where the sections of

313

marble dressing joined. The cracks were thin, no more than half an inch wide in places. Rain swept over him, making the handholds slippery. Waylander paused and opened and closed his left fist, trying to keep the fingers supple. Then he pushed on.

A figure appeared on the balcony just above him. Waylander froze. Lightning flashed over the bay and the assassin saw in its fierce light a nightmare face. Hideously stretched at the temples, the head was triangular, with huge almond-shaped eyes. The texture of the grey skin was scaly, like that of a serpent. Then the creature moved back from the balcony and into the tower beyond. Waylander gripped one of the stone balcony rails and hauled himself up. Lifting the crossbow from the clip at his belt, he vaulted the rail then dived into the room.

Something bright flashed by his face. He rolled to his right. A second burning missile flew past. Coming to his knees, bow raised, he saw the creature's hand come up. A ball of fire appeared in the palm. Waylander shot swiftly. The bolt slammed through the fiery globe, embedding itself in the shoulder of the creature. It leapt forward, then spun, its huge tail raking out. Waylander threw himself to his left. A sharp claw missed him by inches. He shot again. The bolt sliced through the creature's face. It reared up, then fell heavily. Waylander notched the upper string of his bow and slipped another bolt into place.

The creature lay still.

Suddenly Waylander felt immense pity for it, and a powerful yearning to befriend the beast. He knew, in that instant, that it could not be evil, that it desired only love and friendship. He could not believe that he had come here to kill it. The creature rose slowly and turned. Waylander relaxed. Then his eyes fell upon the bodies around the walls. In the corner he saw a dried-out husk. Braided golden hair clung to the skull. He knew the style of the braid. The corpse had once been Norda.

He looked back at the creature. Never in his life had he known such love as he felt now. From somewhere deep in his mind he recalled Ustarte telling him about the charm-spell used by Deresh Karany. The creature was closer now. Its tail swept round, the claw glinting in the lantern-light.

'Will you die for me?' asked the creature sweetly.

'Not tonight,' said Waylander. With a huge effort of will he raised his weapon and touched the trigger. The bolt tore through the creature's neck. Deresh Karany gave a terrible cry. The spell broke.

Waylander dropped the crossbow and drew a throwing knife, which he hurled into Deresh Karany's chest. The creature screamed and rushed at him. Talons snaked out. Waylander dropped to his knees and flung himself to the right. The tail lashed at him, throwing him against an oak table. Waylander came to his feet and drew his shortsword. The tail swept up. Waylander's blade cut deep into it. A high-pitched scream sounded from Deresh Karany, who backed away, his tail oozing blood to the floor. 'You cannot kill me, mortal,' he said.

'But I can bring you a world of pain,' answered Waylander. Another knife sliced through the air, plunging deep into the creature's biceps.

Deresh Karany backed away once more, and began to chant. Waylander had never before heard the language. It was guttural and harsh, yet powerfully rhythmic. The air in the room grew colder as the chanting grew louder. The walls began to vibrate. Shelves came crashing down. Realizing that the creature was summoning a demon, Waylander hurled himself at him. Deresh Karany spun, his blood-smeared tail whiplashing out.

The assassin was thrown across the room. He landed hard, striking his head against the wall. Groggy now, he struggled to rise. A bright light was forming by the far wall. The stone began to ripple. In desperation Waylander drew another knife and hurled it with all his might. It hammered into Deresh Karany's outstretched hand. Waylander heard him grunt with pain. For a moment only the chanting ceased. Then it began again. The cold intensified. Waylander shivered. Fear swelled within him. Not fear of death, or even fear of failure. But fear itself, undiluted and pure. He felt the unseen presence of something so primal, so powerful, that all his strength and guile were as nothing against it. Like a blade of grass trying to withstand a hurricane.

His limbs trembled. Deresh Karany screeched with laughter, the sound bizarre and insane. 'You can feel it, can't you?' he shouted. 'Where are your knives now, little man? Here is one for you!' The *Ipsissimus* pulled the throwing knife from the flesh of his face and tossed it towards Waylander. It clattered on the floor close by. Plucking the other blades from his flesh, he casually threw them

315

down. 'Quick, gather them up,' he said. 'I will enjoy watching you use them against the greatest of demons, the Lord of the Pit. Do you feel honoured? Your soul is to be devoured by Anharat himself!'

The air around Waylander vibrated. Terror, pure and undiluted, swept through him, and he felt a desperate need to escape this place.

'Why not run?' mocked Deresh Karany. 'If you are fast enough his wings will not be able to catch you!'

Waylander hefted his sword, anger coming to his aid. He was still unsteady on his feet, but he prepared himself for one last attack.

A dark figure appeared in the rippling wall, then ducked down and stepped into the room. Its skin was black and scaled, its head round, its ears long and pointed. As it entered it raised itself up until it stood more than ten feet tall, its head just below the rafters. Black wings stretched out, touching the walls on either side. Fire burned in the demon's eye sockets and flames flickered from its wide mouth. A sickening odour filled the room. Waylander recognized it. It was the stench of decaying flesh.

'I summoned thee, Anharat,' said Deresh Karany.

'For what purpose, human?' came the response. As it spoke, fire billowed from the gaping mouth, curling up against the skin of its face. The words hung in the cold air, echoing around the rafters.

'To kill my enemy.'

The Demon Lord's burning eyes fastened on Waylander. Ponderously he advanced across the room. As his taloned feet touched the ornate rugs the cloth burst into flame. Smoke rose around the creature.

Waylander flipped the shortsword, catching it by the blade as he prepared to hurl it into the breast of the demon.

The beast paused. Its head arched back and it began to laugh. Flames roared from its mouth, the sound causing the room to tremble. Waylander threw the sword. As it left his hand it burst into flame then flew up to plunge into one of the rafters. The Demon Lord swung to face Deresh Karany. 'Ah, but this is a good moment!' he said. 'I have always loathed humans, Deresh Karany, but you I hold in utter contempt. Did I not warn you that this gateway would be protected? Did I not tell you that only the death of three kings would open the portals? Did you listen? No. Hundreds of my people have been slain, and now you have the effrontery to call upon Anharat to kill a single human.'

'You must obey, Demon!' shouted Deresh Karany. 'I have followed all the ancient rituals. To the last detail. Ten deaths I have given you, and the incantations were perfect. You have no choice but to accept my order.'

'Oh, this is exquisite! You are a skilled sorcerer, Deresh Karany. You know all the laws governing the Summoning. And what, pray, is the prime law?'

'There must be a death. That is the price! And there he is, Anharat. Kill him, and the ritual is complete.'

'And how many times can a man be killed?' asked the Demon Lord, moving slowly towards Deresh Karany until he towered over the *Ipsissimus*. Waylander stood silently by. Deresh Karany tried to back away. The wall stopped him.

'I don't understand,' he said, his voice shaking. 'Kill him – and go!'

'I cannot kill him, mortal. For he is already dead. His heart no longer beats. His body stands only because a magicker laid a spell upon it.'

'No. This cannot be!' shouted Deresh. 'You are trying to trick me!'

'The prime law,' said Anharat. 'There must be a life.' His huge arm snaked out. Sharp talons crunched through Deresh Karany's body, hauling him into the air. As Waylander watched, the Demon Lord tore open the sorcerer's chest, ripping out his heart. Yet still Deresh struggled. 'Even better,' said Anharat. 'You have mastered the art of regeneration. You will wish you had not. For now it may take a hundred years for you to die.' A blast of flame roared from the demon's mouth, engulfing the beating heart in his hand. Ponderously he turned and moved back to the rippling wall. Deresh Karany was still struggling as Anharat ducked down and stepped through.

As the portal closed Waylander heard one last despairing scream. Then there was silence.

Kysumu had never fought better in his life. He was the representative of humanity in a battle to save his world, and pride flooded his muscles with a power he had never before experienced. *This* was what he had been waiting for his entire life. To be the instrument of good against evil, to be the hero. He was unstoppable, and fought beside the *Riaj-nor* with a chilling ferocity.

At first they clove deep into the superior ranks of the *Kriaz-nor*, driving towards the great arch. It was a curious sight and, even as he battled, Kysumu found it wondrous. Above him the sky was lit by

317

moon and stars, and yet sunshine was beaming through the gateway, casting a golden light upon the stark ruins of Kuan-Hador. Intermittently dark-blue lightning would ripple across the opening, filling the air with an acrid smell.

The *Riaj-nor* had hacked and cut their way forward. Four warriors burst through the *Kriaz-nor* lines and sprinted towards the gateway. A dozen *Kriaz-nor* gave chase. As the grey-garbed warriors reached the portal they hurled their blades towards the golden light. As the swords crossed the opening they flared with a brilliance that dazzled the eye. Blue lightning tore across the huge arch. To Kysumu it seemed fractionally darker than before, but still the sunlight from another world streamed through. Unarmed now, the four *Riaj-nor* had turned and flung themselves at their enemies. They were cut down in moments.

That had been almost an hour ago.

Now the lightning was pale, and within its flare Kysumu could see white streaks. Only around thirty of the *Riaj-nor* were still fighting, and though they had taken a terrible toll on the enemy they were still outnumbered two to one. Ren Tang had fallen moments before, cut down by two *Kriaz-nor*. As he fell, his chest pierced, he reached out and pulled one of the warriors in close, ripping out his throat with his teeth.

The sound of thunder rumbled from some distance away, as a storm broke over the Bay of Carlis. The wind changed and a light rain began to fall over the ruins. Kysumu's grey robes were saturated with blood, and now the rain made the ground slippery beneath his feet. Yet still he fought with controlled frenzy. Two more *Riaj-nor* forced a way past the enemy, running at the gateway and throwing their swords towards it. As the blades disappeared the white streaks faded, the lightning becoming a blue so deep that the sunlight could no longer shine through. Three *Kriaz-nor* fighters peeled back from the battle, killing the unarmed warriors, and taking up positions directly in front of the gateway, ready to cut down any who broke through.

Song Xiu killed two warriors, then darted through the gap. Kysumu ducked under a slashing blade, disembowelled the wielder, then ran after him. But before they could reach the gateway a group of *Kriaz-nor* cut them off. Back to back Kysumu and Song Xiu struggled to defend themselves. The remaining *Riaj-nor* swept forward to aid them. Many were killed.

318

Only a dozen made it, forming a defensive circle. They were exhausted now.

'It would take no more than one – maybe two blades,' said Song Xiu, during a momentary lull in the fighting. He swore and cast an angry glance at the stone arch. They were so close now that their faces, and those of their enemies, were bathed in blue light. One warrior tried to fling his sword over the heads of the *Kriaz-nor*. It spun towards the gateway, but an enemy warrior leapt and caught it by the hilt. The blade shivered and broke.

Song Xiu stared venomously at the remaining *Kriaz-nor*, who were standing now some ten feet away. They were equally weary. 'One last charge,' said Song Xiu. A movement caught Kysumu's eye. He glanced to the left.

Low to the ground, moving behind a ruined wall, was a crawling figure. Kysumu saw the edge of a wolfskin jerkin. Suddenly Yu Yu Liang surged to his feet, sprinting towards the gateway. The three *Kriaz-nor* stationed there ran to block his way.

Yu Yu leapt at them, his sword cleaving through the air.

'Now!' shouted Song Xiu.

The *Riaj-nor* charged. Kysumu lost sight of Yu Yu and joined Song Xiu and the others. They threw themselves at the enemy. The *Kriaz-nor* did not give ground, nor could the weary attackers force them back.

The battle was being fought as if in a dream, the movements of the warriors slow and sluggish. Finally both sides fell back and stared malevolently at each other. There were only eight attackers still standing, and fourteen *Kriaz-nor*.

In the lull Kysumu looked around for Yu Yu. He knew what he would see.

His body lay close to the gateway. His sword arm had been severed. The *Rajnee* blade lay beside it. Kysumu felt sick with grief. Then he saw the body twitch. The *Kriaz-nor* guarding the gateway had moved forward to stand with their comrades. None of them could see Yu Yu.

Kysumu watched as Yu Yu rolled to his side. There was a ghastly wound in his belly, and his entrails had spilled out. Even so, he began to crawl, leaving a bloody smear upon the rocks. Reaching out with his left hand, Yu Yu gathered up the fallen sword. He groaned as he did so. One of the *Kriaz-nor* swung round. Yu Yu flung the blade into the gateway.

There was a searing burst of brightness, accompanied by a high-pitched hum that made the ground vibrate. The blue lightning ceased to crackle. Instead a silver sheen covered the gateway.

The *Kriaz-nor* turned suddenly and raced towards the arch. Thirteen made it through, but as the last warrior crossed it the silver became grey rock. At first it seemed that the warrior had merely stopped in the gateway, but then his body slid down the stone and flopped to its back. He had been cut in half.

Kysumu ran to where Yu Yu lay. Gently he turned him. Yu Yu's eyes were open.

'Oh, my friend,' said Kysumu, tears flowing, 'you closed the gateway.'

Yu Yu could not hear him, and Kysumu gazed down into the dead face. He hugged Yu Yu to him and sat rocking back and forth. Song Xiu moved to his side and sat down. For a while he was silent as Kysumu wept. Then he spoke. 'He was a good man,' he said.

Kysumu kissed Yu Yu's brow, then laid him back on the ground. 'It makes no sense to me,' said Kysumu, brushing away his tears. 'He could have lived. He didn't want to be the *pria-shath*. He didn't want to fight demons and die. So why? Why did he throw away his life?'

'He did not *throw* it away, human. He *gave* it. For you, for me, for this land. Why do you think he was chosen? If the Source had wanted the best swordsman he might have picked you. But He didn't. He wanted a man. An ordinary man.' Song Xiu chuckled. 'A ditch-digger with a stolen sword. And look what that ditch-digger achieved.'

'It just makes me sad,' said Kysumu, reaching down and stroking Yu Yu's face.

'It makes me proud,' said Song Xiu. 'I shall find his soul in the Void, and we will walk together.'

Kysumu looked into the warrior's face. Song Xiu's hair was grey, his face ageing. 'What is happening to you?'

'I am dying,' said Song Xiu. 'We are out of time.'

Kysumu swung round and saw that the other *Riaj-nor* were all stretched out on the ground, unmoving. 'Why?' asked Kysumu.

'We should have died thousands of years ago,' Song Xiu told him, his voice no more than a whisper. 'We knew when we returned that there would be only days left to us. Yu Yu Liang made it worth the price we paid.'

320

Song Xiu lay down. His hair was white now, the skin of his face as dry as parchment. Kysumu moved to him. 'I am so sorry,' he said. 'I . . . misjudged you. All of you. I have been a fool. Forgive me!'

The *Riaj-nor* did not answer. A breeze blew across the ruins. Song Xiu's body shivered and turned to dust.

Kysumu sat for a while, lost in thoughts and bittersweet memories. Then he took his sword and dug out a grave for Yu Yu Liang. He covered it with stones, then sheathed his weapon and walked away from the ruins of Kuan-Hador.

Waylander gathered up his crossbow, and his knives, and moved down the stairs to the lower library. Keeva was sitting there, but there was no sign of the two warriors.

'They left,' said Keeva, rising and putting her arms around the Grey Man. 'How are you feeling?'

'Like death,' he told her, with a wry grin.

'I heard the . . . demon,' she said. 'I have never been more terrified. Not even when Camran took me from the village.'

'That seems a long time ago now,' he replied. Taking her hand Waylander made his way down to the terrace steps where he found Ustarte waiting.

'The gateway is closed,' she told him. 'Yu Yu Liang died to seal it. Kysumu survived.'

Waylander glanced around him, seeking the body of Eldicar Manushan. 'He is dead,' said Ustarte.

'Truly dead?' queried Waylander. 'I would have thought the fall would have killed him.'

'He had some regenerative powers. They could not withstand being struck by a bolt of lightning.'

'So it is over,' said Waylander wearily. 'That is good. Where is Matze?'

'He is still tied in the cellar. Keeva can release him. You and I have to go to the stables.'

'Why there?'

'I have one last gift for you, my friend.'

Waylander smiled. 'I can feel death approaching, Ustarte. My blood is flowing sluggishly and your spell is wearing off. I do not think this is a time for gifts.'

'Trust me, Grey Man.'

Taking his arm she led him back into the palace.

Keeva ran down to the cellar to free Matze Chai. The old man was naked and tied to a chair. He looked up as she entered, and stared at her quizzically.

'I am here to free you,' she told him. 'The Grey Man has killed the sorcerer.'

'Of course he has,' said Matze. 'And what, pray, possessed you to come to me without bearing any clothing for me to wear? Does a little peril make people lose all sense of good manners? Untie me, then go to my rooms and fetch a suitable robe and some soft shoes.'

Keeva shook her head and smiled. 'My apologies, Lord,' she said, with a bow. 'Is there anything else you require?'

Matze nodded. 'If any of my servants have survived you can tell them to prepare a sweet tisane.'

The dawn was breaking as Keeva made her way to the stables. She found Ustarte sitting on a stone bench under a willow tree. The two *Kriaz-nor* warriors were beside her. There was no sign of the Grey Man. 'Where is he?' she asked.

'He is gone, Keeva. I opened a portal for him.'

'Where did you send him?'

'Where he always wanted to be.'

Keeva sat down. A great sadness settled upon her. 'It is hard to believe,' she said, 'that there is no Grey Man. He seemed somehow . . . immortal, unbeatable.'

'And he is, my dear,' Ustarte told her. 'He is only gone from this world. Waylander will never truly die. Men like him are eternal. Somewhere, even as we speak, there is another Grey Man, preparing to face his destiny.'

Keeva glanced at the two warriors, then back at the priestess. 'And what of you? Where will you go?'

'We do not belong here, Keeva. Now that I am no longer using most of my power to thwart Deresh Karany I have enough energy to take us home.'

'You will go back to the land of Deresh Karany?'

'The fight is over for you – but not for me. I cannot rest while the evil that spawned Deresh Karany still thrives.'

Keeva turned to the warriors. 'And you will help her?'

'I think that we will,' said Three-swords.

EPILOGUE

USING A STIFF BROOM TANYA SWEPT THE DUST FROM THE hard-packed clay floor. As much rose around her as was pushed out through the door. Dakeyras had carved designs in the clay, and around the hearth he had created a mosaic with coloured stones from the streambed. Last year's crop had barely supplied them with enough coin to last the year, but Dakeyras had promised that with the first profits from the farm a real floor would be laid.

Tanya was looking forward to such a time, though, as she gazed upon the mosaic, she felt a stab of anticipated regret. She had been pregnant with the twins when Dakeyras had returned from the stream with the sack of stones. Six-year-old Gellan had been with him, full of excitement. 'I found all the red stones, Mama. I picked them all,' he said. 'Isn't that right, Father?'

'You did well, Gil,' said Dakeyras.

'You also soaked your new leggings,' Tanya told the boy.

'You can't take stones from a streambed without getting wet,' said Dakeyras.

'That's right, Mama. And it was fun getting wet. I almost caught a fish with my hands.' Tanya gazed into the boy's bright-blue eyes. He grinned at her and her heart melted. 'All right,' she said, 'you are forgiven. But why do we need a sack of stones?'

For the next two days Dakeyras and Gellan had worked on the rectangular mosaic. Tanya remembered it fondly; the laughter and the joy, Gellan squealing with delight, Dakeyras, his face smeared with clay, tickling him. And when they had finished she recalled them stripping off their clothing and having a race to the stream, which Dakeyras let the boy win. Those were good days.

Tanya put down her broom and stood in the doorway. Gellan was out in the meadow with his wooden sword, the twins were asleep in their crib and Dakeyras had gone out hunting for venison. The day was quiet, the sun bright in a sky dotted with puffballs of white cloud. They looked like sheep grazing on a field of blue, she thought.

It would be good to have venison. Supplies were low, and though the town storekeeper extended them credit Tanya was loath to fall further into debt.

People had been kind. But, then, Dakeyras was a popular man. Everyone remembered him as the officer whose prompt action had saved the community from the Sathuli raid. He had fought with distinction, and he, and his friend Gellan – after whom they had named their son – had been awarded medals. Gellan had remained with the army. Tanya often wondered whether Dakeyras regretted becoming a farmer.

His commanding officer had come to see Tanya the day after Dakeyras said he wanted to resign his commission, telling her that he felt her husband was making a grave mistake. 'He is that rarest of animals, a natural fighting man but also a thinker. The men revere him. He could go far, Tanya.'

'I did not ask him to leave the service, sir,' she said. 'It was his own decision.'

'That is a shame,' he told her. 'I had hoped it was your idea, and that I could persuade you to change your mind.'

'I would be happy with him whether he was a soldier, a farmer, a baker . . . But he told me that he had to leave the service.'

'Did he say why? Was he unhappy?'

'No, sir. He was too happy.'

'I don't understand.'

'I can say no more. It would not be right.'

He had still been confused when he left. How could Tanya have told him what Dakeyras confided to her? The fighting and the killing, which dismayed most men, had begun to fill Dakeyras with a savage delight. 'If I stay,' he said, 'I will become someone I do not want to be.' In the end his commanding officer had convinced Dakeyras to take a year's sabbatical, while still holding his commission. That year was almost up.

Tanya walked out into the sunshine and untied the ribbon that held her long blond hair in place. Shaking out the dust, she moved to the well, and slowly drew up a bucket. Reaching out, she dragged it over until it rested on the stone wall. She drank deeply, then splashed water to her face.

'Riders, Mama!' shouted Gellan.

Tanya turned towards the north and saw a line of horsemen making their way down the slope. She wondered if they might be soldiers, but soon saw that, although they were heavily armed, they were not from the Drenai garrison.

She walked back towards the house and waited for them by the porch.

The first of the men, riding a tall bay, drew rein. He had a long face and deep-set eyes. Tanya, who liked most people, found herself vaguely repelled by him. She glanced at the other riders. They were unshaven, their clothes dirty. Alongside the lead rider was a man with Nadir features, high cheekbones and slanted eyes. No one spoke.

'If you would like to water your horses,' said Tanya, 'you may use the stream. It is a little further back into the trees.'

'We didn't come for water,' said the long-faced man. He stared at her, his eyes glittering. Tanya felt both anger and fear as his gaze flowed over her. 'You are a pretty thing, farm girl. I like a woman with good breasts. I think you can supply what we need.'

'You had better leave,' she said. 'My husband . . . and his friends . . . will be back soon. You are not welcome here.'

'We are not welcome anywhere,' said the rider. 'Now, you can do this easy or hard. Best to know that I gutted the last woman who chose hard.'

Tanya stood very still. One of the twins began to cry for food, the sound high and keening. Little Gellan had moved closer. 'What do they want, Mama?' he called.

The long-faced man turned towards the Nadir. 'Kill the brat!' he said.

A blast of cold air swept across the riders. Horses reared and were brought under control. Tanya turned her head, and saw another horseman. She had not heard him approach. The riders were all staring at him.

'Where the Hell did he come from?' she heard someone ask.

'From the back of the house,' said Long-face. 'Where else?'

Tanya stared hard at the newcomer. There was something familiar about him. He was old, his face masked by grey stubble. And he looked tired. Dark rings circled his eyes. He heeled his horse forward, and Tanya saw that in his left hand he held a small black crossbow.

'What do you want here?' asked Long-face.

'I know you,' said the newcomer. 'I know all of you.' Shock rippled through Tanya as she heard his voice, though she didn't know why. He moved his mount closer to Long-face. 'You are Bedrin, known as the Stalker. You are a man with no redeeming features. There is nothing I have to say to you.' The crossbow came up, and Long-face pitched from the saddle, a bolt through his brain. 'As for the rest of you,' continued the rider, 'there are some who can still find redemption.'

Tanya saw the Nadir draw his sword and heel his horse forward. A crossbow bolt slammed through into his throat, and he, too, fell to the ground, his horse cantering past the man, who continued to talk. There was no hint of emotion in his voice. He might as well have been discussing the weather. The seventeen remaining riders sat their mounts, almost mesmerized by this deadly, grey-faced stranger.

'It is fitting that Kityan should join his master,' he said, casually reloading the crossbow. 'He lived for torture, to inflict pain on others.' He glanced at the remaining raiders. 'But you,' he said, pointing at a broad-shouldered young man, 'you, Maneas, have better dreams. Back in Gothir, at the village of the Nine Oaks, there is a girl. You wanted to marry her, but her father gave her to another. You were heartbroken when you rode away. Would it help to know that her husband will drown this summer? She will be alone. If you return to her you will sire two sons and a daughter.'

'How do you know this?' asked the young man. 'Are you a wizard?'

'You can think of me as a prophet,' said the man. 'For I know what is, and what will be. I have seen the future. If you kill this woman and her children, Maneas, you will still go home. You will still wed Leandra, and she will bear you the three children I spoke of. And then one night this woman's husband will find you. He will have been searching for nine years. He will take you into the woods and put out your eyes. Then he will stake you to the ground and build a fire upon your belly.' Tanya saw all colour drain from the young man's face.

The newcomer's hand swept out, pointing to a thin, middle-aged man. 'And you, Patris. No matter what happens here today you will leave this band and journey to Gulgothir. You will seek to fulfil a dream you have had since childhood, to begin a business, designing jewellery for the nobles, wonderfully wrought rings and brooches. You will discover that what you thought of as talent is, in fact, genius. You will find happiness and wealth and fame in Gulgothir. But if this woman dies her man will find you. He will cut off your hands, and your body will be discovered impaled upon a sharp stake.'

He fell silent, and they waited. Finally he spoke again. 'The luckiest of you will survive for nineteen years. But many of those years will be lived in terror. You will hear of the murders of your comrades. One by one. Every day you will stare into the faces of strangers, wondering if the faceless killer is one of them. And one day he will be. This is the truth.

'Now it is time to make a choice. Ride from here and live. Or stay, and know the endless torment of the damned.'

For a moment no one moved. Then the young Maneas swung his horse and galloped back towards the north. One by one the others followed until only a swarthy, round-shouldered man remained. 'And what of me, prophet?' he asked. 'Is there some happiness I can find?'

'There is *now*, Lodrian. Now you can journey to Lentria. You will find a village and, short of coin, you will seek employment. A young widow will ask you to repair her roof. And your life will change.'

'Thank you,' said Lodrian. He looked down at Tanya. 'I am sorry for the fear we caused you.' Then he rode away.

The rider slowly dismounted. Tanya saw him stumble as he did so, dropping his crossbow to the ground. He took several steps towards Gellan then fell to his knees. Tanya ran to his side, putting her arms around his shoulders. 'You are ill, sir,' she said. 'Let me help you.'

The man swayed and, with difficulty, Tanya lowered him to the ground. He lay back, his head surrounded by the fading spring flowers of the meadow. He looked into her eyes.

'Do I know you, sir?' she asked.

'No. We have . . . never met. But I knew a woman once, who was . . . like you.'

'My husband will be home soon. He will help me get you to a bed. We will send for the surgeon.'

His voice was weaker. 'I will not be alive when he returns.'

She took his hand and kissed it. 'You saved us,' she said, tears in her eyes. 'There must be something we can do for you!'

'Let me see the boy,' he whispered. Tanya called out to Gellan and the child moved forward nervously. The man looked up at him. Tanya saw him relax, and upon his face appeared a look of utter contentment. He smiled at the boy. Then his eyes closed, his head lolling to one side. Tanya sat beside him, holding his hand.

After a while the child spoke. 'Is he sleeping, Mama?'

'No, Gil, he is dead.'

The sound of a galloping horse came to her. Fear flared and she spun round. But the raiders had not returned. The rider was Dakeyras. He leapt from the saddle.

'What happened here?' he asked. She told him of the raiders, and of the arrival of the grey-faced man.

'They were going to kill us all. I know it,' she concluded. 'He saved our lives, Dak. I'm sure I've seen him somewhere. Do you recognize him?'

Dakeyras knelt by the body. 'He looks familiar,' he said. 'Perhaps he was a soldier.'

Little Gellan ran to him. 'He killed the bad men, Father. And he made the others ride away. Then he lay down and died.'

The sound of a baby's cry came from the house. Tanya rose and went to feed it.

Dakeyras walked to where the stranger's crossbow was lying on the ground, and lifted it. It was perfectly balanced, and beautifully made. Extending his arm, Dakeyras loosed both bolts. They flew exactly where he aimed them, slamming into the fence post twenty paces to his left.

Tanya walked out into the sunlight, holding one of the twins to her breast.

Her husband was holding the bow.

She shivered suddenly.

'Are you all right?' he asked.

'Someone just walked over my grave,' she said.